"Hig
exam ... character." –
Daily Telegraph
"Meticulously constructed." – *The Spectator*
"Espionage fiction with a difference . . . reads a lot more authentically than many books of this genre." – *The Scotsman*
"A warm and memorable thriller which captures the imagination fully." – *Irish Times*
"A chilling portrayal of the small, ordinary spy." – *Daily Telegraph Magazine*

The Spy Who Sat and Waited

R. WRIGHT CAMPBELL

SPHERE BOOKS LIMITED
30/32 Gray's Inn Road, London WC1X 8JL

First published in Great Britain by Weidenfeld &
Nicholson 1975

First Sphere Books edition 1978

Dedicated to
Maggie Starr, who urged this story to be told as a book, Liz Wallace, who believed in and protected it, Ned Leavitt, who applied judgement in the final fashion of it.

Filmset in Photon Times

Printed in Great Britain by
C. Nicholls & Company Ltd
The Philips Park Press, Manchester

Some months prior to the cessation of hostilities between the principals engaged in the Great War, prior to the historic signing of the Armistice on November 11, 1918, in the Forest of Compiègne, a secret communication was sent to selected agents throughout the world by the German chief of intelligence. It read in part:

> Soon the government of his Imperial Majesty Kaiser Wilhelm II will sign an armistice with the enemy.
>
> You are ordered to maintain your cover.
>
> You are ordered to make known your status to the control assigned you and to your control only.
>
> You are ordered to obey future orders and instructions to the letter.
>
> This infamous surrender has not been achieved by superiority of arms or men, but by treachery and betrayal from within.
>
> We shall not forget the lessons learned in this conflict.
>
> The Reich will endure.
>
> The Reich will one day take its rightful place at the head of all nations.
>
> The Reich will rise again.

This communication condemned an unknown number of loyal Germans to a strange shadow life.

CHAPTER 1

Upon the occasion of Germany's surrender, Wilhelm Oerter felt little relaxation of the tensions of war. In his role as clerk in the Dortmund Trading Company he'd never had occasion to suffer the trenches or engage in combat. In that regard he'd never known what it was really like.

On the other hand, now that the living were returning to country, home and family, he'd been ordered to stay on in Berne, Switzerland, for an indefinite length of time in order to wind down the undercover intelligence operation.

In due time, freshly into the year 1919, the secretarial staff that had handled both the legitimate and the clandestine aspects of the cover organization were allowed to return home. Thirty days later Wilhelm's superior gave over the keys to the offices, the petty cashbox and the inventory of furnishings into Wilhelm's hands and gratefully returned to Germany.

Wilhelm went to the office every morning at nine, lunched from one to two and locked up for the night at six. There was nothing to occupy him. He was simply waiting for someone to release him from his duties.

On a morning in April he found a letter lying on the carpet beneath the mail slot. It bore no postage and had obviously been hand delivered. It suggested a rendezvous in a small riverside tavern. Wilhelm arrived before time. He valued punctuality. He was seated near the window when an acquaintance passed in the street and waved to him. The man entered the restaurant.

Wilhelm felt the sensation of irritation along the backs of his hands. This chance meeting might very well prove awkward. He must be got rid of before his appointment arrived.

The intruder stopped at his table.

'Good afternoon, Mr. Oerter. You remember me?'

Wilhelm got to his feet and bowed slightly.

'Of course. Mr. Goldman, isn't it?'

The man beamed with great pleasure at having been remembered. Wilhelm decided to add to his pleasure.

'You're a traveler in perfumes and essences.'

Goldman patted his impressive stomach. His fat, rosy cheeks grew even rosier, his pink scalp, shining through close-cut white hair, pinker.

'I was employed in that fashion and in other ways.' There was a shrewd merchant's twinkle in his eyes. 'May I join you?'

'I regret that I'm waiting for someone.'

'Yes.' Goldman sat down and rocked about, making a comfortable nest for his rump. 'I'm the someone you're waiting for.'

For a long moment Wilhelm stood unmoving. This revelation was startling and disconcerting. On the occasions when they'd had small dealings concerning import-export, the man sitting before him had given the impression of clownish incompetence. He'd conducted his affairs as though no war were in progress, bargaining intensely, but with good humor, for every penny of profit. Wilhelm had known that Goldman carried the occasional document, not meant for transport through regular channels, as he himself sometimes did. The activities of Dortmund Trading included the collection and delivery to Germany of certain intelligence. They often made use of such casual messengers, salesmen and travelers whose cover was genuine and loyalty to the Fatherland certain.

Wilhelm had been privately amused and somewhat contemptuous of the man. He also had an indulgent affection for him as one might have for a half-witted but gentle relative.

'I am your control,' Goldman smiled and broke the spell that held Wilhelm in thrall.

Wilhelm bowed again, sharply, and silently clicked his heels.

Goldman made an exaggerated O of astonishment with his cherubic lips, grinned broadly, and then frowned – all in a brief tick of time.

'For Christ's sake, put that nonsense aside. Sit down. You've ordered your lunch?'

'I was waiting for your arrival, sir.'

'Very polite of you. Very courteous. Doesn't old acquaintance allow you to call me Martin or, at the very least, Goldman?'

He snapped open the menu with one hand and raised a finger of the other to gain the waiter's attention.

'This is very good. Soup.'

He leaned over the table a bit as though imparting a secret.

'Since the fall of Germany, salads have become popular in the restaurants. The French influence, would you say? I don't know. These little obeisances to the conqueror may have deep significance.'

'Sir?'

'You don't understand? Of course not. Well, for example, when attacked by the superior male, the weaker baboon turns his back and bends over to show his ass.'

'The males, too?' Wilhelm asked.

'The males, too. It is a gesture of subservience.'

'I don't understand, sir. The baboons. The salads.'

His companion waved the whole subject aside with a gesture.

'Very obscure analogy. Most devious and obscure. You see, I was a professor of psychology before I became engaged in my present occupation. I became a spy late in life.'

Wilhelm glanced quickly at the waiter who had at that moment taken his last step to the table and was standing with a mixture of attentiveness and boredom on his face.

'Soup, soup, soup. Yes?' asked, cajoled, ordered Martin Goldman.

'A coffee.'

'Watching your weight?'

'No, sir. I'm just not hungry.'

'So. One soup, bread, butter, chicken, potatoes.'

The waiter wrote it all down.

'This is squash? Summer squash so early?'

The waiter shrugged, indicating that he had no knowledge of matters so esoteric as the raising of vegetables.

'No squash. Cabbages, yes. A stein of beer. I'll order something for after . . . after.'

The waiter went away, and Goldman laughed with great pleasure.

'This spying is hungry work.'

'Sir?'

'Will you stop jumping out of your skin every time I mention the word? Let's not make a silly charade out of this business. Would you rather I left the papers, the money and your instructions in a hollow tree? Relax. You're a young man. And stop saying sir.'

Wilhelm nodded his head and began to say 'Yes, sir,' but caught himself in time. Goldman regarded him with a kindly and quizzical eye.

'You're a very serious young man. Stiff almost. I remarked upon that to myself the very first time we met. I thought it was because you were a new boy feeling a bit self-important, though uncomfortable, in your duties. But I see now that it is a chronic condition. You must learn to relax.' He reached over and patted Wilhelm's hand. 'Just exactly what were your duties?'

Wilhelm felt himself tighten. There was a slightly patronizing, even taunting note to Goldman's voice, but there was no meanness in it.

'I was principally engaged in translations. I speak three languages besides my own. French, English and Italian.'

'I speak five. Forgive my boast.'

Wilhelm knew that he had been judged and somehow gently deflated. He spoke quickly.

'I was not boasting. You asked me what I did. I told you. But surely, if you're my control, you know my skills and capabilities?'

'No, no. This position is new to me. I've not had the time to do more than skim your dossier.'

'But you were working for Intelligence with the rest of us?'

Goldman shook his head and snorted through his nose in amusement.

'Let us say that I was working for the same government but that I was not, in the strict table of organization, a member of your group. I ran a few errands for you, and in that regard I was. On the other hand, I wasn't.'

Wilhelm frowned. Goldman's conversation had a way of slipping about from dark to light like a fish in the shadows of the sea.

'I was a spy that spied upon other spies. Ah.' He held up one finger, having found the most felicitous description of himself.

'I was an efficiency expert. You didn't suspect that the fat, funny old uncle was a master spy?'

'I thought you were what you pretended to be, a salesman.'

'Well then, you're at least one that I can definitely prove was taken in by my disguise.'

He placed a finger to his lips and rolled his eyes toward the waiter, who approached the table and placed a large bowl of steaming broth before him. When the waiter went away, Goldman bent down with effort and retrieved the bulky briefcase he'd placed on the floor near his chair and settled it in his lap. It was heavy and worn but well cared for. A small brass plate informed: 'Martin Goldman, Representative. Metal Fabrications.'

He shined the brass with his sleeve and looked up at Wilhelm from beneath his brows.

'You see I've changed my business.'

He opened the case and removed a small envelope file enclosed by a wide red rubber band.

'Here we are, Mr. Hartz.' He offered the file across the table.

'What?' Wilhelm responded in confusion and made no attempt to take it.

'We've created a whole new person for you and a new name to go with it. Do you like it?'

Wilhelm shrugged.

'You're right,' Goldman laughed. 'It's a small matter. Take it. Take it.'

Wilhelm snatched the envelope and quickly concealed it in the pocket of his overcoat.

Goldman grinned, pursed his lips and blew bubbles with repressed laughter.

'Has my first name been changed as well?'

'No, no. We don't want to fill your head with too many new facts, do we?'

Goldman saw that the stiff young man didn't take gentle jibes with any considerable grace.

'It's a marvelous thing being provided with a new identity. It's as though one were reborn with an unblotted coat of arms. There are some advantages to being ordered underground. Perhaps you have a wife or girlfriend you'd like never to see again. You don't have to tell me.'

Goldman busied himself with the soup, bread and butter.

'Butter,' he cooed. 'We will see it in Germany again.'

He said nothing more until he'd completed the meal. He decided to forgo a sweet but ordered a brandy with his coffee.

He rolled the liquor around his mouth. He looked like a contemplative teddy bear.

'I offer you a piece of shopworn wisdom so simple as to be inexpressibly profound. Never let tomorrow's plans of great moment ruin the pleasure of today's meal.'

He burped delicately behind his hand.

'There are those in Germany who take no comfort from

the reality of peace. Already they are up to their ears in plans for the next adventure. They change those plans as often as a whore changes her knickers. The allusion is apt.

'They are full of righteous anger at the character of our defeat. They burn with the shame of a great betrayal. They nourish dreams of vengeance and fantasies of retribution. They have the money to implement their dreams and fantasies. Money is easily understood. So?'

He removed a thick envelope from his briefcase and handed it over.

'There is enough there to accomplish two things. First to keep you warm and fed while you make preparations for your entry into your target nation. The process might well take as long as a year. I suggest you establish yourself in Zurich. Sever all ties with friends and acquaintances in this city. Establish your bona fides as a Swiss citizen. Take employment if you can find it. It would be well to supplement these funds so that you'll have as much cash as possible when you reach your destination. You will need money to establish yourself in business. That is the second thing.'

Wilhelm held the heavy envelope on the tabletop.

Goldman pointed a finger. 'Now that is money and should be concealed, my dear Mr. Hartz.'

Wilhelm swiftly and clumsily stuffed the envelope into his pocket.

'Tenderly, tenderly,' Goldman murmured.

He then handed over still another envelope. This one was made of gray paper and bore no mark.

'This is a map of the route to be taken over a span of months to your new home. The Orkney Islands. I am sorry. They are very cold, very stormy and the people very tight-mouthed. It comes from clenching their assholes against the wind.'

'Scapa Flow,' Wilhelm murmured.

'Indeed. The impregnable harbor for the British Home Fleet. I would say, without being privy to those plans devised in high places, that the leaders of the next war would like to prove it vulnerable as early as possible. The expectation of such a coup gives our present leaders great pleasure. Chess is a wonderfully intriguing game. Chess with human pieces is an obsession.' He made the reflection with a sadness in the voice.

'You don't seem to take any of this very seriously,'

Wilhelm said. It would be hard to say whether it was censure or dismay in his own voice.

Goldman regarded him for a long moment.

'I am a man living in a world not of my making. I am filled with the quiet desperation of the undecided. I may extrapolate, draw conclusions upon little evidence and much fiction, but I can never know the truth of the situation, the value of the action or the desirability of the consequences. I have done and will continue to do such things, in the name of duty, that I cannot entirely agree with. Until, that is, some basic moral principle of my own is compromised. If that time comes, I will find out then what I will do. More important, I will survive for this day, this year and as long as I am able.'

Wilhelm drew back from the anger that lay behind the still mild eyes. Goldman was not quite done.

'Tell me, in your youthful inexperience of life and fervent patriotism, are you so certain of the righteousness of what you are about to do?'

Wilhelm suddenly felt like a small boy, and a wave of dependent affection flowed through him. He wanted desperately to call the man Uncle and to beg his help.

Goldman seemed to sense the sudden release of barriers in the younger man, a relaxation of manner. He was aware that Wilhelm's stiff-necked isolation was a product of youth and fear. The anger in Goldman gave way to a compassionate desire to draw Wilhelm out and elicit his confidence. With it all a certain professional gleam remained.

'How serious are your doubts?'

'I'm not certain I have the capabilities for the things that might be expected of me.'

'No special skills are required. In this last war most spies were whores, thieves or confidence men. Why was this so? First, the existence of such a thing as a spy was anathema to the aristocratic military of all nations. Second, they had access to information and understood the devious ways of intrigue. From this moment, we shall find that, while still clandestine, intelligence organizations will gain a certain respect. There will be as much need for clerks as for assassins, for men who have the patience to wait, perhaps fruitlessly, as for active saboteurs. What are your feelings for Germany?'

'I love my country.'

Goldman smiled as Wilhelm bristled.

'Of course, you do.'

'But have I the dedication that's required?'

'None is required. At least not passionate, fanatic dedication. Have you other dreams?'

'What?'

'Do you want to be a lawyer, a businessman, a farmer, artist, doctor, minister?'

'I haven't any particularly valuable skills or any grand designs for my life.'

'Indeed? Then you are eminently qualified for the job. It's a job. A living. Some security.'

'Will this mission be of any real value?'

'How would I know? What can I tell you? I'm not a recruiting officer or a fabricator of strategies. But I tell you this. Your choices are these. You may leave here with the papers and the money. You may lose yourself and make a life wherever you wish. You can return them to me now and go home to see the mother you may never otherwise see or hear from again. However, if your loyalties to the Fatherland are such, you can accept this post. If you are wise, you will fashion a life for yourself and worry about affairs of great moment only when they are thrust under your nose. I would also have a large piece of apricot torte because I've decided this is no time to watch one's weight.'

He raised a hand and snapped his fingers for the waiter.

'I will join you,' Wilhelm smiled. They were suddenly old friends.

Wilhelm entered a life of celibacy and silence more rigorous than that imposed upon an eremite. He dared no friendships, allowed no affections. He was a prisoner of Zurich for six months. He sought employment as Goldman had advised, but with the vast commerce of professional neutrality no longer thriving, Switzerland was suffering a mild unemployment. However, he was fortunate in receiving occasional employment as a translator of technical journals. Wilhelm's loneliness remained painful and his anonymity secure.

In due course, when he felt comfortable in his new skin, he traveled by easy stages through France to Calais and on to Dover. Later he traveled the length of England and Scotland. At last, in the spring of 1921 he penetrated the Orkneys.

He searched out Kirkwall, the county capital on the main

island, for a likely location for his business and listening post. It was a fairly busy place, but on a day's outing to the smaller town of Stromness he found a tavern, the Sailing Master, up for sale.

Mr. Cromarty, the owner of the establishment, was a fair and honest Scot.

'I can make no promise of splendid success. With the war over and done, thank God, the place has become quiet again. There were weekend trippers come to see the sights, and perhaps they'll be back again. On the whole, we serve the fisherfolk, sailors and the occasional drummer visiting the ship chandlers. It's a warm and friendly pub. The owner's flat upstairs is snug enough.'

'My wants are modest. A simple living,' Wilhelm murmured.

'After a lifetime here,' Mr. Cromarty compared, 'I fancy a look at the lights of London or even Paris, perhaps. I got half well off during the war. The staging base for the Grand Fleet was here at Scapa Flow.'

'I know.'

'The young lads and some service lassies favored the Sailing Master.' Cromarty smiled in remembering. 'When malt and hops were scarce, I made a cider that pleased them well enough.'

Wilhelm sat quietly, wondering where the legend of the dour Scot had come from. He found it not uncomfortable to listen to the old Scotsman rattling on. Wilhelm had the gift of patience.

'You'll not see any great increase of trade here again. The war's over and the damned Huns beaten down for good and all.'

Wilhelm felt a rare burst of anger. It shook him and left a trembling in his hands.

He regretted the automatic awakening of national pride. He must learn to dissemble more skilfully.

'I would like to buy your business,' he said softly.

'Then a drink on it.'

Cromarty lifted his mug.

'Cheers.'

'*Prosit*,' Wilhelm responded.

Mr. Cromarty gave no reaction to Wilhelm's lapse into his mother tongue. After all, the Swiss, Cromarty knew, spoke a kind of German.

A simple deed was drawn by the local solicitor; hints, advice and a set of keys passed from Cromarty to Hartz; and the sum of the purchase in Swiss francs and English pounds passed from Hartz to Cromarty.

That first night of occupancy Wilhelm placed a rocking chair by the fire in the small sitting room. It was to be his haven, his nation in a foreign land, his remembering place against the isolation that, even in the first hours, threatened to suffocate and engulf him.

In a gray metal box he put away a birth certificate proving that one Wilhelm Hartz had been born in the Swiss canton of Uri on June 12 in the year 1885. There was also a certificate of graduation from elementary school, another from secondary school, and a third for his completion of studies at St. Galen Commercial College. Another document attested to his participation in the compulsory militia of Switzerland. Passport, visas, immigration applications – all were placed in the box along with several letters from mother, father and girlfriend, a sprig of dried wild flowers, a carved bit of slate. Such things as a man might carry with him as touchstones of memory. All were fabrications.

Until this time his associations had been so few and casual that he'd never been required to be careful of questions about his previous life. Now he must wear the false face at all times. He must, as nearly as he was able, automatically respond to everyone and everything as Wilhelm Hartz, Swiss national.

The townspeople and fishermen had proved wary of strangers and slow to camaraderie in the time-honored tradition of island people. Wilhelm made no extraordinary effort to be enfolded by them and, in that instinctive and natural reserve, discovered the key to acceptance. His quiet self-sufficiency, even austerity of manner, struck echoes in their hearts, and they recognized him as one of their own. Wilhelm found a certain solitary contentment in the passage of a year and a few undemanding friendships as well.

He'd fallen into simple and predictable habits. At the eleventh hour of the night when his customers had left the smoky warmth of 'The Sailing Master – Will Hartz, Proprietor' and had gone their separate ways to hearth and home, he would turn out the lights of the tavern and traveler's inn and go out into the sea-wet narrow street that led down to the rocky shore.

At the end of the dark mole he sat down. The massive

rocks were rough and familiar against his legs. He filled and lit his pipe and stared out upon Scapa Flow.

His attention was called by the scrape of a shoe upon the rocks. He knew the familiar step.

John Kendrick, accompanied by a series of soft, explosive sounds, settled himself alongside Will. The north winds and the spindrift had long since invaded his body. Even his hair, curling from beneath a knitted cap, seemed whitened by sea spray.

Wilhelm extended his tobacco pouch.

'Thanking you,' John said in a strongly burred voice.

They regarded the Flow. The well-sheltered waters, ringed by the Orkney Islands, stirred peacefully. They were not much disturbed by the skeletal superstructures of the German war-fleet lying scuttled in the deep.

Three years before, in June, 1919, apparently by pre-arranged signal, the crews of the interned ships of the German Imperial Navy had opened the seacocks and sent their own vessels to a watery grave.

Eleven battleships, five battle cruisers, eight light cruisers and a number of destroyers were sent to the bottom. The rusting hulks lay there, unretrieved, unsalvaged. They, too, seemed content.

'A ship's graveyard is a sorrowful sight,' John offered.

'Will the salvagers ever finish clearing the hulks away?'

'In time.'

A ten-minute silence sat with them. It was their comfortable way. John broke it.

'It's blowing chill. Used to it, are you?'

'At home, in Switzerland, the wind sweeps down from the mountains. At their feet, white wild flowers are scattered about like snow droplets.'

'Miss home, do you?'

'I believe I would miss the sea far more.'

John rose amid a new series of comforting sounds. He stood on the rock like a small troll.

'Will you come home and take a cup of tea? My sister, Molly, would be glad of the company.'

'Thank you, no. There are things to be done before bed.'

'You'll take supper with us Sunday then?'

'I thought to go to Westray Island to see the ruins of Noltland Castle,' Will hedged.

'That pile of stones has lain there three hundred years. It

will be there yet awhile. It's been a year since you've come to our village, Will. You've come to be a friend. As slow as we folk are to call a man that, it means something to us.'

'I feel that, John.'

'Then come you Sunday. You need a woman-cooked meal. Think on it at least.'

Kendrick offered his friend the door to refusal. He had no way of knowing what it was in Will that led him to embrace a life so solitary and without homely comforts. He was reluctant to ask.

'I'll think about it, John.'

Wilhelm knew he wouldn't go to Kendrick's come Sunday.

The sailorman walked off waving a hand by way of good-night. Wilhelm sat awhile longer, turning the word 'woman' over in his mind and on his tongue. He felt the shape of it in his loins.

In the past, when the incredible human loneliness he sometimes felt sole heir to threatened to overwhelm him, the haven of a woman's body had been possible to him. But now, captured in the small fears of self-revelation, the stern austerity of the discipline he was engaged upon and the dictates of his own sense of honor, there was no woman of the islands he might touch. He was as alone as any on a mountain.

CHAPTER 2

Toward the end of June Will received a letter from Martin Goldman. Even before he opened it, he expected there was some urgency in it. It wasn't considered wise or prudent to communicate in any but the most normal fashion. The letter Will held had been made somewhat noteworthy, to the deckhand of the mail packet who hand delivered it, if to no one else.

The man stood there tucking his blouse into his trousers as though seeking occupation for his hands, which were exceedingly large for the rest of his ill-formed slender bulk. They were the hands of a priest or a murderer, excessively eloquent. Even so there was an awkward moment before Will got their message. He searched in his pocket and handed over half a crown.

'Please accept this with my thanks, Mr. . . .'

The name escaped him, and for a moment he wondered if he'd ever heard it. He was aware that the man was regarding him with a birdlike brightness in which challenge lay.

Will remembered the odd remark passed between his customers in the pub concerning the fellow.

'Wiley,' he said.

The man nodded his head as though justice had been done. He nodded again and left in a rush as though called away on important matters.

The note from Goldman called for a face-to-face meeting at Aberdeen.

Will booked passage on the packet at once. The following dawn, leaving the Sailing Master in the care of his cellarman, Wee Jock, he set sail for Inverness.

The sluggish dirty ship carried a mixed bag of goods: wool, sea products, goats and swine. It carried a few passengers as well. Among them this day was a man from Kirkwall who joined Wilhelm at the rail.

'Mr. Hartz, is it?'

Wilhelm smiled and nodded, but gave no other encouragement for conversation.

'My name is Simmons, traveling in block and cordage for

the firm of Danby and Frickett of Aberdeen. But I make my home in Kirkwall. I took a pint at your pub in Stromness more than once. Had business with the chandler, Donney.' He extended a flask. 'Will you have a dram with me?'

Wilhelm shook his head and patted his stomach.

'A poor sailor, are you?' the man asked cheerfully.

A poor damned, enforced celibate, Wilhelm thought. For some time, since long before his arrival in the Orkneys, he had been denied the comfort of a woman. This voyage would serve double purpose.

'To Wick on business?' Simmons pursued.

'No, to Aberdeen.'

'Well, that is a lucky happening. We can share a compart ment on the train.'

'I have some bookkeeping to do on the train.'

'Just carry on. I'll not disturb you. I don't mind a quiet companion, someone to share the odd moment with.'

It was obvious that Simmons, the complete salesman, intended to natter on and on. Wilhelm grimaced and begged to be excused. He went into the enclosed lounge. After a short while he really began to feel ill. The smell of oil was thick in the confined space.

He picked up a London *Times* lying beside him, left there by a passenger without the habit of thrift. His casual gaze fell upon a headline that sharpened his attention. It was news of Germany. The Foreign Minister, Dr. Walther Rathenau, had been assassinated. A hail of bullets and exploding hand grenades had killed him. It said that Chancellor Joseph Wirth's government was marshaling the liberal element of the nation to the defense of the young republic. Organized labor, represented in both Socialist parties, had answered the call at once. Announcement had been made that the government was to establish extraordinary courts for the trials of nationalist plotters. It feared a reactionary coup d'état.

In one of many small items meant to note the sidelights of the major news story, it was mentioned that one Adolf Hitler, the obscure leader of an equally obscure organization of disgruntled war veterans, known as the National Socialist German Workers Party, had issued a rather rambling statement which ended with the exhortation 'Germany, Awake!' No further attention was paid.

Wilhelm laid the newspaper in his lap. He was ashamed to admit, even to himself, how little he knew of the affairs of his country. He felt sympathy for the dead man who had been so closely identified with the rehabilitation efforts of Germany. He intuited that the cause of the free republic had suffered a severe blow, but this feeling had no basis in intellectual analysis. He was disturbed that labor was so closely identified with the Socialists and he possessed an ingrained fear of Communism in any, even the mildest, form. It was equally true that he feared the reactionary militarists and nationalists. He cursed himself for being a man without convictions.

On the train, Wilhelm buried himself in a small black notebook. It contained no business matters. It contained names, birthdates and odd facts concerning people of Stromness. It remarked on their tempers, their finances and their political sympathies. Wilhelm was gifted with Germanic thoroughness. He was known as a thoughtful man who never forgot the natal day or important anniversary of a customer or friend. He was also gifted with kindness. As he worked, he became vaguely aware that Simmons sat, comfortably enough, regarding him.

'No intrusion intended, but your accent. I fancy myself a good ear, but I can't exactly place yours. German, is it?'

'Swiss,' Wilhelm replied. A nagging fear slipped into his mind. Were the British aware of the secret paper dispatched to German agents and spies? Were they alert to possible threats to their future security? Was every foreign-born resident of Great Britain subjected to some measure of surveillance? Or had they, instead, fallen under the spell of weariness and complaisance that was sure to follow after a debilitating war?

They detrained in Aberdeen, Wilhelm reluctantly walking beside Simmons. The salesman, the journey done and Wilhelm's attention no longer taken by a black book, plunged at once into his meaningless chatter and oppressive courtesies.

'Do come along with me and take tea. I'm buying.'

'I have not the time.' Wilhelm knew he sounded irritated and was sorry for it.

Simmons stared at him for a short moment, deciding whether or not he should take offense. He chose not to and raised his hand in a jaunty gesture of good-bye. Turning on his heel, he walked off.

Wilhelm glanced at his pocket watch. He was somewhat before time for his appointment with Goldman.

He walked the distance to the rendezvous as though he were a common citizen out for a pleasant stroll, and arrived in good time at the small restaurant called the Albatross located on a small lane just off the High Street.

Goldman sat, shrunken into the shadows, at a small table near the kitchen. Such a modest selection of accommodations was sadly out of keeping with his normally flamboyant manner. His hair had faded back from his forehead. It was now a white tonsure, a narrow band just above his ears. He had allowed the remnants of his hair to grow long.

He stood to shake hands as Wilhelm approached. He seemed to have lost a bit of weight. His suit hung upon him as though the body within were very tired. He was scarcely the same man Wilhelm remembered. Suddenly Goldman smiled, and the man he had been laughed from his eyes.

'So, my friend, you seem none the worse for that island's weather.'

'I find pleasure in it.'

They sat down, amenities done, the smile fading on Goldman's face and leaving the stranger there.

'I wish I might say that I find pleasure in my post. I live in London, do you know?'

Of course Wilhelm knew. He nodded.

'Filthy weather there,' Goldman went on. He drew his chair closer and laid a hand on Wilhelm's arm. It trembled there.

'This direct contact is not very good spy procedure, is it?' he said conspiratorially. 'Of course it is not. But the spy business goes badly. At first I had all manner of funds to parcel out to my agents and to maintain my cover while going about my real business. I lived in a fine flat on Cadogan Square and dined at Simpson's on the Strand. I even had membership in one or two modest but very respectable clubs. Then the money from Germany began to shrink to a trickle.'

The whine of a much beaten and put-upon dog entered his voice.

'I protested, naturally. I was told that I must practice a greater measure of austerity, to curtail expenditures.

'I was told to make the bicycle shop pay its own way,' he said with massive indignation.

'Bicycle shop?' Wilhelm responded.

'My cover. A shop in Bayswater. So much for the rewards of the academic life. I was a professor, you know?'

His voice grew clotted with frustration and sudden rage.

'Can't they understand? There is so much correspondence, so much detail work. I have more than forty operatives to run.'

Wilhelm felt moved to comfort the hand that clutched at his sleeve.

'These days is there so very much to be done?'

'These are the days of organization, establishment. It's easy enough for you in that warm, snug tavern you own. But I have the concerns of all of you on my shoulders.'

Suddenly, without a break, he became affable.

'Is it a nice place you have?'

'Yes.'

Goldman looked down upon Wilhelm's hand on his own. He released Wilhelm's sleeve and quickly reversed the positions of their hands. He became the approving uncle.

'Excellent, excellent. And the women? You've made some pleasurable liaison?'

Wilhelm smiled, almost sheepishly, and shook his head.

Goldman leaned back and waved his hands. 'I must not pry. No, no, no.'

Goldman was silent for a long time, a strange smile on his face, as though he were remembering soft arms and limbs from long ago that once had warmed him and filled him with desire. Wilhelm wondered again at the reason for this meeting. Goldman was acting like nothing so much as a lonely man who simply wanted to chat awhile with an old friend. Even an acquaintance would do.

Wilhelm finally broke the silence.

'Have you eaten?'

Goldman returned with the startled look of a man who comes face to face with his executioner. He ignored the suggesion.

'What it comes to is this. Money is needed to continue our good work. Since the funds are unavailable from the usual sources, I have been ordered to call in the loans given to the agents to establish their bona fides.'

'Surely they were not loans? Surely the money and the identities they bought were normal expenditures.'

'Yes, naturally, but we are none of us in this for the money, are we? Is it not for the Fatherland we exile ourselves? It is. Our country now asks a greater sacrifice.'

'Does our government expect us to be efficient if we must struggle for a living? That takes all of one's time these days.'

Goldman's face flushed with anger or with the impatience of teaching a dull student.

'The government cannot officially or unofficially fund us. Don't you read the papers? Germany changes leadership almost weekly. She is being torn apart from within. Our superiors are above the fight. Quietly waiting. And they are short of money.'

'Whom then do we work for?'

'For Germany. For the greater Germany.'

'I know. But who are our leaders?'

'That I cannot say.'

Goldman raised a hand diminished in its command, and the waiter idled over to the table. Goldman ordered a very light dinner. Wilhelm ordered the same meal.

'Don't you read the papers?' Goldman suddenly repeated.

'Yes.'

'Assassination, murder, riot, rebellion. We can only wait until there is one leader. But we must wait for the sake of the nation. Rathenau was murdered yesterday.'

'I know.'

'He was a fine man. He was a Jew.'

Wilhelm didn't know how to respond or if he was meant to.

'I am a Jew,' said Goldman.

'I supposed as much.'

The meal came and was eaten in uncomfortable silence. It seemed to depress Goldman anew. His mood shifted from moment to moment.

'Now to matters of money. You've done well?'

'I make a living. I'm afraid there would be no way of returning the original money short of selling the tavern.'

'No, no. That would never do. Your post is vital. Two hundred pounds? You could raise that?'

'Half, perhaps.'

'You must do it then. For the present, give me what you can.'

'Mr. Goldman, if I were expected to bring money with me, why didn't you inform me in your letter?'

'Didn't I? So many details. So many.'

Goldman stared at him. Wilhelm felt embarrassed as he did when a beggar accosted him. He reached into his pocket and removed his purse. He removed two five-pound notes and offered them.

Goldman took the notes and folded them until they were very small and placed them in his vest pocket. His eyes never left the wallet.

'You have enough for the rest of your journey?'

'Sufficient. I have a few purchases to make.'

'Of course. I understand.'

Wilhelm wondered how deeply in trouble with his superiors Goldman was. How much had his expensive flat in Cadogen Square and meals in fine restaurants eroded the money given him for more important pursuits?

'I will make out a check for the balance.'

'No, no. Good technique demands that we have as few records and bits of paper, as few public transactions as possible floating about. Is it your intention to return directly to Stromness? You said something about purchases. Perhaps your bank . . .?'

'My principal account is in a bank in Glasgow.'

'How quickly could you manage the round trip?'

'The day after tomorrow.'

'We could meet at the railway station at eight in the evening. Will that suit?'

'Yes.'

'Settled then.' He seemed to relax and to swell a bit with a burden removed.

'Now tell me things. The mood of the people. Are there any disgruntled ones that might prove useful to us in the future?'

They talked for a short while. Wilhelm had the feeling that Goldman had absolutely no interest in what he had to tell him. That he was tolerating his part in a ridiculous but necessary charade. He himself felt irritated and foolish. What possible use could these scraps of supposition have to a secret group without present power or plan of action? He, too, felt they were playing at a child's game and desperately wanted the fantasy to end.

They danced through to the end of the pavane.

Goldman insisted on paying for the meal. On the street he hailed a taxi and, as though belatedly recalling his manners, offered Wilhelm a lift to his destination. He seemed happy for Wilhelm's refusal.

Wilhelm felt strangely lost as he watched the taxi move off down the roadway.

CHAPTER 3

Another train carried Wilhelm toward Glasgow. He thought of Goldman. The painful look of frayed respectability about him. The pitiable attempt at a certain raffishness of manner that echoed hollowly against the backdrop of his obvious fear. It seemed to be the terror of a running hare pursued by hounds. Would the loose, nebulous organization they both 'worked' for have the means of disciplining a wayward servant? Wasn't it only the stubborn loyalty of its members that kept it, however loosely, together?

He was suddenly shaken, nearly overwhelmed, by the idiocy of this essentially ridiculous condition he found himself in. A sensible man would make a new connection in Glasgow and go on to London. He would then secure a passage across the channel to France. He would board a train or trains until he reached Bavaria. He would take an oxcart or go afoot to his home. He would begin to gather events to himself. There had been few enough events to remember, it was true, but he would gather them all the same, no matter how small and trivial. He would collect enough to allow himself to admit that he had lived.

There were so few to remember.

As a schoolboy in Bavaria, the son of a minor official in the municipal government of the township of Garmisch, his scholarship had been mediocre, his athletic triumphs pitifully few. He pleased his instructors with his obedience and quiet demeanor. He was notable among his fellows for his scrupulous honesty and demanding sense of honor. He had been told often enough by his slightly comic martinet of a father that he was a part, even if distant and obscure, of a great Junker family. His was, therefore, a soldier's discipline. His every action was dictated by an unwritten book of rules and an imaginary pitiless clock in his father's keeping. It was joked about by his schoolmates that he even 'jigged' Fat Gerda by the numbers. He had bitterly regretted the need to line up with others of his schoolmates and fumble between her sweaty thighs. He had looked on it as a necessity – an act engaged in for reasons of health. A boy of fourteen is mightily concerned with facial blemishes, virility and his general physical well-being.

Gerda had taken her pay in play toys and candy or, often, just in her swinish pleasure. Wilhelm had developed an abiding distaste for the commerce of sex.

In the years to come he had frequent recourse to it, but that was long after first innocence was past, long after the shine of adolescence was gone. The adventures of that time had been small ones lived in the confines of a small and quiet town. It was so placid that a letter received by his father in the late spring of 1902 was enough to be a matter of celebrity.

The postmistress had noted the heavy cream-colored vellum of the envelope. It bore a heavily embossed family crest and an honorable cachet, instead of a stamp, at the corner. The cachet was a privilege given by the Kaiser to respected and valued servants of the Crown.

Katy, the Oerter maidservant, was afraid to take the letter from the mailman. After some discussion he slipped it through the door slot, somewhat disturbed that such a notable document should be treated in such a plebeian manner. Frau Oerter held a conference with Katy, who was friend as well as servant, and it was decided that she should remove the mail from the basket and place it on the hall table in the usual way, but that the object of so much attention should be placed on the silver dish used for calling cards on formal occasions.

Toward evening the foot traffic outside their door increased perceptibly, and many curious glances were cast at the modest brick house. Wilhelm arrived home from the Gymnasium, where he had been involved that day and all that week in final exams. This night his father and he were to talk of his future. The excitement generated around the letter captured him, too. The household waited for the father to come home.

Otto Oerter walked toward home in sharp cadence, as on parade. He swung his walking stick very slightly. Too great an arc was considered effete and Parisian by those who knew such things. He tipped his hat to passing ladies and gentlemen on a carefully weighted scale. The air space between hat and head indicated Oerter's estimation of their social importance. He was espied from the window as he turned up the walk. Katy ran to put on a small dress apron. At the door Otto made a show of noting the time on the face of the heavy gold hunting watch. His wife opened the door and received into her hands his bowler and stick. She kissed his cheek, and he patted hers.

His heart leaped when he saw the impressive letter, but he made calm show of sorting through the rest of the mail, perfunctorily casting aside that which he considered of little importance. Two envelopes were put aside along with 'the' envelope to be read after the evening meal, as was his unchanging custom.

The meal was filled with tension and soon completed. In the parlor Otto made a show of putting on his pince-nez and with slow deliberation read the other communications first. His wife sat on the edge of her chair, hands folded in her ample lap. Wilhelm stood behind her, and Katy hovered discreetly in the doorway. Otto slit the envelope with the paper knife and carefully unfolded it. He read it through once and then again. He glanced at Wilhelm, unable to conceal the flush of pleasure on his pinched face. Two spots of color glowed high on his cheeks. His household reacted to the sign of profound agitation like hunting dogs at the sound of the horn.

'This concerns you, Wilhelm,' he'd said. 'Please to sit down.'

He glanced at Katy half-hidden in the entry.

'Since Katy will, perhaps, have one less room to clean, one less thoughtless boy to pick up after, she should come into the room and hear this.' He smiled his permission for Katy to stand just inside the doorway. He was a man not without humor or kindness. He polished his glasses on the fine cambric handkerchief plucked from his sleeve.

'So. This correspondence is from his excellency Herr von Sonnedorf: "My esteemed Herr Oerter. It has come to my attention, through Cousin Ludi, that your son, Wilhelm, has reached the age of seventeen and has successfully, if not brilliantly, completed his courses in the Gymnasium. No matter. I consider efficiency and obedience superior qualities. Brilliance often is the cause of disorder.

' "I have no male issue and no grandsons, nephews or cousins of my name to fulfill my hopes and traditions. Your connection with the family, though distant and not in direct line of blood, nevertheless urges me to suggest you send young Wilhelm to me for the summer. At the end of that time I shall decide on his future. Perhaps a cadet school or suitable training for a diplomatic career. We shall see. In all events, I feel certain this opportunity for your son will not be unwelcome." '

Otto removed his glasses and fixed Wilhelm with a benign stare. 'His excellency goes on with small family gossip. So, Willy?'

His father called him Willy only in his most expansive, generous and self-important moods. Willy had kept his silence, knowing no response was being asked for, no decision of his to be made.

'I will reply at once. What an opportunity, Willy. I expect you should leave for the ancestral home in Spremberg within a fortnight.'

Wilhelm later had had the opportunity to read the letter for himself, without his father's knowledge. There had been no family gossip, of course, and this distant and ancient relative by marriage had certainly not addressed Herr Oerter as 'my esteemed.' How like his father to assume more petty respects and honors than had been extended. How like him to decide without any consultation that Wilhelm would be eager for such an apprenticeship.

The letter from the aristocratic Von Sonnedorf proved to be a devise designed to secure an unpaid servant to act as companion to the old man during his sojourn at the spa of Baden-Baden.

The general proved to be an ancient kept alive by excessive humidity and heat.

Their first meeting set the tone of their relationship. The old man lay in a huge canopied bed, in a room made a sweltering miasma by the heat of a roaring fire though the month was June. Von Sonnedorf looked like nothing so much as a great, nearly shapeless troll that had fed too long on toadstools and was in danger of becoming one. He was breakfasting on a dozen large burgundy grapes. Wilhelm noted, with wonder, that they had been peeled and seeded.

'Come closer, boy. Am I to shout at you?' Wilhelm stepped closer.

'Your quarters are satisfactory?'

'Yes, Granduncle.'

They were not. His room was a closet only just on the proper side of the hotel servants' quarters.

'I am not your uncle, grand or otherwise. Our relationship is so tenuous as to be of no consequence.'

So much for his father's pride of family.

'Yes, your Excellency.'

Von Sonnedorf cleared his throat. It had the dry, rustling sound of bats' wings. His laughter, Wilhelm was to discover, simply sent more bats into flight.

'Can we settle on mein Herr or Herr von Sonnedorf?'

Wilhelm nodded dumbly and found that was all that was ever to be expected of him.

In Glasgow the freighters wallowed like great whales along the Rothesay dock, Clydeside. Wilhelm was setting out to satisfy the second of his reasons for the excursion.

He walked along the wet cobbles, through the narrow, tortuous streets. The lamps, streaked by greasy mist, shone fitfully, and gooseneck fixtures, curved over scabrous doorways, scarcely illuminated the signs marking grog shops, decaying hotels and seamen's rests. The whores leaned, sprung-hipped, against the dirty buildings, their spiked heels little protection against the damp.

'Care to come home, luv?' The voice was time-racked and woolly with gin.

Feeling a sick reluctance, Wilhelm peered into the shadowed doorway. The old whore stepped into a better light. Her scarlet mouth stretched in a terrible clown's grin. It had the deadly evil of the rictus sardonicus that marked self-destruction by strychnine. Her eyes glittered like the spiny stilettos of the sea urchin. The white powder she used stopped below the point of her chin, leaving her skinny throat pitifully exposed. Wilhelm murmured an apology that sounded like a retching. He walked on, followed by her laughter touched with madness.

Two prostitutes, bolder, lustier, blocked him.

'A penny a kiss. Gi' me five bob and take what you wish.'

The other one touched her crotch. 'I've got a warm spot for you, dearie. In my heart,' she brayed.

A flamboyant woman with carrot-red hair stepped in front of him. Wilhelm felt panic rising in his throat.

'Please, please,' Wilhelm protested weakly.

Wilhelm took a few stumbling steps backward away from her caressing hand. Then he began to walk off briskly.

'Here now, you stuck-up bastard. Don't go shopping in a

market where the fish ain't to your fancy,' she screeched after him.

Wilhelm began to run. A pinwheel of pain flickered around and around in his chest. He stopped beneath a streetlamp. His nose was filled with the odor of cheap scent. He blew into a white handkerchief that smelled of laundry soap.

He turned to the sound of a small voice, a somehow pleasing compound of the raveled breaking tones of a small girl and the throaty imitation of a grown woman.

'You mustn't run so. It's a cold night, and you'll catch your death.' She was very thin. Fragile. Her face had the paleness of alabaster, somewhat luminescent. The paint she had applied was muted and somehow touching.

'I was just – it is to say,' Wilhelm faltered.

'I know. Regular sharks they are, snapping at a man's heels. No part of the lady about them. I wouldn't try to play their cheap games.'

'Are you then –'

'My time's for hire, yes. Call me Meggin. It's really my name.'

'My name is Johansen.'

She regarded him from beneath astonishingly thick lashes. She evaluated his dress and his manner, the slightly halting, accented, deferential tone of voice. No ordinary customer. She altered her course slightly.

'Understand, I don't spend my time with just every man. I mean it's more that I'm lonely than anything.'

My God, Wilhelm thought, do I look that naïve? To this sad child, do I look like an infant fresh from his mother's tit?

'May I buy you a coffee then?' he said gruffly.

'I won't have a thing to do with Chinks or Lascars. Won't even say hello to nigger sailormen.'

'I can see you're a virtuous girl. Tea perhaps?'

'Well, now,' she demurred, 'that will take a bit of time, won't it?'

'I would not expect your company for nothing.'

'Half a crown then,' Meggin chirped briskly.

Wilhelm nodded sharply and placed his hand beneath her elbow.

'Not for the whole night,' Meggin quickly amended.

Wilhelm wished she would play her part as he had imagined it. Always imagined it. Why did the romance he composed always turn into a farce?

'Yes, yes. We can arrange the fees and surcharges as we progress. Coffee or tea, then?'

'And a bun for afters,' she lisped archly. She bumped her tight, apple-hard buttock against his thigh.

The tearoom was tiny and spinster prim. In what might be considered the most Scottish of all cities, it made motions toward English properness. The small napkins were folded in grayed peaks, the water stains scarcely showed on the cutlery. The proprietress smiled a lot and fussed with her back hair as she sat near a small cashbox. It was a small place and somehow cozy.

Meggin took a long time removing her thin wrist-length gloves. Wilhelm noticed with a surge of pity that her knuckles were red and chapped. Her hands fascinated him. They had a bird life all their own. They were ladylike and graceful. The mechanics of her profession, the flirting eye, suggestive smile, had left the life of her hands untouched. Without false manners.

A slight color, not of the wind or of paint, rode on her cheeks, high up beneath clear blue eyes.

Wilhelm captured one of the hands in his own.

'Does this place please you?' he asked as one would ask a favorite niece or grandchild on holiday with a favorite uncle or granddad.

'I don't often come to the High Street. Cabs are terribly dear, and I don't fancy trams much. Why did you want to come to this part of town?'

'I thought you might like it.'

'Clean and very neat, in'nt it?'

The waitress stood by the small table, her hands folded below her thin chest.

Meggin looked at the bill of fare, pursing her lips like a child before the counter of a sweet shop.

'Please,' Wilhelm said, 'anything you like. Anything at all.' He was beginning to feel festive.

'I just don't know. A savory?'

'By all means. A rarebit, yes? Tea? Of course, tea and cakes. Many little cakes.'

Wilhelm looked at the shiny-eyed girl. He realized his smile had become a grin and was glad of the sense of holiday he felt.

'You are very young.'

'Not very.'

'How did you ever –' He paused, reluctant to pry.

'I knew you would ask. You look the kind of man who always asks how a girl like me came into this work.'

Wilhelm gestured, begging her to disregard his lapse of courtesy.

'Oh, I don't mind. It's just that every girl's story is much the same, in'nt?'

She glanced up at the return of the waitress. When the woman left, Meggin said, 'I have no family. No school to speak of.'

She giggled suddenly. 'Shall I be Mum?'

She poured the tea carefully.

'Milk?'

Wilhelm shook his head.

'Sugar?'

'*Citron*, please.'

'Lemon. I know that word. French, in'nt?'

She poured her tea half full of milk and added three teaspoons of sugar.

'I mean, girls will say there is no work and they have to eat. Or she's been ruined by a man who said he loved her,' she said between bites of the savory. 'Or there was a nasty evil older brother or an uncle or even a father.'

'Please, I should not have asked.'

She dropped the subject at once. 'Have a cake. They're very good,' she said and touched his hand. 'You're a foreigner?'

'Swiss.'

'I was given a little cuckoo clock what came from there. A sailor gave it to me. A sailor in the Swiss Navy.'

'The Swiss have no navy,' Wilhelm smiled.

'You see how men lie to a girl?' she said in mock anger. 'But after all, I do have the clock, don't I?'

A ship's horn sounded from Clydeside. She turned her head sharply. 'Are you ready to go to my place?'

'Perhaps we might take in an entertainment together. There is a music hall?'

'Quite good, too.'

'Well, then.'

'You understand, in our profession we have a saying. "Time is money." '

Wilhelm felt a sudden stricture in his throat.

'Of course. The saying is common to most – professions.'

The variety 'palace' was pleasingly colorful and garish. Tea and cakes, chocolates and buns, even ale and bitters could be purchased by the patrons of the more expensive box seats. An array of edibles occupied Meggin's hands and mouth. The comic turns occupied her eyes and her laughter. The place, the people, the performers were happily unsophisticated. The hoariest joke, most obvious pun drew waves of deep gut laughter from the audience. Frequently they talked back to the actors onstage. They were often far wittier.

Wilhelm laughed along with the others. He had a need to. He didn't find them particularly amusing. He primed the pump of good feeling by deliberate laughter so that he might finally laugh spontaneously.

His eyes fell often upon Meggin. She giggled and burbled and slapped at his sleeve.

The comics raced about at a furious pace. They were joined by a blowsy, bespangled woman. Her body was aging beneath the glow of greasepaint. Her tights-encased legs were still handsome.

Meggin glanced at him sidelong. He noticed a stronger blush flood her cheeks. She seemed in distress.

As he would of a child, he immediately thought of the bizarre variety of things she had fed into her skinny body. He leaned forward.

'You are not feeling well?'

'It embarrasses me. That woman there. Oh, I've been to music halls before, but I don't think it's very proper for a woman to show her legs like that in public.'

CHAPTER 4

The stockings Meggin wore were of black cotton lisle. They were rolled to a point above the knee and fixed there with a threepenny bit twisted and secured. Her coat and hat were carefully hung up in a small, nearly empty cardboard wardrobe.

She still wore her gloves against the cold as she stooped to light the inadequate cannel-coal fire laid in the grate. She made little bird noises as she moved about fussing at a few skinny-legged dolls dressed in satin. They had small painted mouths and vacant eyes. She turned a photograph of some nearly forgotten sailor to the wall. It was her small fantasy that the man was her fiance gone to sea, but not lost to her. She waited for his return.

She removed her dress. Her chemise was soiled. She'd not bothered to rinse it out the morning before. Her clients took little enough notice. She removed it.

Her breasts were no larger than two oranges. She sometimes despaired at their size, knowing them to be bad for business. She tried to compensate for the lack of them in other ways.

Men came back to her often, seeking her tense, answering thrusts and strangled cries. They left, certain they had truly aroused the whore, that the professional act had become real and pleasurable to her. The belief puffed them up mightily.

For some men, and for an extra fee, she used her lips and tongue on their genitals. It repelled her, but her very reluctance and tentative explorations led them to believe that she had never done it before, that passion had driven her to the added intimacy.

The chill roughened the flesh of her upper breasts and made the nipples pucker and cringe. She modestly covered herself with a gaudy dressing gown.

Wilhelm stood by the window of the tiny bed-sitting room set high up among the eaves of the crumbling tenement. The fog massed along the waterfront streets. He couldn't see very far across the roofs of the city. He felt confined, but safe, in a milky cage.

'You can take off your coat. It's warming up a bit,' Meggin ventured.

Wilhelm removed his coat and hat. His silent preoccupation made the streetwalker a bit nervous. She took his overwear from him. His pale-blue eyes seemed to reflect the least ray of light and were deep the way cold seas are deep.

He removed his jacket and undid his tie.

'You can put those things on the chair.'

She helped him with the collar stud at the back and was for a moment shaken with a remembrance of the short crisp hairs on the back of her father's neck when she'd been a little girl and helped him dress for work. He was gone these past four years. Dead in the Paupers' Hospice. Dead of cheap drink and lost ambitions.

'Would you like a cup of tea? The kettle's on the hob.'

'No, thank you.'

'A little tot of whiskey or a glass of port? The port is from Portugal.'

'Yes, that would be nice.'

She brought him the wine. He sat on the chair in long woolen trews, one sock still on.

She got into the bed and removed the covering robe.

'Will you come to bed?'

Wilhelm put aside the glass of wine, went to the bed and lay beside her. They were strangers preparing to enter into the most intimate of human exchanges. She was puzzled and somehow discomfited. She touched his hand tentatively. He clasped it to his chest. After a moment she moved it down his body opening the buttons of the shirt as she went. He called up a memory of the first urgent passion of his boyhood. It became present lust. He took the frail, thin body of Meggin.

Meggin drew up to him, crying softly. The cries were true ones.

He was quickly spent.

'Please, again,' Meggin said urgently. 'I'm really good, you know. Men tell me I'm very good.'

'Yes, little one.'

He stroked her hair and pressed her head into the hollow of his shoulder. The coal fire glowed weakly. Meggin shuddered.

'Put something on. You'll take cold,' Wilhelm said.

She left the bed and put on her chemise. Wilhelm regarded her with sadness in his eyes.

She returned and snuggled against him. A clock struck, and Wilhelm gestured in irritation.

Meggin spoke suddenly. 'A shopgirl can make two pound a week. The fact she's a "respectable" working girl don't stop the chief clerk or the delivery boy from grabbing and pawing at her in the stock room. A housemaid makes even less, eats worse than the house pets, has no time of her own, and if the master of the house is too old or too afraid of his wife to pinch her behind, there's a pimply-faced boy around to make it black and blue.'

She rushed her words, hoping to distract him. She didn't want him to leave. Wilhelm left the bed and began to dress.

'You do keep yourself fit, don't you?' She endeavoured to flatter. He made no answer.

'Truth is, some girls have a hard time of it. Up from the farms and villages to the city. There's times when there's no work to be had, but that's small excuse. Do you know why most girls whore? Because we're lazy, most of us. We whore for the easy money.'

Wilhelm was having trouble with his collar stud. Meggin left the bed. She stood behind him and fixed it. Impulsively she threw her arms around his waist and hugged herself to his broad back. In the moment she felt very much the wife sending her husband off to work. She turned him around and did his tie.

'It was a very nice time you showed me this evening.'

'I enjoyed it very much myself.'

She helped him with his vest.

'I want you to know I never felt that you were paying for my time.'

Wilhelm touched her cheek and smiled mechanically.

'I felt like we were walking out together,' she added.

She buttoned his suit coat and brushed an imaginary bit of dust from a lapel.

'Mr. Johansen?' She lifted the edge of the name shyly. 'Will you tell me your first name?'

'Carl.'

She kissed him lightly at the corner of his mouth. He walked to the door, his coat over his arm, his hat in his hand.

'I want you to know I like you,' she whispered.

Wilhelm turned at the door. His glance surveyed the poor room, the nearly dead fire, the satin pillows taken from the bed and neatly stacked on a chair. He pitied the screen that obscured the washstand. The brush and comb and mirror upon it. The enameled metal basin and pitcher. The second basin of water purpled with permanganate. She hadn't washed her genitals with it.

A heavy desire filled his chest, to protect the miserable little thing that shivered slightly. The dawn washed her with a music hall's approximation of moonlight.

'I didn't try to fool you,' she said.

'Perhaps I wanted to be fooled.'

He slept alone in a modest hotel close to the financial district. The next day he withdrew a hundred pounds in cash. He kept an account separate from the funds secured in the bank of Stromness. When he played the role of the spy, he considered it his escape money in the event of discovery. Or perhaps the price of his freedom from his duty? Occasionally, as today, in the role of the modestly successful proprietor of a small inn, he thought of it as a nest egg. He felt put upon having to reduce his account by the amount of Goldman's request.

The train rocked its way toward Aberdeen. Upon the announcement of service in the dining car, he unaccountably decided to indulge himself. He never ate on trains. He was a frugal man by nature and upbringing.

On the way to the dining car he thought he caught a glimpse of Simmons in a compartment. He quickly averted his head. He had no desire to be bored to death on the return journey. Besides, he felt a deeper antipathy than simple boredom toward the garrulous salesman. He gave no further thought to it, however.

He dined sparingly but with unusual pleasure on a small cutlet with mashed peas and boiled potatoes.

On the way back to his car, he once again averted his head when he passed the compartment in which Simmons might be seated. Wilhelm had no wish to satisfy his curiosity as to the accuracy of his recognition. He napped fitfully until the train chuffed into the station at Aberdeen.

It suddenly occurred to him as he stepped out of the railroad car that Goldman and he had not mentioned a spot within the train station to meet.

There were several platforms. Would Goldman expect him to make contact with him on the platform serving the trains going south? Or, since he was to receive money and there was a certain courtesy involved, would he have intention of coming to Wilhelm?

The passengers flowed around him as he considered the petty problem. There was the fact that Goldman was his superior, and therefore, protocol demanded that Wilhelm seek him out.

He smiled wryly. Of such affairs of great moment was fashioned the profession of espionage.

He walked slowly to the kiosk closest to the main entrance, and purchased a newspaper. He looked up and down the platform which was quickly cleared of the discharged passengers. There was no sign of Goldman's bulky figure.

He looked across the way. Across four sets of tracks. In the near distance the whistle of a passenger train announced its approach to Aberdeen. There were many people waiting for its arrival on the Southbound platform. He methodically surveyed them, his eyes moving from left to right. At the end of the sweep he could see the smoke of the steam engine rising above the roofs of the warehouses. His eyes moved back along the line of people stirring, milling about, moving in closer to the edge of the platform.

There he was. Goldman was standing about five feet back from the track well. He craned his neck. He looked like a great tortoise surveying a beach. The train roared into the station mouth.

Their eyes met. Goldman shouted and moved forward. He waved his arm frantically to capture Wilhelm's attention. He had a great, broad smile on his face. Even from the distance, it seemed a grin of inexpressible relief.

The crowd massed up around those points where the doors would open when the train came to a full stop. Wilhelm raised his hand to acknowledge Goldman's presence. There was a surge in the mass of humanity around Goldman. He pitched forward onto the track and under the drive wheels of the engine.

The screech of the brakes, the shrieks of the people, the hiss of steam – all melded together in one crash of sound. Above it all, Wilhelm thought he heard Goldman crying out.

Wilhelm stood stolidly. His hand was still upraised. He lowered it slowly and looked dumbly about. He thought of leaping onto the tracks and running to his friend, but he stood still.

In the crowd around the point of the disaster there was the

momentary glimpse of a face. Wilhelm thought it was Simmons, but the face moved away in a tick of time and was lost to his view.

Wilhelm hurried to another platform, and the train that would take him back to Inverness and the sea passage home, with a choking fear in him. It was the fear of unforeseen death which carried with it the atmosphere of human fragility. As he sat and waited on a hard wooden bench, the feeling left him slowly. It seemed to leave his body through the soles of his feet and the tips of his fingers.

The journey to Stromness was only a passage of time. He thought of the jovial man he had first met, so dramatically changed in appearance and manner by the time of the last meeting. He realized, with a strange tightness in his chest, that he had, in some fashion thought of Goldman as a friend. As a link to the homeland.

The death of the man, the murder perhaps, clearly defined the fact that Goldman was not simply trying to balance the books of his stewardship. He had been a man on the run, desperately gathering up what funds he could for his escape and evasion.

Was it Simmons he had glimpsed in the crowd? Was Simmons an enforcer? An assassin for the shadow force of which, he himself, was such a tiny and insignificant part?

How must he proceed after this tragedy? He had no one to contact except the mail drop in Switzerland. He would write a letter explaining the facts as they had occurred to the best of his knowledge. He did not know whether to mention Simmons, since he could not report his involvement with certainty.

In the morning the small fishing craft pulled into Stromness.

Three old men sat cross-legged on the quay, gumming their pipestems and mending the seines. They were the three ancients of the community often called the Witches of Endor. They were happy men in their way.

In such closely related societies there is work for the youngest and the eldest, and very few are left to feel alone and useless.

'Morning, Will.'

Siever Scarff raised a gnarled hand, and Wilhelm touched the brim of his hat. He walked on, strangely plodding for a man of thirty-seven years.

‘A strange one is Will Hartz,’ Handy said.

‘Quiet in himself in a rare way,’ Booth added.

‘Never known him to pass more than the time of day with a woman,’ said Scarff, pinning the point.

‘Most every spinster in all the town has her cap set for him.’

‘Gives them just a nod and a good day is all.’

‘He’s been asked to take tea up to Kendrick’s cottage from time to time.’

‘Ai, Molly’s a handsome woman, and keeping house as the sister of a man isn’t the same as being the wife.’

‘Will’s not yet taken tea there.’

‘Would I were twenty years younger and Molly free to marry.’

The old men turned their faces to the pale sun. Memories of women and wives warmed them.

‘It’s not the natural way for Will to act. What does the man do alone in bed these cold nights?’

‘These German types is cold, odd folk. Met my share during the war. Captured seamen and all,’ Scarff said.

Handy pinched his own cheek. ‘So have we all. So have we all. Besides, Will is a Swiss. They was neutral.’

‘And there’s the man’s trouble.’

CHAPTER FIVE

The letter to Switzerland was written one evening in the first week of June, 1922. Wilhelm fashioned a report that told the bare bones of the incident. He described the summons from Goldman and his control's request for funds. He told of his journey to secure what money he could, his return and the tragic accident in the train station as he remembered them.

He could say little more with certitude, for the more he examined what had occurred, the more he realized he could in no way offer his surmises, his beliefs or his suspicions concerning Simmons.

Having sent the report and requested further instructions, he tried to put the matter from him. But a constant, though slender, rage seemed to occupy a dark part of his heart and mind.

One hot summer's day there was excitement in the streets of Stromness. Children were running and adults hurrying down to the quay. It was on to noon closing, and when his customers left to search out the reason for the excitement, Wilhelm followed along.

Nearly the entire town was gathered about a spot close to the mole which was the place of Wilhelm's nighttime contemplations.

A great shark had become entangled in the nets of one of the boats of the fishing fleet. It had been killed after a great struggle. Usually such predators, unacceptable by the island people as food fish, were cast off to be devoured by the very fish they devoured. This one, however, was a monster of its kind.

Wilhelm found a place next to John Kendrick. They gazed at the great fish lying like a great slab of molten steel upon the rocks. It was quite dead, yet seemed to radiate a terrible, elemental danger.

'Ugly devil,' Wilhelm said.

'Sixty foot of hellish fish,' John agreed. 'Greenland shark it is come down from the Arctic waters. Rare enough, and never have I seen one of this size.'

The children threw stones at the carcass and beat it with sticks while their fathers laughed and told them to give the devil hell.

'Fishermen hate sharks, do they not, John?'

Kendrick nodded his head.

'They've reason enough, they believe. Sharks ravage the schools and destroy the nets.'

There was a gentle questioning tone in his remarks.

'You don't hate them, John?'

Kendrick took a long, thoughtful moment before he answered.

'They are there in the sea doing what they were given to do. I'm not sure I'm a wise enough man to say which thing is good and which evil. Every creature does what is asked of it by its nature. It can't always reason out the purpose behind its acts.'

Later that night in the small sitting room, Wilhelm felt comforted by the incident and by the words his friend had spoken. He had made the necessary report. He could not hope to assess the good or bad of what had transpired. He would do what he must do. The first, indeed the only, order that had ever been impressed on him was that he should simply sit and wait until called upon to serve.

It was a simple command not at all simple to execute.

Months passed. The tavern's business went well. He found he could no longer refuse John Kendrick's invitations without being unforgivably rude. He took tea upon three occasions at Kendrick's cottage and treated the sister, Molly, with neutral politeness and regard.

On Friday, November 9, 1923, Wilhelm realized with something akin to physical shock that he had, these past months, nearly forgotten that there was a world in turmoil outside the Orkney Islands. More important, that his own crippled nation was being racked by brutal inflation, inner dissension, assassinations and despair.

The public room was filled with talk of the news that Adolf Hitler had overthrown the republican Bavarian government of Von Knilling. General Ludendorff had been declared the Commander in Chief of the 'National German Army,' which was believed to make of him the virtual dictator of Germany. There was speculation that General von Seeckt, who was loyal to the republic, would order the Reichswehr to march against Hitler's forces.

'Let the damned Germans kill each other off,' someone suggested. It seemed to be the general temper of the gathered men.

Wilhelm went to his rooms with a great impatience storming in his blood. Events of great moment were afoot in Germany. The people were shouting to be heard. The people were marching. He longed to be with them instead of buried away in this northern tomb. He wished desperately for a letter from Switzerland. He wanted to be told that a new superior had been assigned him and that he was not forgotten.

By the next day the revolt of the Hitlerites was broken and their leaders discredited. The attempt at a coup d'état was called the maddest farce pulled off in memory by the same people and newspapers that had been crying fear of war the day before.

A week later Wilhelm received a visit from Mr. Simmons, no longer a traveler in block and cordage. It was a few minutes before the afternoon closing that he appeared in the doorway.

'A pint of the best,' he said, and chose the stool at the far end of the bar to settle himself upon.

Wilhelm placed the mug of bitters in place on the bar top.

'You've been very patient,' Mr. Simmons offered.

Wilhelm dried his hands with a bar rag and regarded Simmons with a neutral stare.

'You've taken the lack of communication with rare calm. You haven't flooded your correspondent in Switzerland with questions and displays of panic. Such restraint has served your reputation very well.'

Wilhelm's eyes did not shift even a fraction, though a tumble of thoughts were charging through him. It was indeed apparent that the suspicions he once believed foolish were true. First, that Simmons was a fellow spy. Wilhelm's first error had lain in the fact that Simmons was no operative for the British but was a comrade of his own. Secondly, he had indeed seen Simmons on the day of Goldman's murder. Simmons was, in fact, the murderer.

He noted the subtle change in the manner of the one time drummer in ship chandler goods. Where once the man had been unpleasantly garrulous and even fawning, now he was assertive and somewhat arrogant.

'Was my reputation ever in danger?' Wilhelm asked. He felt a deep distaste of the man's arrogant manner.

'Everyone is under surveillance. It is necessary. We are creating a secret force whose loyalty and resolve must be beyond suspicion.'

'To what or to whom do I owe this loyalty?'

'To Germany,' Simmons said with some force, and then glanced around with hurrying eyes.

'Whose Germany?' Wilhelm asked.

'What?' Simmons replied, staring at Wilhelm vacantly.

'I mean to ask, the Kaiser's Germany?'

'The monarchy is done for.'

'The Bolshevik Germany then? Or the Republic of Germany?'

Simmons straightened himself, and his neck grew rigid.

'Do you play word games with me?'

Wilhelm replied very softly in a voice of utter reason.

'No. I only wish to know whose voice I am to listen to. How am I to know if you represent the constituted authority I have sworn to serve?'

'How else would I know of your existence?'

Wilhelm spread his hands wide to attest to his good faith.

'The British must have counterforces.'

'They've gone back into their shells.'

'Indeed? Are you a German?'

'I consider myself so.'

'But you were not born in Germany or raised in Germany?'

'My father was a Rhinelander. My soul is German.'

Wilhelm had an almost overwhelming desire to laugh.

'I served the Fatherland in the Great War,' Simmons went on. 'I was given my present post for that service.'

'You killed Goldman,' Wilhelm interjected softly.

'He was an opportunist, a recidivist, a traitor.'

'But highly placed?'

'Mistakes are made. He was a professor. Intellectuals are rarely trustworthy.'

Better stolid fools like me, Wilhelm thought.

'He proved to have Communist sympathies. He was a Jew. Neither is to be trusted,' Simmons added.

'In our line of work no one is to be really trusted,' Wilhelm offered.

'That is true,' Simmons agreed.

‘Then why should I trust you?’

They looked at each other for a long moment. When he finally spoke, Simmons’ voice had a crisp edge to it.

‘You’re asking proof?’

‘Should I be less than cautious? After all, it seems that I have been following the orders of the wrong man.’

‘You will be contacted and given assurances,’ Simmons said stiffly.

‘Ah, assurances,’ Wilhelm breathed and smiled with great loathing upon Simmons.

Wilhelm’s simple doggedness was infuriating Simmons.

‘I want you to check on the sympathies of one Bostock. He may prove useful at some future date.’

‘This man is the island sot. A brute. Useless.’

‘You will allow us to make such decisions.’

‘I will wait for the assurances you’ve promised.’

‘If it’s in your mind to make some independent investigation of me in Kirkwall, let me tell you that my headquarters have been moved to London.’

‘Ah,’ Wilhelm said cheerfully, ‘you’ve gone into the bicycle trade.’

Simmons said, ‘What?’

Wilhelm felt the loathing clot his voice. ‘Did you murder Martin Goldman so you might improve your position? Did you kill a man without question of guilt or innocence because you wished to leave Kirkwall for the larger stage of London?’

Simmons rose stiffly.

‘I did what I was ordered to do by my superiors.’

‘Without personal ambition? Without hope of the reward?’

‘I followed the demands of duty,’ Simmons snapped. He turned suddenly. His heels beat a military tattoo across the floor, and he was gone.

‘Ah.’ Wilhelm leaned back as though he had found the answer to a most profound and perplexing problem. ‘Duty.’

He had done his duty to his father’s fiction of aristocratic family connections. He’d spent that summer in Baden-Baden doing his duty as footman to old Von Sonnedorf. He was his dog’s bone.

He entered the university with the celebrity of the Von Sonnedorf name as a cachet. Such patronage and his stolid, unsmiling demeanor were misinterpreted as aristocratic arrogance.

He knew it to be the fear that he seemed plebeian, gross and insular to his fellow students. He built his wall to protect himself against their derision. In the first year he made no friends and was much alone.

So it came as a great surprise when, at the beginning of his second year, he was asked to join a fraternity.

He wrote to his father to tell him of it, and his father wrote a letter in return that made no attempt to conceal his pride in his son.

The ceremonies of initiation were held in the upstairs room of a town beer cellar. It was long and narrow. At one end was a deal table with six chairs, one for each of the fraternity officers, set along one side of it. At the opposite end was another table nearly obscured by shadows. It was piled with equipment of a sort that looked vaguely athletic. The wall opposite the entry door was nearly covered end to end by long tables fashioned of carpenter's trestles and common doors. These were loaded with steins and dishes of sausage, a small keg of beer and round loaves of black bread. There were forty straight-backed chairs for the common membership.

There were eight nominees. They had been instructed to arrive at such-and-such an hour. At first they were the only souls present in the room. Within minutes a senior student, wearing an outlandish helmet and a velvet cape, entered and instructed them to line up in the center of the room two by two. Wilhelm found himself with a tall, pale boy in the second rank. The caped master of ceremonies lit the candles in the sticks at the officers' table. He lit more that were fixed in sconces upon the walls. Disturbing shadows were thrown about the room.

Suddenly it seemed filled with young men. The members of the fraternity were gathered, the officers seated, the ceremonies begun.

The new pledges were informed with great ceremony and at length about the long and honorable traditions of the fraternity of which they were invited to become members after a suitable testing of their own honor, will and courage. Such a fellowship was not to be entered into with reservations but with the deep resolve that the brothers would be loyal one to the other until death, if need be.

Wilhelm could not help thinking of the lodge of which his father was a member. The outlandish costumes. The pompous, juvenile secrecies. The handshakes and the passwords. The organization had always seemed to him a suitable excuse for men to gather and boast together and drink together.

The introductory ritual seemed to go on endlessly, and Wilhelm developed a nagging itch at his crotch. The dry, superior manner of the president did nothing to enliven or to speed the proceedings.

Wilhelm allowed himself to sink into lethargic waiting.

With a start he became aware that the preliminaries were over. The members of the fraternity had moved to the sides of the room. They straddled the chairs or stood on one leg propped against the walls in what they believed to be a properly nonchalant manner. Many had already provided themselves with steins of beer. One of the prerogatives of membership seemed to be the right to carry a personal tankard about, emblazoned with the fraternity coat of arms on the one side and the man's name, or personal coat of arms if he could claim one, on the other.

Certain young men, named as seconds for the evening, went to the table in the rear, and each returned with a set of equipment.

Wilhelm and the other new aspirants were set in two lines facing each other some two yards apart, face to face, and four yards distant shoulder to shoulder.

Wilhelm noted with surprise that shreds of fear glittered in the pale-blue eyes of the man opposite. Wilhelm glanced around, hoping to gather some idea of what was going on by the attitudes of those about him. He was regretful that he had not listened more closely to the president's words.

He was handed a jerkin made of rough linen, heavily quilted, a pair of steel goggles fashioned with elastic webbing to hold them over the eyes and a wooden stave roughly worked to the shape and length of a saber.

His second aided him. He laced the tunic behind Wilhelm's back. He adjusted the goggles so that Wilhelm had a maximum of vision through the slits cut into their faces. He handed the wooden saber to Wilhelm and stepped away. The young men faced each other, peering about like light-blinded bats. They shifted their feet uncomfortably. A laugh, high-pitched and short-lived, issued from the pale man opposite.

The president sat upon the council table, one booted foot planted on the floor, the other dangling idly. A brother hurried his tankard into his hand.

'Now, gentlemen,' he began in a low voice, 'the finest tradition of this fraternity is the honorable duel: the giving and the receiving of wounds in man-to-man combat. The tradition is laid in history, in the jousts of the Teutonic Knights. On this field a man's courage is tested. He who flinches from the blade is not fit to stand shoulder to shoulder with his peers. He is a man without courage and honor.'

Wilhelm now gave the youth his full attention. He was fascinated by his drawling voice.

'The scars you may receive are badges of honor. They are carried with pride.'

Wilhelm noticed that the president's face was unmarked.

'Some of you,' the president went on, 'are familiar with the use of the saber. Others are not. And so you will have the opportunity of practice and training. But please to understand that it is not our purpose to produce great swordsmen. Our only purpose is to test our resolve in the face of injury, our courage in the face of possible death.'

Wilhelm looked around at the assembled fraternity brothers. There were a few who bore scars upon their cheeks or brows. Either most were uncommonly lucky or skillful, or the ritual of the duel was an occasional affair. He knew the university officially frowned on such ceremonies. Unofficially, they turned their eyes away.

They reminded him of a crowd of village layabouts clustering about a dogfight. He felt laughter welling up within him.

The blow landed on his padded shoulder a second after he became aware of the downward sweep of the wooden stave. It startled him, and he jumped back, knowing he looked clumsy and foolish. There was a small ripple of laughter.

'So our young Mr. Oerter doesn't even deign to defend himself,' the president drawled. 'Courage, indeed. But we expect when the true steel is placed in your hand that you will not give your opponent an easy victory.'

The members laughed again. Wilhelm felt a strange quiet grow in him. He heard the wooden saber clatter to the floor. He removed the goggles.

'This all seems damned foolish to me,' he said.

There was the gasp of held breath and then a heavy silence. The president quirked his head as though he had not quite heard what Wilhelm had said.

'I fear I don't quite understand your meaning.'

'It's a game for children.'

The silence shattered into voices of contempt, derision, protest and hate. Most of all, hate.

The president spoke in a low voice to his chancellor. The young man walked the length of the hall and returned with a tunic, a set of goggles, and two heavy basket-hilted sabers.

Wilhelm's sense of inner quiet had left him. It was replaced with a painful metronome in his chest. He watched dumbly as the president set aside his glass and allowed himself to be outfitted. He did truly look like a knight being armored for combat.

'Now we shall play a game for men.'

He took the saber from the chancellor. Wilhelm's second thrust the other into Wilhelm's own hand. The pledges fell back to join the others. The president stepped quite close to Wilhelm.

'On guard.'

He whipped the saber upright before him above his head, his forearm in front of his smooth pale face.

'Paul,' he said.

Wilhelm's second moved a step closer.

'Upon the word you will commence the duel. Each round will be timed to the duration of one minute. The duel will end when one of the combatants retires from loss of blood.'

He raised Wilhelm's stiff arm over his head. The president stood unmoving, steel held high, until his salute should be returned.

Wilhelm wanted to say something, but his throat closed about the words. He felt like gagging. Fear? He thought not. Shame? Perhaps. Frustration? Most certainly. Why had he been thrust into this ridiculous posture? Why must he be the one to refuse to take part in a charade? Most of the others, he was certain, would willingly have given over the nonsense. Or would they? Was it not, instead, essential to their sense of identity? A comparatively felicitous badge of courage.

The president's blade flashed down. It seemed oily in the candlelight. Instinctively Wilhelm caught the blow on the hilt of his saber. A pure, clear note rang through the narrow room.

The president lifted his sword arm again and drove forward. Wilhelm was disturbed because he could not see the man's eyes. He fell back, catching the slashes as best he could. He was in it now with nowhere to go. Trapped in a mode of behavior he thought stupid. But in it all the same.

He felt the blade wrenched from his hand and watched the arc of light lining the president's saber as it descended toward his unprotected face. He threw up his arm. The blade stopped short of the mark. The president returned from his position of attack.

'A child's game, is it?' The president eyed Wilhelm coolly.

'I do believe so,' Wilhelm heard himself say. He tore the tunic from his body and dropped it with the glasses upon a convenient chair as he went out.

After the fiasco in the dueling fraternity's salle, he spent hours, even days, in pursuit of his motives.

He brutally asked himself if he'd been terrified of the pain that would be inflicted. He knew that he was not some masochistic damn fool who went about seeking injury and agony. He was touched, as nearly everyone was, with the almost amusing fear of the dentist's chair. He turned his head away when a needle was poked into his arm. Yet he had, more than once, endured severe pain with stoicism and what appeared to be nonchalance. But he'd never had fantasies of proving his courage by allowing a fox to gnaw at his entrails or sticking his hand into a fire. Until this moment.

In a foolish desire to prove his courage, he slowly extinguished a burning cigar on the back of his hand.

Wilhelm grasped his hand and looked up at the remembered pain. He became aware of Simmons' absence and remembered his abrupt exit. He'd left, Wilhelm thought to himself, propelled no doubt by duties of great urgency.

He closed up and walked to the quay to collect his mail from the packet. There was a five-pound tin of his special blend of tobacco, a narrow box marked 'Fragile,' another tin filled with Swiss candies, three letters and two Christmas cards.

Two of the letters he folded and placed in his pocket. He

knew what they contained or, rather, what they did not contain. He was always amused at the sheets of fiction, evidence of the German love of organization, detail and subterfuge. These small evidences supporting his fictional life in Switzerland seemed highly comedic.

The third letter was addressed in delicate flowing script. The hand of a woman. It was a communication from the authority in Germany. London had apparently been bypassed altogether. In obscure business and personal references he was informed that his control had been assigned. He would be contacted by Mr. Simmons, who was known to him by brief acquaintance on one or two occasions. Wilhelm smiled. He was foolishly happy for a moment that the obnoxious Mr. Simmons had arrived before receipt of the letter. He glanced out to sea where the mail packet, carrying his control off and away, chugged across the waters of the Flow.

'Mr. Simmons,' he murmured, 'I would like to tell you that I rather liked Mr. Goldman. He had a happy laugh from time to time.'

The last of the letter was composed of a few more chatty paragraphs designed to render it innocent if suspicious eyes were to read it. It was signed 'Heidi.'

Wilhelm thought of the fictitious 'Heidi.' How pleasant it would be if there were really such a girl in some toylike village. He examined the writing, delicate, yet precise, with all the refinement of copperplate script.

It was the hand, no doubt, of some aging lady, a minor factotum of some small wartime bureau now engaged in new and dreary enterprise. Did she believe that she was part of a great movement to restore the glory of the Reich?

Or perhaps it was the pen of an ex-customs guard with a great love of protocol and uniform. Was he now entitled to wear some insignia-blazoned coat and trousers with a stripe along the seams in the privacy of his rooms?

Wilhelm was drawn from his thoughts by the sounds of pleasant commotion. Children came skipping, laughing, quarreling, running, frolicking down the street. School was over, and this was the day of the mail boat's arrival. They raced toward Wilhelm, shouting his name, babbling about the mail. They stood in a semicircle around the bench upon which Wilhelm sat. Their faces were brightly flushed. Anticipation surfaced in their twinkling eyes. Their uncontrolled smiles contrasted with their customarily shy, almost somber manner with adults.

'So, school is out and everyone is very happy? Study and learning is useless, is it not, Sean?'

'No, sir, Mr. Hartz.'

'Then you enjoy school. You could scarcely tear yourself from it. That is so?'

Their heads bobbed. 'The mail packet came,' another boy ventured.

'Indeed it did. Did you get any mail?'

The children giggled and puffed out their cheeks at the prospect. The little boy lifted his shoulders in embarrassment and delight.

'The mail boat did indeed arrive this morning. And what importance should I put upon that?'

There was a babble of small sounds from which Wilhelm plucked the word 'Switzerland.' 'Switzerland? Have I heard of such a place? Where, I wonder, is it?'

'In Europe,' half of them shouted.

'But surely we are in Europe now.'

'In the Orkney Isles. That's where we are,' many replied.

'Orkney? Orkney? Sounds like a sty full of piglets.'

'In Scotland.'

'Ahhh.'

'In Great Britain,' Sean yelled.

'So that is where Switzerland is not, hey?'

'In Europe. In the mountains. In the snow. Near Austria. Near Italy. Near Spain.'

'Near. Near. And also near the moon. Well, I am not the schoolmistress, am I? Still I would ask you what Switzerland is famous for?'

'Mountains! Clocks! Sweets!' came tumbling out.

'For what?' Wilhelm pretended not to hear.

'Sweets! Sweets! Sweets!'

He portioned out the candy among the children. They ran off holding the sweets, each one wrapped in bright-colored foil. 'Not till after supper, mind,' Wilhelm called after them.

He held out his hand filled with the sweets to the last child who hung back from the others regarding everyone with detachment. Her eyes flicked away as though seeking an avenue of escape.

'Julie, wouldn't you like some, too?'

The twelve year old clasped her hands behind her back tightly.

'Come. Won't you sit and have a wee chat with me? If you have the time, of course.'

She perched next to him and carefully smoothed her skirt over her bony knees. Her eyes upon him were as solemn as a kitten's. Wilhelm lit his pipe.

'May I?'

'Please,' she murmured.

'It has come to my attention that someone of my acquaintance is very soon to have a birthday.'

'Who?'

'Why, Julie Bostock, I believe.'

'That's me.'

'So it is.'

'I'd near forgotten my birthday,' she said.

He nodded. 'I often forget mine. Or try to.'

'How did you know about my birthday?'

'Friends should find out such things. Will you have some sweets now?' Wilhelm extended his hand. Amid the colored foil nestled the small, slim box. Julie touched it with a tentative finger and glanced a question at his eyes.

'A special kind of sweet. Open it.'

Her fingers removed the brown mailing paper and revealed white tissue wrapped in a yellow ribbon. He could see the small pulse beating in the hollow of her neck. She removed the wrapping gently and paused again before opening the box. Wilhelm's own anticipation made prickles along the backs of his hands.

A tiny wristwatch lay in a bed of cotton. The corner of Julie's mouth twitched uncontrollably, and great crystal tears welled in her eyes.

'For your birthday. A small token of our friendship. Shall I put it on for you?' She nodded. He fixed it to her wrist. It hung loosely around the slender bones so like the twigs of a young birch. He made a gruff and jolly sound.

'A bit too large, is it now? I will take that home with me and make it smaller.'

Julie withdrew, placing her wrist against her neck. 'No, please!'

'As you wish. You will grow into it soon enough.'

Julie stared at the watch, struggling to believe the truth of it. 'Must I . . . tell you gave me this?' The child knew her father would pawn it for a bottle. She was already wise to the need for a hidden place. A dark place for her few treasures. A secret place her thoughts and her soul's desire.

'No, little one. No.'

She stood and walked a few paces from him. She turned, her face filled with intense love, her birdlike chest and arms trembling with unexpressed need. Displays of affection were alien to her.

CHAPTER 6

Two months later Wilhelm read with small interest of the trials of General Ludendorff, Adolf Hitler and eight other conspirators in the *Putsch* of the past November. It was noted from the outset that Hitler, Ludendorff and the others seemed not to take the trial very seriously.

By the fifth day of the trial the court, Germany and the world were growing weary of it all. Hindenburg laboriously read a prepared speech, fifty pages in length, to the tolerant court. Hitler went on for hours, lashing out right and left at Catholics and Jews, friends and foes. It was a display of Germanic patience and thoroughness that had overtones of a musical comedy turn.

It was generally agreed that their violent actions had succeeded in blackening their own cause and strengthening the position of the republic they sought to overthrow. The failed revolutionary was, at last, convicted and incarcerated in Landsberg Prison. Wilhelm was pleased to note that the German government and the German people were punishing the ridiculous upstart and adventurer. It was a fleeting opinion, expressed to himself, before he gave his attention to the improvement of the Sailing Master's business and services.

On a day in spring Wilhelm pedaled his bicycle along the pathway upon the westerly cliffs that comforted Stromness from some small amount of the Atlantic weather. He carried a small bunch of a variety of daisy, white-petaled and yellow-hearted. Each had a black dot in its center, slightly askew, like a drunkard's eye. Reaching the Kendrick cottage, he leaned the bicycle against the neat stone wall and removed the clip from his pants leg. He pulled out the crease to its morning sharpness.

The newly whitewashed face of the house was eyed with two windows half-curtained with sea-blue cloth, and the door, the upper half left partly ajar, was painted the same color. The sod and grass roof sat like a helmet, high-browed in front and sloping toward the back so that the farthest eaves sloped to the ground. The Kendrick cow was on it, nibbling at the fresh-growing grass. John appeared in the doorway, his heavily roped arms bared to the elbow.

'Welcome! Welcome!' He opened the door full wide. The largest room was sitting room and dining room and partial kitchen all in one. It glowed like a freshly scrubbed child's face. Molly was bending over the fire as she prepared the meal, her face flushed and tendrils of hair curling damply at her neck.

Wilhelm had been a few times in this room for tea or a man's hour of chat with John Kendrick. This was his first formal visit. Molly was still, in every real way, a stranger to him. Her appearance he knew well. How many evenings had he lain in bed describing her to himself? She was late on in her twenties, but even on this island, where most maidens were promised or wed, indeed delivered of one or more children by their eighteenth birthday, there was nothing of the spinster about her.

She was very nearly as tall as Wilhelm and, in fact, stood a good six inches above her brother. The masses of dark hair were pulled behind her ears and settled in a comfortable shape she rarely fussed or poked at. Her lips were a bit thin, with little curve or tilt, and her chin was somewhat too aggressive. Her nose was undistinguished. She could be called neither beautiful nor plain. She might be called a 'handsome' woman. Only her eyes were exceptional, large and luminous, at once direct and elusive.

'Molly, come along, girl,' John called, as though she were at least a field away.

She walked forward. 'Your sleeves, John.'

He laughed and began to roll them down as a gesture to gentility and hospitality. Wilhelm raised a hand in protest, asking him please not to bother or to stand on ceremony. He faced Molly's outstretched hand and offered the flowers. There was a moment's pleasant confusion that ended in laughter.

'Welcome to our home, Mr. Hartz.'

'Thank you for having me.'

'The flowers are lovely. I thank you.'

Wilhelm nodded. Molly went into the pantry to fill a jar with water and place the flowers. Wilhelm watched her as she returned across the room to set the jar of flowers upon the window ledge where the sun puddled like yellow butter. He admired the strong sway of her hips, the thrust of her breasts. He felt John's hand on his shoulder and ducked his glance as though he had been caught at something forbidden.

'A dram for the appetite, isn't it?'

'Just the one now. Supper's nearly on,' Molly said.

Molly placed a small joint of lamb, roasted potatoes, bowls of vegetables, a great loaf of warm bread, a slab of pale butter and another of lard upon the table.

'Now then,' she said, and went into the larder once more, shortly returning with a great pitcher of cellar-cooled ale.

'I dare say Mrs. Lind doesn't cook like this for you!' John nearly bellowed. Molly sharply, but shyly, admonished him by speaking his name in a certain tone of voice. She colored prettily.

'Mrs. Lind is jolly and round. She makes steak and kidney pies, scotch eggs, a rarebit and, sometimes, a shepherd's pie,' Wilhelm said.

'And very good they must be, I'm sure,' said Molly.

'They please my customers.'

'And you end up with a cold pudding or a scrap of pie for your dinner.' John urged Wilhelm to fill his plate nearly to overflowing.

'Does she do supper for you as well?' Molly asked.

'No.'

'How do you feed yourself then, Will?' John asked.

'I make myself a chop. Fry potatoes.' He shrugged as though to say it was of no consequence.

'Pity. Good food is a prime pleasure of life. Feeding, fishing, fighting and –'

'John!' Molly warned.

'– and frolicking. They make up the good life.'

Wilhelm felt his eyes water with suppressed laughter. The whiskey suddenly smelled very strong in his nostrils, and the roots of his hair seemed to tingle.

'I should say I am not doing very well in the living of your good life. My cooking could hardly be called good food. I have never fished in the sea except once or twice from the jetty. I don't believe I've had a serious fight in my entire life.'

'Nor has John,' Molly interrupted.

Wilhelm babbled on, out of control. 'And as for frolicking, very little of that. Next to none.' Who was the damn fool chattering on in such a way? Himself. 'None,' he finished lamely. He took a long draft of ale to cool his tongue and looked at Molly and John with such a hangdog air that they both burst into laughter.

'We can take care of the food easily enough,' John roared. 'Tuck in.'

He proceeded to eat in the manner of good and simple men: with unalloyed pleasure, single-mindedly. Wilhelm ate with more restraint, but his obvious enjoyment pleased Molly immensely. She pointedly ignored John's occasional smiling glance, avoiding the implication in her brother's wicked grin that she could very well supply the fourth ingredient necessary for the good life.

There was Peggotty pie for afters and large mugs of tea, the men's generously laced with whiskey, Molly's with a bit for the flavor of it. Molly had dropped the 'Mr. Hartz' and had, passing over her brother's use of the name Will, called him Willum instead. It was a subtle mark of affection.

'Do you often hear from home, Willum?'

'Oh, yes. My sister writes upon occasion. My father less frequently. I have letters from a friend as well.' He touched his breast pocket, indicating he kept them with him.

'They miss you?' she asked.

'They urge me to return, yes.'

'Do you ever consider it?'

'I come from a small village at the foot of the mountains. There are mountains all around except to the south. There is a valley there. It gives a feeling of great safety. That is enough for some men.'

'This is a small, safe village.'

'Yes, but the sea implies wider freedoms, greater horizons and the promise of adventure.'

'Then you will someday choose to leave?'

'I am afraid I like my adventure close to the comfort of a warm hearth. I dream of danger within easy reach of the teapot.' Will laughed self-deprecatingly.

John had listened to their talk in comfortable silence, nearly dozing like a well-fed cat. His eyes enjoyed the sight of his well-loved sister and his admired friend. What a pair they would make. He stirred himself.

'I've had my adventures and dared my dangers. Just damned uncomfortable they are as a rule.'

'Would you rather never to have had them?'

'No!'

'Ah. You are a man born to his proper time and in his proper place. I –' He paused. The pause became a silence.

'Do you believe you were born in the wrong time and the wrong place?' Molly murmured.

'Yes, I believe so.'

His answer was to his own constant question. The one he lived with. They couldn't know that he was not a mountain Swiss displaced from his own country. He was a Bavarian German alienated from his people and his place by circumstance and duty. He was not a refugee or a man seeking his livelihood or his fortunes in some foreign place he might hope one day to make his own. He was a gypsy actor living one part, telling of another and remembering a third. Will shook himself. He must avoid such confusing thoughts and be the Swiss he claimed himself to be.

'Why did you leave your homeland?' Molly asked a second time.

'In my village,' he said, 'there are many guides to lead climbers up the mountain. I have no head for heights. In my country we are famous for clocks, toys and confections. I haven't the eyesight for the first, the sense of humor for the second, and I have absolutely no taste for sweets. We are, of course, also known as a nation of hotelkeepers. I suppose I'm fulfilling my heritage, after all.' He laughed, and the others joined him. John undid his belt and heaved a great sigh.

'Please, Willum, be comfortable.'

Will removed his jacket and undid the buttons of his vest. He, too, sighed hugely. The two men, laughing, patted their stomachs in broad caricature of fat men well fed.

In the following hour Will's glance often fell to the shadowed places between Molly's breasts and in the valley of her skirts between her thighs. How wonderful it would be if John were the visitor who would shortly go into the night air and pedal his way above the sea to a lonely space while he, Will Hartz, innkeeper, respected citizen, beloved friend, householder and husband, would lock the doors and snuff the lamps and go to bed to gentle sleep upon the warm pillows of his wife.

CHAPTER 7

A wind blew, setting the sign of the Sailing Master into violent motion. Any mainlander would call it a gale, but to the Orkney Islanders, it was little more than a vagrant breeze. It was cold enough, all the same.

Within, the taproom was misty with warmth and tobacco smoke.

'A pint, if you please, inkeeper,' Daniel Collier called.

Will pumped the tap handle with four quick, short strokes, then filled the tankard with two long, smooth pulls. He felt especially good this night. Saturday week he was to take Molly Kendrick to an entertainment. John had predicted a touch of rheumatism for himself, and they were to go alone. The prospect of being close to Molly filled Will with pleasure, though he admonished himself to carefully space out their meetings so the townspeople would not whisper it about that they were walking out together.

He understood the dangers very clearly. In such a tight society, an unwed woman too often seen about with an eligible male was considered to be in a state but one step removed from serious courtship. For such a relationship to be aborted without reason or explanation, never to reach wedlock, exposed the woman to the most acute humiliation. Since no relationship with any woman could end in marriage in the foreseeable future, Will felt he must be most circumspect and honorable.

'A bonny night, Will.' Wee Jock grinned as he hustled along the bar deck, serving up a quip with each pint. Will regarded his helper with affection. He stepped down the length of the bar when his tavern owner's sense told him customers were dry. John Kendrick, Samuel Barnstall and daniel Collier were sharing rounds and conversation together. Will pulled three pints.

'And one for yourself, Will,' Daniel offered.

'Thanking you,' Will answered.

'There, Will,' Samuel noted. 'It's the proper tongue you'[e beginning to speak. You'll be a Scot in tartan before long.'

Will nodded, pleased, and settled his elbow upon the shelf

of the passway between the pub and the family room at the back. He listened with pleasure at the flow of words as the men told tales.

'There was one English lad I remember well. A ruddy-cheeked boy with a west country slant to his speech,' John said. 'A farmer's son from Wiltshire. Had never seen the sea. Strange, that, with Devon so close. The corvette he was on was sunk, and his sister ship picked him up. An hour later that one was struck by a sub and sent to the bottom as well. He was rescued by a destroyer that survived heavy shelling, a crippled rudder and severe casualties, yet made it safely into Scapa Flow. A month later he shipped out on a coast freighter as passenger. He was to have home leave. The vessel sank without a trace.'

'The death at sea is clean,' opined Samuel.

'Aye. I was in the bloody fields of France, half mole, half mud puppy.' Daniel shivered.

'Did you have your chance at Paris?'

'I did. A weekend's permission once. It was lovely, lovely. There was a girl. She taught me the words to that French song.'

'Is that all she taught you of the French?'

'There were other things.' Daniel grinned.

They all broke up in bawdy laughter. Will, smiling broadly, turned to the pass-through to accept a summons from a customer. Ian Bostock, glowering darkly, brushed a three-fingered hand over a spiky head of hair.

'A large whiskey.'

'Mr. Bostock, it is nearly closing. You should call that the last,' Will replied.

'Tend your bottles, saloonkeeper. A large whiskey, damn it, and tell those sea gulls to shut up. War stories, is it? What the hell do they know about it?'

'A damn sight more than you do, Ian Bostock,' John snapped. 'You spent your war on the beach.'

'And you. You did as well.'

'I served my time and watches on the coastal patrol.'

'Bloody great deeds of bravery. What German ship would have come right into the jaws of the British Grand Fleet? None, that's what.'

'Were you ever sober long enough to stand a deck?'

Bostock held up the mutilated hand. 'There was reason.'

He implied, with drunken disregard of the fact that

everyone knew he had lost the fingers in a stupid and besotted accident on a tangled line, his wounded hand had been the result of some great deed of courage.

'Yes. Yes,' he said as though reluctantly keeping the secret of his bravery from them.

Will held up a hand to Kendrick, whose kindly face had grown darkly red, and said softly, 'Mr. Bostock, I give you this one drink. It is the last.'

'Like hell. This is a public house. As long as I have the shillings to pay for it, you'll serve me.'

Kendrick could no longer hold his anger. 'Pennies you took from your wife's purse. Food you took from your children's mouths.'

Bostock glared at him with impotent rage.

'Take your whiskey to your table,' Will interposed quickly. 'And Mr. Bostock, I will not serve you anymore. Not tonight. Not any night.'

Bostock transferred the look of hate to Will. 'Bloody foreigner. Bloody Hun.'

'Go to your table. I tell you to do this thing.'

Bostock picked up his drink. The spittle had gathered at the corners of his mouth, making him look mad and vulnerable. He made his way back to a small table, nearly stumbling into an elderly couple that were enjoying a quiet glass before bedtime.

Will stepped down the bar to serve a customer. His attitude was unconcerned and neutral as though the unpleasantness had never occurred. The sick anger within him was coolly masked, but his eyes were dangerous and alive. It was virtually impossible to ignore Bostock's continued mumbling. His bitching went on, rising frequently in loud complaints, falling to unmanly whines, soaring to shouted obscenities.

'Bloody warriors, is it? Fucking, ball-less beach marines! Let's sing those old fighting songs, mates. Pack up your bloody troubles. What the hell they know about troubles? Do they have half a dozen spitting, puking brats crawling around, mouths open like goddamn featherless birds wanting their bellies filled? While you – you were fucking little bundles in France.'

The old man and his wife stirred uneasily and flushed with unprotected weakness. Clutching his pint of ale, the husband was conscious of his brittle bones and cordlike veins. And his wife cried inside when she looked at his impotent face: the young man staring out of the old eyes, weeping.

Will went through the one door to the hallway and the second into the lounge. His pace was unhurried.

'I'd have been in the fight if I could. What do any of you know? Pack your bloody troubles up your bloody asses!'

Will paused at the window of the pass-through to urge the men in the pub not to interfere. He simply said, 'Please,' and raised a hand, then turned to Bostock. The side door opened, and Julie entered.

'Julie, you shouldn't be here,' Will said.

'Mum wants my Da home. Baby Richard is coughing. He has fever,' she said, all the while keeping her stolid glance upon her father.

'Damn the wife. Damn the kiddies. I could have done things. Traveled. Gone to China. India. The Windward Islands.' Bostock's voice grew soft and husky, somehow attractive. 'Built me a hut of palm thatch on the shores of white sand. Listened to the warm seas as they washed my feet. Warm sun, warm things, that's what a man needs.'

Kendrick and the others were gathered at the door.

'Da. Da?' Julie called softly.

'A whole world I could have had,' the slovenly drunk conjured. And his vision found a place in the hearts of all the men.

'A thousand ports of call.' A few men smiled. 'A thousand women smelling of powder and perfume. I could have had all that.' The silent echoes of all the company's unspoken hungers agreed.

'You're wanted to home,' Julie said.

Bostock staggered to his feet and leaned over the table on widespread arms. 'Had it all except for you and the bell that bore you!' Bostock shouted.

'Be careful, Mr. Bostock,' Will warned.

'Except for you, hear? Damned lonely island. Damned woman's smell. Damned cunt smell!'

'Enough!' Will nearly shouted, and then more softly, more reasonably: 'You're wanted at home, Mr. Bostock.'

'Shut up! Can't you see what I'm trying to tell you? I'm not what I seem to be.'

'We understand.'

'Don't you know I'm a Viking? Where is my home?' The cry was that of a lost animal. 'I could have found it except for the smell of a girl on the one warm night of a thousand cold ones by the sea.' He stared at Julie with the curious intent desire to communicate that marks the drunkard. 'I made you that night. I built a cage for myself that night.'

He lashed out in deadly rage, wanting to destroy his child, the betrayer. Julie's contempt was another presence in the room. Will stepped between them.

'I said enough!'

Bostock lunged against Will, unaware of the encircling arms, wanting nothing but to beat the girl. He flailed wildly against the restraint as though swimming through the surf. Will calmly, dispassionately, punched Bostock in the stomach. Bostock gasped and retched, and Will, almost gently, pushed him back into the chair. The drunkard's imbalance sent him clattering to the floor, taking chair and table and glass with him. He reached his knees. He prepared to attack. Bostock, for all his self-abuse, was still capable, in his rage, of dealing out serious injury to Will or, worse, forcing Will to hurt him badly.

Will looked down at him with resigned sadness. There was cold determination as well. He was no longer the kind, gentle, even shy host of a warm and friendly pub. He was an efficient man under stresss. A man who placed necessity and duty above all. It was clearly his duty to end the violence. Efficiency demanded violence to achieve that end.

He punched Bostock in the face as the man rose to the attack. Bostock slammed up against the wall, his nose spurting crimson, his eyes unfocused.

Will turned to John Kendrick. 'Please. You will take him home?' Kendrick, Barnstall and Collier helped Bostock to his feet and moved him out into the night.

'I am so sorry,' Will apologized. He glanced at his watch. 'And now time, gentlemen. Time, if you please.'

He looked at Julie, still standing there. 'Go along home, Julie.' Her steady regard was unsettling. 'I'm sorry I had to strike your father.' Julie smiled a small, ragged, bitter smile. She wasted no love on the man who had accidentally conceived her.

Will trembled with sick reaction when, at last, he was alone. He tried to settle himself the familiar chores of closing time. Wee Jock could be heard rattling around in the cellar below. Will emptied the ashtrays and cleared the glasses from the tables.

He saw himself as he passed the back mirror elaborately engraved with eagles and heather by the distillery. He wondered at the calm, impassive face that looked back at him, for he felt no such calm at the core of himself. He felt, instead, a grinding frustration. There was so little he could do for the little girl, Julie. Her solitude and pride and dignity reached out to him. He was ravaged by the desire to help her. Yet his face was impassive. No, stolid. That was, by far, the better description. Stolid.

His father had often mistaken the patient passivity, calling it stupidity or wrongheadedness.

Wilhelm had felt stolid, lumpish, incapable of movement or flight when he stood before his father's desk. It was on the occasion of the first holiday following his disgrace at the fraternity. He was not invited to sit down.

'You have failed in your duty,' his father said. 'You have failed your mother.'

Better to be bloody than to suffer a mother's tears, Wilhelm thought.

'You have failed your fellow students.'

Better to be a sheep among sheep.

'You failed your university.'

Wilhelm wanted to point out that the university officially frowned upon the drinking and dueling fraternities, but he knew that would be viewed as a legalistic device to avoid the truth of the real world.

'You failed your patron.'

Perhaps he would, in summers to come, be denied the privilege of washing the old fart's feet, Wilhelm thought.

His father's pride spared Wilhelm the exposition of the greatest failure of all. He had failed to measure up to his father's dream of him.

The situation had the air of a trial *in camera*. But Wilhelm had known this was to be no trial. His father had already condemned him. He was there to have sentence passed upon him. His father stared at him for long intervals between his words. He was forcing Wilhelm to drop his eyes.

Though he truly wanted to show himself contrite, respectful and subservient, Wilhelm discovered to his dismay, that he'd developed the habit of returning anyone's stare and, even now, couldn't let it go.

When his father leaned forward to begin the wholly

imaginary ceremony of breaking the sword and tearing the badges of rank away, Wilhelm was startled by the sight of a riding crop in his hands. The silly man doesn't even ride a horse, he thought, and suppressed the nearly uncontrollable desire to laugh in the face of the man who'd sired him.

'You have an explanation?' his father asked, as though Wilhelm were some cowardly officer who'd lost a regiment of men in the storming of a wedding cake.

'I saw no reason to accept one wound or more on my face in what seemed a child's game to me.'

Crack!

The riding crop came down upon the wood of the desk. His mother personally polished it every day. It sounded like a rifle shot. Wilhelm flinched involuntarily.

'You saw! You decided! You criticized an honored tradition! Did you decide it was child's play when you were asked to join the fraternity? Did you sneer at the rules when you lifted the beer stein with your comrades? Or did you come to this conclusion when you were threatened with the small pain?'

'I accepted the invitation into the fraternity because I thought it was expected of me and because –'

Crack!

'Because it was expected,' his father sneered. 'But you decide on the limits to be placed upon your responsibilities and your honor.'

'I considered the issue and –'

Crack!

This is a damned silly investigation, Wilhelm thought with a sense of sacrilege. How the hell am I to answer or explain with that damned silly quirt marking up the desk? It will take one hell of a lot of polishing to put it right again.

'Enough. You refused to accept the discipline of your caste. Just as the peasant must obey the lord of the land, the lord himself must always hold his honor uppermost, and he must, even when painful, accept his duty.'

Crack!

I didn't even get the first word in that time, Wilhelm remarked to himself.

'So you are a man who considers, a man who decides. And what have you decided about the university?'

'Sir?'

'Do you believe you deserve to return to it?'

'I would be glad of the opportunity to continue my education,' Wilhelm said carefully.

'Do you mean to tell me you wouldn't rather escape the scene of your disgrace?'

'I will do my best to make up for it.'

'You are not afraid?'

'No.'

His father stood from the desk, walked around it and positioned himself in front of Wilhelm.

'We shall see.'

He raised the leather crop and started a lashing blow. Bare inches away from Wilhelm's cheek, he stayed his arm. It began to tremble. The tremor fled for a moment throughout his body; then he turned on his heel and faced the window. 'Get out of my sight.'

At the door, Wilhelm paused and looked back at his father. He seemed to have aged in those moments and stood, his shoulders slumped, looking out of the window of his modest home.

Wilhelm realized in the instant that, as from time immemorial, his father only wished that his son should grow up to accomplish those things he himself had once dreamed of. The symbol, not the deed, was important; the title, not the skill.

Two days later, standing before his distant, so very distant, old relative, he had the same thought and accepted the justice of Von Sonnedorf's pride in his medals.

'I tell you truthfully, young Oerter, that I never thought much of that silly custom of saber scars.'

He paused a moment and slipped into a brief reverie. Probably, he was bitterly regretting the fact he was not of an age where he could happily, triumphantly, accept such wounds.

'There was no such custom in my days at the university. We prepared for the more serious business of war. War deals out bullets in the belly, not mere scratches on the cheek.

'But there is something of far greater importance at issue here. You set yourself up against the accepted tradition of your fellows. You disregarded the command of the group conscience. It would, therefore, be easily believable that in a time of peril you would disobey the direct orders of a superior because you judged that he was in error. No military organization can be run on that basis. I hope you can understand that. Obedience! Obedience! Obedience!'

Duty! Duty! Duty!

Why not, instead, act in the service of love in all its many forms?

Wilhelm became aware of his own face in the mirror. It was no longer stolid. It was screwed up like the face of an infant threatening to cry. But no tears came, and his face was instantly composed when Wee Jock returned from the cellar.

Wee Jock spoke as he went through the ritual of leaving.

'The brown ale needed doing. I tapped a new keg.'

'Very well. Everyone is gone?'

Obviously they were, unless someone was hiding in the pisser. The housekeeping of life was as mannered and fixed as court protocol.

'Only the glasses to be washed up,' said Wee Jock.

'You go along home.'

'Thanking you, Will.'

Wee Jock hesitated. Will was sure Jock thought some comment should be made concerning the fight. There was little enough excitement in Stromness to mark the passing of the days. He said nothing.

'Good night, then.'

Jock left to return along the night streets to home.

Will washed and dried the glassware. He thought of Wee Jock, so secure within his circumscribed life: a passive and affectionate husband, a doting, gently authoritative father. A man who found his pleasures in small tasks, victories in the extra shillings he earned in such part-time labors as serving bar in the evenings.

He found himself suddenly irritated with his chores. He felt as though he were cleaning and setting a home to rights that he would never live in, that would be surrendered in some unknown but imminent tomorrow to strangers. He left the unfinished, foam-etched mugs, dried his hands and poured himself a brandy.

He shut down the lights one by one. After checking the locks a final time, though there was little or no need for such precautions, he plodded up the narrow staircase to his quarters.

The kindling in the grate beneath the cannel coal caught quickly. The fire rose to do battle with the damp and the chill. He sat down close to its comfort.

What in the hell was he doing in this place? He'd struck and harmed a poor, foolish drunkard threshing against the terrors of lost dreams and fled youth. Didn't he himself often wish to declare himself? To tell everyone, the world, that he was not the man he seemed to be? It had nothing to do with the deception he lived with. That seemed ludicrous, even innocent, in the face of life's complicity. No. To reveal the brave and youthful aspirant of life that dwelled within his rather stodgy figure, that hero that every man saw himself to be before capricious circumstance, unilluminated responsibilities and badly understood duties came along to place a yoke about his neck – to fulfill this heroic self-image at least once – was the privilege Will desired. But then, he wondered, were there many men who fashioned their own destinies and clearly saw the path they meant to travel and the consequences of their actions? He thought not. In that general condition of humanity there was some small solace. To be a sheep among sheep. But at least those animals that followed the Judas goat onto the killing floor had the company of their fellows.

He was alone, so alone.

CHAPTER 8

The three-colored poster announced a program of moving pictures presented by one George K. Devlin, showman and lecturer. The exciting presentation was to be Charlie Chaplin in *The Kid*.

Such entertainments rarely came to the Orkney Islands and even on those occasions were offered in Kirkwall, the capital. But, as the incomparable Mr. Devlin was to inform his audience, he had decided to take his traveling motion pictures into each town and hamlet of the British Isles.

During the afternoon closing, Will cycled to the poor dwelling of the Bostocks. The thatch was rotting and rank with mold, nearly fallen away. Refuse scattered the dead ground cover. Mrs. Bostock told him her husband was in bed.

Will passed through the communal room. It was filthy. Three scrawny chickens pecked at their lice. Three scrawny children scratched at theirs. They looked at him with the eyes of startled and defenseless night creatures.

The woman's eyes bore the same resignation, a look of a pain so fierce and of such long duration that it was no longer pain but a familiar companion. Her belly promised her another hell of birthing. Her breasts sagged in protest. Once her breasts were as Julie's, scarcely budding. Once her face, if not beautiful or even passingly pretty, had been as open and glowing and eager for love as Julie's often was when Will gave his shy and dignified affection to her.

In the sleeping room of the parents, the one where all these sorry children had been conceived in the fruitful but reluctant belly of this poor, thin woman, Bostock lay. His eyes were half closed in stupor or in half sleep. A cloudy bottle of slum, the tailings of the beer kegs usually sold to farmers as a feed additive for a pittance, sat on the floor amid the sticky stains of a hundred such bottles.

Bostock stirred at Will's greeting, and a flash of surly anger sparked in his eyes. But the anger couldn't rise above Bostock's torpor.

'Why do you come to a man's home without his bidding or invite?' Bostock rasped.

'There is to be a moving picture shown in Stromness this Saturday evening. I would like to take Julie. A small pleasure for the child.'

'So you would, would you? You would take my darling Julie to the moving pictures. They show them in the dark, don't they?'

Will held down the wash of anger. It shook him badly.

'Miss Kendrick will be with us.'

'An old one and a young one. It makes for interesting prospects. Is that the secret of your private life, foreigner? I've wondered about you. Everybody wonders about you and your ways about women.'

'I ask you to say no more. I am in your house. If you go on with this filth, I will be forced to call you out.'

Bostock remembered well his encounter with Will.

'Julie has her chores to do of a weekend. What with school all week, she has little enough time to earn her keep.'

Will's eyes were dangerously lidded. The heat of his anger had been replaced by the chill of loathing. He was in his most formidable mood, one rarely experienced in his usual condition of careful self-discipline.

'I will pay you for her time away.'

Bostock was emboldened by the easy victory. 'You'll pay me. You'll no longer ban me from the Sailing Master.'

'I understand that you would want me to back down before the others. In another man I could sympathize with the need to preserve one's dignity. But,' Will added carefully, 'I have no intention of catering to you in my tavern. I will give you a few shillings to spend elsewhere. That is all.'

The lights went out abruptly. Every makeshift plank bench was crowded end to end. Indeed, there were those latecomers who found room for only one buttock, and some who found no room at all. Even now the room was growing slightly steamy from the breath of so many bodies. There was, too, the odor of rarely used perfume on the women and fish on the seamen. The sharp, acrid tang of the carbide lamp added its own grace note.

The titles appeared on the stretched, bleached cloth screen, and then Charlie Chaplin of the baggy pants, the bamboo cane, the outrageous shoes and derby, the apologetic mustache began to stumble, with achingly vulnerable optimism through the sad comedy. He met with Jackie Coogan, 'The Kid,' cap too big and flopping over his ears. The audience responded with sighs and low cries of empathy and understanding.

Will glanced at Molly, who sat straight-backed, leaning slightly forward. The great masses of her hair had been piled up, and a small frivolity of a hat perched on top of it. Tiny beads of moisture dewed her upper lip. Her hands tore at a small handkerchief.

He glanced at Julie, sitting next to him on his other side. Her eyes were luminous in their solemnity. She too leaned slightly forward, suffering pleasurably for the tramp and the waif and, perhaps, envying a poverty and lack of privilege she would herself happily embrace.

The audience existed in a suspension of time and place. Their eyes glistened with reflected light like the eyes of people mesmerized or newly dead. They were still, yet animated. They watched Chaplin and the Kid walk down the dusty road. The film racketed through the sprockets of the projector, and the screen went white. The houselights came on, revealing the people of Stromness hypnotized and vague-eyed as the flickering images continued to live in their memory. They looked at one another as people do freshly awakened from sleep. The applause began and continued for some time to the accompaniment of smiles and expressions of approval.

Devlin appeared in front of the screen. He raised his arms.

'Ladies and gentlemen, please retain your seats. You have just enjoyed George K. Devlin's latest presentation of that fabulous entertainment, the moving picture.'

He was treated to another round of applause. He accepted it with admirable modesty. It was obvious to all who witnessed his pleasure and pride that George K. Devlin had written the story, directed the players, operated the camera and, indeed, by some magic acted out all the roles. Even the female parts.

'The projectionist is presently preparing the machine for the showing of the *Pathé News of the World*. This is an unannounced, added attraction brought to you in keeping with George K. Devlin's policy of bringing you the best entertainment and educational film available regardless of expense. All right, Harry?'

The machine stuttered, the lights went out, and the newsreel appeared. It caught George K. Devlin on the off foot as it were, and he talked rapidly to catch up with the pictures.

'And so, ladies and gentlemen, George K. Devlin brings to you film of the late great War, now happily concluded. I will supplement the film with pertinent commentary.'

The film of the Great War was spotty at best. There were brief glimpses of the leaders of the principal nations. The shot of the Kaiser elicited catcalls. The footage of King George drew cheers. The impresario limited his comments to flowery descriptions of scenes that needed no description.

Stained and scratched footage depicted men at war; the turtlelike tanks lumbering across the muddy fields of Flanders, infantrymen vomiting from the trenches amid bursting fragmentation bombs at Chateau-Thierry; a cavalry charge badly underexposed and overdeveloped. Wilhelm watched the shadows that once were men fall wounded or dead at the Argonne and felt a vague sense of loss commingled with shame.

His own military career had been without incident, remarkable only in the fact that it was so unremarkable.

Eight months after the double humiliations of the lectures delivered by his father and Von Sonnedorf Wilhelm left home to begin his compulsory military service. It was only then that his father had placed his hand upon his son's shoulder, with sadness and regret for the lost young officer that might have been, and called him Willy in an affectionate way.

'Preserve our honor. Never turn your back on your duty.'

Wilhelm preserved the family's honor. There was nothing to threaten it. He did his duty. By diligent application to mediocrity and anonymity he rose to the rank of corporal. At the end of the two years he experienced a strange thing. He remembered each of the days in great detail yet he felt as though he had been vividly told the events of someone else's life. He was transferred into the Landwehr, the reservist army.

He came home to his mother's grateful tears, Katy's floury embrace and his father's ill-concealed regret that he hadn't risen higher.

They sat together, in a measure of adult equality, to discuss his future career.

'It saddens me to say,' his father lectured, 'that you appear to have no special talent, no brilliance. I can't hold you to blame for that.'

Oh, but you can, thought Wilhelm. You believe it to be my fault, my most grievous fault.

'However you are not a stupid young man. Apparently you are simply a man without ambition or great aspirations. Through the regard in which I am held by people of some influence, I've secured an interview for you with the postal inspector in Stuttgart. A position in the civil service is not to be looked down upon.'

And, Wilhelm added to himself, a uniform goes with the job.

He cleared his throat and waited for permission to speak. His father gave it with a nod.

'I prefer to teach.' His father, after long consideration, nodded his head. Such a profession did carry with it a certain dry prestige.

'I've obtained a post in a small private academy in Stuttgart.'

'Who was your means of introduction?'

'I obtained it myself through correspondence.'

It was apparent that his father was somewhat annoyed that one of his basic precepts, the use of influence, had been dispensed with and that Wilhelm had accomplished this connection without consultation with the head of the house. He dismissed his son with a curt nod of the head and gave his attention to other matters.

Wilhelm reached the door.

'Willy,' his father said, 'you must buy a new black suit.'

In that first year as an instructor of languages at the boy's academy he walked, day after day, in a rarely varied routine. The pathways of his life might have been described as a square. One corner was the Spartan room above a tailor's shop in a market street where he made his purchases for his simple meals. The second was the modest schoolground enclosed by a fence in a once fashionable, now decaying district of the city. The library and, occasionally, the concert hall across the boulevard from it composed the third corner. The last was the armory where he served as a reserve soldier in the name of the emperor.

His habits became so regular that the merchants began wrapping his day's purchases the moment they caught sight of him. From the butcher, a pork cutlet on Monday, Wednesday and Friday; a slice of veal on Tuesday, Thursday and Saturday. From the greengrocer, turnips on Monday, potatoes on Tuesday, mustard greens on Wednesday, beets for Thursday's meal, beans for Friday's.

On Sundays he had sausage and sauerkraut in a beer hall.

He was respected by the students at the school. They soon discovered that he was impervious to pranks, whether they were prompted by maliciousness or affection. The boys learned that he had a disconcertingly bland manner of staring at them. Since he remained an unknown quantity, they preferred not to tamper. He was the only one of the instructors who had no nickname.

His fellow teachers soon decided, unanimously, that he was a poor companion, a worse conversationalist, and that, since he patently had no liking for women, grown men or small boys, he preferred large dogs or country ewes. But even this nasty observation died swiftly. It is difficult to spend much time defining or describing a vacuum.

He was, by far, most appreciated in the library, among people who valued their own thoughts and their solitude, among the professionals who made the cataloguing of books their life's work.

During those weeks of random scholarship, which were merely another means to isolation, he scarcely noticed the dark-haired plainly dressed woman at the long oaken check-out counter. Her name, Miss Spector, overheard upon occasion, made small impression upon him. Once or twice, he later remembered, he'd asked her help in searching out a particular volume, and she'd simply nodded. But one day he was almost startled at the sound of her voice.

'I've never seen anyone with such a diversity of interest,' she said in a throaty, sensual voice that contrasted sharply with her severe hairdo and pale complexion.

He looked up and found himself being candidly regarded – and perhaps challenged – by the clearest pair of eyes he'd ever recalled seeing.

He found himself stammering, and before he was aware of his purpose, he found himself asking her out for a coffee.

For six months or so following that first afternoon, the relationship proceeded no further than the coffee. He found himself constantly fascinated, nearly mesmerized by the implied sexuality of her voice.

One evening chance placed two excellent seats to the current opera at the concert hall in his possession.

Going to collect her in the extravagance of a taxi, he was taken aback by the woman who met him at the door.

She'd touched her lips and cheeks lightly with color. Her eyes had been framed and enhanced with subtle shadows. The dress she wore could not be called an evening gown. It was a clever and practical compromise: a dress that could be worn to weddings, celebrations and funerals as well.

She invited him in to meet her father. For some reason, Wilhelm had given no thought to her manner of living outside the library. He simply assumed she cooked and sewed and slept in a room similar to his own, adding only a doll on the bed and a jar of flowers to indicate a woman's presence. He was somewhat unprepared for a tastefully furnished house belonging to a member of the merchant class.

He was equally unprepared for the menorah and the father who wore the skullcap of the pious Jew

The introduction and the few passing comments were brief. Ruth kept an eye upon the passing moments and the waiting cab.

Wilhelm had never had much association with Jews other than the brief exchanges in normal daily commerce. He'd held no opinions about them one way or another. He simply noted to himself the briny smell of the house which seemed strange to him.

He scarcely heard the opera. All through the evening he was painfully aware of the weight of her thigh against him and the many subtle pressures of her fingers as she prompted him to share some enjoyable performance or aria.

She insisted that they walk back to her house. She refused his invitation to a late supper or even a glass of wine, insisting that the wine of her father's house was far superior.

Without realizing the progression, Wilhelm found his life being ordered by the subtly persuasive Ruth Spector.

She urged him to greater care in his appearance and cajoled him into the purchase of a new suit, pointing out, justifiably, that the one he habitually wore was turning greenish at the elbows and knees from too much wear. She even obtained the new garment at a wholesale price through a friend of her father's who was in the garment trade. He also found himself, without realizing quite how it came about, with an overcoat and a black homburg as well.

She possessed a great talent for subtle manipulation. He

soon discovered she had the sterling qualities of organization, thrift, simplicity, loyalty, intelligence, obedience, culinary skill, housekeeping excellence, and impeccable taste. She revealed each one like a great magician beguiling and enchanting her audience with one casual marvel after the other.

It became the unvarying custom for Wilhelm to take his evening meal at Ruth's house. They became, in most ways, a family. Ruth gently urged him to learn what he could of her father's wholesale stationery business. He did, indeed, agree to put in three evenings a week at the warehouse.

It was decided that Wilhelm should move into the extra bedroom in the Spector household. While continuing his teaching duties, he would further his own education with a view toward the necessary degrees and credentials that would make him an attractive candidate for a university post.

One day Ruth revealed to him a discreet method of passage to her room without fear of disturbing her father's sleep.

Wilhelm was very nearly done in by her assault that night.

She revealed the final marvel, her body, her passions and her amatory skills, in one great rush that enveloped him. He thought of the legends of the succubi that sucked the life from one's being and understood the glory of such a dying. Her breasts demanded his attention. Before he was sated with their salty savor, she'd offered him the dimples at the base of her spine, the hollows of her neck, the satin purse between her legs.

She pulled the pins from her hair and bathed him in their waves.

Her tongue explored the chambers of his ears and made him feel they were triton shells from the sea. Her lips traced the creases where leg met torso in the slow way of an explorer adventuring along a favorite questing place, reluctant to have the journey end. Her teeth plucked gently at the coarse hair of the sack that held an incomparably aching desire.

Over all there was the threnody of a passion that delightfully promised never to be sated. It sounded in her incomparably sex-tuned voice that sang songs without words.

When it was done and he was done, he wondered, as they lay together, at the powdery dryness of her body.

She smiled up at him and murmured, 'I've often watched

you as you listened to my voice and wondered if I could match the promise it had. I think sometimes you doubted the librarian could fuck you like an insane mare.'

The bluntness of the remark so startled Wilhelm that he laughed foolishly in self-defense.

That evening, Wilhelm was to discover, was in the nature of notarizing a contract of betrothal between them. Part of the agreement was to be his continuing studies and future achievements.

During the ensuing months she allowed no familiarity other than a chaste kiss between them, and that at no other time than in the presence of her father or some other relative. He met many of those. Many were apparently much disturbed that Ruth should be promised in marriage to a Gentile.

He found himself being inexorably driven into a profession, a marriage, a commitment to a life he'd not really chosen.

At the conclusion of his reservist obligations, he voluntarily transferred into the ready reserve. He allowed his commander, Captain Blendheim, to believe that it was his persuasiveness that had prompted the decision. He allowed Ruth to believe that her advice that continued public service would mark him as a responsible and civic-minded educator was the deciding factor. He realized that it gave him a place of escape, a haven from the all-inclusive and detailed ordering of his life by his bride-to-be.

He faced the activation of his unit and the subsequent declaration of war on August 14, 1914, with a feeling very akin to relief.

On the night preceding the mobilization, Ruth gave him a graphic reminder of what he would be missing and what he would come back to.

Truly, he often lay writhing in tortured recall on his lonely cot in some lonely place, but when he was granted a few days' leave from time to time, he found urgent business elsewhere. He fed his appetites in a soldier's way, casually and at a cost.

The letters between them grew fewer, the passages in her letters designed to inflame his passions had cooled to ashes, and sometime before the cessation of hostilities, Ruth had married a young man of her own faith who suffered with hernia.

He never saw her again.

Will came to himself with a start, drawn out of that distortion of time called reverie in which entire lives can be compressed into brief moments, by the laughter of the people who surrounded him. His eyes caught the image on the screen, but his ears missed Devlin's commentary.

A remarkably comic figure, dressed in a trench coat, had reached the topmost step of the entrance to what was an official building of some sort, turned to the crowd and removed a shapeless fedora. The reason for the laughter was clear. The man wore a smudge of mustache and possessed a ridiculous manner of movement. The resemblance to the figure of Charlie Chaplin was sharp and very funny.

He leaned toward Molly. 'What is this?'

'That man Adolf Hitler. Something about a trial for some foolishness he was involved with in Germany.'

By the time Will returned his attention to the screen new laughter was greeting the appearance of bathing beauties being arrested in a place called Atlantic City, New Jersey.

The lights came on, the people stood to 'God Save the King.' Will sang as lustily as any of them.

Julie was seen safely home. It was a courtesy to her semi-grown-up estate.

The jiggling of the cart and the patient tattoo of the island pony's hooves were pleasant sounds as Will drove Molly home through the clear, moon-bright night. Her body swayed comfortably as she gave herself to the jostling of the rig. Her solid thigh and soft breast seemed to give kisses to Will. Every touch implied more than simple friendship.

Will felt himself grow tight against his desire. His nature intuited and feared a confrontation. Molly touched the hand holding the reins, bidding him to stop.

She looked out across the great expanse of Scapa Flow. Will found great interest in the pony feeding on the bark of a gnarled tree.

'There was a time I hated that cold, barren sea,' Molly murmured.

'Do you still?'

'I'm an island woman. Part of it. Hate and love don't really apply. Twice I thought to leave Scapa Flow.'

Will sat in silence. A pulse started in his throat. Molly, he knew, was about to reveal something of herself. He knew such a revelation was, to these independent, enduring people, a precious gift, an overture to even greater giving.

'I was young. Only a few years older than Julie Bostock. I was filled with dreams of a constant sun, with dreams of great cities.' She laughed lightly at herself. 'Somehow I put the two together and made London the Camelot; that cold and rainy place. But then Father was lost at sea and Mother grieved and needed me. Finally, she sickened and I couldn't leave. John was off, away. His postcards became my adventure.'

Will felt a terrible touching of the secret places of their hearts.

'Then the war. Mother died, but still I couldn't leave. John, then, would be alone. We had grown together, for near the end of her illness, John had come home, and after her death he stayed on. He was growing old. There was need for each other.'

Will knew he must ask the question. To ignore it would be to indicate that he guessed her purpose. To speak of it would, perhaps, open a door he preferred left closed. Yet it would be asked.

'Why did you never marry?'

'First, I was a dreaming young girl seeking escape. Then a dutiful daughter. Then a choosy, proud young woman, sensitive in her spinsterhood. Island women marry young, if at all.'

She left the cart and walked to stand within the shadow of the tree. Will hesitated, then followed her.

'In the middle of the war, I found a love,' she mused. 'He was serving on a ship of the line, but he was really a displaced scholar. I had no learning to match his own, but he often said I had the ways to nurture the flowers in his lonely academic tower. He sailed out of the Flow and was lost. A torpedo sank his ship forty fathoms. That was the second time I thought to leave Stromness. Somehow I believed I should find him in some university with his books. I reached Edinburgh, but it seemed to me a great machine that ate people.

'Willum, I'm content with this village. I've no thought of far places any longer. I accepted this place as my lot in life long ago and tried to be content. I put aside thoughts of men – of a man. But I haven't forgotten what a good man is like.

You're a good man, Willum, and since you came, I'm no longer content.'

'Please, Miss Kendrick,' Will pleaded, but once begun, Molly had no way of stopping.

'I'm not a virgin. I gave my dead love that. But that won't put me off. My name is Molly, and I'm a strong woman. Time may have cheated me, but I'm all the things that make a good wife. I need a husband to make it truly so.'

'Molly, please don't,' Will begged, painfully embarrassed.

'My hair is thick and long. It's a pretty sight when it's taken down for bed. My eyes are clear. I'll never need spectacles. I'm not beautiful or even good-looking perhaps, but I have strong teeth and good digestion.'

'My God, you're not a horse.'

He turned away, but Molly grasped his arm in a strong hand and turned him to face her. She looked him squarely in the eye.

'I have rough big hands from the salt water and strong soap and scalded fish, but they could be – want to be – soft and gentle. And, Will, under these petticoats and skirts and common cloth, I have a body a man could find warmth and comfort and strength in.'

'It's not proper you should –' Will cried out in his hurt for her.

'– sell myself to you?' she finished. 'Why not? Marriage is a bargain at our time of life. An exchange of benefits and virtues – and faults. I know what kind of man you are. I know the husband and father you'd be.'

'I say it's not right –'

Again she cut short his words. 'Is it right that I should lie abed without a man to warm my back? That you should take your sleep alone? You live like a priest. Why?'

'Perhaps I'm not so certain of this world.'

'An island woman is not sure from tide to tide.'

'I have thought of returning home one day.'

She would have none of his temporizing. 'I'm strong enough to travel.'

Will thought how stupid he must sound to this woman who, against custom and inclination, offered him a relationship he deeply desired and, perhaps foolishly, could not accept. He walked slowly back to the cart. After several moments, Molly followed, and he helped her to be seated.

'You must think I've shamed myself. Indeed, perhaps I have.'

Will shook his head. 'You've made me wonder about the reasons people do things. Or rather, the lack of reasons.'

In his lonely room, a glass of brandy close to hand, Will gave himself up to the contemplation of the anatomy of honor, of duty, of one's given word and sworn oath. How much compliance was unthinking, unreasoning habit? How much was simple faith? The faith of a man who believes the sun will inevitably shine though the lone eclipse of the sun seems interminable and irreversible? How far must one go to keep a promise given to an abstraction when the arm and living body in the hungry and demanding present cried out with a clearer voice for satisfaction?

Hindenburg had been elected President of Germany. The old warrior was not some half-mad adventurer like that posturing fool Hitler on the screen, plucked from the extreme right or left of the political spectrum. He was a symbol of the Fatherland. He embodied all that was best in the German character. There was a feeling in the halls of power that his ascension might mark the stabilization of his country, an end to strikes, violence and assassination. In the old monarchist was the promise of steady Teuton diligence and efficiency, hard work and obedience.

If this were so, then he must come to terms with the enterprise in which he was engaged. Goldman had died for nothing. Would Wilhelm Hartz/Oerter live for nothing? His mind plodded along. In the end there was, of course, no answer or immediate decision, only a great weariness. The evening with Molly had left a sense of anxiety as well, a depleting distortion of serenity. A second and a third glass of brandy had no effect.

He went into his cold bed. He lay curled up on his side in a fetal position, hoping to hoodwink his body into sleep. Masturbation did nothing to relieve his tensions.

CHAPTER 9

The routine and chores attendant to the Sailing Master grew oppressive to Will in the heat of the summer. The silence of the nighttime jetty did nothing to still his soul. He was torn by reflections on two women: the Ruth who had set out to manipulate him into marriage and the Molly who had offered herself, without reservation, in a manner so simple and direct that it had shattered Will's false content. His nights were filled with erotic dreams of the two of them, separate and as one woman, enticing him, torturing him with their lips and breasts and thighs, bringing him to climax at last in the midst of the dream, to awaken to a soiled bed and an overwhelming sense of shame.

His friend John remarked his irritability and agitation. He suggested a long workday at sea to still the pangs that ailed his friend.

Will saw the wisdom in it. The simple wisdom of hard work as the anodyne, haven and comfort of simple men. It was true, he thought, that nothing else could be quite so cleansing to the body and the soul as the wash of salt spray crashing over the gunnels of a small working boat and the play of muscles in conflict with the sea.

He accepted the proposal and went the next morning to the quayside, boots on his feet and a slicker over his arm. The mail packet was moored at the dock, having arrived the evening before and stayed over till the day. The man Wiley leaned on the rail. Will waved in common greeting, but the deckhand's attention was elsewhere. Will turned to look at what so captured the sailor's attention and marked upon his face a look of such delight. He heard the crash as he saw the pony fall to the cobbles. The small, sturdy animal had fallen in the traces, tipping the cart and knocking the driver to the cobblestones.

The pony thrashed in a frenzy of pain, beating its head against the cobbles. Blood crimsoned its expressionless, patient face. It made no outcry. A shaft had splintered and somehow had pierced its side. Before the driver could recover or Will reach it with the thought to kill it and release it from its pain, it had killed itself. A splintered spear of wood had thrust itself into its lungs. Will was on his knees, reaching for its head, when a great gout of blood marked the end of life. He looked up at the sound of sharp, chilling laughter. The man Wiley was roaring with a sickening, lustful pleasure.

Will ran the distance to the mail packet and climbed the gangway with his hands red with blood. He took Wiley's throat in a fury of loathing with his bloody hands meaning to choke the life from him. Wiley was first dismayed and then fought against Will's grip. He managed to release them long enough to speak.

'Simmons wouldn't want me dead.'

Will's hands fell to his sides, immobilized by the sudden revelation that the sadistic creature staring up at him was somehow enlisted with himself and Simmons in the same cause. He felt John Kendrick next to him, grasping his arm, drawing him away and soothing him. Wiley grinned as Will allowed himself to be led to John's boat. He was still grinning and fingering his throat when the fishing craft was headed toward the open sea and Will turned back briefly to see the sadist standing there.

He knelt over the side and washed his hands in the cold water. His rage was washed away as well. An hour later he faced the wind and the spindrift blowing off the turmoil of gray-green and flashing white.

He turned to look at John at the helm and smiled a broad smile of wildest delight.

Kendrick took the stubby blackened pipe from his mouth and shouted, 'Haul nets!' The two men of his crew leaped to the lines. Will discarded his protective, glistening oilskins and joined them. John stayed at the wheel, holding seaway and shouting orders and encouragement.

All about them other boats of the fishing fleet of Stromness bent to the task of harvesting the sea. An ancient, rhythmic chant rose from the men, from the decks, from the breast of the ocean and challenged infinity.

When, at last, the writhing, glistening harvest was drawn alongside, John placed his hands to the nets as well. The two men laughed into each other's faces. The trailing lines were secured to belaying pins. With long-handled dippers the four men scooped, pivoted from the waist and dumped the silver alewives into the keeping well. It demanded the grace and skill, the musculature of a ballet dancer. Will stumbled frequently and nearly lost his scoopful of fish. Twice he nearly lost fish, scoop and himself.

In the labor there was the wonderful alternation of thrust, pull, balance, the lift of weight and the sensual relief when the burden was cast aside. Then it was taken up again.

Later, the boat heavy with a fine day's catch, Will and John sat on the deck leaning against coils of rope smelling pleasantly of salt and tar. They had been a full day at the harvest, and now, soothed by the heartbeats of the engines, they took their ease with the idle pleasure given to men who have worked hard. Their downturned pipes were badges of their fraternity. Will moved to resettle his rump and made a sound, half groan, half laugh.

'A bit of a twinge?' John sympathized.

'Moving a few barrels of ale about doesn't do much for the muscles. I'll feel this week for several weeks more. But, oh, Lord, how I enjoy it. I thank you for letting me come along.'

'You're a good fisherman. You do your share. If you ever decide to give up the Sailing Master, you have a berth with me.'

'That would be a good life.'

John regarded Will from beneath the hoarfrost of his brows.

'It might be we could make a partnership.'

Will returned silence to his friend. The implication was too clear. Partners. He and John. Will and John and the boat. Molly and Will, John and the boat. The family.

'Will you take supper with us tonight?' John asked.

Will made a grimace of comic pain, though he regretted the need for acting out such a transparent subterfuge.

'Thank you, no. I think a very hot bath, and then, if I am able, I should work the pub. Wee Jock has had the responsibility of it by himself all day. In his busy world that is too long to be steady at one chore.'

John made a show of refilling his pipe.

'Did something go amiss between you and Molly?'

'Nothing,' Will answered with a frown.

'She won't speak of it either.'

'Please.'

'Will, we've known each other a good long time now. Island people are slow to accept strangers. But now you're one of us. Everyone considers you an Orkney man. That's no small gift to give a man, even if it's not wanted. Men try to speak straight to one another. Sometimes it's a burden and not a gift for a friend to care. Has it to do with the letters you receive from Switzerland?'

Will wondered what John would think if he told him of Simmons, the mail drop, the cover story, the blank pages, the coded messages saying nothing. He wondered what he would think if he knew the only thing that had saved Wiley from great injury was the revelation that he, too, was apparently in the service of German espionage.

'They are letters from friends.'

'A woman in particular?'

'There is a woman,' Will lied.

'I thought as much. We might be secret sort of people, but the need to protect our privacy doesn't extend to the post-mistress.' John grinned. 'She noticed one address is written in a female's hand. The two of you have plans for the future?'

Will shrugged. 'Our families. We were children together. It seemed to be understood that we should marry,' Will went on. 'I was restless. I wished to try other things. Here I am.'

Will felt a sadness for the fictional Heidi waiting back there in the Swiss mountain snows. 'It's not normal for a man to be without a woman,' John opined.

'It's a hard discipline,' Will agreed.

'These trips you take every few months or so,' John ventured delicately. 'It's to satisfy a man's needs?'

Will nodded and felt easy for the moment because he could tell this much truth to his friend. 'It's not always adequate. I most usually regret the necessity.'

'It's no weakness. A man. A woman. A happy fuck. Or an unhappy, hurried one, for that matter. It's nature's way.'

'But in God's way, it must be sanctified by marriage.'

'I'll buy you a collar and hymnal for that remark,' John said and Will blushed at the sour-sweet silliness of his own statement.

'Marriage is best, no doubt. It pleases the woman and gives her a brave face. It pleases the man as well. A wife fills the hollow beneath his wing. I had my Rose for a time – and it was a good, too short, time. It was the best time of my own life. Having her prepared me for now, just as all the hell raising of my young, lusty days prepared me for the time with her. I'm fair contented these years because of a store of memories she left to me, along with a pair of slippers in needlework she was making for me just before she died.'

His eyes layered and deepened and no longer reflected the sea. Instead, they seemed to reflect the paler blue of moonlight. Will sat silent, holding himself away – alone. John was not alone. He shook himself and coughed. He looked to the point of the mast and remarked they were passing near the outer shoals.

'I married late on. I sailed in big ships and touched the world's ports of call. I took and enjoyed the women. But there came a time when only one woman would do. And none would do but one who was part of home. This has become your home, Will.'

'You say you all consider me an Orkney man – but I haven't grown totally into that feeling. I mean to say I feel most welcome and part of everything here. But my home still tugs at me from time to time.'

'Understandable. Natural. But you're a settled sort of man. You need a woman. Your own woman. Molly's surely every bit of that.'

'I've thought of it. Truly.'

He looked directly into John's eyes, not knowing how to finish his thoughts in words. John nodded.

'I understand, and I'll say nothing to Molly of this. Hold off on thoughts of marriage then. But, Will, do what your feelings tell you to – with or without the vows.'

'You suggest I have an affair with your sister?' Will said.

'My God, you're shocked. You don't believe that would be the brotherly thing to do. No, Will, I don't suggest you have an – affair – with my sister. I tell you to bed her. Molly's no virgin. There was a young sailorman during the war. He didn't survive it. I think he was the only one she'd slept with, but she was gone from the islands for a time, and I can't be sure. The point is, she's a warm, loving woman, and it's not right that her body should be a waste and a burden to her.'

'She's too fine a woman to be deceived.'

'She'll know what you're about and, if I read it right, will welcome the chance to become a much-needed habit for you.'

'But a casual –'

'Affair?' John chuckled. 'What a starchy, lamps-out, under-the-blankets word that is. I'm talking of a healthy, joyful, rollicking fuck. I tell you this, Will: A woman would rather be wedded than only bedded. But she'd rather be well fucked than famous for her virtue.' He moved lightly to his feet and turned to the rising moon. 'I say no more.'

John was as good as his word. He 'said no more' about the distance Will allowed to remain between himself and his sister, Molly.

In a curious way the courtesy of John's silence left Will unsatisfied. A part of him wanted John to broach the subject once again. He took time from the tavern to go out with the fishing fleet on one more occasion some weeks later. It was his unexpressed hope that John would feel it proper, in that stronger intimacy they seemed to share at sea, to introduce Molly into their conversation. John remained mute. Having once had his say, he was done with it.

The letters from Switzerland became fewer as the year slipped through autumn and on toward winter.

The first snow fell in the deep hours of the night. Will was in his rocking chair thinking of Molly. He thought of her as someone well loved who existed in some distant past. He thought of her and of John in their separate sleep unmoved by the sadness of the snow.

In midwinter his friend, John, was absent from the pub for three days running. It was another day before Will found out he had taken to his bed with icy pains in his chest. By the time Will decided he must go to see his friend in his illness, despite the discomfort of being in the same room with Molly, his friend was back on the same stool at the end of the long bar. His nose looked pinched, but he seemed well otherwise.

Winter gripped the islands and then let go all in a rush. It was spring. Another year had passed.

The closing of a pub at nightfall is a sad thing. A room so warm and filled with the sounds of life suddenly becomes a box of echoes. Noises that went unheard before clatter and crack, sigh and toss all around. When a man clears his throat or coughs, it sounds like the embarrassed nervous response of a mourner sitting before the casket that holds the corpse. Homely sounds of water running into a copper sink, heavy glasses greeting on the bar top, a chair scraping as it is put into place, lonely and unoccupied by a human being, become a threnody of lost dreams.

Will went about his work of the last clearing up of the day. When it was done, he bundled into his greatcoat and stepped out into the wet street. He hesitated a moment and turned as though the empty tavern had whispered to him. He walked on down to the sea and out along the mole a short way. He settled himself on the rock that, so familiar, welcomed his company.

A small dory was pulled up on the shale, and a pleasure craft was moored a few hundred yards offshore. It seemed to Will a beautiful but flawed boat. It was painted a pale blue except for the bowsprit some distance aft. There it had been painted white in imitation of a cloud formation so that it might appear, in the proper light at the proper time of day, to be sailing in the skies themselves. Its name, *Limbo*, was lettered in gold leaf. Its sails were of an uncomfortable dark gray, reefed now, but even in the moonlight somehow more funereal and despairing than black might have been.

He'd viewed it during the day and found it to be a bit too fine, too sharply lined. There was a mincing, dissolute quality about it. But perhaps Will was simply projecting his impressions of its owner and skipper on it.

The man, dressed in immaculate whites and already carrying a cargo of liquor, had come into the Sailing Master some weeks before. He himself had used the sailorman's phrase and declared happily that he was 'three sheets to the wind.' He drank rapidly and without apparent pleasure. His attempts at conversation with the 'Witches of Endor' were affable enough on the surface, but his lips seemed always on the point of a contemptuous and patronizing sneer. The three old men accepted his offers to drink and played the parts of taciturn old sea dogs. He seemed to delight in their quaint ways but all the while seemed like a magician trying to astound himself with a magic trick, the secrets of which he already knew.

It was clear that he was a wealthy young man with nowhere to go.

Will had seen him once in the late afternoon talking to Julie. He'd paused and stood ready for a moment to intervene in case the stranger became an annoyance to her, but Julie, grown to more womanly ways, yet still possessing the solemnity of childhood, had listened with slightly averted head and downcast eyes. Then she'd turned and walked up the main street of Stromness and never turned to glance back.

Will heard the soft scrape of a footstep and, reacting to the custom of years, reached into his pocket for the tobacco pouch. In the instant he remembered that John was in bed early in the evening of late. He turned to see if his ears had simply recalled the footsteps of a thousand nights of friendship and talk.

Julie stood a short way from him. Her figure, etched by the moonlight, told him for the first time that she had flowered and grown.

'Julie, out at this hour?'

She regarded him with a look of soft pain.

'Come sit with me a moment,' he said. 'Have a chat with me, and then I'll walk you home.'

Julie came closer and sat beside him. 'I'm not going home.'

Will knew then that he had sensed a parting at the sound of the footfall, and it had been that which saddened his soul.

He tried to see into her eyes, but those eyes, usually so direct and full of candor for him, were averted. He gently took the cameo of her face in his hand and turned it toward him. One side of her face was puffed and a bruise that covered much of it was beginning to color. 'I see,' Will said.

'Only that he beat me again? Worse than that. Worse than that this time.' Her voice rose and fell as though threatening a storm.

'He was drunk again?' Will asked, and felt foolish for asking. He was aware that words, questions, were often used to delay the truth and avoid the answers.

'He's always drunk. With Ma dead, he tried to make me take her place.'

With a start, Will realized that the death of Julie's mother had caused only the slightest ripple in the community. That she and her memory had passed from the island that had borne and known her with less attention than would be given the flight of a gull.

'Tonight he got stumbling, crying, sobbing drunk. He called me Sarah. He begged me to forgive him. It was disgusting.' She shuddered and held herself with her thin arms. 'Then he tried to use me in bed,' she whispered, and then nearly shouted. 'He tried to fuck me! And all the time he was calling me Sarah. The dirty pig knew who I was well enough.'

Still she didn't cry.

'Where will you stay? Will asked.

'There's no place for me here. I'm sick of Stromness anyway. Sick of these islands.'

It was then Will saw the torn traveling bag at the beginning of the mole.

'I want to see lights and cities. I'm young and pretty.' The last word lifted – a question. 'I want to enjoy it.'

'You are pretty, Julie. Who told you that?'

'Men.'

'When are you leaving?'

'Tonight.'

'How are you leaving?'

'With a man.'

The owner of the sky-blue boat stumbled on the shale beach. His white trousers and shirt were dirty, and somewhere he had lost his yachting cap. He looked around and hallooed.

Julie stood up.

'Will you write?' Will asked.

'I don't think so.'

She took a few steps away and lifted her arm. She poised her wrist in the air for a moment.

'The watch fits me.'

'Yes, I see you've grown into it.'

CHAPTER 10

With the passing of the winter of 1928, Ancient Booth passed away as well. For the first time, many people of Stromness learned that his Christian name had been Horatio.

Old Siever Scarff and Handy sat on the rocks by the sea and kept a space between them as though Ancient Booth were still with them. They were the first to sight the auxiliary sail of an excursion steamer that had been reported off the Pentland Firth.

When the small steamer tied up at the dock, three dozen or more young men and women disembarked. Nearly all wore white trousers or skirts and blue jackets with German silver buttons.

'Students they are,' said Scarff.

'Don't I know that?' Handy growled. 'Norwegian or Danish, I'd say.'

Scarff shook his head knowledgeably, for his hearing was less impaired than Handy's. 'No, German.'

'It's all forgotten then. The war.'

'All forgotten – again.'

The students walked up the pier toward the town and the crescent of townspeople.

'Ah, well, look there,' Handy noted. The children of Stromness, with that special shyness of Orkney children, giggled behind their hands, bright spots of color blushing on their smiling faces. Little girls peeked from behind the skirts of their mothers or older sisters, and little boys rammed their hands in their pockets and teetered on their toes with studied nonchalance.

The slender moment was broken when a German girl extended a bit of candy to a child and when a German boy took the picture of a girl just in her budding years. Then there was much joining of small hands with larger ones, a gabble of voices, the universality of laughter.

'Lovely, lovely. Boys and girls together,' Handy murmured.

'It is to remember,' Scarff softly added.

There was a time when the two groups of strangers

flowed together. Then they began to fragment. The German girls tended to stay together under the direction of a bespectacled, pinch-mouthed tour leader. She had no doubt lectured the group on their responsibility to prove themselves neat and orderly guests and not to leave bad impressions on the provincial and isolated towns and peoples they were to visit.

A few girls managed to detach themselves, and these gathered a covey of scampering little ones, who vied with one another to show the visitors the really important points of interest within walking distance, like little Harry Barlow's pirate cave.

A few others stayed close to an equal number of boys. They were but mildly interested in the histories of any of the areas they had visited on the outing.

The boys went off in twos and threes to examine things for themselves.

Three of the young German men stood on the cliff overlooking the graveyard of the scuttled German fleet, somewhat depleted in numbers by the salvagers, but still in evidence.

The tallest of the three wore a yachting cap unlike the student caps of his companions. He was obviously the kind of boy who listened carefully, made his own decisions and proceeded to do as he wished without further consultation with anyone. The other two boys were as clearly followers and idolators.

The shortest boy, thick-chested and gross-featured, narrowed his eyes and in attempting to look like an eagle succeeded in looking like a pig.

'They should have fought!' he said in German.

'Speak English, you damned fool,' their leader snapped. 'Do you think nine years would make German sound pleasant to these people?'

'I am sorry, Günter.'

Günter's gesture of forgiveness was expansive and ended with his hand placed with carefully measured camaraderie on the thick boy's shoulder. 'No matter. Come, we find a rathskeller.'

'Hey!'

Günter laughed lightly at his own lapse. Chosen ones can afford to be generous. 'I mean – a pub.'

Günter Prien, Karl Kramer and the quiet Hans Emling,

students, went along to the Sailing Master in the late afternoon.

Young Prien stepped up to the bar and placed his foot on the brass rail. He was flanked on either side by his lieutenants. 'Three lagers, please.'

'We have bitters. You would call it beer. There is stout, light ale, dark ale. . . .'

'Three bitters then,' Günter ordered, without asking the others their taste.

'Pints or half-pints?' Will asked.

'Pints, yes.'

Will poured the heavy glass mugs full and set them, neatly lipped, upon the bar.

'You will join us?' Günter asked with a slight, courteous nod of his head.

'Thank you, no. It is too early in the evening. You understand?'

'Your accent. You speak German?'

'Schweizerdeutsch.'

'Ah, you are from German Switzerland.'

'No, I am from Switzerland.'

There is something powerful in this man, thought Günter. Something lies behind the face of the jolly innkeeper.

He extended his hand in a hearty, schoolboy fashion. 'My name is Günter Prien.'

Will took his hand and shook it with Teutonic abruptness. I wonder, he asked himself, if this is one of the casual travelers in the fashion of Simmons. No. He was only a boy not yet fully grown. But still he had the haunting feeling that this handshake was somehow a prelude to another, graver relationship.

He did not give his own name. It was, after all, clearly stated on the sign over the door.

'You travel on your holiday?'

Günter took a map from the pocket of his tunic and opened it as though preparing a lecture. 'You see, we went first to Copenhagen. Then to Kristiansand. It is a boat tour.'

Will smiled and nodded.

'Then to Bergen, the Shetland Islands and, so, to here, the Orkneys. We leave tonight for Glasgow. I regret we cannot stay over a day or two and see more of your beautiful islands, but it is not possible. The accommodations are not numerous enough.'

'Perhaps another time.'

'It is to be hoped for.'

'And what will you do for the rest of your school leave?'

'I also regret to say that we leave the boat in Glasgow and travel by rail to Liverpool. A day there and then to Southampton, where we shall cross the Channel to France – and so back to Germany.'

Will was struck by a nearly overwhelming weakness and longing. 'Home,' he murmured.

'Yes, home, to Germany – to Garmisch.'

'Bavaria.'

'You know it?'

'I – have visited. A long time ago. Did the war change it very much?'

'The war changed nearly everything,' Günter said, as though he had long deliberated the subject. 'But we have rebuilt, and Germany is once again becoming as it was. Germany is recovering. I drink to these good and peaceful times.'

As he lifted his mug, immediately followed by his companions, Will raised a hand to ask for a moment's pause. He quickly poured himself a glass of port and raised it.

'To these peaceful times.'

The boys toasted 'these good and peaceful times.' At the very sound of the words, a certain assurance struck Will.

The look of the three young men, dressed so neatly in white and blue, their scrubbed, shining and open faces, their candid attempts to establish threads of communication and friendship – all vividly enforced the thought that grew in him.

Would this new generation of Germans possibly want to turn away from the good tasks of rebuilding the Fatherland and restoring it to prosperity? Would they refuse to seek the promising future and the hope of recovering something of the pleasant past in order to march again? Could they refuse peaceful opportunities in order to resurrect the old arrogance and futile ambitions of war? It seemed an impossibility. Such aspirations of conquest were insane.

Will felt flushed and elated, very nearly drunk on the single glass of port.

'Come you will join me now.'

He refilled the mugs and tipped the bottle of port over his own glass.

'Tell me of your plans,' Will said to young Günter in

particular. He found the boy handsome, good-mannered, admirable in every way. He was a perfect example of German youth.

'We will leave the boat at Glasgow, as I say –'

'I mean the plans for your life. Will you be an attorney, a doctor, a merchant?'

Günter smiled. He seemed grave and mature.

'I intend to make a career in the Navy.'

His two companions nodded, announcing their intentions to follow their friend into the service of their country.

'Admirable.' Will grinned. 'Drink. You find the bitters not to your taste?'

The three young men drank to prove the goodness of the brew and to please the tavern owner.

Will raised a finger. 'Wait, wait. Perhaps I have something more to your taste.' He disappeared behind the counter. There were the sounds of bottles nudging one another. Günter looked at Hans Emling and raised his brows. Will reappeared with a dusty, half-empty bottle.

'Schnapps. From Germany itself, yes.'

He quickly poured three glasses over the protests of the boys.

Will's eyes were shining. They seemed bluer in his flushed face. He chattered away and refilled his glass. He drank schnapps now with the boys, who themselves were getting drunk.

John Kendrick entered the tavern. He was dressed in his best suit. He waved a hand at Will, who scarcely glanced at him. He went to the end of the bar and stood waiting for service.

'Excuse,' Will said. He seemed reluctant to leave the company of the German boys.

Günter Prien took the opportunity. He felt himself tipsy but still in control. 'We must be on our way.'

He extended his hand and pumped Will's hand twice. Karl and Hans went through the formality as well. Will watched them leave with regret.

He served John, who looked after the German youths curiously.

'Fine boys,' Will said.

'Young, and that's a good thing. Perhaps they'll grow up differently from their fathers,' John commented.

Will felt a sharp lance of anger, of hate. He almost

protested the veiled insult to the German people. He looked at his old friend, and the anger fled from him.

'Are you dressed for a wedding or a wake?' He laughed.

John grinned and brushed the vest of his best suit. 'I'm off to Glasgow on business. I managed a passage on the excursion boat.'

Will raised his glass. 'To these good and peaceful times.'

CHAPTER 11

A night of restlessness came to an end with a certainty that burst upon him as a seedpod explodes into the sunny air. Hope-filled promises flew out, and all things became possible.

At the next day's noon closing, Will rushed out to the High Street. He bought new linen, a new shirt, a hat. He threw frugality away and bought a new suit.

He spent more than an hour with the barber.

He bathed twice before dressing himself in his new clothes. In his excited expectation he found himself sweating too much.

He treated himself to a double shot of schnapps, emptying the bottle.

He restrained himself from speeding along the cliffs on his bicycle. He didn't wish to sweat more and so to offend. He wished to make the visit casual and unplanned.

He stood before the door of the Kendrick cottage, holding a nosegay of flowers and feeling like a schoolboy. All around him the atmosphere had the marvelous clarity of twilight. On his way he'd seen six brown pelicans flying in a wedge, and that, as everyone knew, was the luckiest of signs.

The door opened.

'Willum!'

The world held the sound of pleasant surprise and amused curiosity.

Will removed his hat, extended the nosegay and giggled foolishly.

'It was such a lovely evening. I gave the care of the Sailing Master over to Wee Jock and walked along the seafront. The sun seemed to fill the universe as it set. There was a long moment when the line between sea and sky disappeared and a sailboat beating its way home seemed to be sailing in the heavens.'

Molly could not help but smile. 'It seems to have made a poet of you.'

Will giggled again and regretted the weakness. But despite himself, he rambled on without control over his tongue.

'Yes. Yes, it's not the proper way for a stolid Germanic

type, is it? No. Well, I walked and walked, and it became dusk, and I walked some more and – I find myself here.'

Molly's beautiful eyes twinkled. 'I see that your bicycle followed you. How clever.'

'Oh, yes, it is a most intelligent bicycle. John is home?'

One of Molly's eyebrows tilted in mock sympathy.

'You hadn't heard he'd left for Glasgow? He's been gone since yesterday.'

'Really? How foolish of me. I am forgetful. Is it age? Is it happiness?'

He grinned at Molly to demonstrate just how foolish he was. She smiled affectionately as a woman will smile at a child wrapped in fantasy or a man who is slightly tipsy, reproving, yet amused.

'Willum, have you been sampling your wares a bit more than usual?'

He started to make a small show of protest, but his laughter bubbled through. 'No, no, I swear to you. But it is a prospect to be considered. Do you invite me in to have a small drink?'

Molly stood aside and placed her hands behind her back to remove her apron. As he turned to face her inside the room, she pulled him slightly forward by his lapel and sniffed his breath.

'Am I not to be trusted?' Will asked with feigned indignation.

'I'm letting you into the house, Willum.' Molly chuckled.

Molly went to the sideboard and took out the stone jug. She pinned him with an appraising eye and poured out a generous dollop of whiskey. She gestured him to a chair by the open window where he might enjoy the onshore breeze and handed him the glass there. She placed the flowers in a pitcher of water and took the chair opposite him. The north star appeared.

'Thank you. Thank you. Thank you,' Will murmured.

His eyes had the depth of moonstones reflecting the last light, and Molly touched the pulse at her throat. His voice had the timbre of a man at prayer.

'What is it, Willum?' she asked, wanting so much to be allowed in.

'I suddenly realized today that I am home.'

'Yes.'

'A man can live many years in one place and not be home.

Echoes of other places keep him in a kind of enchantment. He goes about his daily work, scarcely seeing – afraid to build any new memories. Therefore, everything remains strange to him, and he is always a stranger. I say it badly.'

'No, Willum, you do not.'

He relaxed visibly and unbuttoned his coat.

'Yes, I am home.'

He took a lingering sip of the whiskey and lost himself in the tang of smoky peat upon his tongue.

'Another?' Molly asked.

'Should I?'

Molly went to the sideboard to fetch the jug. Will turned to enjoy the movement of her hips.

'Consider it a celebration. Consider it a homecoming,' Molly said gaily.

'Then you must have one with me.'

She returned with the crock and another glass and poured both glasses nearly full. They drank, and she coughed a bit. They laughed.

'Yes,' Will said with exhilaration. 'A man comes to an age when he must begin to build small traditions for himself, for a family.'

He stood and walked across the room as though about to energetically harvest a crop of such traditions.

'To store up memories and moments. To be able to recall, when old age comes, the taste of holidays and the smell of the changing seasons and the sounds of voices that are loved or were loved.'

He paused before the hearth and fingered a small music box. He opened it, and it played a gay little air. He closed it with a start, realizing that this had been a gift from Molly's dead lover.

'When you store up memories, you mustn't be afraid of them or saddened by them, Willum.'

Will returned to the chair. He found himself unable to stop talking.

'A man must decide to put away all the errors of the past. All the obligations to things that are withered and gone. He must savor the present and make a book to be read in the future.'

He spoke for a long while. He spoke as he had never spoken to another human being, as he spoke to the sea or the shadows of his room. He spoke until the last wash of light fled from the window seat and the dark fell.

But he could not bring himself to reveal the hidden purpose of his life in Stromness.

The river of words slowed and stilled in the night. He turned his head toward her slowly as though fearful that an expected beloved image would have disappeared in the dark.

Molly held up one hand as though in benediction, bidding him be still for a bit. She took him by the hand and led him into her bedroom. It seemed filled with the clean smell of soap overlaid with heather. She lit an oil lamp and placed the flame low. She sat him upon the bed and unbuttoned the top of her blouse. A certain smile touched her mouth. She removed the shirtwaist. She unloosed the bow at the neck of her camisole. As she lifted her arms to remove the garment, she turned her back.

'Will you undress yourself, Willum?' she murmured and went from the room.

Will removed his clothing. He pulled back the counterpane and bent to smell the sharp sweetness of the wind-dried sheets. He lay down and felt their gentle harshness along the length of him. He turned his face to the window, pleasuring himself with anticipation.

The lamp illuminated his features with a light so soft and subtle that his reflection in the darkened pane was devoid of lines about the eyes and mouth. The hint of jowls and the texture of coarsening skin were veiled. The gray that dusted his hair was no more than the shine of moonlight. He was a young, young man in the window glass. He heard the whisper of her step. He delayed a moment longer before turning to see.

Had there ever been a love bride quite so beautiful? Her breasts were such as to nurse titans. The column of her neck seemed carved of rose marble. Her belly mounded with promise. The lamplight excited auburn sparkles in the fall of hair that cascaded to her waist, in the thick moss at the root of her belly.

She held a flannel nightgown in her hand, having decided to cast aside even that convention.

She brought her riches to the bed. Her touch gave a sweet sickness to his body. Her tongue filled his mouth with the taste of honey. All the poetry of his imaginings were over-hued with a single blazing thought. He was to take this woman and make her his own!

He touched the points of her breasts softly with the very

tips of his fingers so she might feel the trembling there and know the quality of his desire. He caressed sonnets along her shoulders, back and thighs. He whispered songs without words to her.

Her large, good hands clasped him and drew him close to her.

He became aware of his face constricted with the intensity of his desire. He struggled to create the means to culminate his passion. The distortion of his face became that of anguish.

He employed every device, at last, that he'd learned at the breasts of unnumbered whores.

Molly's body pressed to him urgent and demanding. It touched and fled away. It was welcoming, passive, fierce, compliant, searching.

Will's body failed him. He strained with effort and flogged his mind with fantasies, recollections and brutal imaginings. His whole being crouched in a rictus of frustrated will. Molly seemed to relax all in a rush. She was offering him the luxury of time and trying to remove the urgency of her need that well might threaten him. But panic tightened his enveloping arm, and she rejoined his struggle gently but with strength. Finally she made a space between them. His failure left a slender snail track on her thigh. He was overcome with shame. He turned away and plunged his face into the pillow.

'My God, no,' he cried. It was the strangled cry of a drowning man.

Molly touched his shoulder. 'Willum, don't.'

'God knows I want you. I've wanted you for such a long time,' he explained.

Molly wisely and instinctively salved his failed manhood with soft words. 'Perhaps that's the cause of it, Willum.' She sat up in the bed. 'So much wanting.' She caressed his back lightly with the tips of her work-worn fingers.

Defeat and despair captured Will. She was treating him with tenderness and consideration. It was, strangely, the very worst thing she could have done.

He protested weakly, his words muffled by the pillow.

'Hush, Willum, hush. Then, too, you had a lot to drink.'

How many excuses will she find for me? he wondered bitterly. He turned his head away from the smell of her sweet sweat on the linen coverlet.

'Yes, perhaps that is it,' he agreed dully.

'Turn over,' she ordered gently. She lay back herself and placed her hand on his chest. 'Rest a bit.'

She closed her eyes. She could not help thinking that the grand seduction had been something of an adolescent farce. She quickly put aside the thought, scolding herself for her lack of charity.

But, damn him! Damn his orderly manners! Damn his concern with my acceptance in this bloody small village! Damn his propriety and delicate feelings, his gentle ways and gentlemanly consideration, his sense of honor and his careful treatment of me! Damn, damn, damn his frightened cock!

She settled herself to the quiet task of soothing his fears, restoring his pride and stiffening the vital member.

But Will remained impotent.

'Are you awake, Willum?'

He became aware that her hand was no longer on his chest, that she had relaxed into the bedding as the tension of her desire had left her. She was now simply drained, though unsatisfied.

'Yes, I'm awake.'

'We're not children. We know these things happen. Wanting too much. Trying too hard. One – or the other – too tired or –'

'Excuses?' Will interrupted irritably. 'Must we make excuses?'

Molly felt a sudden surge of venom. After all, the failure had been his; the humiliation hers. She scolded herself at once. No, the humiliation was far more terribly his.

He touched her hand. 'Like a dog, I snap at my own tail.' He laughed sharply. 'Not an amusing comparison. I thank you. It is kind of you to reassure me.'

'Must you speak in such a formal manner?' she murmured.

'The foolishness of pride. I must tell you I am not usually impotent.'

He thrust a leg out from beneath the quilt that half covered them. She turned her head sharply to look at him.

Don't be a fool, Molly girl, she thought. Of course, the things the women supposed must be true. Certainly it was to bed a woman that he went on his frequent journeys.

No matter. To hell with him then. She'd played the wanton, but she'd be damned if she'd play the whore.

Will sat on the edge of the bed and shook his head.

'That was a stupid thing to say. I sound like a schoolboy crowing about past performances. Forgive me.'

Molly felt an infinite sadness. She felt that any expectations between them had fled. She intuited that no amount of logic, tenderness or common sense could bring back that precious, hopeful moment. How easily it might have been a beginning and not an end.

'I'm not quite sure what I'm supposed to forgive.'

CHAPTER 12

Will found no way to comfort his soul in his failure. He fought off, with a sense of the dishonor to Molly in it, the need to take himself to the body of a whore and in that sorry way recapture proof of his manhood. He told himself that he was a fool to doubt, or fear for, his virility because of a single night's failure to gain an erection. But the wisdom was buried in some nameless fear.

At last he fled. The following day he begged passage, on a fishing vessel which left him on the Scottish coast. He traveled for a long time on more than one train. He found himself in London. Perhaps there was the thought in the back of his mind that it was but a short voyage across the Channel to France. From France to Germany and home. Away from the Orkneys. Away from his trusting friends. Away from Molly.

He walked, that first night, along the Thames Embankment. The dark, turgid river complemented the sorry rage he felt in himself.

Molly would not leave his mind. She seemed to walk beside him, murmuring words of comfort for his failure, but he imagined a gleam of contempt in her eyes. His failure with her had been the most humiliating failure of his life.

But then, it had been natural enough, innocent enough. He had expected a performance from himself based on the fantasies of a thousand nights. His body had laughed at the vanity and had played a monstrous joke upon him. It had told him to stop playing the fool and act the grown-up. He did, in truth, have nothing to be ashamed of.

Molly had been gentle and willing, comforting and wise. She had been everything he had imagined she would be and more.

He felt a lift of the heart, and he turned his steps away from the despairing river.

He had only to visit Molly once again. To let her know with all the passion in him how much he loved and desired her. He would ask her to walk out with him. They would enjoy a sensible, not too long courtship. They would enter into the ways of lovers in good time. They would be married, and she would tease him at times about his flattering, if awkward, eagerness.

He found himself in the outskirts of Soho. His legs were aching. He turned to the street, seeking a taxicab. He was eager to gather his few belongings from the hotel and return to Stromness as soon as possible. No cab offered itself, and he began to walk rapidly home.

He was forced to stop his progress at the doorway of a low ginhouse. Two drunken sailors and a single painted prostitute staggered from the place and blocked his way. He politely retreated a step and made to walk around them. By force of habit, he even tipped his hat to the woman.

'You're a gentleman, luv,' she rasped. 'I could do with one.' She made an elaborate show of keeping the sailors on their feet.

'You see how it is, dearie. They're not much use.'

'There are two of them,' Will pointed out rudely.

'Four of them wouldn't suit a big girl like me in their condition.'

She looked at Will levelly. There was more than a touch of challenge. She was big, and though she was well past her prime, an animal vitality had left her body comparatively untouched by the life.

'Two, in that condition, should be more profitable.'

'I don't fancy that sort of thing. I believe in giving value for money,' she snapped.

'Then name the price.'

They regarded each other like enemies. She hated him fiercely. He suddenly and irrationally wanted to beat her to her knees. With contempt. With violence, if need be. She narrowed her eyes and smiled.

One of the seamen was not half so drunk as he pretended. The other, a fresh-faced boy, was scarcely drunk at all.

'Belt up and get you out of here, you bloody toff,' the older sailor ordered.

Will didn't honor him with the slightest glance.

'Go along, you,' the boy piped.

Will smiled at the whore, seeing the feral eagerness in her eyes. She was a woman to be bought, used and paid, but it in no way lessened her feminine atavistic desire to see male animals fight over her.

'Crawl around some other gutter if you want to get

dirty,' the senior commanded. 'Stay here and you'll get bloody.'

The boy giggled nervously, reacting to Will's calm. The older, heavier sailor jolted Will's shoulder with a stiff arm. Will kept his eyes on the whore's for a last moment, then thrust out at the red face of his antagonist.

The man staggered back. Will moved in with short, choppy steps. His walking stick was held unused in his left hand, but at each step his right hand punished the sailor. He struck short, brutal blows meant to injure seriously.

The man fought to gain his balance, to get his weight shifted forward so he might set himself to return a punch. When he had achieved that purpose, Will smashed him in the face. The sailor's nose seemed to burst, and blood masked his nose and chin. The man still kept his feet. He tottered finally and fell to one knee, where he vomited onto the roadway.

Will turned to the boy who stood immobile. Will pulled his fist back to strike. The whore gave a sharp yip of intense pleasure.

The boy's face seemed to collapse in fear, pain and terrible regret. He turned and ran.

In the whore's hot, airless room, Will battered away at her body with his own. He punished her woman's flesh as she gave as much as she received, clawing at his back with ragged nails, leaving bloody tracks. He poured out filth into her ears, and she screamed 'Yes!' to goad him on. He kneaded her breast till she bit her lip and cried in pain and pleasure. He slapped her face. Her head rocked from side to side, her sweaty hair making pencil lines across her cheeks. He came in a final, long-delayed rush.

Within moments his body became alive with invisible insects. He looked at the repellant orange-peel thighs spread in defeat. He began to cry.

Will stood on the deck of the mail packet. His hands were thrust deep into the pockets of his coat. They were clenched there as though holding onto something vital to his life. A storm, which had not struck the sky overhead as yet, was coursing through the bowels of the sea. The deck pitched and rolled. Will adjusted easily to the shifting plane beneath his feet and, bareheaded, faced the spray.

He felt a great loathing of self. He'd dishonored the intention to court and marry Molly in the very moment he'd assured himself that it was a destiny both possible and proper. He was harsh in his judgment of self but allowed, sensibly, a long look at the extenuating view. He'd been threatened in his manhood. He'd reacted in a boastful, perhaps adolescent way in proving himself on the whore's body. It was done. He was no longer doubtful of his potency.

His hands slowly opened in the pockets of his coat. He felt a tension drain away similar to the release that tears had brought at the end of the sexual act. He knew he could never have traffic with women for pay again. The resolve fashioned on the Thames Embankment was still valid, still strong within him. He felt a strange creeping of the skin of his neck and back. It was an animal awareness of something loathsome. He turned sharply around prepared to fight or flee.

Simmons smiled at him from beneath the edge of a wide-brimmed fedora that began to drip necklaces of water drops as the sky suddenly released its burden of rain.

'What an unpleasant day this has turned out to be, Mr. Hartz.'

'What are you doing here?'

Will's voice was filled with the suspicion that Simmons was there for the express purpose of watching him. Had Wiley alerted another agent in the port of Scotland? Had he been under surveillance all the way to London? Had his liaison with the whore been remarked?

Simmons smiled a quirky grin.

'I'm traveling to Kirkwall. I have business there. And what are you doing here?'

'I'm returning from London.'

'And did you have business there?'

Will regarded Simmons balefully. Simmons regarded Will cheerfully but was no less an enemy.

'You went to visit a woman perhaps? Very discreet, keeping your amatory activities so far from home.'

'That's none of your affair,' Will said sharply and was sorry for the defensive tone in his voice.

'It might well be. I hope you're not too garrulous with your whores.'

Will offered no response. Simmons' manner changed and was suffused with heavy camaraderie.

'Here, old fellow, am I blaming you? It must get damned lonely for you living among strangers.'

'They're not strangers. That is the sad fact of the matter.

I've lived in Stromness many years. I live in Stromness, but I'm not of Stromness. I cannot pursue a life in any normal fashion.'

'That is part of the common condition of those in our profession.'

'It is uncommonly painful and uncommonly lonely.'

'You should marry. Pursue an average, normal life. In point of fact, it would make your cover even more secure. There is something very suspect about an eligible man, a man of some substance, living in such an isolated society, remaining unmarried.'

'Are you suggesting that I involve a woman in my deception?'

'Naturally not. Tell her nothing. At least not at first. Not until you've brought her around to your way of thinking, slowly and subtly. Teach her and any children you might have. Women and children are very malleable. Their loyalties are simple ones, and they are practical creatures. They have an abiding trust in the person who butters their bread.'

Will could fashion no reply. Like most big lies, Simmons' game plan had a core of good sense buried in it. He should proceed as though he would spend all his life in Stromness, as indeed he might. If a man's dedication was to a thing larger than himself, why shouldn't it be larger than those who might come to love and depend on him? It was a ruthless view and one that made his good soul cringe.

If they married, Molly and he, and if he were called upon to fulfill his vow to the Fatherland, how, then, would she react when the truth was made known to her? Would she consider her life and her will bound to him? No. He knew his steadfast Molly. With her honest islander's eyes she'd see truth fairly with no regard for her own security or comfort. If her love of the British nation was untested and undefined, her love of her small spot of earth nested in cold seas was fierce and pure.

'I could not live two lives.'

'We're already doing it.' Simmons gestured widely. 'Do as you please. Your domestic arrangements are your own concern. Perhaps you're right to do as you do, after all. We have only one duty: to prepare for that day when the burdens of reparations will be repudiated, the occupied territories restored and the infamy of Versailles avenged.'

'Do you really believe any of that will ever come to pass?'

'Are you saying you do not believe?'

Wilhelm shrugged. That was the very point about which he spun. What did he believe?

Once returned home, Will struggled to resolve the problem of his own indecisiveness. He would think it through carefully for the thousandth wearying time. He deferred the confrontation with himself in this way. He delayed the necessary and desired visit to Molly's cottage. As time passed, he feared a rejection because of the delay. Time eroded his intention to act forcibly in the name of his own happiness.

In the fullness of summer, though the sun was warm, Will felt a chill reluctance in his bones the many times he left his lonely bed in the early dawn. He had taken to tramping through the gorse and bracken, over each rocky prominence and shadowed glen on the island. He was a man waiting for an event he believed would never come to pass. His life was a held breath.

He deceived himself and contrived to forget the passage of days, waiting as supplicants, fools and children do for fate to offer an unmistakable sign and show the way.

In late autumn, while on one of his early-morning rambles, he came face to face with Ian Bostock. The man confronted him, by chance, on a narrow path running along the bank of a small stream. He stepped back defensively, one arm raised in protection against a blow. Then he straightened himself with a defiant air. His lip curled, ready to offer an insult, but he hadn't the courage for that.

He was unshaved, and the sick smell of him carried even in the cold, sharp air.

'Have you any word of Julie?' Will asked. He kept his voice pleasant and without a trace of the overwhelming pity he'd suddenly felt.

Bostock seemed startled by the civility. He was emboldened to stay and chat. There were few enough who would give him the time of day.

'A letter from that twit of a girl? Not likely. Work your fingers to the bone,' he said, lifting his mutilated hand. Seeing it there, he laughed foolishly.

'Work your fingers clear off, and what thanks comes of it? None. Runs off like the little slut she is. I did my best. Bad blood. Like her mother. A filthy little whore is what she is.'

he said with great injury and vehemence. He looked at Will carefully. The man had been a friend to the girl. Perhaps he had gone too far.

Will shrugged his shoulders again as though in sympathy. 'The young people must make their own way.'

Bostock sighed for his lost child. He nodded his head, considering the great pain she caused him. His eyes searched the ground, hoping to find a way to ask Will for the price of a bottle of slum. When he looked up, Will was gone, walking off down along the stream.

Well, he thought, the foreigner hadn't assaulted him. Knew better than to try that on when he, Bostock, was sober and well prepared to defend himself. In fact, the man had been downright civil to him. A small victory. Perhaps one evening he would saunter into the Sailing Master. Perhaps he would be allowed the company of that warm place again.

Will walked on around the bend of the stream, fighting down a powerful need to be sick. The man offended him in every way, and now he had engendered pity as well. He wondered what took Bostock out into the hills at such an hour. The island whore had a cottage nearby, but even old Meg, herself lost to drink and depravity, would keep her door locked against Bostock unless he had more than sufficient funds to pay for her time.

The man had acted surreptitiously, even guiltily. In need of drink or money, had he gone to Meg's hovel and been turned away? Had he gone there to steal or worse? Rebuffed, had he done her an injury in desperate anger?

Will found himself, suddenly, before the whore's cottage. The windows were stuffed with rags to keep out the wind and cold. Empty, rusting tin cans and all manner of garbage were piled in the yard space. The thatch was moldy and gave off a sour stink.

All at once, the aging slattern appeared in the opening of the half door. She grinned and tucked in her filthy blouse so that the cloth was stretched over her dugs.

'Come for an early roll in the hay, luvvie?' She grinned.

Will stood transfixed. He stared, his mouth agape at the spectacle. He turned and ran. He was violently ill in a small copse of slender birches.

Good God, he thought, he'd felt a stirring of sexual desire. Not for the dirty, scabrous slut. For woman. Any woman.

He rushed back to his rooms and bathed himself. He

scrubbed his body with harsh wood wool and chastened it with frigid water.

He darted about his cramped, untidy quarters, dusting and polishing with a housewife's vigor and purpose.

He bathed again and was finally still within himself.

The stillness and reasonable content lasted for a long, long span of days.

CHAPTER 13

On a harsh cold day filled with the threat of storm Will sat on a stool behind the bar and complimented himself on keeping a good, clean tavern.

I am a good, clean, quiet man. I have one talent, apparently. I have patience. I find it irritating, but not too difficult, simply to sit and wait.

He glanced up at the clock on the wall. The morning hours of opening were nearly half gone and not a single customer. Not a face. Not a voice. Will took his spectacles from his pocket and began to polish them industriously with his handkerchief.

He heard the door open behind him and felt the icy hand of the wind at his back. He quickly folded and repocketed the eyeglasses.

Siever Scarff shuffled with patient effort to the barrail. Mister Handy had died while playing a game of drafts in the Sailing Master, and Scarff was left quite alone. His steps had become slower in consequence.

Without a word, Will placed the board and counters in front of Siever.

He raised his watery eyes to Will's, blinking furiously several times. 'Damn foolishness, isn't it? A half of bitters, if you please, Will. We played drafts every morning – Handy, Booth and me. Fifteen years near enough.'

Will pulled a pint of stout and set it up.

'Now, no, Will. A half of bitters, if you please.'

'Stout is better for you, old man. Would I have you die of shock not having your morning pint of stout?'

'I remember those games, thanking you, Will.'

'And so do I.'

'Old Handy went out peaceful, they say.'

'But you were here, Mr. Scarff.'

'So I was. So I was. Holding my hand when he fled, he was. Gripped my hand that last second like to break it. He died a young man right then.'

Siever looked up at the clock. He noted the decorations with a snort of disdain.

'Merry Christmas. Damn foolish. World's not very merry.' He picked up a box of checkers and the board and carefully tucked them under his arm. He grasped the mug of stout in both hands and started the long six-foot voyage to the table.

'Not very merry.'

A few evergreen boughs, browning at the needle tips, some red holly berries and tarnished gilt letters made a brave and tawdry show on the wall around the clock.

'1930 – Merry Christmas.'

Will replaced himself on the stool. The ticking of the clock was loud in the pub. From time to time, at long intervals, there was the sound of a game piece being moved, followed by a pleased chuckle as Scarff approached victory over his ghostly opponent. Nearly an hour crept by before the door opened again.

A woman entered. She stopped three steps inside the warm room and shivered within her sailorman's heavy short coat at the change from the cold outside. She set down a carpetbag, much frayed and faded, and removed the shapeless cloche on her head. Her hair was marcelled tightly to her small skull in the fashion of the cities. It looked like a helmet of cheap brass. Her mouth, bold and scarlet, twitched into a parody of a smile. It seemed uncertain, defiant, yet afraid. The bright spots of color hadn't been caused by well-being or the wind.

Will held up his hand and answered the smile politely. 'Pardon me. Ladies are not allowed in the public bar. If you care to –'

He stopped in mid-sentence and put on his glasses. The heavy makeup made her face that of an old clown, yet he could see now that she wasn't a woman, but a girl. He knew those steady, candid eyes.

'It's me, Mr. Hartz. Julie.'

'Julie,' he echoed, and then hurried out from behind the bar and down the length of the pub toward her.

She unbuttoned the coat with red, chapped, clumsy fingers. Will's fingers hurried to help hers, to undress her as one undresses a child come in from a winter day's play.

'I saw the lights and I saw the cities. Well, three of them. Glasgow, Liverpool and London.'

Will frowned at the sharp fluting edge to her voice. He undid the last button. She was wearing a brightly colored dress tightly cut to her thin body. It was a tinsel green. He glanced at Scarff, who was still unaware that they were not alone, and led her to the family saloon.

'When did you arrive?'

'Last night.'

She stumbled a bit, and Will tightened his hand on her.

'You've been home then?'

'I went to the old house,' she corrected. 'The kids asked me for money for food and coal. The old man asked me for money for whiskey. I don't have any money, so he showed me the door.'

Will refrained from clucking his tongue. It was a bad habit of the aging and helpless.

Julie sat down in the chair Will held for her close up to the dead fire. He began to help her remove her coat, but she clutched it tightly about her.

'I'm still cold.'

'I'll light a fire. We both can use one. Not much need for an extra fire in this room lately.'

He squatted to light it. The dry scraps of driftwood caught at once, making friendly sounds. Will rose, favoring his right side with a comforting and supporting hand. The sea winds are rusting me a bit, he thought.

'Take off those wet shoes and stockings, Julie. I'll bring you a towel to warm them, and I'll make you a nice hot drink.'

'A rum toddy would do nicely, if you please.'

There was a whore's coquetry in her manner. Will frowned at her. She looked up sharply, then dropped her eyes.

'I'm of age,' she said, with more than a touch of defiance. Will turned away and went into the bar. He placed a copper kettle on the gas ring, poured a little lemon squash into a glass, added one, then another spoonful of sugar, and took down the bottle of rum.

'I suppose you have a lot to tell me. I'll be interested. So much traveling. Well, at least you are home now,' he chattered on in a loud and cheerful voice.

'Will you please stop saying home!' Julie shouted shrilly. 'I've come back to my filthy birthing place like a sick dog.'

Will poured a tot of rum filled to overflowing into the glass.

Siever Scarff raised his head and looked into the present. 'You said something, Will, did you?'

'Just talking to myself, Mr. Scarff.'

'Better watch that, Will. Sign of old age,' the octogenarian said, and returned to his game.

Will stood silent until the steam began to rise from the kettle's spout. He placed the full glass upon a tray and, with it, one towel heated in the remaining water and another that was dry. He returned to the family lounge and placed the tray on the hearth.

Julie was huddled up all within herself, hugging herself desperately. Without comment, he knelt to one knee and washed her face of the paint and powder until something of the solemn, tender child emerged.

'Where did you sleep last night?' he asked with a flat and casual air.

'I walked. I walked along the cliffside. I walked along the shore. I sat at the end of the mole.'

'On such a night?' he said, as though amused at a child's prank. He dried her face, even behind her ears, and she laughed. He dried her small feet with hands of pity.

Oh, no, Julie thought, this old, foolish bastard thinks he's Jesus Christ washing the feet of the beggars. I'm afraid I'll puke up all over the old cock's gray head.

Her throat constricted in shame. Damn it. Will I cry? she asked herself.

'We'll find you a place,' Will promised.

'Who'll have me?'

'We can find you a room in town, certainly.'

'You sweet man. Don't you understand? I've worked in a house of prostitution. I was a streetwalker. A whore. There's not a woman in this town that would give me leave to sleep in the pigsty or in the outhouse.'

'That can't be true,' Will protested.

'I tell you that it is,' Julie answered from the depths of her wisdom.

'What will you do?'

She shrugged eloquently and took several small gulps of the hot toddy.

'The world is going to hell, Mr. Hartz. Even the prostitutes suffer competition from shopgirls and discharged serving maids. The streets are full of girls and women who'll go to a man's bed for half a night's rest on a straw mat or a warm bowl of soup. There's a worldwide depression, haven't you heard? So – I came back to this lost corner. At least, I'll be no stranger to this particular kind of misery.'

'What will you do?'

'I'll set up shop in some abandoned cottage, I suppose. I'll give old Meg a bit of competition.'

Will rose to his feet without effort, distressed and agitated beyond his usual stolid control. He compared the waif sitting beneath his gaze, still a child in his heart, to the old prostitute he had seen but days before surrounded by the accumulated filth of years and a thousand men. Old Meg, who sold herself for ale and pennies to a scattering of drunken, lustful sailormen and the lowest forgotten man. To this girl's father when he had the price.

'No!' Will shouted, startling even himself. 'You will stay here. At least for the present. Until something can be arranged. Things will be better for you. I will make it so.'

Julie looked at him, and she believed it. Have I set out to trap this kind man into an act of charity? Julie wondered. Have I really planned to play him for a fool? This man who was the first of so few to show me a kindness.

She stretched out her wrist. The little watch circled it. 'No matter how bad things got, I never sold this. I never even put it into pawn.' She prayed he understood, for there was nothing more she could offer.

Will smiled, briefly, for fear he would cry. 'There is a small room under the eaves. A little bed, a table, a chair. A mirror, yes, and a jar for flowers. It could be a cozy place. It will, at least, be a place to rest.'

'You know this could make trouble for you.'

'The women will have something to wag their tongues about for a while. But sharp tongues seldom do a lasting injury.'

The front door opened. A finger of cold wind rushed through the barroom and even to the fire itself. The man and the girl shivered as one and laughed as one.

'Rest and enjoy the fire. At midday closing, we'll build your little nest.'

That evening the taproom of the Sailing Master was almost crowded. In these hard times it was a condition to be remarked upon. Wee Jock was pulling tankards of brew at a good pace. He'd come on at opening without any request from Will.

'It's not Friday or Saturday, Jock,' Will remarked.

'Felt in the need of a little man chat,' Jock replied. 'Might as well busy myself. No wages expected or asked for, Will.'

The family room in the back was nearly filled as well. There were even a few housewives who rarely, if ever, showed their noses in a pub.

In his innocence Will attributed the activity to the approaching holiday season. Christmas was a good time, after all, even in the worst of times.

When Julie entered the barroom from upstairs, it all became clear to him.

The chatter concerning the high cost of food and coal, the poor market for their fish, the disturbing and seeming helplessness of the government, faded and died as every head turned to the doorway.

Julie stood in the doorway like a child who fears that she is intruding on an adult celebration, yet wants very much to join it. Color washed across her face, which was, Will was inordinately pleased to see, freshly scrubbed and nearly devoid of paint but for a hint of color on her lips. Her emotions lightly crimsoned her slender neck, her thin chest and shoulders, which were revealed discreetly by the peasant blouse she wore.

Will went to her and spoke softly. 'You should be asleep, or at least, resting.'

'I want to do something. I want to help.'

'It's Julie, is it?' John Kendrick said in a jolly way of greeting. 'Come back to the nest, have you, Julie?'

Julie smiled prettily. 'Back to see how you old sea gulls are doing.'

The reply drew a burst of laughter far greater than its wit merited. In the laughter was the unmistakable sound of welcome.

'I daresay we'll be a disappointment to you after all those fine gentlemen in the city,' Daniel Collier opined.

Will's jaws tightened, but he immediately relaxed, knowing that he was being sensitive to a possible insult when nothing but kindness was intended. Julie, certainly, understood the intent of the banter.

'Tell us then, girl. Which were the better men?'

Julie stepped up to the bar, folded a cloth and wiped up a spill of bitters on the wood. 'London men are careful to take your arm when crossing the street. Liverpool men try to grab your leg. And Glasgow men keep their hands on their wallets.'

The laughter was fuller. The men gave themselves to their enjoyment of the banter.

From the family room the women craned their necks like so many chickens, trying to capture a glimpse of Julie. They came to the pass-through one by one, and ordered refreshment singly in order to secure a better look.

Julie made up a tray of small smoked herrings and shrimp, cheeses and rounds of bread. She took it into the family room to give them, once and for all that night, a good long look at a fallen woman.

She smiled at them and spoke softly. She did not presume on her acquaintance with them. An older woman touched her hand in the loving way the old touch the young. 'I had no chance to tell you that I sorrowed for your mum's death,' she said. Julie, in a rush of thankfulness, bent over and kissed the woman's dry and dusty cheek. She rushed from the room back to the rougher smiles and welcome of the men.

The women murmured among themselves and opined that life had been hard for young Julie Bostock. Only God could judge the measure of her sins. She was, after all, a child of the islands – returned.

It was not until three days before Christmas Eve that Bostock ventured into the Sailing Master, at a quiet time of the day's custom.

Away from the gloom and fear of her homecoming night, away from the cold and dark, Julie looked at the man who had fathered her with detachment. She saw a man who wore failure as a cloak. His back seemed bowed, not with labor, but with the will to cringe. His hands seemed always clawed in the attitude of a beggar. His nose was pinched across the bone. His eyes were ravaged by bad drink.

He saw a woman grown.

'Well, now,' he said. 'The governor not up and about?'

'Mr. Hartz mentioned he won't bar you from the place any longer. So if you want to order a drink, I'll serve you.'

'That's a cold way to talk to your father, isn't it, girl?'

'We'll have no talk about that.'

She stared at him, waiting for him to buy. She remembered the night that had finally driven her from this place. She placed her hands behind her back and made the most of her breasts. His eyes flickered there, and desire flared, then dimmed with shame at the thought. She turned to the shelves and removed a bottle of the best whiskey. She poured a double tot and placed it before Bostock.

He grinned. 'Well, well. Whiskey. It's not my usual sup.'

Julie leaned across the bar and fixed him with her eyes as he fought with his own to keep them from staring down her blouse.

'Drink it, old man. It is for having something to do with me being born. It's payment for the right you had, through accident, to call yourself a father. It's the price of the debt between us. Paid in full and be damned.'

Bostock started to protest with anger. She cut him off at the root of his tongue. 'Choke on your words. A nod from me and you'll be thrown out in the cold again. Don't make any sly remarks to Mr. Härtz. Don't make any suggestion it's your right to allow me to stay here or that you put your well-loved daughter into his keeping.'

'And what will be in it for me?'

She pointed to the glass. 'There it is. The first and the last for free. Paid in full, I said.'

'As you say, daughter.'

'No. Julie. You can call me Julie, because that's the friendly way the patrons call the barmaid.'

In the months that followed, Will's life took on a new and in most part comfortable pattern.

Julie alone often took care of what small custom the tavern enjoyed during the day. Will found a new, if placid, pastime for himself, visiting those places of historical interest that dotted the islands.

On various spring days, Will spent quiet hours in the cool gloom of St. Magnus Cathedral in Kirkwall. He sat beside the legendary Dwarfie Stone on the island of Hoy. He rambled around the fortified tower for which the island of Burray was named. He visited the Carrick house on the tiny island of Eday where the pirate John Gow was taken in the king's custody in the year 1725.

At first he begged the short voyages from anyone sailing to any place in the islands. Then he bought a small single-handed sailing craft. He became, the men of Stromness agreed, a better than fair sailor.

He spent a pleasant afternoon in the village of St. Margaret's Hope on South Ronaldsay. It was there the 'Maid of Norway,' Queen Margaret, had died.

He was seated on a stretch of lonely beach, breaking the morning's fast with the lunch Julie had made up for him. He thought of the events that he'd read of that had surrounded the short life of the little girl who had been the titular queen of

Scotland in that past age. She had been the daughter of a king, Eric II, of Norway, and of the Queen Margaret who had been daughter to Alexander III of Scotland. When her mother died in the first year of little Margaret's life, the lairds of Scotland had decided that if her grandfather should die childless, the crown should pass to her. Two years later Alexander was killed, and the toddler was a queen. The English king, Edward I, who was embroiled, as were all the crowns and heads of Europe, in the struggle for power, arranged a marriage between the infant and his son. Margaret was six years of age and surely unaware of the maelstrom of intrigue that swirled about her tiny person. She sailed from Norway to the Orkneys and died there in September of the year 1290.

A tiny life in a tiny bit of time, Will thought. A tender and trifling pawn in a game she could never have understood, if indeed anyone truly did.

How many little lives, he wondered, have been ruled, commanded, thwarted, twisted, brought prematurely to an end without the consent or even the understanding of those who had been given the life of God or nature? Clearly he himself was a number on some page, a mere dot of an i in some tangle of files and ledgers no one could make head or tail of.

The letters from 'Heidi' continued to come. The handwriting was changed, but they came. They never offered any information. No direction for his efforts. They simply gave assurances, over and over again, of the importance of his role in the future of Germany. He was told there was a master plan. He would be pleased to know just what in hell his role was in the least part of that plan.

He walked down to the shale beach and grasped the prow of the sailboat. To push the small craft into the sea took no more effort than skipping a stone across the waves. He grunted and placed a clutching hand to his side. He grimaced at the pain of the stitch beneath his ribs.

I am, he thought wryly, no longer a young man.

CHAPTER 14

If winters in the islands are cruel, then spring is an expectant stirring in the heart and limbs.

Julie sat in her small rocking chair by the window of her tiny room, looking down the narrow street of Stromness toward the sea. The bright promises and sweet smells of spring made her restless. A warm indolence within her centred in her loins.

Since she was a small child, Julie had never been a stranger to sex or its many manifestations. She had witnessed with ears and eyes her father, sometimes begging, sometimes demanding, sometimes raping, twined with her mother upon the bed or even upon the floor. By the time her own breasts had begun to bud and her menses flowed, she regarded the act without particular distaste – except that the coupling of her parents was scarcely a love act – nor with any pleasurable expectations.

The drunken wastrel, owner of the fairylike sailing craft, who had taken her maidenhead was simply an extension of her father's drunken fumblings at her. Only his possession of the beautiful boat had overlaid the act with any pretty moments.

She'd accepted prostitution as an expedient, a necessity. The act made no emotional demands on her. She was not even very successful, for that independence of spirit and honesty of heart that had always marked her refused to allow her to manufacture those groans and cries that were the stock-and-trade of the headliners in the whore's profession.

She'd never thought of looking to sex for any pleasures she might gather from it herself.

She was known among her sisters of the streets as a 'dignified, quiet and nearly dead fuck.'

Perhaps, not so strangely, this quality eventually gave her a certain celebrity among those several men who found the facsimile of death sexually stimulating.

She'd never been sickened by their aberrations. She'd never catered to it. She didn't care one way or the other.

They were invariably gentle, and that was a kind of extra reward in itself.

The haven she'd found in the warmth of the Sailing Master these past months, the nest she'd made her own beneath the eaves, the safety she'd discovered beneath Will's wing – all conspired to alter her cynical and bitter attitude toward the world.

She reveled in Will's old uncle attitude toward her, the way he watched so carefully that no one should insult her in any least way, the way he smiled proudly at her cheerfulness and industry.

But she was young, and though someone who is ill may lose the taste for food, only the terminally ill refuse it indefinitely. She placed one hand down the bodice of her nightdress and felt her small breasts. The nipples grew hard, chilly with desire. She placed the other hand between her thighs and held it there with the pressure of her loins and buttocks.

Will sat in his room reading his paper. An election had been held in Germany, and Hindenburg had polled some seven million more votes than the National Socialists. Expert observers predicted that it marked the peak of the Nazi drive for power and that the party would soon be eliminated as a political force.

He reached for his brandy glass and found it empty. The decanter was empty as well.

Here now, old man, he thought, you drink alone too much. He rose and went out into the hall, the decanter in his hand. He shuffled downstairs to refill it.

Julie heard his door open and went to her own door. She could hear his slippers descending. She stood there scarcely moving, shivering slightly. She caught the almost inaudible clink of bottles. Long moments later she heard the creaking of the stairs as Will made his way back to his room. Carefully she judged his progress.

At the right moment she opened her door and stepped out into the gloom at the head of the short flight of steps leading to his rooms. She padded swiftly, on bare feet, and turned the corner to proceed below to the pub.

Will's eyes had been cast down at the stair treads. He looked up sharply as they very nearly collided. Julie pretended to be startled at the confrontation and gave a little gasp. Will's hand went out to steady her as she seemed to totter slightly.

'I'm sorry, Mr. Hartz. It's so dark.'

'Yes, yes, it is. I was downstairs to. . . .' He gestured vaguely as he turned away.

Julie moved a half step closer. When he turned back to her, his hand brushed her breast.

'I was thirsty. I wanted to. . . .' Julie blurted out her words, all in a confusion with his.

They laughed nervously.

No. She'd had enough of men pawing her about and using her, Will told himself sharply.

What the hell does the old fool want? Julie thought with a feeling of irritation. Does he need me to lift my gown above my head and put his hand on it?

'You don't sleep very well, do you?' Julie sympathized.

'When one gets older,' Will answered.

'You mustn't say that. You're not at all old. I won't hear you say it.'

'You should go to your room. Even the very young need their sleep.'

'I find it very hard to sleep these days past. It's spring, Mr. Hartz. The happiest spring of my life.'

'You might catch a chill, all the same. The night air.' He placed his hand on her shoulder to urge her to turn around.

Julie drew closer. 'The only chill I feel is the chill of loneliness.' Her head was tilted back. He was on the step below her, but even so she had to look up at him, and she knew this had an irresistible appeal to men. She moistened her lips so they became faintly wet like a child's. Will's hand tightened upon her. She kissed him softly and felt the tremor of his mouth.

Oh, my God, you poor lonely man, she thought. His arousal was so evident as to be painful to her. She felt the desperate need for a man. She wanted Will's bed.

'Julie, Julie child. I'm twenty-five years older than you.'

'That's no argument or reason.'

'When I asked you to stay, it was to offer you protection – security.'

'Give it to me then. I'm not a red-nosed child to be given a wristwatch.'

She took his reluctant hand in hers and drew him toward his rooms.

'I'd like a brandy, wouldn't you?' she said.

In the morning the sun fell like butter across the faded carpet in their bedroom. Often in the morning, Will had awakened feeling that the bed was only half full. This morning, when he felt nothing beneath his searching hand, he felt sharply that it was half empty.

Julie padded in from her bath. She was quite naked, and little drops of sparkling water still clung to her. Will propped himself back upon the pillows, the comforter pulled up to his waist. He glanced down at his chest. Silver hairs had appeared there, but blond as he was, they were scarcely to be noticed. He was not old. He was not a young man, it was true. He was better than a young man; he was a man in his prime, and he knew he'd served the woman well. He glanced to the side. His tousled hair gave his face the look of a mischievous imp full of good lechery.

Julie sat on a small bench before the dressing table, watching herself in the mirror as she piled her hair on top of her head and fixed it there with a pink ribbon. Her buttocks and back were rosy with bed and bath. The movement of her arms, lifting her small breasts, was a marvel to Will. He wondered if any gestures of a woman were more beautiful than those she made when at her morning's toilet. She caught his admiring appraisal in the glass, and she smiled with equal deviltry.

'And what for breakfast?'

'Yes, that for breakfast,' Will answered.

'You've had me the once for morning wake-up tea.' She spun around facing him, keeping her knees close together. 'Now what will it be? Rashers and eggs?'

'Sausages, I do believe, and many cups of coffee.'

'Coffee's terribly expensive. Tea for breakfast.'

'No, woman, I said coffee.'

She ran tiptoe to the bed and kissed him on the nose. 'How you do blow your bugle,' she said. He tried to envelop her in his arms, but she escaped from him, crying, 'No, no, no. I must go to my room and get dressed.' She ran from the room, and Will peeked beneath the covers at his erection.

Two weeks slipped by that were a marvel to him. 'The sleeping snows of winter make the rushing rivers of the spring,' he murmured aloud. The old saying of his native mountains really meant that, just as an old dying tree produced a last bountiful crop, so the failing libido of an aging man, once thawed, tended to produce a crop of vigorous lust. He looked at the truth of himself.

Julie's warmth had stirred desires, carefully insulated and put away, to burst forth in urgent life. He must make a journey to the city. He must glut himself on women. He was determined that he and Julie must not sleep together again.

He went to the bed and lay down to rest his burning eyes for a moment. He would find the opportunity to explain the matter to her during the afternoon. He pretended not to hear the light tapping on the door. When he sensed Julie within the room, he pretended sleep.

At the closing, while they worked together, washing and drying the glasses, he stumbled into an attempt to make clear his feelings. 'I meant to say –' he began.

'I'm sorry, Mr. Hartz. I didn't hear you.'

'No, no. I was thinking to myself.'

'And spoke out loud.'

'Yes. I mean to say that what has occurred between us.' He found himself abandoned by his tongue. 'I don't want you to think that I feel our –'

'Making love, Mr. Hartz? Making love is what it's called,' Julie said with marked innocence.

'I know that it was the spring and the loneliness you felt in me. I know it wasn't simple desire for an old man like me.'

Julie chose not to make comment. Let him say what he felt he must say.

'You mustn't think it's required of you while you work here and live here.'

'I'd never think such a thing.'

'We were both mightily lonely. Myself more than you. What has happened must not continue.'

She stood regarding him with large eyes. Dear man, she thought.

'You understand?'

'Yes, sir. Quite,' she said.

Will waved a hand and went away to the cellar to prepare a new keg for the morning. By the time he returned, Julie was gone from the taproom.

He paused at the door of his room and cocked an ear to the room above. There was no sound or stirring. He went into his rooms, feeling greatly weary and gently sad. Hungry, too. He had missed his supper.

Julie stood by the window of his sitting room dressed in

her best frock. She'd moved his table from the place before the grate and placed it at the window. Supper for two had been laid out. A candlestick, set in the center, cast a small glow over the cold meats and cheeses. There was a decanter of port. She smiled tentatively and gestured that he should sit down.

Though he did not take her and she made no attempt to rouse him, they slept together in his bed. Will savored the soft length of her along his side before he went to sleep. Julie's hand rested, bird light, upon his chest.

Bit by bit, Julie's few possessions came to join Will's in his rooms. Her few dresses came to hang beside his suits and sweaters in the closet. Her slippers sat next to his in the bottom of the cupboard. A new chest was purchased to accommodate additions to her wardrobe.

She'd placed a woman's touch about the rooms. Curtains had been sewn and covers on chairs renewed in bright, fresh colors that seemed to bring April into the winter rooms. She moved furniture about but allowed Will's rocking chair its familiar place before the fire. She bought a standing lamp for reading, protesting that if left to his own ways, he'd be blind long before he became middle-aged. Will accepted the gentle flattery and the wonder of having things done for him.

He bought her a small dressing table where she might attend her morning toilet. It was white and trimmed with gold leaf. There was an oval mirror large enough so he could pleasure his eyes with the sight of her breasts lifting as she combed her hair.

In January of the year 1933 he read with some interest, but as though it were a report of a foreign nation, the ascendancy of Adolf Hitler to the chancellorship of Germany. That funny little man with the Chaplin mustache.

He was informed by letter from Switzerland that his control would still be the man Simmons. He saw nothing of the hateful man and was glad of it.

It was Christmas Day in the evening, one year since Julie had returned. Will looked up from the paper as she entered the room. Peering over his spectacles, he looked an old tabby cat.

Julie had plaited her hair, which she had allowed to grow. It fell below her shoulder blades. She wore a flannel nightdress and one of Will's old dressing gowns. She leaned, sprung-hipped, against the doorjamb. Will frowned at the sight of the glass of whiskey in her hand.

'Yes, Julie, is there something wrong?'

Her voice sounded brittle and defiant when she spoke. 'Because I'm having a drink at bedtime?'

'Ah, perhaps it will warm you.' He returned to his records and made a notation. He heard Julie slip into bed. It was a pleasant, domestic sound.

'Are you coming to bed?' Julie asked.

'In just a moment.'

Her bare feet banged down to the floor. She strode across the room to him and snatched the pen from his hand. Will looked at her in mild surprise.

'I've been to see the doctor!'

'Then there is something not so good?' Will asked with honest concern.

'For God's sake, speak like an Englishman. You've been here long enough.'

'You are ill?'

'Haven't you heard me throwing up my breakfast?'

'No. No.'

'No, of course not. Too damned busy daydreaming. Sailing your silly boat. Scratching in that ledger. Reading books. Too damned busy to care.'

'What is wrong?' Will asked reasonably.

'I'm going to have a bloody baby is what's wrong, you bloody damned fool!'

'A child?'

'Yes, the little darlings that usually come when a man takes his pleasure with a woman night after night.'

Will removed his glasses slowly and began to polish them carefully with his handkerchief.

'Well, you've had your fun,' Julie said, nearly in tears but bone sharp. 'Now are you going to leave me to pay the piper alone?'

'No. I would never do that.' Will looked at her solemnly. 'We will do what is necessary,' he finally added.

'Let's do. I'm no more pleased than you are. I never intended to be trapped in this part of the world. If you give me the money, I can go to London. I know a doctor there.'

Will stared into Julie's face, trying to read something there. Julie instinctively took a step backward and felt the desire to flee for the sake of her life. She'd never seen rage so completely, so instantly, take possession of a human face. She'd never before witnessed rage as cold as death.

'You would destroy the infant? You would abort it?'

Julie stuttered badly when she tried to reply, any pretense of outraged injury shredded and tattered. 'I can have it and put it in for adoption,' she finally managed.

'You know people who traffic in children as well?'

Julie began to tremble, and her face collapsed. She looked like a sorry India rubber doll. 'Oh, my God, my God, my God,' she wept.

Will went to her and gently urged her sorrow and her fear into his shoulder. 'We will do what is necessary. What is right. I will go to Kirkwall and make arrangements for our marriage.'

Julie clung more tightly to him. 'Oh, Mr. Hartz.'

A wedding at the church was never considered, indeed never mentioned. Will went to Kirkwall to inquire about the legal necessities. He decided to look into the matter of citizenship, which had been implicit in the instructions under which he'd lived these years. A thought struck him briefly. Was he finally seeking naturalization because his impending marriage was a commitment to a loyalty deeper than duty to his oath to Germany? Did he wish to be a British citizen because he was taking a Scottish wife? He took no time over the illumination of such a consideration.

In the office of the registrar of the district he was mildly surprised to discover that a Mr. Cockburn, a man he knew passingly well, was the duly appointed servant of the Crown.

'Good morning, Mr. Hartz. So you find me at me work.' Mr. Cockburn welcomed Will. 'What service can I perform for you?'

'I have a double purpose. Citizenship and marriage.'

'A double good fortune.' He arranged forms, note pad and pen on the desk top. 'Now which shall be first? There is, of course, no need for you to be a British subject in order to marry. However, it does require a bit of additional red tape. The tangled threads of bureaucracy, necessary for the common good, I'm sure.'

'My intended wife is native-born,' Will ventured.

'Yes. But to what benefit to the immediate circumstance? Now if she were the husband and you the wife, it would be simple enough. You see, the alien wife can become a citizen by the simple act of marriage, but not the other way around.'

Cockburn's button nose turned rosy, and he broke out in a queer sort of laugh that was infectious. Will laughed as well and extended his hands in a graphic gesture of helplessness and trust.

'You've resided in the United Kingdom in the last twelve months? Of course you have. Of course you have. Was it three months ago we shared a glass at the Fox and Grapes? Yes, and perhaps another three before that I remember you told me of your intention to back Pertinent in the Derby and I thumped for Irish Dana. Is that right? Is that right? Yes, it is, and Irish Dana won. I had half a crown on it. Never wager more than half a crown. Sensitivity of office and all that, you know? But a tiny flutter can't be considered heavy gambling, can it? No, of course it can't.

'You've resided in the United Kingdom for an aggregate period of four years? Yes, you have. We've known each other nearly ten, is it? Yes, ten.

'You're Swiss, aren't you?'

Will managed to fit in a word of agreement.

'I'm not prying, you understand,' said Mr. Cockburn. 'Simply part of the task.

'Are you of good character? I would say the best. Sufficient knowledge of the English language? Definitely. Intend to reside in the United Kingdom or the colonies?'

'Stromness is my home.'

'Well, certainly, that takes care of that. I intend to facilitate and speed up this entire process. Even we minor servants have a few tricks of the trade.'

Will murmured his appreciation and admiration.

'And now, a few more questions on a more tender subject. You're not already married, are you?'

Will shook his head and smiled at the arch look on Cockburn's face.

'And the intended bride is not?'

Will murmured.

'Neither one a certified lunatic? Silly question that, in a way. I mean, after all, it would be a matter of record. Your intended isn't under sixteen years of age?'

'No.'

'And very sensible, too,' Cockburn said.

Will wondered what the remark meant. Apparently

Cockburn was in the habit of giving judicious opinions on just about everything.

'You're not within the prohibited degrees of consanguinity? Blood relationship,' he defined.

Will didn't bother to tell him he knew the meaning of the word.

'Or affinity? Relationship by marriage?'

Will was fascinated by the obvious pleasure the little man took in the precise formality of the documents to be filled out. It was, he could understand, a security and a certainty that all was right with the world. 'Quite done!' Mr. Cockburn said, and wiggled his nose like a rabbit.

After a bite to eat and a pint of ale at the Fox and Grapes, Mr. Cockburn shook Will's hand as though conferring knighthood upon him and assured him that all things would be in order for the double celebration of citizenship and marriage within a month. Five weeks later Julie and Will were married.

CHAPTER 15

It was April in the year 1934. Will had taken his small craft out for the pleasure of it. Julie had affectionately said that pregnancy was a hard thing for some prospective fathers and Will had been working far too hard building an estate for a future heir. He was to have the day to himself, and if he were late returning, no matter, she would open the pub for the evening custom.

He did lose track of time and was forced to tack his way back to Stromness after the sun had set into the sea and the prevailing winds had shifted to an offshore breeze. It was a small challenge of seamanship that always pleased and exhilarated him. He arrived at the Sailing Master well after dark. It was a quiet evening. There were few customers. He greeted everyone and walked back to the family saloon in the usual habit of things.

He saw Ian Bostock first, sitting facing the room at the table farthest away. He was in deep conversation with a well-dressed man who seemed a stranger to Will. Yet there was something about the shape of the head and the set of the shoulders that sent a shock of anticipatory unease through his heart. Bostock glanced up and broke off his intent conversation with a broad smile of greeting. He raised his mutilated hand in a gesture of familiarity. His companion turned toward Will, and the reason for his instinctive rush of anxiety became clear.

Simmons sat there, looking prosperous and smug. Bostock beckoned, and Will approached, for there was nothing else he could do.

'I think you know Mr. Simmons, Will. Of course you do,' Bostock said. His voice ill concealed a vivid challenge for Will to be less than gracious to his father-in-law. Bostock intended to take some liberties, and Will feared the reason why.

'Come along, sit down and let us stand you a drink, Mr. Hartz.'

Will stood there. His need to know what had transpired between the two of them was stronger than his desire to show them his independence. He sat down but refused the drink.

'You know each other?'

'Only just met,' Bostock said. 'I mean to say, met face to face.'

Will waited for clarification. Simmons' eyes were fixed on him.

'Mr. Bostock and I found we had opinions in common about certain matters.'

'And how did you discover that?' Will asked.

'We subscribed to the literature of a certain organization that has long held the belief that the destinies of Germany and Great Britain are, because of common goals and heritage, inextricably wedded.'

'I didn't know you had any interest in political philosophies,' Will said to his father-in-law.

'Any thinking man has an interest. After all, this last war wasn't the finish of things. Nothing was really put right. Germany's been badly used and through no fault of the British people.'

'Well, I am not a political man. I am an innkeeper with a wife who is about to have a child, and that is enough to occupy me.'

'You seem annoyed with us, Mr. Hartz,' Simmons said. He'd raised a small mustache that seemed to be a smudge of charcoal beneath his nose. It gave a weakly evil look to his face when he smiled. It looked simply foolish otherwise.

Will stood up. 'I'm simply saying I have no interest in your political points of view. I am a Swiss and a neutral by upbringing and inclination.' He turned to leave the room.

'Mr. Hartz, I've engaged a room for the night with you. Perhaps we can have a chat at the end of the business day,' Simmons remarked, and did nothing to mask the fact that it was, in truth, an order.

Will nodded and went to the bar. He avoided any further contact with Simmons and Bostock. Bostock left at closing quite drunk on the free drinks Simmons had provided.

According to the laws and customs of the country, a traveler was entitled to treat an inn like his own home, within reason. He was allowed to drink past the licensing hours. Simmons stayed on till the clearing up was done and Julie had gone to bed. He'd removed himself from the family saloon to the bar. Julie's footsteps faded above, and there was the slender sound of the door closing.

Will placed his hands on the bar. 'Can you tell me what damned foolishness you're engaged in with Bostock?'

Simmons grinned in anger. 'Don't forget yourself. Remember I'm your superior. I came here to make a suggestion to you. I believe you should investigate the possibilities of buying into the Fox and Grapes in Kirkwall. It has far more value as a listening post than this quiet tavern.'

'You could have easily offered such a suggestion in the mails. I want to know what game you have with Bostock. I told you clearly that he is the village drunk. . . . A failed creature with nothing but hate, envy and impotence in him.'

'Exactly.'

Simmons spoke the word as though Will had, through stupidity, made a miraculous quantum leap toward the understanding of his own brilliant recruiting techniques. Will refused to enter into the game, and Simmons was moved to speak again.

'How do you think an organization such as ours finds its rank and file? From the failures, the malcontents, the whiners, the fools. Those who are easily puffed up with small secrets and empty honors. The childish who long desperately to destroy the father figure. The cynical, the cowardly, the self-seekers, the greedy.'

'This man Bostock is a drunkard and totally undependable.'

'So? He's a useless fixture that everyone ignores. He has eyes and ears. People will speak in front of him as they would in front of an old dog lying in the corner.'

'To what purpose at this time?' Will nearly shouted in his frustration. 'What is he to overhear? What scraps of useless information might he possibly gather? To whom will it be reported, and to what use can it be put?'

'We are building an organization without precedent in the history of the world.'

'There has been espionage before, spies before.'

'There has never been an apparatus such as we are building.'

'We? Who are these planners you confer with?'

'Men next to Hitler himself.'

Will blew an impatient blast of air through his nose. He threw his hands from the bar as though giving up an argument with a lunatic.

'How much have you told Bostock?'

'Are you interrogating me?'

'I have to know how to treat the situation, do I not?' Will asked reasonably.

'I've told him nothing except that I am a man interested in his views. I've suggested he secure employment at the naval base at Lyness. It might prove of great value in the future.'

'I wish you the best of British good luck. The man could never hold down a job, even if he could secure one.'

'We'll see. In any event, he will be a listening post. He'll have perfect knowledge of other malcontents since he is one himself and they, most usually, take comfort from one another. He has no idea his sympathies will in any way be used against England, though I don't think it would matter much to him if he could do the society he believes failed him an injury.'

'What have you told him of me?'

Simmons widened his eyes. 'Nothing.'

Will thought to say that there was that impudence in Bostock's manner toward him that suggested he'd received the hint that Will was somehow in league with Simmons. He decided it would only multiply the confusions of the conversation and let the remark die in his throat. Instead, he made a comment of warning. 'The man is not a fool.' He'd had enough of the night. 'I am going to bed.'

'Husband, I'm getting round and heavy,' Julie said.

They sat in the sitting room, Will in his rocker and Julie in a wing chair, her back well supported with pillows, her feet up on a footstool. He grinned at her affectionately.

'Will, why are you so friendly with that man?'

'Man?'

'It sticks my throat to say father.'

Will put aside his paper. 'I am not very fond of Bostock, that is true. Yet he is your father, and you are going to have a child that is something of his flesh and blood.'

Julie made a strangled sound of disgust.

'No, no, please let me try to explain. I know I say it badly. Perhaps there is no way to explain it really. He's not been good to you at any time in his life or in yours. At least in no time that you can remember. Yet is he a truly bad man or a stupid one? Did he hurt your mother and you because of cruelty and arrogant strength or because of weakness and failure?'

'Sometimes you're as stodgy as the minister.'

'I don't preach charity or suggest we turn the other cheek. I only say he grows old, and the bitterness of lost things burns in his belly. I'm not friendly to him. Only civil.'

'You give him money.'

'For your brother and sisters. I see to it that very little is wasted.'

'You're a good man, Will.'

He avoided the compliment with a wave of his hand.

'Would you like a cup of tea with honey in it?'

She smiled at him fondly. 'And a bit of lemon.'

'Yes, and a bit of *citron*.'

'That's French for lemon, isn't it?'

Oh, yes, little innocent prostitute, he thought.

Julie grew hugely round, and she gently but firmly turned away Will's sexual overtures as dangerous and improper. Will honored her feelings and gave thought to the expansion of his business holdings. He went to Kirkwall to have a conversation with Mr. Dowdy, owner of the Fox and Grapes.

They arrived by slow steps at an agreement that would be mutually pleasing if the transaction were consummated. In that event Will would be the principal partner, though Mr. and Mrs. Dowdy would continue to occupy the apartment above the pub as long as they wished. They considered together a proper house that Will might purchase for his family if the move were made. In the way of island people nothing was settled at first meeting, and yet, somehow, everything was settled.

In the first week of August Julie Hartz was delivered of a boy.

Looking down at the small form cuddled next to his child-looking wife, Will thought how helpless they were nearly lost in the covers and pillows of the bed. Like two nesting chicks. A great warmth suffused him. Julie grasped his one finger with her whole hand and drew it to her mouth. She kissed his hand moistly and smiled from the edge of sleep. The midwife shooed him out of the room.

Will went away to the room beneath the eaves in which he had slept for the last few weeks. He sat at the window, looking out across Stromness to the sea and made plans for his son. He had a sharp desire to see his own father.

All at once he knew that his father was dead. He had never

been informed. In fact, he had never received any word from his family. It was another of the extraordinary demands made on men in his line of work. But he knew most certainly his father was dead. He ran down the short flight of steps into their bedroom and for a long time stared down upon his sleeping wife and child.

The next day but one, Julie brought his breakfast to him in the bed they again shared.

'What is this foolishness?' he scolded.

'The bearing of children is hard work for a man at times. Especially the first. It is your first?' she teased.

'That is debatable. It seems I had my first when I married a child bride.'

'No child me, Willum. And an island girl to boot.'

She offered the breakfast to him, buttering the toast and pouring the thick, black coffee he pleasured himself with.

'All the way to the downstairs to the kitchen. All the way upstairs with the heavy tray. It is not good.' He was very pleased. He took a bite of bread and a sip of the hot coffee. 'I have been thinking of taking a proper house. All rooms on the one floor. Perhaps an inside toilet, even.'

'It would be nice but a terrible expense.'

'Not so. I've done well. I've even had talk with Mr. Dowdy in Kirkwall with the view in mind of becoming, at first, his partner and later moving there. Would you like that?'

Julie looked about the room and patted his rough hand gently. 'I'll think on it. But you're my husband, and I'll do what you wish.'

'It would be better, I think.'

The infant gave a small cry. Julie took her hand from Will's and moved to the crib. She lifted the child to her breast. It was immediately soothed and grew quiet. She returned to the bed and sat in the chair next to it.

'I never thought to ask. Are you a religious man?'

'When I was young, I went to pray. It's a good thing for the young to go to church.'

'I never. But I think it's a good thing. Have you a special faith?'

'I hold no preference. Are you of the Scottish Kirk?'

Julie first nodded, then shook, then nodded her head. 'I've no way of knowing. There was no church or God at all in our house. But it's a good faith, I should think.'

'Yes. The boy will be christened in the Scottish Kirk.'

Julie laughed and tickled the baby's chin. 'We shall want a name.'

'*Gott in Himmel*,' Will nearly shouted. 'I have not even thought of it.'

'Will we name him William? Wilhelm seems a bit –' She searched for a word.

'Harsh,' Will supplied. 'William is a good name, but perhaps someone in your family?'

Julie shook her head quickly.

'A decision of such great moment should not be made over morning coffee. Shall we think about it?'

'I like William.' She stood up and replaced the infant to its bed. 'Eat, old man, and rouse yourself. You've another mouth to feed,' Julie said and hurried from the room.

It was a morning full of pleasures.

By afternoon a cloud was cast upon it. Will remarked to himself that John Kendrick had not yet come to see his son. It was Abel Ewen who brought the news that Kendrick's sickness had settled in his chest again and he was abed.

Within the next three days, Will, by stealth and careful observation, reckoned when Molly would be out of the house for an hour on necessary errands. When he saw her leave with bonnet and basket, he was touched by the signs of fatigue that marked her strong body. So much of her life had been fashioned of selfless nursing and care of others. He took the opportunity to go in to his friend. He felt like a skulker and a thief, but all these long months since that fated, foolish night, Molly had clearly avoided him, and he honored, indeed agreed with, that intent.

Kendrick lay in the ancient bed, rough-sawed and hewed by his great-grandfather's hands. His hair had lost any trace of color. It seemed more nearly transparent than white. It had lost the crisp bold life of the man. The bones of his face seemed sunken upon themselves. His hands were so large as to belong to a man twice his size. They were scarred with the cuts of line and the penetration of hooks. They lay, pallid sea creatures, on his wasted chest.

'John, old friend,' Will murmured, reluctant to rouse him from his rest.

John opened his eyes. They focused slowly. He turned his head and smiled a pale smile. He reached out one hand.

'Hey, oh, Willum. So it's you?'

'Yes, I've come.'

'I'm glad for it. I feared I'd not see you again.'

Will knew better than to protest John's recognition of approaching death. It was a measure of a man to know the Reaper when he appeared and to extend his hand with dignity and patient resolve.

'You've had a son.'

Will nodded.

'I would have come to see him.'

'I know that.'

John regarded Will for a long time. Will could see the question in the eyes. What had gone wrong between my dear sister and my dear friend? Will felt his own reluctant tongue forming the answer or at least an explanation, but John slipped off into sleep.

Will sat for half an hour with John's hand clasped in his own. He left the cottage before Molly returned. From a screen of trees, he saw her arrival with the doctor. Was there a third dark shadow with them?

He went home and quietly told Julie that it was his wish that the child be given the name John.

CHAPTER 16

John Kendrick was made of the granite rocks of the island. He was made of the fierceness of the Atlantic in winter storm. He was as fierce and as patient. All his long life he had fought to wrest a living from a harsh and demanding discipline. In his death he fought as well and as quietly. He died on the first day of the new year.

Two old women were summoned to the cottage. They washed his poor wasted body and dressed it in clean linen and his good black suit.

Four of his friends fashioned a casket of weathered wood. They shaped it lovingly for his last bedrest. They planed it smooth and polished it with wax. They fixed four wrought-iron handles to its sides. They placed a black cross on its lid.

They placed his body in the coffin. The two old women folded his hands and brushed his hair a last time. His hair had remarkably sprung to renewed life out of final death. It curled crisply about his ears and brow.

The coffin was placed in the parlor upon a trestle. The structure was a miniature of the trestle upon which they placed their new boats before launching.

Fisherwomen prepared earthenware pannikins of food. Stoneware jugs of whiskey were brought by men to refresh the mourners.

At nighttime, two candles were lit, one at each end of the bier. John Kendrick's friends came in great number.

Molly sat with the women in a place by the window, and the people went to her to murmur soft solace.

Will came. He stood with his hat in his hand beside the body of his old friend. From the corner of his eye he was aware of Molly staring at him. At a moment when she was alone, he went to her and sat beside her. They were silent for a while.

'John was my best friend.'

'Yes.' Molly's lips were tight, and small bitter lines were formed at the corners of her mouth. She knew herself to be well and truly alone and youth gone. She felt anger toward this stolid, embarrassed man sitting next to her.

'Julie wishes for me to send her condolences.'

‘She’s not well?’ It was an accusation of cowardice.

Will fumbled. ‘She doesn’t like to leave the baby with anyone but me.’

Molly turned her gaze directly upon Will and fixed him cruelly. ‘I wonder if I’ll ever understand.’

Will felt panicked and useless. There was nothing he could say. ‘Circumstances. Duty.’

It was the wrong thing to say. It suggested the truth. That his marriage was one of necessity. It was a dishonorable thing to suggest about his wife, even if true.

‘We must never forget our duty, even if we do forget our good sense.’ She cut deep, meaning to.

Will stood. He assumed himself properly punished.

‘If there is anything you need . . . anything –’

‘I will manage . . . alone.’ Molly cut him short, and there was no more left to say between them.

On March 1, 1935, the Saar Basin territory was returned to Germany. It was a confirmation of Hitler’s policies and an affirmation of his strength.

On the same day, Will Hartz received an unexpected visitor. There was nothing obtuse or complicated about the approach of the man who bore with him an unmistakable air of authority. He simply waited until Will came to serve him.

‘Mr. Hartz, I would like to speak with you privately. I have news of a mutual friend, a Mr. Simmons.’

Will knew at once a demand upon his obligation to the Fatherland was to be made. He came out from behind the bar.

‘Jock, I’m off for a breath of air.’

Will grabbed his sailorman’s jacket and went to the door. The man followed him. They walked in silence down to the wintry mole.

‘You’ve been in correspondence with Switzerland questioning the activities of Mr. Simmons?’ the stranger said.

‘I wanted clarification of his authority. Some of his innovations seemed ill advised to say the least.’

‘You made that judgment?’ The tone was bland. His opinion couldn’t be read in it.

‘I was afraid he might have been, or would be, indiscreet.’

‘Yes.’

‘I feared he might attempt to manipulate a local and in so doing jeopardize my cover.’

‘The local would be this man Bostock?’

'Yes.'

'Your father-in-law.'

'Unfortunately.'

'This Bostock has given indication of knowledge concerning your true purpose here?'

'Not directly, not in so many words, but he's presumed to treat the relationship between us with far more intimacy than I've ever allowed. There seems a threat in it.'

The stranger withdrew into himself for a long moment. The silence grew oppressive.

'I can't condone your criticism of a superior, but in these unusual circumstances I believe you should know that Simmons has indeed recruited Bostock.'

Will expelled a grunt of disgust.

'I make note of your disapproval but insist you have no right to it. Simmons was the executive in the field. It was his decision to make.'

'Blind obedience?'

The man considered a moment. He turned his eyes slowly and fixed them on Will. The words dropped one by one, individually forged.

'We expect you to follow your orders and instructions without question, certainly.' He went on in a voice tinged with a kind of weary regret. 'I find it distasteful to have to explain the facts of life to an agent. The necessity for the explanation suggests that his utmost loyalty and unquestioning application to duty is suspect. It can well plant a seed of doubt and urge a reexamination of his value. Why did you come into this profession?'

'Profession?' Will echoed dumbly. He had never thought of it as a profession or something one chose to do as one would decide for a career in medicine or law.

'You were the son of one Otto Oerter, a minor functionary in the civil service in a small town in Bavaria. Garmisch, was it not?'

'Yes.'

'Your career in school was undistinguished, but your family had some remote association through marriage with one of the aristocratic Junker families. Through the influence and good offices of the late General von Sonnedorf, aide of Steinmetz and hero of the Saar' – there was veiled contempt in the emphasis of the words – 'you were given the opportunity to enter a prestigious university.'

Will wanted to tell the man to stop this recitation of his past. It offended his sense of privacy deeply to know that somewhere there was a dossier that many people, even Simmons perhaps, could leaf through and draw conclusions about Wilhelm Hartz/Oerter.

'If memory serves, you were invited to join a fraternity. You disgraced yourself by refusing to stand up to their honorable custom of giving and receiving the slashes of a saber in supervised combat.'

'I was not afraid.'

'A matter of principle?'

Will shrugged, unable to give an honest evaluation of the feelings he'd had those many years ago. The stranger began to laugh. There was something bizarre, even obscene, about it.

'Don't be ashamed. It was the high point of your life. It might interest you to know that the Führer frowns upon such duels and illegalized them.'

It was not a compliment. The point remained that Wilhelm Oerter had refused at a time when it was expected of him. The laughter stilled, and the lips abruptly composed themselves in an instant.

'You stuck it out despite the disdain of your fellows and finished two years of study. You were called upon to serve your compulsory military service. You achieved the rank of corporal and finished your service in the Department of Supply and Administration. It was noted that you kept exceptionally neat records.'

The man was deliberately baiting him. Instinct told Will not to rise to the bait. He knew the man's eyes were on him covertly. His own eyes remained without expression.

'You were placed into the reserves as required. You made an abortive attempt to study the law. Your father, I'm sure, had great aspirations for his only son. He saw the facts of the matter, however, and was about to secure a position with the Postal Department for you when you surprised him by securing employment as a teacher in a small private school.'

A second summit in my life, Will thought.

'You made no mark for yourself but apparently attracted the attention of Ruth Spector, a Jewess. You were saved from what would have undoubtedly been a disastrous marriage by the Great War.'

Will flinched as each revelation proved him to be a man totally undistinguished in any least way. Only a few times in his life had he asserted his own will in any meaningful circumstance. For the rest, he had allowed himself to move along paths of little resistance. In large part, he continued to do so. His objection to Simmons' procedures seemed petty, even presumptuous, in the face of the record of an ineffectual life. The stranger touched his sleeve. For a moment, Will thought it was a gesture of sympathy. It was more likely a means of recalling his attention.

'You made a friend in the reserves of a Captain Blendheim. Upon the advent of war, he was promoted to the rank of major, and he, in turn, promoted you to the rank of sergeant. In civilian life he had wide contacts in the banking and mercantile world. The authorities of the time seemed to believe this fitted him to set up an intelligence operation in neutral Switzerland. He suggested you as his noncommissioned aide. You spent the war in civilian dress and in safety.'

Will felt drained. He felt as though he had appeared before the authority of Judgment Day and had been found desperately wanting.

'Do you know why I've inflicted this painful recitation upon you?' the stranger asked softly.

Will shook his head. His throat was clotted, and he found it difficult to speak.

'To tell you that you are, in all ways, an unremarkable man. So are we all, in most cases, unremarkable men. But there is a glory that can be yours, and that is the collective glory of the Fatherland. It is because you are unremarkable that you are admirably suited to the task we've chosen for you. If you came to us without dedication or conviction, you have strong reasons for them now. Do you see?'

Will managed to say yes around the relief and gratitude that welled in him.

'Yes, you do understand. You must know this as well. You have not the strength of will to direct your own feet or to question the actions of those above you. The Führer directs the steps of all. We are his children. So. From this moment you will be taking your orders directly from me.'

Will was confused. 'Does that mean to say that Simmons –'

The stranger raised his hand and smiled a warning smile. It said, 'Have you forgotten the lesson I just gave you so soon?'

'Let the man Bostock believe what he will. Say nothing, but allow a friendlier relationship to develop.'

'My wife will resist that, I think.'

The stranger stared at Will with something akin to shock. The look said how strange he took it that a man would be concerned about the wishes of the wife.

'How do your negotiations for the public house in Kirkwall go?'

'These people are very slow, but it progresses.'

'It's essential that the deal be completed. In the event of war, Kirkwall will be, by far, a more valuable listening post than Stromness.'

Will knew better than to say that such a thought had never entered his mind concerning the expansion of his business.

'If immediate cash will facilitate, it will be provided. You will do everything possible to close the matter upon your return.'

Will felt a sudden weakness in his legs. Now we come to it, he thought. He waited for the revelation without comment.

'You will travel with me tomorrow morning on the boat to Scotland. You can accommodate me at your tavern for the night?'

'Yes, there is a room available. What is this venture?'

'You will be told in good time.'

'How can I explain such haste?'

'To your wife? You will tell her that you go to the mainland on business. Simple. You are raising the necessary funds to acquire an ownership in the Fox and Grapes. Simple.'

'We have a child,' Will said desperately seeking an escape. He realized in the moment he was like a small boy who hoped to prevent a beating by crying that his finger was broken.

'And the child has its mother.'

'Is it only to Scotland that we are to go?'

'You will arrange for a journey of two weeks, perhaps more. he affair should be completed by then. I trust your passport is in order?'

The stranger fixed Will with his disconcerting stare once again. The eyes were prepared to read a final judgment on him. His loyalty and dependability were being tested. Perhaps it was only that and not a matter of great moment that would jeopardize him in any way.

Will said nothing, and they returned to the Sailing Master.

The stranger gave Will leave to call him by the name Conrad. On the journey across the North Sea to Wick he kept to his cabin and allowed Will no opportunity for conversation.

A seagoing motor launch was waiting for them and speeded them on to Aberdeen. There an aircraft rose from the earth and took them on to London.

It was Will's first experience of flying. It gave him no great anxiety. He was far too obsessed with renewed fears of what manner of mission this might be.

In London, on the third of March, Conrad took Will to a small flat in a mews. The apartment was above a space still used to stable horses. It was cold, and the flat was unheated. They sat in their overcoats. Will stared at the puffs of their breaths in the nearly empty room.

Conrad sat in stony silence, unmoving except for his hands. Their agitation proved to Will that his companion didn't possess the gift of waiting.

Conrad stiffened. He turned his head very slowly from side to side. The resemblance to a snake was acute. His eyes shone milkily. He had responded to a sound unheard by Will. He snapped his finger softly and pointed to the single dim bulb glowing from its socket in the ceiling. Will stood to pull the chain that brought the dark. Moments later he heard footsteps on the stair treads. He felt tight within himself. He glanced at Conrad, an unmoving figure in the dark. A key turned in the lock. A figure stopped in the lozenge of lighter gray in the hallway.

'Conrad, we have come.'

Conrad snapped his fingers again. Will turned on the light. Simmons stood there. He was dressed in work pants and shirt with a black sweater pulled over it. He wore no coat. He had a peaked cap on his head. He grinned. He looked very fit.

'So, Mr. Hartz, you have come as well?'

He waved a hand toward the man who had entered with him. This one was dressed in suit and tie. There was an air of slovenliness about him. The faint electric light picked up the shine of grease marks on the glasses he wore. His hair had been disarranged by the wind, and he hadn't bothered to brush it into order with his hand.

'This is Harold. You can call him Harold.'

Harold grinned and revealed long, stained, horselike teeth and an amount of gray gums. No one extended hands to be taken in greeting.

'You were a little annoyed with me, were you, Hartz?' Simmons laughed.

'That matter has been dealt with,' Conrad snapped. 'We will get on with it.'

Simmons seemed to stiffen, but he laughed again and shrugged. The seat of authority was clearly established.

'Sit,' Conrad said.

There were only three chairs. There was a moment's confusion of protocol. Simmons began to sit in the chair closest to hand, but at Conrad's glance he chose the one Will had occupied instead. Will sat down in the third chair. He had moved too swiftly in order to establish the fact that he would not be treated as an underling. He felt foolish for it. Conrad, at the last, remained standing.

'You will proceed to Paris by boat train. Here are your fares.'

Conrad extended the tickets. Simmons very nearly snatched them from his hand. Will was amused. Apparently Simmons found it equally necessary to establish himself as the leader of the mission.

'You will time your arrival to arrive in Basel on the seventh day of this month. It will be like a homecoming for you, Mr. Hartz.'

Will felt a rising surge of hope that he might still escape this duty. 'Sir, my experience is with Berne.'

There was tic of confusion in Conrad's eye. Someone had apparently made a clerical error in Will's dossier.

'Do you know Basel at all?'

'Yes, but only as a casual visitor.'

'It is enough. You carry the passports of both a British and a Swiss citizen. That is a large part of your value in this matter.'

Will found himself somehow chastised. He mumbled an apology.

'You will arrive on the first day of a city-wide festival. There will be a masked carnival in the streets on the third day of the celebration.'

Harold farted. He grinned with great unconcern and waved a hand in easy camaraderie.

Conrad took no notice. 'You will be met by one Rudolf Schroeder, a journalist, in the grill room of the Adlon Hotel. Only one of you will make the initial contact.'

'I will decide,' Simmons said.

'He will give you further directives and apprise you of your subsequent actions. That, I believe, is all.'

'But what are we supposed to do when we arrive in Basel?' Will asked. The remark was totally ignored. Conrad passed the authority to Simmons by a formal sharp shake of the hand. Simmons nearly stumbled to his feet reaching out for it. Conrad pulled out the light and left the room.

Harold lumbered to his feet.

'The train leaves at nine tonight, Harold.'

Harold nodded and left the room. Will wondered for a moment if the man were a mute.

'I am told you didn't approve of my recruiting your father-in-law,' Simmons said from the darkness.

Will could imagine the man grinning whitely like a Cheshire cat in the gloom. His anger seemed like a third presence in the room.

Simmons lowered his voice and hissed, 'I know you would like to punish me. But you must learn, Hartz, that you are a soldier like any other. You are under orders. For the duration of this mission, at least.'

'And then?'

'Conrad will take over your control. I have been promised better things. Nine o'clock, Hartz. Don't be late.'

Will walked to the door, feeling frustrated and impotent.

'*Heil Hitler*,' Simmons said in a voice so low it could scarcely be heard.

For the first time, Will realized he was working for a man named Hitler he had never seen, as certainly as he was working for his Fatherland. It was not to be thought about. Hitler was the constituted authority in Germany. Justice would prevail. When all else failed, he must remember that his only discipline must be that of duty.

At the railway terminal, Simmons, now dressed as a petit bourgeois businessman, gave them their tickets. Will felt like a schoolboy about to set out an an excursion. Harold carried a briefcase of sorts. It was wider and longer than the usual.

They boarded the train. Simmons and Will shared a compartment with an Anglican priest, a nurse and her six-year-old charge, and two young men in the uniforms of the Home Forces. Harold was nowhere in evidence. Will sat opposite the solemn-eyed child, a boy with black hair and a tender pale complexion. The child stared at him with the frank assessment of the very young. Will made a small face, and the boy grinned shyly, deciding that the big bluff man across the aisle was the stuff of which friends were made.

Before long, Will had introduced the child into the intricacies of cat's cradle played with a length of string. On the boat across the Channel, in the overheated lounge, the boy fell asleep against Will's side. Will felt the weight of the child with pleasure and imagined him his own son six years grown.

He would teach him to sail at just about this age. They would together explore the caves and coves of the islands. He would teach John to fish from the mole, to splice a hook to a line, to spit away from the wind. He would watch his son grow straight-limbed and steady on the rocks in a northern gale or on the deck of a fishing boat beating its way back from the sea. He would see to it that John had the world of books and knowledge at his command. He made a note in his small black book to buy a set of child's encyclopedias upon their return to London. His education would be wide-ranging and adventurous. He would be prepared for the life of his choosing. He would not, Will hoped, be a publican. He would certainly not be a spy.

They arrived in Basel on the seventh according to the schedule. Simmons and Will went to the separate rooms that had been engaged for them in advance at the Adlon. Harold was still not to be seen.

Will opened his suitcase and put his clothes neatly away in the closet. He felt soiled and weary. In the absence of any other instructions, he ordered a bath and went down the hall in robe and slippers. He took a long soak and amused himself with the Berne newspaper he had purchased from the desk.

When he returned refreshed to his room, Simmons was sitting in the one chair near the window. Simmons frowned, displaying some impatience.

'Where have you been?'

'That would be obvious.'

'You will keep yourself in readiness at all times from now on. We cannot schedule this affair around your bathing habits.'

'I am prepared to follow orders,' Will snapped. 'But I expect to be told what is required of me and when.'

Simmons gestured vaguely. It was in the way of an apology. It was apparent that he was anxious, even somewhat afraid now that they were embarked on the enterprise. An enterprise Will still knew nothing about.

'After you've dressed, you will please go to the grill room.

At the end of the bar a man will be seated. A man with thinning hair and a large dark mole beneath his left eye.'

Will almost smiled. He wanted to ask if the mole was real or a bit of disguise.

'To identify him further, he will have set a small case such as is used for carrying business cards on the bar top. It is made of green morocco leather.'

Good heavens, Will thought, this is turning into a very bad pantomime.

'You will take the chair beside him.'

'Which side?' Will asked. He kept a straight face.

'No matter.'

'Suppose the seats either side of him are occupied?'

Simmons looked at Will sharply, sensing that he was having his leg pulled. 'You will wait until a seat is available. You will ask the bartender if he knows how to make a Singapore Sling.'

'Is the bartender one of us?'

'Of course not.'

'Suppose he doesn't know what that drink is. I do not.'

'No matter. Drink what you like. It is only to tell Rudolf Schroeder that his contact from England has arrived. When he hears you ask for the cocktail, he will present you with his card. You understand all this?'

'Clearly.'

'He will give you the address where we will meet for the final briefing.'

Simmons stood up stiffly and moved to leave. He paused. 'You will not find this so very amusing, Herr Hartz.

As he dressed, Will thought that he didn't find it amusing in any way. There were certain comedic overtones, but he was not amused.

The interior of the grill room was dimly lit with amber bulbs in wrought-iron chandeliers. There was a feeling of an expanse cluttered with red velvet, smoky wood and leather well seasoned by time. He blinked his eyes to get used to the gloom and thought randomly that at least the lighting effects were according to form. Most of the spy literature he had ever read for light entertainment seemed to employ dimly lit locales for atmosphere.

The bar itself was practically empty, though many of the small tables were occupied with the early luncheon trade. He found himself counting the house and reckoning the number of beef and kidney puddings, cheese rarebits and portions of shepherd's pie required. He smiled and walked down the length of the bar to the place where a man with thinning hair and a nearly black mole beneath his eye, yes, the left eye, was sitting.

The bartender stopped before Will ready to give service.

'Do you know how to make a Singapore Sling?' he asked.

'Yes, sir. Gin, lemon squash, some fruit, a bit of sugar and a dash of grenadine for color.'

The concoction sounded quite sickening.

'I think not. Perhaps a whiskey with a small split of Vichy water.'

The bartender nodded pleasantly, accepting what he believed to be a salesman's small joke, and moved off to fill the glass.

'You've had some experience in the Far East?' Mr. Schroeder inquired as an opening wedge to conversation.

'No,' Will replied. He scarcely knew what light chat was expected of him. He felt like an actor not very well up in his part.

Schroeder opened up the leather card case. It was not of green morocco. It was tan pigskin. Did this mean that the man whose card identified him as Rudolf Schroeder was an impostor?

'Something is wrong, sir?' Schroeder asked.

'I was looking at your card case. I was thinking of getting one in green morocco leather.'

'Yes, of course, of course. I lost it. I bought this an hour ago. It is very difficult to find special leather card cases upon such short notice. Believe me, I am Rudolf Schroeder.'

Any facsimile of a friendly chat with a recently scraped-up acquaintance was thrown away. Schroeder spoke sharply. He was a man under some strain. He downed the last of his drink in one gulp.

'The address is on the back of the card. An hour after dark tonight.'

With that he left. Will examined the back of the card. He remembered the area. The street was one off the main avenue at the lower part of the business section. It was a district that was gone to seed, at least as much as the Swiss allowed anything to go to seed. Will giggled uncontrollably. There was a certain madness to this business. He steadied himself with the whiskey. He threw it to the back of his throat and swallowed it in one go. It was unlike him.

CHAPTER 17

They gathered that evening just after twilight at the moment when the streetlamps came on. The meeting place was a small office in a building posted as condemned and due to be razed.

Harold was apparently the first one to arrive. When Will and Simmons entered, he was sitting in the grayness picking his teeth. He grunted at them by way of greeting.

There is something ancient, monolithic and elemental about that man, Will thought. His apparent sloth seemed to conceal a well of energy. He was like a vast capacitor storing electricity, waiting for the touch that would release the deadly spark.

Close to the center of the room was a small deal table. Simmons drew three straight-backed chairs around it. He turned on the green shaded bulb that was suspended above it. He took a map of Central Europe from his suit coat pocket and spread it out.

The door opened, and Schroeder entered, an eye and a nose at a time.

Simmons instantly acquired a certain manner as though he had suddenly donned a uniform. 'We are ready then?'

Harold brought his chair up to the table by placing a hand under it between his legs and hitching it forward. He stayed a few feet back from the edge of the table as though he were a spectator to it all.

Simmons looked at Schroeder, commanding him to begin.

'I've kept Jakob-Salomon under surveillance this past month. He's a man of fairly regular habits. But with this business of the carnival, he might have made arrangements that I would have no way of predicting.'

'You're familiar with the cafés and restaurants he frequents?'

'Yes, they are the places the liberal journalists gather in. I myself am welcome in all of them and count most of them as my friends.'

'Including Jakob?'

Schroeder hesitated. The note of pride in his voice in the seemingly casual allusion to the fact that he had successfully hoodwinked the liberal community into believing he was one of them was replaced by one of doubt.

'No. I've made overtures, but he seems to sense I'm not what I pretend to be. He's like a fox. Very wary and very private.'

Simmons glanced at Will. 'Now you see why we've risked bringing you here. We can't depend upon Schroeder leading this man down the garden path.'

'What man?'

'This Jakob-Salomon.'

'Someone seems to be in error about me in this matter. Totally in error.'

'You deny having known a Jakob-Salomon in Berne before the Armistice?'

They were all three of them looking at him as though he were proving himself a traitor and, as such, ready to be disposed of.

Will touched his forehead begging recall.

'God damn it, I tell you I don't know this man you speak of.'

They continued to regard him impassively. Wondering at the reason behind his display of irritation and impatience, perhaps?

Suddenly memory flooded in upon him. 'Yes, yes, I remember him now.'

Simmons smiled, and Will was ashamed at the sense of reprieve he felt.

He remembered a dark face much like a hound's. The man, a journalist, yes, had once done a favor for him.

'But we weren't friends. He did me a small service. At least it was small to him.'

He remembered a very solitary man.

'Would you recognize him if you saw him again?'

'I'm sure I would not.'

'That's of no consequence. Schroeder will point him out to you.'

'I continue to wonder why I am here,' Will protested.

'You can easily renew the old acquaintance. It will seem natural.'

'Surely anyone knowing enough about this Jakob could pose as an old acquaintance after so many years.'

'Perhaps, but memory is an immeasurable attribute. This Jakob-Salomon is a journalist, and they have notoriously long and detailed memories.'

Simmons turned back to Schroeder, dismissing Will. 'What sort of man is he?'

'A very private person. He doesn't make friends. He is cordial but aloof with nearly everyone.'

'But a little more aloof with you.' Simmons grinned.

'In any event, we can hope that he will not be celebrating this holiday in the bosom of some innocent family?'

'We can assume that, yes.'

'Where does he live?'

'In a small hotel, the Deinerhof, three blocks from the Adlon. Here.' He touched the map.

'What time does he emerge from his fox's burrow in the morning?'

'He takes morning coffee about seven thirty in a small café across from his hotel. Here.'

'That might be your opportunity for a first contact,' Simmons remarked to Will.

'He doesn't take a leisurely breakfast,' Schroeder said by way of naming a flaw in Simmons' game plan. 'He takes a hurried cup and goes off to his office.'

'With whom is he associated?'

'He free-lances. He sells to many English and French journals. He is considered by many to be an acute analyst of German politics.'

'His office?'

Schroeder located it on the map. 'He shares it with three other journalists. It's only a place to get his mail, to keep his files and typewriter and to make use of the telephone.'

'Lunch?'

'A rathskeller near the office.'

'Where is that?'

'Here on the Freiestrasse, close to the main railway station.'

'Excellent.'

'You intend to take him across the border by train?'

'That is none of your business.'

Schroeder accepted the rebuff without a word. Tight-lipped, he waited, insisting on being asked specific questions.

'After the midday meal?'

'Wherever a story he is working on might take him. Government offices and the like.

'Does he observe a usual end to his workday?'

'At five o'clock he returns to his hotel.'

'Yes, and then?'

'Perhaps he bathes. Perhaps he naps. I don't know

'What time does he surface again?'

'Eight o'clock. He goes to his dinner.'

'Alone?'

'Almost invariably except on Friday.'

Simmons waited for him to go on.

'He goes to the Jewish temple and prays.'

'I hope he says a good one tomorrow night.'

Harold laughed briefly, then subsided.

'The same restaurant each night?'

'Yes. In fact, the same rathskeller where he takes lunch. It would be better to take him after dark.'

'I want only his itinerary from you, Herr Schroeder. I will make any command decisions. Go on.'

'He moves about after that, going to one place and another. There is no pattern to the places that he visits, though he will almost invariably take a nightcap at a small café called the Quill.'

'Is there anything more?'

'I think not.'

Simmons leaned back in his chair. Harold was done picking his teeth and was now exploring his nostrils with a delicate little finger. Somewhere on the river a tugboat sounded its foghorn. Simmons leaned forward and placed his hands on the table.

'Tomorrow morning, at seven o'clock promptly, Hartz will meet you on the corner of this intersection near Jakob's hotel. Will that afford you an unobstructed view of the hotel entrance?'

'Yes.'

'You will take care not to be seen, since Jakob-Salomon has no liking for you. You will point the man out to Hartz, and you will go at once to the Hotel Adlon, where we shall breakfast in my rooms. Understood?'

'It's very clear.'

'Then good-bye until the morning.'

Schroeder hesitated. He was offended at being dismissed before the business and planning were completed. He thought better of making a protest and left without offering to shake hands.

Simmons waited until the door had clicked shut and Schroeder's footsteps faded away down the stairs.

'I don't like that man. Now, Hartz, when Jakob enters the café, you will follow a few moments after. Order a coffee and a pastry. Allow Jakob to see you. I mean to say, I want you to make no effort to avoid being seen. If he recognizes you, it will make the meeting seem the more favored and remarkable. If not, you can give him a glance or two as though a memory disturbs you. But make no approach.'

'I'm not much of an actor.'

'You can look puzzled and pensive. You usually look that way in any case. If he approaches you, make much of the chance meeting and contrive to arrange a meeting at lunch or dinner. If he does not, let it go for the time. A man waking himself up with a quick cup of coffee and off to the day's problems might not be eager to take up with an old friend.'

'Acquaintance. Acquaintance only.'

'As you wish.'

'Perhaps he'll have no desire to talk over old times at all.'

'He knew you as a young clerk in a German trade bureau during the war. He might have well been astute enough to reason that you were an agent for the German government, though in a most minor post. He did you a small service. He sees you again some years later. Again you are in Switzerland. He will connect the two and read the possibilities. He'll want to probe for evidence of any suspicions he might form. I'm sure you'll find that he thought of you as a great friend.'

'If he does form such suspicions, won't that endanger this entire endeavor?'

'Not at all. How many men do you think stay in the service of their countries between wars? No, he'll only have the thought that such a thing might be possible. And, journalist that he is, he will pursue it. He will discover that you emigrated to the British Isles and became a citizen. By that time he will see his possibilities of an intrigue disappear, but he'll have committed himself to being hospitable, and you will have ample reason to spend some of his time.'

'If there is no contact in the morning?'

'You will return to the Adlon and we will try again at noon.'

'Suppose he does have other plans for the day? Suppose he doesn't act according to habit?'

Harold showed his teeth. Simmons smiled.

'We'll know where he is at every moment.'

The next morning dawned gray. The sky over Basel was heavy with clouds, and by the time Will set foot out of the Adlon to hail a taxi a light, penetrating drizzle had begun to fall. He had dressed with care in his best suit. He wore a dark gray homburg that lent distinction to his somewhat-stolid face. He wondered if he had dressed himself as the successful businessman he truly was in order to impress Jakob if he was recognized right off. Small vanities.

Schroeder was waiting for him in the doorway of a tobacconist's. His eyes were red-rimmed, and heavy pouches dragged beneath them. When he said good morning, his breath was fetid. He was nursing a hangover without a doubt. He stared down at his shoes, which were much worn and badly stained. He glanced at Will's boots, which were highly polished and were resisting the spatters of rainwater.

'There might have been a better and more comfortable way for me to make the identification.'

'Perhaps. But it seems to be a small concern.'

'I'm well known here. Anyone passing by in an automobile could see me standing out here in the rain and wonder why.'

'You're a journalist. They would expect you were pursuing a story.'

'I'm hungry,' Schroeder said petulantly, as though that were the summation of the entire matter. He glanced at his wristwatch. He referred to it with annoying frequency in the next thirty-five minutes. Will had long since discovered that clocks robbed a man of contentment.

When a dark, spare, hurrying figure left the entrance of the small hotel, Will finally looked at his own pocket watch.

'That's the man?'

'Yes.'

'Five minutes tardy.'

'Do you recognize him?'

Will looked at the man intently. From the distance there was little to recommend him to his memory.

'I think perhaps there is something about him I recall. Perhaps that's only because I'm meant to.'

Schroeder seemed to hesitate as he had the previous evening. Again there was the attitude that he was somehow allowing the matter to run its course away from his supervision.

'Good-bye then.'

Will watched him as he hunched his way off down the street. Will stepped out into the rain. He stood there for some minutes, suddenly finding it fresh and enjoyable.

Inside the café Jakob was the only patron. His coffee was just arriving as Will selected a table for himself within the man's view. Jakob read a newspaper and scarcely glanced up. He had a strong face with a prominent nose. Will did remember him because of the eyes. They were large and luminous and were filled with a sadness such as histories possess.

Will ordered a modest breakfast in a normal voice which seemed loud in the small, sleepy room. Jakob looked up again with a line of irritation between the dark eyes. He was impatient with what he considered an intrusion. Will caught his look and smiled. He nodded politely, one early riser to another. Jakob's mouth twisted a trifle, and he returned to his paper. He looked up almost at once. His frown had deepened a bit. Will felt the beating of his heart strong at the base of his throat. He felt momentarily giddy and sick. Jakob gave an almost imperceptible shake to his head, revealing his thoughts, and finished his coffee in a gulp. He left a coin on the table, folded the paper into his pocket and left. Will kept his eyes on the newspaper with which he had provided himself. The bell above the door tinkled. Will looked up and watched Jakob move off down the street, head up, unaware of the weather.

Will returned to the Adlon. He went at once to Simmons' rooms. Schroeder had been there but had left shortly thereafter, and Simmons was alone. He was wearing a dressing gown of rich fabric and ornate design. The remains of breakfast were shoved to one side of the chair in which he sat.

'Success?'

'I thought I remembered him. I thought he had his memory jogged as well, but I can't be sure. There was something in his manner. I believe I struck a familiar note, but he couldn't capture it.'

'Excellent. It's a good beginning.'

He looked out of the window. 'Filthy day.'

'Is there anything else?'

'No. Have you had your breakfast?'

'Yes.'

'Another cup of coffee?'

'I think not.'

'All right then. At noon we'll send you off to the rathskeller near the train terminal unless I receive a report that he has changed his usual pattern. I think this next chance meeting will be enough to restore his memory.'

'If not?'

'You'll have to make the approach. Three chance meetings in one day would be a little more than we could expect an astute and suspicious man to accept.'

Will thought that even two, so widely and oddly spaced, would be enough to cause suspicion. Simmons seemed to read the thought.

'Check-out time is two o'clock. I think it might be best if you checked out now and went to the Deinerhof. A business-man would choose an inexpensive hotel in case Jakob inquires. It will also explain you're going to the same coffee shop for your breakfast.'

'I think I'll rest for an hour first.'

'As you please. See me here or in the grill room before twelve.'

Will returned to his room and lay down. Surprisingly, he fell asleep almost at once and awakened after two hours. He packed his bag and informed the desk that he wanted his bill made up.

He went to Simmons' rooms, but his knock on the door brought no answer. He left his bags at the desk and went into the grill room. Simmons was there. Obviously the leader wanted to know that Will was prepared for the second attempt.

'If you arrange to be sociable with him, call me at once. But don't make personal contact with me. You won't see me again until the affair is well under way.'

Will took a taxi to the rathskeller. Inside it was incredibly noisy, though not exceptionally crowded. The place was, however, well enough filled so that stranger was sharing a table with strangers. Perhaps I won't even be able to find him, Will thought hopefully. No one could fault me for that. A sweating waiter took his coat and hat. He gave them to the wardrobe woman. Will gave her a coin and retrieved them at once. He was a careful man, and the hat was nearly new.

He followed the waiter through the room, murmuring apologies as he bumped into other patrons in his passage through the alleys made by the closely spaced tables. The waiter looked around for a suitable place. Will saw the empty chair at a table for four occupied by three people, obviously strangers to one another. He recognized Jakob-Salomon still plunged in his newspaper. With the pressure of anxiety in his chest he ignored the table indicated by the waiter and went to sit beside Jakob-Salomon. The waiter shrugged and followed to take his order. Fate had closed the last door upon him.

He refused the menu and loudly gave his order of knackwurst, potatoes and sauerkraut.

'To drink?'

'Beer.'

Will sat down with apologies more profuse than were required. He occupied the empty chair next to Jakob. His quarry's meal arrived, and the journalist put aside his paper for a moment. He looked at Will and could not conceal a startled look of surprise. Will smiled and said, 'Good afternoon.'

'Yes. We've met.'

'I have the same feeling.'

'This morning in the coffee shop.'

'Yes?'

'The shop across the way from Deinerhof.'

'I'm staying there for a few days.'

'Of course, this morning. But there is something else. I mean to say I have the feeling we've bumped into each other before this morning. To meet you so soon again is strange enough, but I have this sense of *déjà vu*.'

'So do I.'

'You're a citizen of Basel?'

'No.'

'Of course not. Why would you be staying in a hotel?'

'I might have had a fight with my wife.'

Will laughed heartily at his own joke. Jakob laughed, but it was brief, and the puzzled look remained on his face.

'You live in Switzerland?' Jakob asked.

'No, I'm here on business only. I live in Great Britain.'

'Surely you're not English.'

'Naturalized.'

'You must think me very rude asking all these questions of a stranger.'

'Not at all.'

'Still, I feel I know you.'

'Your schnitzel will get cold.'

'Thank you.' Jakob applied himself to the plate before him.

Will's luncheon arrived moments later. Service was rough but fast. The food was good and plain, but even the first few bites lay heavy on his stomach. They ate in silence. Jakob never once looked up from the table.

'Oerter.' He looked at Will triumphantly, the knife and fork poised in midair.

Will nearly stumbled in his reaction to the unfamiliar name.

'Yes?'

'Heinrich Oerter?'

'No.' Will grinned, fully in control of this new game.

'Tell me then.'

'Will. Wilhelm.'

'Of course. Now test your memory.'

'I have no talent.'

'So. I am Jakob-Salomon.'

Will allowed himself a look that suggested an effort of memory. And then he allowed the lamp to light.

'Yes. Berthold.'

'Well, isn't this a wonder? We met during one war and we meet again before another.'

'War? I know nothing of this.'

'It will be upon us. I guarantee, unless something is done about Germany and about this Hitler.'

Will sliced a bite of sausage for himself.

Jakob continued, 'Don't be offended. You are German, I know. So am I.'

'I'm not offended. I'm German by birth, but I'm British now.'

'We met in Berne, am I right?'

'Yes. It seems a long time ago.'

'Better days. The old days always seem like better days.'

'We were young.'

'You worked, I seem to remember, for a German trade bureau.'

'That is correct, and you were a young newspaper reporter.'

'Now I'm an old newspaper reporter.'

Wilhelm smiled and answered the unspoken question. 'I am no longer a clerk. I own a small tavern and traveler's inn.'

'In what part of Great Britain?'

'In Scotland, really. In the Orkney Islands.'

'And you are no longer a spy?'

Will looked at Jakob sharply. The man's eyes were shrewd, but at the moment they seemed clear and bland. They seemed to overflow with humor all at once.

'I was never a spy,' Will said mildly.

'I know. I know. A small joke. A courier perhaps? A messenger? There were very few Germans in Berne at the time who were not doing double service for the Fatherland. I was even called upon once or twice.'

'We were young.'

Jakob-Saloman laughed aloud. 'You'll take dinner with me?'

'That would give me pleasure.'

'Yes, we'll talk of old times, and I'll show you a bit of the town.'

'Most kind.'

Jakob tapped his forehead with an open palm. 'This is Friday, is it not? Of course it is. I'm afraid I won't be free this evening.'

'I understand.'

'No. No, I'm not thinking of withdrawing my invitation. It's simply that in my old age I find comfort in weekly worship. I go to temple regularly now. It's soothing to my soul. Will you be free tomorrow night?'

'Yes. My business should keep me here that long and longer. I have no friends here, and hotel rooms do get confining.'

'Say no more. We'll meet in the lobby of our hotel on Saturday evening at eight. You have a friend.'

In such a fashion the creature stepped into the holding trap.

CHAPTER 18

Will reported to Simmons at the first opportunity. He used a public telephone booth instead of making the call from his room for fear his conversation might be overheard by the switchboard operator.

Simmons was delighted with the arrangement.

'You've done very well. Did he propose a restaurant?'

'I didn't think it would seem proper to ask.'

'Very properly considered. Well, tomorrow evening we will see to it that Herr Jakob-Salomon pays a visit to his Fatherland whether he likes it or not. You are free to do as you please until tomorrow evening. If Jakob calls you to change your appointment for any reason, inform me at once. Make certain that you arrange another meeting with him for dinner. We must consider all possibilities. You will be under surveillance from the moment you leave the hotel tomorrow. At the proper moment I will approach you. We will greet each other as old friends, and we will find a reason for me to join you or to at least share a taxi to wherever Jakob intends to take you. Is this understood?'

'Clearly.'

'So enjoy yourself then. But I would suggest that you take very little to drink and that you refrain from using the services of any women.'

He hung up before Will could frame a retort to the double insult. The remarks suggested he was irresponsible and undependable, or was it simply Simmons' odious character that demanded he enforce his authority in the most offensive way?

Will returned to his hotel. The city held no savor for him. He occupied himself with projections and considerations of the value to himself and family that might come from his acquisition of the part ownership in the Fox and Grapes. He retired early and slept fitfully. He thrust the thought that he was party to an entrapment that would lure a man to an uncertain fate from his mind. But it was a persistent insect that kept returning. He found solace in the rationale that Jakob Salomon was evading the authorities for disloyal and anti

German reasons. The man was a traitor to the Fatherland or very nearly so. He would do what was required of him, but he ardently wished he knew more of the reasons behind the entire matter.

His mind was prisoner of his body and would not rest. His body was prisoner of his mind and fashioned chains and fetters of the bedclothes. Before morning he rose and bathed himself with a cloth at the washstand. He dressed in the pale light of false dawn and went out into the damp streets. He walked for a long time and found himself at the edge of a small park fenced with wrought-iron pickets. The top railings were made of twisted cartouches of iron that traced intricate patterns against the brightening sky. The gate was open. He walked in and spread his handkerchief upon a bench wet with dew.

A black sedan pulled up at the curb just outside within his view. It looked official, and he was momentarily frightened. A man left the back of the car. Will immediately recognized Conrad by his bearing. It was military and precise. Will glanced at the man behind the wheel. He thought it was Harold, but the shadows within the car were deep, and he couldn't be certain. The car pulled away slowly, and Conrad walked briskly to the entrance of the park.

He joined Will on the bench. 'I've come to apprise you of certain details of this operation. You are, no doubt, surprised to see me here.'

'Very frankly, I am beyond the attitude of surprise.'

'I find that a very favorable response.' Conrad examined Will as one would a horse or dog, testing its temper and willingness to be used. 'I think, after this, you'll no longer be called upon to leave your post in the Orkneys. I'm sure there will be no call for it. The organization was allowed to develop in a fragmentary manner without strong direction from a central source. Such autonomy is over now. The inefficient, the poorly motivated, the misfits and those whose total loyalty is suspect will be weeded out. You will be pleased to know I consider you totally reliable.'

I am not particularly pleased to know that, Will thought.

'Once Jakob-Salomon is safely across the border in Germany, he will be taken in hand by our operatives there. You and Simmons and Herr Bochner will have completed your assignment.'

'Herr Bochner?'

'Harold. When the three of you are alone, you will no longer take instruction from the man Simmons.'

Will made no comment despite the fact that Conrad left him the space for one. Conrad seemed pleased by his silence. 'From that moment, you will take your instructions from Harold. You will not interfere in any action he may undertake, but you will assist him if the need arises. Harold is trustworthy and skillful, and I doubt very strongly if he will call upon your help.'

Conrad stood up and glanced out past the fencing to the street. The sound of an automobile approached. 'You've done well so far. Unfortunately, in our profession that's the only commendation you'll receive. I suggest you return to your hotel and check out. You won't be returning there. Check your bags at the central railroad station, and purchase a ticket for the morning train to Paris. Say nothing to Simmons. Meet Jakob-Salomon in the lobby of your hotel as arranged. It would be as well not to mention you've already checked out to him either.'

He walked out of the park. His car paused at the curb at the moment he reached it. He was driven off.

It was clear to Will that Simmons was in disfavor. Was he to be removed from the service? Will avoided the thought, for if the man were marked for liquidation, every human response in Will would urge him to give the dislikable man some warning.

At noon he checked out of the Deinerhof, knowing for a certainty that the eyes that watched him would not be Simmons'. He carried out the instructions Conrad had given him, keeping but a single thought in mind. Soon, very soon, he would be on the Paris train and on his way home.

At a quarter of eight he arrived back at the hotel, having spent the intervening hours in idle wandering. Precisely on the hour Jakob descended in the grillwork cage of the elevator from his floor above.

'Have I kept you waiting?'

'I was just a trifle early. I completed my business and spent an hour or two in the art museum.'

'You should have come to my room for a drink. Well, no matter. Come along.'

They took a taxi to a fine small restaurant overlooking the river. Along the way the streets were filled with masked revelers. Those dressed in bizarre costumes, carrying noise-makers of all sorts and wearing papier-mâché heads of fabulous animals seemed, somehow, more in keeping with the old buildings along the waterfront than those people dressed in everyday wear.

Many of their fellow diners were costumed. There was a festive ambiance to the place.

With his long nose and mournful eyes, Jakob-Salomon, sitting opposite, seemed to be a man out of time. Within that deception he seemed impervious to disaster. Perhaps, Will thought, he will be protected this night. He wanted it to be so.

'I thought a quiet dinner,' Jakob said, 'and later we'll have a drink or two along the way.'

'This is most kind of you.'

'No, no, no. It's my very great pleasure to spend an evening with a man I knew when I was young and things were simpler.'

'We were at war.'

'Yes, but perhaps old wars are surrounded with romance in time. Or perhaps, life was really more simple. At least, I believe, there was code of honor existing in our Germany then. A certain belief in ultimate good. The war that's coming will be more brutal than any the world has known. We're moving sharply toward the edge of disaster. This creature Hitler will make a war that will put Attila and Tamerlane to shame.'

'Are you so certain there will be war? Chancellor Hitler has announced that he is satisfied with revisions to an impossible treaty. He has no territorial aspirations. He has no army with which to fight.'

'It's not difficult to be a great and successful liar when those who listen to the lies wish to believe them. I assure you that within a matter of weeks, perhaps days, this Adolf Hitler will announce Germany's right to conscript an army. My feelings should be hurt. Apparently you don't read my articles.'

Will gestured as though to say that he was a simple man with little knowledge of matters beyond his small community. Jakob-Salomon laughed. It held a bitter note.

'Perhaps your way is best. Apparently those who do read my writings discount them without further consideration. But let's put such talk aside. These matters make up the fabric of my life, waking and sleeping, and I'd rather hide in pleasanter conversation tonight. Tell me, why did you decide to emigrate to England? It's very wet.'

'And the islands are windy and cold,' Will added. He went

on to provide a small sketch of his reasons for going to the Orkneys and his life there. Even as he spoke, he was startled to realize how little he had to invent. Only at the very beginning of his story did he find it necessary to exercise care and to create fictions, for the bulk of his life he spoke of drew without thought upon the true facts.

Jakob-Salomon, a man who through choice, dedication and profession was deeply involved in the events he reckoned was a gathering storm, seemed enchanted by it all. The talk of friends and family and cozy nights protected from the cold outside struck a deep wound of loss in him.

'What would your choice be if there were to be war between Germany and Great Britain?' It was, in the context of the foreboding events, an obvious and honest question.

'I would, naturally, fight for my home and country.'

'Ah, yes. Your home is in the Orkney Islands.'

'Yes.'

'Do you consider it your country as well?'

Will found himself stammering. 'I am a British subject. A naturalized citizen.'

'But don't you continue to think of yourself as a German?'

'Yes, as a German in my birth. But as an *Englander* in my choice.'

'And in your heart?'

Will stared at the journalist. His technique of interrogation was brutal. There was no letup. It seemed to animate him in a way that was pleasant to him. But suddenly he seemed to become aware of Will's discomfort. He broke off the attack and dipped his head in apology.

'I ask myself those questions. I'm a Jew, and I prided myself that the Jews of Germany had been assimilated more completely than they had in any other nation, including England. We not only were accepted but enjoyed every benefit of citizenship in the most civilized country in the world. Now I can see it might well have been because we had given up our Jewishness, our birthright. We had masked ourselves but it wasn't enough. When a goat was needed, we were ready to hand. When a madman's hate was expressed, the German people were quick to take it up.'

'Please, Mr. Jakob-Salomon, I hold no prejudice.'

Jakob-Salomon held up a hand to silence Will's words.

'Of course you do not. Yet you used the world *Englander* a moment ago. It was reflex in a moment when I had backed you to the wall. The expression *Englander* carries with it a certain contempt, does it not? No matter. There is this point to be made. I fight against Hitler, not against Germany, my country.'

He smiled a smile so inexpressibly sad and lost that Will's hand began to reach out to touch his.

'We are, of course, too old to fight. My question was academic in that regard,' Jakob-Salomon said.

They went on to talk of other things. Of remembrances of Germany and the countryside. In a short while Will became silent altogether while Jakob-Salomon, having found a friend from the past, relived his life's sweet moments. There had never been, perhaps, anyone else to relive it with.

Well fed, they went on with the night's adventure. They were already on a first-name basis, and Will had the warm feeling that he had known this man intimately and constantly for a long, long time.

Jakob-Salomon introduced him to the small café the Quill. Here artists and writers gathered for talk and companionship. It was a small place and very crowded. But then it seemed that most places of social intercourse were crowded everywhere in the city.

Will had a vagrant thought. He had often noticed that animals sought the strength of numbers when disaster threatened. Then he noticed a few costumed persons and saw it all as part of innocent revel.

They found a place to stand at the small bar. They were crushed shoulder to shoulder with men and women who seemed determined to be heard above the din. It took a moment for Will to realize that the hand plucking at his sleeve and the voice shouting into his ear was not the result of casual jostling and undirected conversation. He turned. Simmons grinned at him. Will was stricken with the sudden thought that Simmons would address him as Hartz and give the game away, but Simmons almost winked at him while making noises of surprise about meeting good old Will Oerter so far from home. Will steadied his fears after this near miss while thinking that it was just like Simmons to take a little sadistic joy in not informing Will that he was aware of his former name and probably all his intimate past. Simmons obviously took pleasure in keeping him off-balance.

Will made the necessary introductions. Handclasps and smiles were exchanged. It was a night when strangers were taken as friends.

By the time they left the Quill Simmons had insinuated himself into the small reunion. Represented by Will as an old acquaintance from Stromness, he chattered on in humorous fashion about his escape from a sales territory that found him somewhat confined to places of fierce weather to a position that gave him greater latitude. He compared the lonely evenings of the traveling salesman to those of the foreign correspondent. They were privy to the customs of a hundred cities but were never part of them. In subtle fashion he joined Jakob to himself in a brotherhood of sorts. He excluded the comfortably settled Oerter as a breed apart. It was done with many jokes and much good humor. He was, in addition, in possession of private transportation. His business associate, presently lost in the crush, had volunteered to show Simmons the city and was driving him about in his own automobile. Harold was found and introduced as they left the café.

They piled into the small vehicle. Simmons contrived to sit next to Jakob-Salomon in the back. Will sat in the front next to the still-silent Harold, who drove through the throngs in the streets of Basel with practiced skill.

They stopped at a beer hall in the northern part of the city. This establishment was crowded to the rafters as well. Simmons contrived, with a handsome gratuity, to obtain a table against the wall. He overwhelmed them all with generosity. The drinks were soon lined up on the table. Harold drank slowly with a curiously fastidious grace. He held each glass of schnapps between first finger and thumb with the other fingers, fat and gross, fanned out. Will drank sparingly. He was ill with excitement, tension and fear. His untouched drinks were passed along to Jakob-Salomon. Simmons, Will noticed, seemed to drink one for one with Jakob-Salomon but actually tasted each glass and only consumed one in four.

Jakob-Salomon's consumption was steady and considerable. The luminous eyes became shadowed as though glazed with opaque glass. He spoke steadily but with no slurring of speech about the disaster that had overtaken Germany in the shape of Hitler and his Nazis. He spoke of the fearful danger that threatened Europe and perhaps the world.

Will found it difficult to keep his attention centered on the conversation. He was intrigued by a sort of gay, reckless arrogance that Simmons displayed. He would often sharply dispute what Jakob had to say, and then when Jakob seemed on the point of such anger that would put an end to the evening and therefore to the opportunity to spirit him away, Simmons would clap him upon the shoulder and laugh loudly as though they were in perfect agreement.

He glanced at his watch and suggested a change of scene. Jakob-Salomon demurred, pleading weariness and much work to do in the week to come. At last they assembled in the car again. This time Harold sat in the back with the journalist. Simmons drove.

They passed the outskirts of the town. Jakob nodded in the back. Simmons whistled nearly soundlessly between his teeth. A grin was plastered on his face. The automobile left even the suburbs behind. They passed between long passages of sentinel trees.

'What the hell! Where the devil are we?'

Jakob-Salomon snapped to wakefulness and apparent sobriety in a mere shaving of a second.

'I know a roadhouse along this way. I thought the company of some friendly girls would be a proper climax to the evening.'

'I'd have you take me back to the city.'

'We'll just look in on this place I know, will we?'

'No, you'll start back to Basel. Now!'

Simmons no longer replied. The tires made a hissing sound on the tar roadway.

Jakob's voice rose several tones. 'God damn it, Simmons. That is your name?'

'Yes, Simmons.'

'Well, Simmons, I want to return. I'm in no mood for any more drinking or any women tonight.' Simmons glanced at Will. 'Mr. Oerter, can't you talk to your old friend? Convince him that we shouldn't bring such a pleasant evening to an abrupt close.'

Will turned in the front seat, a placatory smile forming on his mouth.

Jakob-Salomon stared at him. Stark fear blazed from his eyes. 'Tell me what this is all about, Oerter.'

Will found it difficult to form a lie. His mouth wouldn't function. He continued to regard the man as though he were in the process of dying and, therefore, curious.

Jakob-Salomon surged forward in his seat. He reached out for the handle of the door. Harold reached across the journalist and grasped his wrist. He was smiling as though the gesture were one of great friendliness and solicitude. Jakob surged forward again. Harold pulled him forward with the hand that held the wrist farthest from himself. Jakob-Salomon stared into his face. He started to scream.

Harold's fist struck him squarely in the center of the face. Blood welled, paused, then gushed from the nose, splashing down the front of his topcoat and scarf. He began to cry in rage or terror. The eyes were wild, and Will had the curious thought that the man didn't feel the pain of the blow. The eyes, swimming, accused, accused, accused! The accusation glowed beneath the surface like phosphor burning in the sea.

Simmons gave an exclamation of disgust and disapproval.

'Good Christ, Harold, did you have to make a mess of him? If we're stopped I'll have to make up a tale.' Simmons was annoyed at the possibility of being put to some small bother.

Will couldn't take his eyes from the ravaged face. The mouth, the carmined lips, the broken teeth gathered themselves for another scream. Harold struck Jakob-Salomon on the jaw just below the left ear. Jakob slumped. His cry choked in him.

The carriage way narrowed. It became a common dirt road. It wound briefly up a gentle rise and reached a clearing. Simmons stopped the car but left the motor idling and the lights on. Answering lights shone from a vehicle not fifty yards away. Simmons left the car, and between them, he and Harold dragged Jakob-Salomon across the clearing toward Germany. The journalist's shoe tips gouged two slender furrows in the dirt. Will, unbidden, trotted behind intent upon picking up the man's feet so his shoes shouldn't be ruined. He bobbed and reached, but the shining shoes eluded him.

Two men in black leather coats took Jakob-Salomon in charge. Harold, without making the request, took Jakob's wristwatch from his dangling arm. He grinned at the two men and at Simmons and put the watch in his pocket. Jakob-Salomon was placed in the back of the sedan. The car backed up, turned tightly and was gone away.

Simmons sighed and rubbed his hands. He was mightily pleased with himself. He had engineered the kidnapping. It had gone off without fuss or difficulty. They began to walk back to their own transport. Simmons threw an arm about Will. They were comrades returning from a night of beer and good conversation. Will felt his body crawl from the contact. Harold shuffled along a step or two behind. He was suddenly, acutely aware that Harold's footsteps stopped. He began to turn. He had expectations of some new horror. He felt Simmons' arm jolt. Simmons pitched forward and lay without moving. A blossom of blood seemed purple in the moonlight. It adorned the center of his back.

Will felt himself grabbed by the arm and hurried the last few paces to the automobile. Harold opened the door on the driver's side and very nearly slammed Will into the seat behind the wheel.

'Get the hell out of here,' Harold said. 'Leave the car at the station and go home.'

Will couldn't turn his head to watch Harold walk away. One incredible and foolish thought occupied his being.

That damned Harold could talk.

CHAPTER 19

On the train to Paris Will felt a sick urgency to be safe at home. He longed for Julie and his child, Wee Jock and the Sailing Master with such intensity that the bones of his legs ached with the desire to run. He felt he could run faster than the train could travel.

He hurried from the train at the Gare de Lyon and secured a taxicab for the ride across the city to the Gare du Nord and the train to Le Havre. It was necessary for him to wait in the station for eight hours. He sat on a bench, moving only twice to relieve his bowels and bladder and to buy a paper from the kiosk that sold newspapers from the major cities of Europe. Of course, that day's paper from Basel had not yet arrived. He took no food or drink but was unaware of the fact.

He slept fitfully on the train. In Le Havre he was forced to spend another night sitting on a hard bench. He had missed his connection with the boat to England.

He became aware of a weakness. The feeling translated into hunger, and he had a sausage roll and a cup of tepid tea. It sat badly, and he had the urge to throw it up, but he waited on, white-faced, stolid and patient. The minor sickness passed.

On the boat, despite a heavy crossing, he fell asleep in the passenger lounge. He awoke with no reckoning of the time or the day.

He journeyed to London and slept briefly again. He discovered his hands were numb, though it wasn't particularly cold. He couldn't find his gloves in the pocket of his coat. He worried briefly about where he might have dropped them.

He felt he had been condemned to journey forever sitting on faded, worn, plush or hard wooden slats. His feet were sore and his legs achingly weary as though he had walked every foot of the way.

He fell into a spiritual malaise, a coma of the senses. He was but vaguely aware that he was on yet another train moving into Scotland. On the voyage across the Pentland Firth he was taken with an overpowering chill. His hands developed an uncontrollable tremor.

He was found wandering along the quayside in Kirkwall.

He was taken to the Fox and Grapes. He was made as comfortable as possible in Mr. Dowdy's bed, and a doctor was summoned. His illness was diagnosed as bronchitis.

The day was Friday, March 15. It had taken him six days to travel this close to home.

The papers were full of the news that Hitler had declared the immediate restitution of military conscription. It was his intention to place thirty-six divisions, three hundred and twenty-four thousand men under arms.

Jakob-Salomon's prediction had come true.

A telephone call was put through to Julie in Stromness. She placed the Sailing Master in Wee Jock's charge and left little John with Mrs. MacClintock. Then she set sail on Abel Ewen's fishing craft to join Will.

She hurried into the sickroom. There was about her an air of great capability as though motherhood had brought with it a fully flowered maturity.

'Hello, old man. Got yourself poorly, did you?'

She stroked the gray stubble of his beard, and he opened his eyes.

Whose small face, lined with concern, was this that hovered palely above him? She had a resemblance to a child he had known and felt a love for. But that child was gone. Perhaps she had returned just this moment in a feverish dream. He smiled and closed his eyes.

'Sleep, you dear old husband,' Julie whispered. She took up the care of him and jealously refused to allow anyone else to nurse him. She sat on a chair drawn up close to the bed and held his hand. When weariness overcame her, she slept on a cot at his feet. Sometimes she rested her head on the counterpane and fell asleep sitting.

In three days his sleep became less troubled. Color returned to his cheeks and lips.

On the morning of the sixth day he woke all at once, weak but refreshed. Julie lay like a doll broken in the middle, her head touching his thigh. He touched her hair and felt a great abiding love for his wife.

Julie woke to a healthy, ravenous husband. She fussed and cooed over him as he ate, as though he were a child who had been pecky at his food and now savored it. Will gave her the gift of playing his part in the charade. He ate until he could eat no more.

Julie went off to bed then, exhausted beyond further enduring.

Will read the paper. There was no mention of the events that had taken place in Basel. He asked no questions about any prior appearance concerning the story in the press. He felt it might seem odd. His friends would have no cause to take special notice of such strange goings-on in a nation a world away.

Will was robust by nature. Once gone, the illness was as though it had never been. He was eager to be truly home. To see his son.

They stayed on a few days more to settle the details of the partnership in the Kirkwall tavern.

On March 24 there was a small item on the BBC news. It noted that the German Foreign Office had informed the Swiss government that Berthold Jakob-Salomon had been arrested on German soil and jailed.

In the pub room that night Will was greeted by his old friends and customers as though he had been gone on a long absence. They were showing him that they knew of his illness and that they were grateful that he had passed safely through the valley of the shadow.

The next morning Julie insisted that Will stay in bed. He allowed her to mother him. He spent the hours in apparent idleness listening to the radio. The commentator of the news captured his complete attention.

'The assistant prosecutor of Basel, accompanied by a police official, arrived in London today to investigate the alleged kidnapping of Berthold Jakob-Salomon, anti-Nazi journalist. The German Foreign Office yesterday announced the journalist had been arrested violating their borders. It now appears that he was the victim of a kidnap plot planned and organized in London.

'Swiss officials discovered that Hans Wesemann, a German involved in the kidnapping and presently in custody in Switzerland, had been living in London intermittently over the past three years as Rudolf Schroeder. In the guise of a German liberal he had won the confidence of British liberals and German refugees in England.'

The news gave Will a terrible fright. Schroeder had seemed a weak straw to him, petulant, vain and unreliable. Would he talk to save himself and implicate Will and the others? A more careful examination in the next day's newspaper which actually arrived four full days later on the regularly scheduled mail packet gave Will reason to believe that the authorities looked upon Schroeder as the ringleader. There was no least hint of the possible identities of any others who must have been involved with him in the conspiracy. They were going ahead with further investigations in Basel. The examination of Schroeder's association in London seemed simple formalities and fishing expeditions.

Even so the fears of those days and the days that followed centered on the possibility that the police were withholding information obtained from Schroeder and were, even now, playing cat and mouse with Conrad and himself for their own purposes.

He stationed himself by the radio at all the hours when the BBC broadcast the news. He feared his anxiety was noticeable to Julie and made every effort to conceal it.

On the thirtieth a statement by the German government news service was announced.

'Salomon, called Jakob, had, according to information received to date, already illegally crossed the Franco-Swiss border and intended also by illegal means to cross over into the Reich in order to meet there certain individuals in his confidence.

'German frontier officials were able to halt him as he crossed the border.'

The announcement served to cloud the issue.

The news broadcast offered no statement from the Swiss government or from any authority in England.

On April 2 the Swiss replied. They said they were steadfastly determined to uphold their sovereign rights in demanding the return of Berthold Jakob-Salomon. They were launching an investigation into the activities of the Swiss Nazi Party and alleged German agents.

The Germans denied the kidnapping on April 10. Their position was that he had been arrested when he stepped on German soil and had been charged with treason.

Five days later the Nazi government dropped the mask of diplomacy. They no longer denied the kidnapping. They admitted the possibility that certain 'patriotically motivated' persons had acted with the intention of placing Jakob-Salomon into the hands of the German authorities. Inasmuch as Jakob-Salomon had come within reach of German jurisdiction without the intervention of official German authorities and inasmuch as he was a traitor to the state, there was nothing they could do but allow the criminal procedure pending against him to take its course.

It was implicit in the announcement that the Germans were giving notice to Switzerland, Britain and those who were preparing to present the case before the International Court at The Hague that, as far as the German government was concerned, the matter was closed. The tragedy and final passion of Jakob-Salomon, anti-Nazi émigré journalist, disappeared from the attention of the world.

It did not pass so easily from Will's conscience. It reflected darkly upon even the brightest of his days.

A short way north along the rocky shore of the island there was a small sandy beach shaped like a lunette. The natives of Stromness rarely frequented it. Being of the islands and therefore of the sea, they didn't view the water's edge as a playground but as the giver of work and life. They found it difficult to understand why holiday makers would spend a day in idleness sitting on the sands or dabbling their feet in the surf.

But Will was a man of the mountains, and the sea never lost its enchantment for him. He found on or near it the deepest content of his troubled life. In the confusions that plagued him the sea acted like a crystal mirror that reflected only the simple fact of his humanity, not the dark inconsistencies of his purpose. Will found himself making time to spend long, lazy days by the shore with his small son.

Julie fussed about them both equally, charging them to take care of wet feet and insisting they stay bundled in coats and scarves, though it was June and summer. She touched Will's hands and found them cold.

They had somehow never recovered their natural warmth even after the passage of many months. She fetched a pair of mittens.

'Here, fit your great paws into these. I can't find your good gloves. Have you lost them, Will?'

She scolded him gently and fondly. Will smiled ruefully, pretending to be an absentminded man.

Later in the sheltered cove the two of them, Will and his son, joined in a conspiracy to remove the encumbering clothing. John went off to play at the water's edge. Will lay down upon the shore, and the sun grew warm on his face and chest. He removed the mittens and held his hands between his eyes and the sun. What had become of the gloves? Had they been dropped in that struggle on the Swiss-German border? Had they been exposed to laboratory tests? Had the label identified them as gloves purchased in Scotland? How many pairs had been manufactured? Where sold? Had the shop-keeper made a record of Will's purchase? Had they traced the gloves to their owner? Had the various authorities accepted the kidnapping of Jakob-Salomon as a *fait accompli*, a political matter rather than a criminal one? Were they now watching him as an undesirable? He shook himself and looked to the safety of his small son through slitted eyes.

Wee John would be two years old before long. How sturdy and bright he'd grown. He moved from pool to pool, across the shallow hillocks of sand, with energetic grace. He threw his head back and laughed at the gulls traversing the sky.

Will called out to the boy just for the sound of the name. The little boy careened across the distance and showed his treasures to his father. Will reached out a finger. John grasped it, and between them they pretended the child drew the man to his feet.

Along the main street of Stromness they walked toward the Sailing Master. At the door of the greengrocer's they met Julie. Will smiled as though most amazed by the chance encounter. He pointed to the string bag.

'Mutton chops,' she said. 'I'll stuff them with clams and breadcrumbs. There's tomatoes and good potatoes.'

'With a bottle of claret, a feast for a king,' Will said, and laughed. They all three laughed and laughed.

In the roadway outside the Sailing Master, Will paused.

'Are we doing the right thing, Julie? Is the move to Kirkwall to your liking?'

'Kirkwall isn't the end of the earth, after all. I know you've got a fondness for the Sailing Master and all, but I suppose it's natural to grow some and to change.'

'But you're not unpleased.'

'No. I'll like it in Kirkwall. It's a vaster place.'

'What a strange word, "vaster," to use about Kirkwall.'

'Bigger then.'

'Yes, it is bigger. Well then, Abel Ewen will take our things over in the morning. We have everything properly packed?'

'Yes, for the hundredth time. Are you sorrowing, old man?

The two places are only the flight of a bird away from one another.'

'Perhaps it's just that change makes me nervous.'

'A proper clam you are. You'd be happiest in one inch of a tide pool with no reason to move at all.'

He allowed that was probably true. They went in to supper. It had been a good day.

It was the day Hitler occupied the Rhineland.

The following morning their personal possessions were transported to Kirkwall by their friend Abel Ewen. There was not enough to crowd the afterdeck of the small fishing craft. Most of the furnishings of their rooms they'd left for the use of Wee Jock and his family. Besides their clothes and cooking pots and such things, they took only their bed and the smaller cradle of John's, a desk and Will's old rocking chair.

In Kirkwall Will had purchased a house at the end of a short path close enough to the town to be convenient, far enough to be unobstructed in its view toward the sea. On three wonderful occasions he and Julie had gone together to Aberdeen and allowed themselves the luxury of buying all that was necessary to furnish the house new.

By evening Will began to feel a sense of great expectation. He was a successful businessman. He was expanding for the sake of his wife and the future of his child and for his own sake as well. He did, indeed, feel that he was taking his family to a vaster place. His old friends gathered in the taproom. A hundred toasts were drunk. Wee Jock and his round, splendid wife insisted Will and Julie should be treated as guests. They served, and the Hartzes sat at a table like visiting dignitaries.

Will had placed the keeping of the Sailing Master in the hands of Wee Jock. They had come to fair arrangement, and Will was certain he was in no danger of being cheated in any least way. It had been decided that Ian Bostock should take the position of barman at a decent wage. That part of the arrangement gave no great pleasure to Wee Jock, but he was an honest man and understood that Will would want to do what he believed right for his father-in-law. Neither was Julie pleased by the situation. She'd developed no affection for her father and often complained to Will of his tolerance of the man. But she was secretly proud of the deep honesty and fairness in Will that would urge him to act toward Bostock in such a generous fashion.

The least pleased of all was Bostock himself. He'd

arrogantly assumed he should properly be the governor of the Sailing Master and Wee Jock helper to him. Bostock arrived late on the night before leaving. He'd gotten drunk somewhere along the way.

'So here we all are. All the friends of this good man, Wilhelm Hartz.'

Julie half turned her back to her father.

He drew a chair up to the table crowding in to establish himself as a member of this particular small ruling class.

'Mr. Bostock, have you been patronizing another establishment?' Will asked, trying to make a light joke.

'Ian. Call me Ian. I will have you call me Ian, Mr. Wilhelm Hartz.'

He emphasized the Germanic sound of the name. Will raised a hand.

'Ian, of course. And you then must call me Will.'

'Fair enough. Will anyone offer me a drink?'

'Please,' Will murmured.

'After all, this is a celebration. Where are you going?' he nearly shouted as Julie stood up.

'To get you a drink.'

'That's a good girl. Make it a whiskey. A double. This is a celebration. Where's my grandson?'

Again he struck hard at the word.

'In bed asleep,' Will answered mildly.

Something of the joy had been taken out of the assemblage. A few murmured good-nights and left, sensitive to the currents of discord.

'My grandson's a braw lad. Looks like me a bit, wouldn't you say?'

'Not by a fraction,' Julie said, and set a glass down before him.

'Well, I say so. Three generations of my blood is here right now, under this roof. Isn't that a wondrous thing?'

A few of the gathering agreed to placate the man.

'But soon my little family will be gone away.'

His face screwed up as though he were about to cry.

'That's a painful thing. A painful thing when one grows old to see his family gone from him.'

'Kirkwall's only a bird's flight away,' Will soothed.

'What the hell do you know of birds? You're a lander.'

'There are birds in Switzerland, after all,' Will responded mildly.

'Old.' Bostock held up the maimed hand. 'Old and useless. At least, that's what my foreign son thinks. Useless to manage for him this small part of a family business.'

Wee Jock cleared his throat. Will looked at him sharply and shook his head. There was nothing for MacClintock to explain or defend. He made a gesture of pouring. Wee Jock nodded and brought a nearly full bottle to the table.

'It's a full day tomorrow,' Julie said. 'Good night all, and thank you.'

She kissed Will lightly on the cheek and went away to the last sleep in the Sailing Master.

'No kiss for your old father? Sicken you, do I?'

Julie's back disappeared. Bostock displayed the hand as though to suggest the mutilation caused his daughter disgust. More of the people left. Though Will had announced his intention to continue on past normal closing and though the announcement had been greeted with expectations of great good fun and a long drink, his friends were leaving. They were folk who sensed the coming of storm.

Will poured Bostock's glass full. The man drank greedily and steadily.

'I've been quiet enough. I haven't demanded my rights.'

'What bloody rights?' Wee Jock burst out.

Bostock whirled on MacClintock, glad of the opportunity to be goaded on to revelation. Will moved swiftly.

'Jock. Take you home now. It's been a long day and another tiring one tomorrow. You'll have your things to move over.'

'There's the cleaning up to do.'

'I'll take care.'

Wee Jock removed his apron reluctantly, but his wife urged him along. She brought his coat and her own.

'Morrow, Mr. Hartz.'

'Yes, tomorrow.'

'I really should stay for the cleaning up,' Jock said.

'No, no, no, please.'

Mrs. MacClintock hurried her husband out. With them the last of Will's friends left as well. Bostock laughed.

'Maybe I could hire out to clear company away. Like a rat chaser or a chimney sweep. I must stink, I must.'

'You do.'

'Watch your mouth, you fucking Nazi.'

'You've got it wrong way around,' Will lashed out. 'It's your mouth you must watch lest it be smashed for the filth, the lies or the idiocy it utters.'

Bostock retreated behind his twisted hand, but liquor gave him a bit of courage.

'Don't play the innocent with me. Simmons told me what you were and what you're here for.'

Will caught the automatic, indignant denial in his teeth. It was just wild enough to have a seed of truth in it. Simmons might well have been that indiscreet. As he sought a response, he saw clearly that Bostock lied. The man had taken a random shot in the dark. Will leaned back with apparent amusement.

'Did he?' Will asked blandly. 'Did this foolish man, Simmons, a traveling salesman, a bore, braggart and gossip, tell you that I am a Nazi?'

'Yes. Oh, yes. You're a fucking German spy.'

'Keep your voice down, Mr. Bostock.'

'You'll call me Ian,' Bostock said in automatic response.

'I will call you what I please to call you. How does this Simmons imagine that I am a – spy? How did he dream up such foolishness?'

'We drank together one night, and he told me.'

'Ah, so two drunken fools told each other lies. He told you he knew this secret. And you, no doubt, told him you had lost your fingers through some act of courage.'

Bostock was silent. Will prodded him.

'This is so?'

Bostock clasped the maimed hand.

'We spoke about plenty of things. We share the same views of the way things are. He said he might have use for me. He told me to keep my eyes clear and my ears open.'

That much Will could conceive as true.

'For what reason?'

'He said he might have work for me. I watched. I watched you.'

Will shook his head in despair.

'Oh, Mr. Bostock, you are a drunken, foolish man. Understand me. I feel sorry for you, and you are the father of my wife. And, yes, the grandfather of my child. It would do me no honor to see you destitute. You're angry, and you imagine lies about me because I've not made you the governor of this establishment now that I am gone to Kirkwall. You lose control of your thoughts and your tongue. That is why I did not make you the governor.'

'It belongs half to my daughter,' Bostock babbled, trying desperately to find a valid argument.

Will smiled and sat back.

'I make you a bargain then. Ask Julie if she wants you to manage our interests here. If she says yes, I will, of course agree.'

He leaned forward, and Bostock retreated.

'She will say no, and then there will be an end to any courtesies between us. My pride would no longer allow me to be kind to you. I would cast you out and away from us altogether.'

Bostock stared at Will, mesmerized by the soft voice.

'If you continue to call me such names or to whisper such lies or to harbor such insane suspicions, I will take you aside before we go. In some lonely place we will be quite alone. I will beat you with my fists. I will leave you crippled and in great pain. The bottle is finished now, Mr. Bostock.'

Will stood up. Bostock gazed at him. He cringed within his skin. He knew Will never threatened, never idly. He rose, staggering, from the chair. He moved toward the door sideways like a crab.

'Forget this matter, Mr. Bostock,' Will said softly. 'Come you tomorrow, and see your daughter and your grandson away. I will call you Ian.'

CHAPTER 20

There seemed to be more activity in the Fox and Grapes than there had been at the Sailing Master. It seemed greater not only in volume, but in energy. The Sailing Master had always seemed to be an extension of a private living room or fireside in a cottage kitchen. It was a place where men gathered for the simplest relaxation.

But in the Fox and Grapes there seemed to be a more active concern with events that transpired beyond the encircling sea. There was a far greater traffic of strangers, salesmen, travelers, merchant seamen and a fair sprinkling of men in the uniform of His Majesty's Navy. After all, Kirkwall was the capital of the Orkneys, and it intended to act like one.

Conversations, even dispute, touched on matters that were social, political and universal. There was the usual leavening of simple gossip as well.

It was exhilarating, but Will missed, terribly, the bright puckish face of Wee Jock and regretted even more the loss of his good friend John Kendrick.

He made a special friend of an ageless ship's captain named Skipper Gatt, who owned a small drifter, the *Daisy II*. He had little of the antic good spirits Kendrick had often displayed, but he was much like John in other ways. He had the same air of giving his friendship after due time but completely, loyally and without question. He was whitened, as John had been, by the touch of the spindrift and the gales. He had a solemn way of speaking because he was much used to being alone.

He brought Will greetings from Jock and small news of Stromness from time to time.

'Bostock has left his job as barman and found himself a place of work at Lyness.'

He never referred to Will's relationship as son-in-law to Julie's father. Perhaps he sensed that it would be no service to remind Will of it.

'That's good news,' Will said.

'A bit of a wonder as well. He's had few enough jobs in his life.'

Will shrugged.

'The service is putting the station there in some sort of working order, I understand. They'll need what casual labor they can get.'

Skipper Gatt nodded his agreement. 'Oh, there'll be work enough for them that wants it. There's plans afoot, they say, to put all of Scapa Flow into readiness to harbor a war-ready home fleet if the need arises.'

'Surely not.'

'It's possible, isn't it, Will? This Hitler fellow sent armed men into the Rhineland only this last March. He broke the last restraint placed on Germany by the Treaty of Versailles.'

Will offered an opinion with great diffidence.

'From much of what I've read of the treaty and its aftermath, many experts seem to agree that the demands were punitive and unrealistic.'

Gatt gave a small laugh that passed through his nose with explosive force. It was a trick of manner John had possessed.

'I don't count myself an expert in such matters. And I don't pretend to think the treaty was fair, though, after all, Germany was clearly the loser. All the same, I don't hold with grinding a man's, or a country's, nose into the garbage of defeat. It's just that the facts are there. Hitler's making noises like cannon. Those people went after Europe once before. They could well do it again.'

Will was called away to serve a customer. When he returned, Skipper Gatt was finished with his pint and buttoning his coat to leave.

'Here's a bit of news. Bostock must have been feeling big in himself with the new job and all. He faced out Wee Jock in the Sailing Master. Called him some filthy names and made vile suggestions as to how Jock secured his favor with you. Jock felled him with a bung starter. He's a gentle man and was sick for it after, but he knocked a bit of salt out of Bostock's mouth.'

He waved a hand and went to the door. Will came around the bar and followed alongside to see him out in a special gesture of regard. They nearly collided with Wiley as the deckhand made to enter.

Skipper Gatt went on down the roadway. Wiley plucked at Will's sleeve.

'Come along. I'd like a word with you.'

There was a touch of command in his voice that rankled. Will was about to protest and put the sorry, twisted man in his place. He thought better of it and followed Wiley. They walked toward the center of town where the small cathedral stood.

Wiley clawed into his pocket and produced a small penny notebook.

'You'll have to start earning your keep.'

'I'm not paid for what I do.'

'The more fool you are then, though I find it hard to believe what with being the owner of two fine inns and all.'

Will grunted impatiently and regretted that he'd found it necessary to protest that he was an unpaid patriot.

Wiley handed over the book. 'You're the listening post, all the same, and now you'll be a gatherer of information as well. Here's four what are with us in this area. That includes one who's a traveler and passes through often. There's a small history of each of them in there. It might prove useful if any change their minds. Read it, remember it, and get rid of it.'

Will glanced through the pages. Bostock's name was not among them.

'There's a man in Stromness who claims he was recruited some time ago. I can't be sure. It's possible he only had a drunken conversation with the agent called Simmons.'

'Is this man Ian Bostock?'

Will nodded.

'I was told about him.' Wiley tilted his head and looked up at Will with a twisted, unpleasant quickening of the lips. 'No need to for you to read about his history. You're married to his daughter, after all. I was to give you this instruction about him. First, I was to tell you that Conrad said you were right about Simmons. That we get a lot of sorry damn fools in this business from time to time. But we've leadership and organization now and it won't happen again.'

'What about Bostock?' Will asked, impatient with the twisted man's garrulity.

'Simmons did recruit him in a half-assed sort of way. He was a little looser with his tongue than he had a right to be. So there's nothing for it but to use this Bostock if we can as long as we can. Do you get the meaning?'

Will rubbed his hands against the cold that suddenly seemed to flood there.

'Who is to say when he's no longer useful?'

Wiley seemed to delight in the burden he sensed he was placing on Will.

'You are, Mr. Hartz. You're the sole judge of when Bostock should be retired.'

'Do these orders come from Conrad?'

'How the hell should I know? I work on a mail packet. I'm just a mailman.'

He laughed. It was the queer laugh that had so enraged Will at the death of the island pony. Will averted his eyes and raised his hands to his ears, to shut out the sound. When he looked again, Wiley was several paces away standing in the open space before the church.

Will envied the 'mailman.' Wiley had no attachments, had gathered no affections. He watched Wiley pass into the cool dark of the church and wondered why he entered there.

In the months that followed Will had occasion to meet, in the way of trade, the men on the list in the notebook. He'd read the brief dossiers and tucked them away in the welter of papers that filled the locked drawer of his desk. To burn the pages at some dark hour and in some clandestine manner smacked too much of the melodramatic to suit him. It was, too, a rather slender reminder of his true calling.

Robert Dennerson was a man of about fifty years of age. He was a quiet fellow with a bitter mouth who occasionally came into the Fox and Grapes for a small whiskey. Will knew him to be a failed doctor who had been unable to fight the twin disasters of alcoholism and chronic bronchitis in the city of London. The alcohol had killed his practice. The lung ailment drove him out of the polluted air of the city. Asthma drove him to the Orkneys, Ultima Thule, and the end of the world. He now made his living collecting and preparing specimens of marine life for sale through a biological supply house in England.

Will poured a glass of whiskey and brought it to Dennerson as he sat in a corner near the window. It was a quiet part of the day. Late sunlight dappled his hands. He looked up at Will with eyes that were veils of regret. He touched the glass with one extended finger.

'Will you sit down, Mr. Hartz? Will you join me?'

'I'll sit with you, but it's too early in the day for me to have a dram.'

Will instantly regretted what might seem a rebuke. Dennerson smiled slightly and touched the ends of his neat mustache.

'A very wise view of things. I offer that as a personal as well as a medical opinion.'

He lifted the glass with great care and took a carefully controlled sip. It was pitiable to see a man sipping slowly at one or two whiskeys when his true desire was to consume enough to find oblivion.

'The authorities have forbidden me the freedom of certain portions of the shore. It might indicate some reinforcement of defenses hitherto unknown to us.'

He'd spoken the word 'authorities' as though it were alum. He'd always been a reactionary in his political views. He would have been pleased if an absolute monarchy or a dictatorship had governed Britain. He had little taste for the common man or common authority. In this fashion he added to his sense of isolation and superiority.

'You've read the newspaper account of the Führer's latest pronouncement?'

'Yes.'

'How did you view it?'

'It seemed reasonable and conciliatory.'

'The kid glove, my friend. He offered cooperation to Eden and Léon Blum, yes, but then he made his declarations. He will have the restoration of Germany's colonies. He will not countenance the spread of Russian Bolshevism into Western Europe. He repudiates, entirely, the admission Germany was forced to sign at Versailles that she was responsible for the Great War.'

He was caught up in the fanaticism that was a reflection of Hitler's fanaticism. He forgot himself and took a large swallow of the whiskey. He choked upon it.

When he'd recovered, he said, 'This is a glorious time to be a German.' He waved a languid hand. 'But, of course, you are a Swiss.'

Will realized with something of shocked surprise that this man thought of himself as a German. It was clear why Intelligence considered him safe. He was unpaid. His loyalty was secured by his belief that he was one of an Aryan, intellectual, counterrevolutionary elite.

Sean Selene was an Irishman and a separatist. He hated England and all things English with a fierce passion. He was two generations removed from County Ulster in the North of Ireland but talked constantly about returning to his homeland and setting it free. He was outspoken and violent in his expressed hates.

He had a newspaper folded and stuffed into the pocket of his jacket when he burst into the pub at evening time.

Will was in quiet conversation with Skipper Gatt. Selene ordered up a pint and declared he would buy a round for all if he only had the wherewithal.

'Failing that, I hope you'll all lift your glasses with me at the news of a brave thing this Adolf Hitler's done.'

'What brave thing?' someone challenged.

'He's taken personal charge of the armed forces and of the foreign policy of his country.'

'What in the hell would you know of such things as armed forces, Sean?'

'I know a thing or two about English guns and the brave lads that beat them out of Ireland.'

'Oh, leave off, man. Will we hear about all your distant relatives who were men on the run during the "troubles" while you and your da and your grandee were safe here in Scotland?'

Selene laughed and finished off the pint. Someone ordered him another, for he was always good for a bit of fun and no one took him seriously.

The man who stood him the pint wanted more of his outrageous opinions.

'Tell us about foreign policy. You should know something of that since you're living here an alien and subject still to the English king.'

'The king and all his little men in striped pants are shaking in their patent leather shoes this very minute.'

'Will you go to join Hitler's new armies, Sean?'

'Well, now. I would but for one thing. I can't abide the taste of their lager beer.'

Martin Deutsch owned a small shop near the center of town where he fashioned and repaired shoes and made other trifles of leather. He came, upon occasion, to the Fox and Grapes and silently drank a beer. He enjoyed beer, and he enjoyed the company of people. He didn't enjoy conversation. He reported small gossips to Will and made a quiet show of deference to him as the local leader. The bits of information were largely of no value. They were passed on with great solemnity. He reported every least thing.

'A sailorman was in my shop today.'

Will waited for him to go on. Deutsch waited for Will to urge him to tell more. Finally Will said, 'Yes?'

'He wanted his boots calked against the wet.'

'A natural request.'

'He said it was because he was off as a civilian instructor on a training vessel.'

'Yes, I see.'

Deutsch waited for further signs of approbation. Will wondered what the man expected in return for the shreds of useless information. Deutsch was paid for his services. His concern was the money, small as it was, and nothing else. He was known as a Belgian. Will knew what others didn't know. Deutsch had been tried by his country for cowardice in the face of the enemy during the Great War and had narrowly missed prison. Now he seemed to want some manner of commendation from Will.

Will felt a sudden flooding impatience and irritation with this fellow he had to cope with.

'Any other news?'

'Mrs. Dranger and her family are moving to the mainland.'

Will almost burst out laughing.

'Do you know,' he asked carefully, 'that German troops entered Vienna at the request of the new Austrian chancellor, Seyss-Inquart?'

'Seyss-Inquart?' Deutsch responded idiotically. He sat there dumbly. He knew some other comment was being asked of him. 'Do you think that is a good thing?'

'Yes. The division of Germany and Austria has always been an artificial one. Now they will be one nation under one leader as it should be.'

Deutsch nodded his head and seemed pleased to have been party to the opinion.

When he left, Will thought of what he had said and he believed it to be true. He felt a lifting of his spirits. All these years of loyalty were finding focus in the accomplishments of Hitler. The man he'd once laughed at no longer seemed a figure of fun. He had proved himself a leader any German should be proud to follow. Yes, these were glorious times in which to know oneself to be a German.

For that moment and for a long while afterward Will kept that newfound pride in one of the many compartments of his mind. He had successfully trained himself to keep the many aspects of his life carefully separate. He had become a good secret agent.

CHAPTER 21

In the conversations that occupied the patrons of the Fox and Grapes in September of the year 1938, there was an expressed indignation laced through with real anger at the arrogance of the new Germany. There was, as well, the subtle bell note of a fearful doomsday tolling. Veterans of the Great War, their memories suddenly freshened by the resurgence of German militarism, feared the new continental involvement that seemed to loom beyond the horizon of complaisance.

On the thirtieth, when the four powers, Germany, the United Kingdom, France and Italy, agreed to the cession of the Sudeten Territory to Germany, a great trembling sigh of relief echoed from the halls of power and throughout Great Britain even to such a simple gathering place of men as the Kirkwall public house.

'What do you think, Will, of this arrangement we've entered into?' Skipper Gatt asked.

'As a traditional neutralist and noncombatant I must say it seems a sensible enough solution. If restoring this bit of land to Germany, if repairing some of the excesses of Versailles can insure peace, it seems well worth it.'

'Little Czechoslovakia lost the territory and had little enough to say about it in those great councils.'

Will smiled at his friend affectionately. Skipper Gatt had that most endearing of all the qualities of the independent and proud island Scots. He hated to see any weak thing put upon. He was the ever-faithful champion of the underdog.

'Besides, I don't believe the way to stop a starving, ravening dog from attack is to tease him with a small bit of the joint.'

'England doesn't seem to be gulled by this talk of "peace in our time." She prepares for war.'

'Then you think there will be war?'

'No. I think Hitler has recovered what he believed was Germany's by right. I believe him when he says he has no further territorial ambitions.'

'I hope so, Will. But somehow I'm afraid the trenches being dug in Hyde Park, plans put forth for the rationing of petrol and talk of universal conscription mean more than the exercise of simple prudence.'

'It might be a sufficient show of strength to deter Hitler even if he has taken the old Prussian dream of conquest for his own. Better safe than sorry in any event.'

Skipper Gatt nodded and returned to a silent brooding as Will walked the length of the bar counter to serve a new customer just entered.

Harry Prester was a salesmen traveling in ladies' corsets and underthings. He was small and thin and quick. He told funny stories with a racy tang to them and was a great favorite among the customers. He was the fourth name on Will's list of agents.

He set a large sample case on the floor beside his stool. He placed the other on the counter top and ordered a pint.

'In here,' he said, slapping the imitation leather of the case, 'is the most amazing collection of garments women have ever draped on their bodies. They're enough to make a man paw the dirt and bay at the moon.'

The men, gathered around him, urged him for a view.

'Here, now, that wouldn't be quite proper, would it? I mean to say these flimsies, naughty but nice, are for the private pleasures of wife and husband.'

He laughed and accepted the drinks urged on him. He winked at Will as though to say, 'See how well I get the ear of these silly fools? See how well I drink at no cost to myself?'

He fiddled and diddled them along, never tiring of the game. The customers gave up at closing time, disappointed on the one face of it but still happily titillated on the other.

Mr. Dowdy went early to his bed. Prester chattered softly to Will as he washed up for the night.

'You know how to work a wireless?'

Will shook his head.

'You'll need some instruction then. Where and when's most convenient?'

'I'm off for Stromness tomorrow. It will have to be now or early in the morning.'

'We'll need a private place to set the equipment up. Any secret hidey-hole available around the pub? Some corner of the cellar?'

'Mr. Dowdy knows every mouse hole and spider watch down there. There's a shed, never used, out near the wall in back.'

'Never do. We'd have to run a power line to it. I imagine it will have to be someplace in your own house.'

Will felt a sudden wrenching in him. One of the walls of the isolating compartments of his mind was to be breached. Another wall. He could see the necessity in serving his oath to Germany of bringing this business into his home. But it would be close to his wife and his innocent son. It seemed to him a monstrous betrayal of their trust.

'I suppose that will have to be. There is a room off to one side in the cellar.'

'Private?'

'As private as one can make a place in a home with a good wife.'

'Nosey, is she?'

'A very tidy housekeeper who abhors dusty, dirty corners.'

'Tell you what. Most married fellows I know take up some pastime or other. A hobby, you see? Sometimes they're serious about it. More often it's just an excuse to have a private place for a quiet drink.'

'I have no use for such a place.'

'Course not. That would be a funny sight. A man what owns a tavernful of whiskey sneaking a drink on the sly. But what I mean is you could take up a hobby that would require a locked room.'

'I have an interest in cataloguing the various plants and flowers that grow upon the islands.'

'That's a start. You collect specimens you wouldn't want disturbed by accident.'

'Perhaps I could purchase a camera to record them.'

'And the necessary equipment and chemicals to develop your own film. That would give you a good reason for keeping such dangerous things locked away.'

Will nodded and felt vaguely pleased with his invention.

'You've a good head for trickery,' Prester remarked. 'Now you can buy the camera and whatever tomorrow. For the present we can pretend I've brought the necessary trays and chemicals and such along from the mainland. Shall we go along to your place?'

At home Julie was at her knitting. When Will explained the reason for the late-night guest, she went along to their bedroom and left them to their toys.

He conducted Prester downstairs and showed him the small

storage room. It was cluttered with bits and pieces of things, but Will had not lived in the house long enough to acquire any great accumulation of things. He cleared a table.

Prester fashioned a kind of safe by the clever manipulation of several small crates. The radio was easily concealed and could be found only in a more than casual search. He tapped into the overhead light source and ran a wire concealed by a crack in the boards overhead to the back of the radio set. He worked swiftly, quietly and with great concentration. He was at home with his specialty. Will wondered idly how many similar installations the man had made.

'This wireless works on a narrow band. The beam is focused and has considerable range for its size. Here's a copy of the Morse code.' He handed over a pasteboard printed with the letters of the alphabet, each one followed by a series of dots and dashes.

'Sit down here.'

Will sat on an upturned crate before the wireless. Prester wired a telegrapher's key to the transmission pole. He fingered it, and the metal sent out tiny blue sparks.

'Try it.'

Will's great fist made clumsy slow work of it.

'It will come with practice. No need to have it hooked up to the set while you learn your way around it. When you're good enough, you'll be given a schedule of transmission times. You must keep the messages as short as possible. We don't want an English monitoring station getting a fix on you.'

Prester straightened up and rubbed his hands together. He took up the second case and opened it. It was filled with the samples of his cover trade. He took out a bit of sheer black cloth.

'A gift for the wife.'

Will was about to refuse. Julie, he knew, was no stranger to such erotic bits of underwear, and he wanted nothing to remind her of that past life. She now wore good, sensible cotton pants and had even grown shy about Will seeing her in such an intimate garment. Perhaps she had grown a bit too prim and matronly. He took the lace chemise and thanked Prester.

Prester bustled into his coat and picked up the cases. 'I'll be through here again. Next time I'll bring some batteries. They'll be short-term backup power in case there's a power failure.'

'There are enough of them in these islands.'

'Exactly.'

After Prester was gone, Will fashioned a hasp and closure from a few bits of scrap metal and secured the door to the storage room with a padlock.

He slept the night feeling the small bulk of the wireless like a weight pinning him to the actuality of his oath to Germany.

In the morning Will set out on his journey to Stromness. It was more than the inspection tour of business that might be usual with a man who owned two establishments.

Skipper Gatt had been witness to some remarkable indiscretions upon the part of Bostock. He carried the tales reluctantly out of deep friendship to Will, for he was no common gossip. Word had come from Wee Jock as well, complaining of the brazen arrogance of the man who let no one forget that his son-in-law was the proprietor of the Sailing Master. It was apparent that Bostock, with money in his pockets from his job at Lyness, could, for the first time in years, buy rounds of drinks shoulder to shoulder with other men. He'd taken up with a raucous filthy-mouthed group of stevedores and dockers, who had been attracted to the Flow for the work that was suddenly available for their gypsy kind. Bostock had arrogantly made the private saloon bar of the Sailing Master the headquarters for the drinking and gambling of his soiled society. The presence was very definitely hurting the local custom of the establishment.

Jock was prepared to throw them out, bodily if need be, but was uncertain in his resolve because Bostock hinted at secret knowledge that would be damaging to his son-in-law.

Skipper Gatt confirmed that, for he had been witness to it.

'What hidden knowledge?' Will had asked him. His friend looked into Will's eyes to establish without doubt his trust in him.

'He hints that you're not a Swiss national. He suggests you're really a German.'

Will had laughed, hoping the hollow fear didn't cause his voice to ring false. 'Some sort of enemy agent?'

'No, no, not that. Not right out, though he hints at that, too. More along the lines that you're a foreigner and worse, a German come here to profit from the people who've lived here all their lives.'

'So.'

'There'll be more of such slanders, Will. Not only from a

fool like Bostock. While this trouble lasts, it will be excuse for people to hate you for making a success where they could not.'

'If it comes to actual war.'

'You'll have a bad time of it.'

'Is there nothing I can do?'

Skipper Gatt shook his head. It was not so much in sadness and regret at what his friend might suffer. It was a clear reading of the nature of men and events. It was something to be reckoned with and not simply deplored.

'You'll not be alone, Will.'

It was a declaration of sturdy friendship and fellow love. It was an open declaration and therefore vaguely embarrassing to the sea captain. He went on without pause. 'For the present you'd best have a talk with Bostock.'

In that talk Will knew he must display the proper anger and indignation at the disloyalty of his wife's father. At the same time he must neutralize Bostock as a threat to his clandestine activities. As he journeyed to Stromness, he puzzled over what level of fury would seem proper for the one, yet not cause suspicion of the other. He could protest neither too little nor too much, and such a careful balance was alien to Will's candid nature.

When Will arrived at the Sailing Master, Wee Jock greeted him with open arms but with a smile that held less than his usual good spirits.

'I've come to do what I can,' Will said.

'Managing a pub can be a fearful thing. And to think I once envied you somewhat.'

Wee Jock seemed about to say something more but, instead, gave a skitterish sort of laugh. It had a devious, oblique quality in it unnatural to the direct little man. Will spoke to express his understanding.

'I've not made it easy for you.'

'Lord, Will,' Jock protested, 'no man could have been fairer than you have been to me.'

'I speak of this matter of Ian Bostock.'

'I haven't enjoyed complaining to you, Will. Sending notes and hearsay like a small boy who can't fight his own battles.'

'You've been patient in this. I have placed a kind of protection around Bostock in this place because of his relationship to my wife.'

Wee Jock attempted a grin to ease the solemnity Will was

displaying. 'In-law troubles. Classic ailments for a married man.' Will grinned back at the little man with affection. 'Well, I've come to effect what cure I can.'

Will hoped that the confrontation which he sought with Bostock could be arranged privately. He himself was vulnerable if his father-in-law was prodded into indiscretions that would force Will to make a bold and public argument with him. According to the principle that it was best to let sleeping dogs lie, he would have preferred no confrontation at all. He knew, however, that to ignore Bostock's rude and oblique insults would stand as proof that something was indeed shady about Will Hartz, the stranger and alien.

He must, for the sake of domestic tranquillity in the Sailing Master and the prevention of any possible suspicion against him, neutralize Bostock cleanly and clearly. How best to do it was the problem. He knew that weak men could be dangerous men. They soon forgot or rationalized any fear they felt, named it caution and found other, more devious methods than direct attack to bring down their enemy. If Will moved with too much energy against Bostock, it might well prod the man to action. He must be subtle and hope that Bostock recognized a serious but veiled threat.

He went over the books with Wee Jock during the noon closing and enjoyed a meal in the MacClintocks' quarters where once he and Julie had lived. There was about the meal the cheerful warmth of homecoming.

Bostock and two of his cronies were the first of the evening's customers. Will was glad of it and intended to get Bostock alone as soon as possible in the family lounge.

Bostock made a great show of surprise at Will's presence and a greater show of giving his son-in-law a warm welcome. All the while his eyes, ferretlike, sought out Wee Jock. His look said that first Wee Jock must see how warmly he was regarded by his daughter's husband and, second, that Bostock was aware Will had come at MacClintock's cry for help and he would pay for it.

'So here you are, and it's little enough I get to see you.'

Will recoiled from his embrace. The man was, so soon in the day, well on the way to being drunk.

'I'd have you meet two friends of mine,' Bostock went on loudly. 'This here fellow is Tanner Pace and this Corly Beechum. Both mates of mine and working partners.' He laughed wildly, and the two rough men, as drunk as he, joined him. There was some secret joke among them.

'This is my very successful and most generous son-in-law, Will Hartz.'

Tanner reached out a great paw. 'What was that name?'

'Will Hartz. Wilhelm Hartz. You'll buy us a drink, son-in-law? You'll show my friends the hospitality of the house?'

Will caught Wee Jock's eye and nodded. Bostock turned his head sharply. 'Three whiskeys.'

Tanner's hand was still extended, unclasped by Will's. The grin remained on his face like a rictus of pain.

'Wilhelm, is it? Like Kaiser Wilhelm, is it?'

Wee Jock made a clatter setting down the glasses to be poured.

'Your whiskey,' Will said.

'I mean, is it a foreigner, even a rich one, thinks himself too good to shake the hand of an Englishman?'

Will hesitated for only a moment then took Tanner's hand and pumped it three times in the formal, Germanic fashion.

'Let go of my dirty paw pretty quick, isn't it?'

'Is everything you say a question?' Will asked.

'What the hell does that mean?'

'It means that a man who asks insulting questions is looking for support from his friends in his provocation of another man.'

'Here, now, I won't have any quarreling between my good friends and my good son-in-law,' Bostock said with heavy joviality. He placed a glass of whiskey in Tanner's hand. Tanner stared at Will.

'You've got a fancy way of speaking for a foreigner.'

'I'm a citizen of Great Britain.'

'You're a goddamn German, is what my friend Bostock says.'

Bostock's face was drained of blood in the instant. He took the whiskey in one swallow and ordered another. He made a show of putting the money for it on the bar top. When he turned, he met Will's steady observation.

'Here now, Will, I never said you was a German.'

'You did, Bostock.' Tanner cut him off at the tongue.

The man Beechum had been quiet all this while, grinning at the quarrel that was brewing. Now he threw in his lot with his crony.

'German or no, Hartz, you're a bloody foreigner, and that's

true enough. You've come here and put up businesses to make profits on the people born here.'

'For Christ's sake,' Bostock interposed shrilly, 'there's no cause for this kind of talk. Here I've introduced you to my own sweet daughter's husband. What will he think of me?'

'He thinks poorly of you, mate. Can't you see the way his nose wrinkles like he's smelling piles of shit?'

Beechum moved in closer to Will, standing shoulder to shoulder with his friend Tanner.

'He's a German son of a bitch and probably worse according to your own words, friend.'

Wee Jock had come silently from around the bar. He held a bung starter in his hand.

Will closed his eyes as though he were infinitely weary. 'I want no disturbance here.'

Tanner and Beechum backed off a pace, not in retreat, but in preparation for battle. Bostock was beside himself in fear and agitation.

The door opened, and Skipper Gatt came into the pub unnoticed. He summed up the meaning of the tableau and made no sound but moved quietly within striking distance.

'Well, how will you have it, you son of a bitchin' German bastard?' Tanner threatened.

Will struck so suddenly no one else had a chance to move. He drove a fist into Tanner's gut. The man fell into Wee Jock who pushed him aside to free his own hand for a blow with the pike he held. Will struck out in a countermovement against Beechum. The man staggered back. Before Beechum could recover, Bostock was on him, pummeling him with short, ineffectual blows. Will dragged him off. Together, he and Wee Jock reached down to collar Beechum and lift him to his feet.

Behind Will, Tanner made his feet. He pulled a sailor's clasp knife from his pocket and revealed the blade. Skipper Gatt picked up the half-full whiskey bottle still standing on the bar and coldcocked him.

They made an arrangement of Beechum, still mobile, and Tanner, dangling over his mate's shoulder, and pushed them to the door. Skipper Gatt made a regretful sound in his throat. He looked at Will.

'I'm very sorry, Will.'

'It's all right. They don't count for much.'

Will turned to Bostock, who stood bent forward as though trying to hide behind his own spine.

'I've never said naught against you, Will. Not things like what they said,' Bostock whimpered. Will took a step toward him. Bostock's mouth opened as though he were about to scream and was suddenly and violently ill. The vomit sprayed about the floor stinking of alcohol and fear. Will took him in hand and led him out to the convenience shed in the tavern yard.

Will held him as he finished retching. Bostock shook his head from side to side with a rolling motion like that of a puppet with a broken string.

'Lost my job. Bloody bastards sacked me and threw me out. I did it for you. I got in trouble for you.'

Will felt an overpowering urge to smash the fool not only for indulging in dangerous gossip about him, but for daring to suggest that they could, in any way, for any reason, have interests in common.

'Whatever do you mean?' Will grated.

Bostock scrabbled into his pocket and withdrew a crumpled piece of paper.

'This is the reason I was sacked out of Lyness.'

Will unfolded and smoothed out the bit of paper. In the dim light he could barely make out that it was a roughly drawn map of Scapa Flow. Bostock's crabbed hand had indicated the open channels into the fleet anchorage. Other marks were clearly the locations of the blockships sunk in the last war to protect the entrances. Their locations were common knowledge. There were other marks that were clearly indications of other concrete hulls that would be sunk in future to tighten the throats of the channels. There were dotted lines and barely legible writing indicating where the submarine nets would be placed.

Bostock, the idiot, had stumbled upon the plans of the Scapa Flow defenses.

Will looked from the paper to Bostock. The man was weaving from side to side and staring stupidly at his shoes that were becoming soaked through in a puddle of his own urine.

'They discovered you preparing this?' Will asked.

Bostock's head snapped up as he made an effort to focus his attention.

'I'm no damn fool. They just found me wandering about in a place that was restricted. I gave them a dumb show, and they thought I was too stupid to know where I was.'

Will smiled softly to himself. Truth was Bostock had been

too dumb to know the value of the map but foxy enough to gather up the scrap of information like a jackdaw for future trade.

He would never know how Bostock had come by the chart, but he could imagine some officer responsible for its security failing to lock it away properly. When he'd discovered that Bostock had apparently blundered into the area it wouldn't have done to report his own dereliction of duty. Bostock was simply let go for drunkenness or incompetence, which was true enough, and no investigation necessary to plague the officer.

'It's worth something to you, isn't it, Will?'

'What possible use would this scrawl be to me? I don't even have an idea of what it is.'

'You know well enough, you German bastard,' Bostock hissed in sudden fury. Will was reminded of the great water rats he sometimes confronted unexpectedly in the dark. 'Don't I know you're a fucking saboteur?'

Will raised a hand to his own face in a gesture both weary and patient. Bostock cried out in terror.

'Calm yourself. I have no intention of hurting you. But you must stop speaking such slanders against me.'

'Good God, Will, I'm with you. Don't you know that? You and me and Simmons all together.'

'Simmons is dead,' Will said flatly.

Bostock began to tremble uncontrollably. He stared at Will in mute horror. 'Did you do for him, Will?'

Will said nothing, instinctively knowing that silence was the more fearsome response.

'Oh, good Lord, Will. It's not much that I want.'

'What do you want?'

'I want a place to rest. A warm corner by the fire.'

'You have a cottage.'

'It's no home to me with the wife dead and Julie gone.'

'You have your other children to care for.'

'The eldest, Paulie, is head of the house now and has no use for me.' Will's reasonable and quiet questioning was acting as reassurance to Bostock. He was quick to grasp the slender hope that he might gain his ends. 'You could give me back my job as barman here at the Sailing Master.'

'You've caused too much trouble for Wee Jock. There's no way for that arrangement to work.'

Bostock grinned to himself. Of course he knew that. He moved a step closer to his goal.

'I can see that. But in the Fox and Grapes?'
Will regarded him thoughtfully for a long moment.
'Julie won't have you in the house. You know that?'
'I wouldn't ask to be invited. Even so I could get a glimpse of my grandson on his way to school or at play.' Tears formed in his eyes at the thought of being a poor, old, child-deprived grandda.
What a pitiful old fraud, Will thought. In this moment he could almost like the shameless charlatan.
'You can find me a bed. In the back shanty. Anywhere,' Bostock pleaded.
'We'll do what we can. Come along.'
A small moan escaped Bostock as he followed Will back to the tavern. The purging of his stomach had done little to sober Bostock up. He begged a drink to steady himself when they were inside, and Will allowed it. He was drunker than ever by the time they returned to Kirkwall on Skipper Gatt's craft. Drunker still when Will put him to bed in the shanty back of the Fox and Grapes. He was still fairly drunk when he scratched upon the kitchen door next morning. Mrs. Dowdy fed him, but there was strong disapproval in her manner.
Bostock kept himself away but found a moment to accost Will.
'Thanking you, Will. I was in a bad way last night.'
Will said nothing but stared at Ian in that same discomfiting way he had in the convenience.
'I busied myself a bit this morning,' Bostock said. 'I cleaned the outhouse summat.'
Will noted the craft that sprang into the man's face.
'That was good of you. We'll make a job for you here.'
'I had a bit of paper in my pocket. Didn't I give it over to you last night?'
Will hesitated, trying to judge how much of the night Bostock clearly remembered.
'You had something. I have no idea what happened to it.'
Bostock patted his pockets as though checking once again. He grinned. 'Well, not to worry.'

That night Will left the Fox and Grapes well before closing. Bostock was in the cellar cleaning up some small accumulation of cartons and the like. There was very little actually to be done, for Mr. Dowdy had always kept a spotless house and Will was, if possible, even more meticulous. It was makework to allow Bostock to keep out of the wind and out of the way of the Dowdys. He seemed to know it and had accepted his supper and a pint of ale with an excessive air of humility and gratitude.

At the supper table Will was about to tell Julie that her father had lost his job and come to Kirkwall, perhaps to stay for a time. Julie anticipated him.

'So the bastard's come, is he?'

Will had never grown used to her angers, they were so rare. He shrugged.

'He lost his position at Lyness.'

'And you've made him welcome.'

'I gave him a place to sleep and something to eat.'

'And now he'll stay on like a cur at the butcher's back door. I don't understand it. None of it. Not at all. This man you choose to remind me is my father was better off left in Stromness.'

'He was causing difficulties with the MacClintocks.'

'Better he should cause difficulties here? What is it in you, Will, that would make you take care of the brute? Do you carry a guilt of some sort?'

'He's your father and young John's grandfather.'

'He is a bastard.'

'I'll see to it that he never bothers you.'

'Oh, I know that you will. But there's an evil about him, and I don't want him near me or my son.'

'He's an old man who may soon die.'

It was the end to the quarrel and an end to Julie's anger. She came around the table and kissed him lovingly for the generosity of him, ill conceived though she thought it to be.

Will was allowed an hour to play with young John, though it was past the boy's bedtime. Finally, when the child's laughter grew a bit strained with weariness, Julie took him to his sleep and prepared herself for bed as well.

'Are you coming then, Will?' she called down the stairwell.

'I thought I might work for an hour or so in the darkroom,' he answered.

'Don't stay up the night,' she said, and Will understood by her tone of voice that she was that night prepared for sleep and not for pleasure.

He went downstairs and unlocked the door to his small photographic laboratory. He sat on a stool and reexamined the bit of paper he had taken from Bostock the night before. He arranged the information in the briefest and best manner. He turned on the transmitter and waited for the tubes to glow. He consulted his pocket watch and at the proper hour he sent the intelligence over the airwaves.

He gave little thought to the consequences of the act but was vaguely pleased that his mission had, at last, proved of some small value.

CHAPTER 22

The actual work of the defenses of Scapa Flow as outlined in the map copied by Bostock was slow to begin. The booms across the Hoy, Switha and Hoxa sounds remained in a condition so decrepit as to render them totally ineffectual. The old blockships, hulls doomed after the Great War to be scrapped but filled instead with concrete and sunk in the Skerry and Kirk sounds, were breaking apart from twenty years of battering surge and storm and the roaring flood race. The flood race itself, moving with fearful power, was still considered the ultimate defense for the fleet anchorage and the naval base at Lyness on the Isle of Hoy.

Elsewhere Britain was gripped in the twin reactions to impending cataclysm, turmoil and malaise. The *Aquitania*'s regular Atlantic crossing was canceled, and she was employed instead to transfer strengthening troops to the garrison in Palestine. The people of London were engaged in a great exodus to the less populated reaches of the British Isles, although London County Council plans to evacuate fifty thousand schoolchildren were postponed. The Royal Navy began mobilization. Still England wanted to believe that Mr. Chamberlain had indeed returned from Munich with 'peace in our time.'

In the north of Scotland town-bred military personnel entrained to form a garrison at Lyness.

A contract was let by the Admiralty to one Will Hartz, tavern keeper and provisioner, to provide light bitters, ales, squashes and suitable foodstuffs for a canteen at the base.

Other tavern keepers in the islands, other provisioners had offered bids on the Admiralty contract. They smiled and shook his hand. They congratulated him on his continuing success. The smiles were of cardboard and the handshakes as limp as dead fish. The words that sounded like 'the best of luck' really meant 'damn your foreign eyes.' Skipper Gatt and others assured him that his friends gave no heed to the whispered slanders against him. Will regretted, with infinite sadness, that they found it necessary to so reassure him, to remind him after so long a time that there were some who thought of him as a stranger and not as an islander. But in a secret part of himself he accepted the pain of conversations interrupted by his appearance, of subtle withdrawal, of friendships weakened as the punishment due him. He was, after all, a deadly stranger in their midst.

The new paradox further complicated his life and his relationships. He had no ground for protest or for righteous indignation. He sometimes wondered how he would react were he truly an innocent victim of their libelous innuendo. Since he had no truth to deal honestly with, how could he dare criticize the envy of those who calumniated him?

How could he dare feel betrayed by someone like Wee Jock? When he went to the Sailing Master intending to offer a partnership to his tavern manager in this new enterprise, Jock acted shy of the matter, reluctant to discuss the details of the operation. After several awkward moments he finally spoke his heart.

'There's something I must tell you, Will.'

Will waited for the man to release his burden.

'I want to tell you I made a bid on the canteen contract for Lyness.'

Will gave the revelation a moment's thought and hid the sudden pang of regret. Finally he nodded.

'You had a perfect right to do so. A perfect right to establish yourself as an independent tradesman.'

'I know that, and I knew you'd say that. The thing that's been soured in me is knowing I did it without telling you first. It wasn't proper or manly, and I'm apologizing for it.'

The damn of his reluctance had broken, and he was discharging himself of his guilty feelings in a flood. Will raised a hand attempting to stem it.

'I've felt badly about it,' Wee Jock rushed on. 'I knew I couldn't rid myself of the pain in my belly till I confessed to you.'

'Please, please. It's not necessary.'

'Perhaps not for you to hear it, but it is for me to say it. None of my own people has ever been as good to me as you have, Will.'

A sick emptiness gathered itself around the words in the very instant of their utterance. The hollowness filled the room. Wee Jock battled with his tongue trying to call back the words.

'I didn't mean that at all the way it fell out. I meant the people I was born and raised with. The island people.'

'I understand.' Will smiled gently. 'I understand that it isn't enough to be called Will instead of Wilhelm, to prepare a traditional haggis for the Christmas feast, to marry an English woman and have an English son, to live twenty years in a lonely place and to trill one's *r*'s.'

'Good God, Will, don't go on this way.'

There were tears in the little man's eyes as round and solid as he was.

Will laughed softly. 'Now I must ask your forgiveness. Here I sit playing upon your sympathies. I say again you had every right to better yourself. I'm glad that you've told me. I know you to be my good, good friend.'

Later Will admitted to himself that he'd made an overt plea for sympathy. That he'd felt mightily put upon. Yet he also felt himself an incredible fraud. He did not admit to himself that failing to mention the partnership in the Lyness enterprise had been a deliberate act of punishment against Wee Jock.

At Christmastime and the advent of the new year good fellowship flourished briefly. When it was past, Will became once more acutely aware of the weakening regard in which he was held by the people he'd known these many years.

He was once again visited by Prester who brought with him a supply of storage batteries for the wireless.

'I'm not certain how many more times I'll be asked to make these trips, Hartz. The closer we get to war, the harder it is for any traveling man to move about as freely as he'd like. I'm of an age where I'll be called up if the English decide, as they will do, that national conscription will have to be enforced to fill the ranks. I may be asked by our people to volunteer before that probability in order to have some small chance of maneuvering a favorable post for myself.'

Will listened patiently. He knew the thought of real war and his engagement in it frightened Prester. If conflict came, Prester might very well find himself fighting against Germans sworn in loyalty to the same nation he'd given his own oath to. There was a certain cruelty in the thought that he might indeed be killed by a German bomb or bullet.

Prester tapped the notebook to which he had transcribed in his own handwriting the coded information he had gathered on this latest tour.

'Dangerous carrying this stuff around. I don't fancy getting found out and shot as a apy.'

'Is there much danger of that?'

Prester jerked his head round like a startled animal. 'Why do you say that?'

'I simply meant your cover seems most secure. You've had no reason to suspect the British are aware of you?'

'No, but in this work how can you ever be sure? I wake up in the night after I've made an illicit contact wondering if the waiter who seemed to linger so close to my table was there to overhear what I said. I trace my steps in my mind over and over again. What did I do before the contact? What did I do after it? Was everything innocent and casual enough? I walk it through until my legs actually ache with the weariness of a long journey. Did I leave some clue for anyone who might be watching?'

Like a pair of gloves, Will thought.

'Or have they been watching me for a long time waiting for me to lead them to others?'

Will shared the man's disease. They both shook themselves as though discarding their shrouds. Prester handed over a small roll of flimsy paper no bigger than a cigarette.

'This is the information to be sent. It's to be memorized and destroyed.'

'And if captured, to be eaten with a dash of steak sauce,' Will said wryly. They both laughed, but the small joke relieved none of their apprehension.

'You are to maintain the normal schedule until the moment that war is declared,' Prester went on at last. 'After that you are to act independently. No information except that which you gather will be funneled to you. No more couriers will be risked.'

It was well after midnight when Prester finally went to his bed. Their mutual isolation and fear made them both eager for what companionship they could give each other that night.

Will walked home carrying the case of heavy batteries. There was a full moon that etched the gnarled, enduring trees along the cliffs and feathered the waves with mantles of luminescence.

He began transmission according to schedule the next night. It was a collection of information largely unintelligible to him. It took under an hour to send it all in short bursts with long waits between messages. When he was done, he set out the trays of photographic chemicals, prepared the enlarger, selected a negative of a bit of sunlit thistle and proceeded to indulge in the pastime that explained the locked cellar room.

The pastime that would have, under other circumstances. given him real unalloyed pleasure but which was, even so small a thing, spoiled by his masquerade.

When all was ready, he turned the lights off and reached for the switch of the red safelight. But something was different. His hand paused. The total, oppressive darkness that he'd become accustomed to was unfelt. There was a nearly imperceptible wash of gray, instead of velvet black. He turned to the single window set at ground level in the basement wall. A slender beam of moonlight glowed there like a shilling piece fashioned of milk. He placed a chair against the wall and stepped up on it so his eye was level with the source of light. It was a peephole that had been carefully scratched out of the black paint he'd used to make the room light safe. He placed his eye to it. A shadow moved in the shadows of the rose vines along the wall. Will felt a prickle of apprehension.

He went out into the silver night. There was nothing there by the wall. He walked to it and out along the path. He went the hundred yards to the place where the road forked one way to the cliffs and the other to the town. He chose the cliffside path. He fancied he heard running feet before him. He reached the cliff. It fell off sharply and sheered eighty feet to a tiny shingle beach. The principal path meandered on along the incline and, after several hundred yards, came to an end down by the sea. Another path, treacherous and nearly concealed. cut by winds from the face of the cliff, reached the shingle in a swifter, if more dangerous descent. It was fully light enough. and Will took that way. When his foot touched the beach, he hurried on to the place where the longer path ended. He waited there, and Bostock nearly hurried into his arms. The man's head was turned, watching along the way he'd come, worrying about pursuit.

He gave a doglike scream.

'What is it, Bostock?' Will asked.

'It's you, is it, Will? Just out for a little stroll in the moonlight.'

'I've never known you to do such a thing.'

'Oh, there's a bit of poet in all of us.'

Perhaps there is, Will thought, and a bit of the young man we all once were. A bit of the hopeful young man. All of us lost young men.

'What are you doing roaming about in the night?' Will insisted.

Bostock retreated a step and planted his feet. There was a challenge to his stance.

'All right, have it then. I was watching after you.'

'Spying on me?'

'You'd know the meaning of the word, you German bastard spy.'

'I might have caught you sneaking about and shot you for a thieving prowler.'

'You'd know about killing, too, wouldn't you?'

Will regarded the man with soft, nearly sleepy eyes. Bostock shifted a step or two to the side. Will was reminded of the way in which wild animals fight. There was a certain casual, languid grace in their combat, a slow and formal pavane in which death was a third dancer.

'Simmons more than hinted at what you were about. I can see now he was right.'

'Who was Simmons?'

'What do you mean?'

'Was he working for the Germans?'

'I don't know. He was working against those who were hurting the English people.'

'Hurting you?'

Bostock waved his mutilated hand in the air by way of answer.

'They never gave you a chance, did they? You could have done something with your life, but those secret men of power at the top never gave you a chance, isn't that it? Simmons was going to help you get your just rewards if you helped him?'

'I'll get some of them now.' Bostock grinned wildly.

'This Simmons was an Englishman then?' Will pursued.

'Yes. I don't know.'

'Perhaps he was a German if he told you he and I were somehow working together.'

'You're a spy well enough. And you probably killed Simmons.'

'If he worked with me for the same cause, why would I kill him?'

'You knew he was dead.'

'Yes.'

Will said no more, allowing the threat to lie there between them, admitting nothing, adding further confusion to the already hopelessly confused man before him. Objectively, Will admired the cool manner in which he entangled Bostock in a tangled skein of contradictions. In truth, his entire body pulsed with explosive anxiety and fear.

Bostock's eyes seemed to clear from the effort of thought. 'I've got the proof. You've got a radio in your cellar. You were using it tonight.'

'What do you want?'

'You admit it then?'

'I asked you what you want.'

Bostock gave over the small pleasure of Will's corroboration of his cleverness at once. He saw the desired victory in reach and was greedy for it.

'I know that Dowdy and his wife are talking of retirement and soon. There's too much custom in the Fox and Grapes for old folks to handle. I want to be made manager with the governor's flat above for my own.'

'I intend to convert the flat into rooms. There's not nearly enough accomodation for travelers in Kirkwall. It will mean a handsome profit.' Will spoke in reasonable tones. One businessman discussing matters of commerce with another.

'A room then.'

Will pretended to consider it.

'It might be arranged in time.'

'Are you trying to trick me?'

'I'm trying not to draw attention to ourselves now that we have interests in common.'

'Interests in common,' Bostock echoed doubtfully.

'We are comrades in more than this matter of taverns. You've known about me for some time. You knew about Simmons. You never reported either of us to the authorities.'

The threat was clear. Bostock hurried to put a good face on the guilty knowledge that was in some degree out in the open.

'What kind of man do you think I am? Would I do anything to injure Julie or little John or their own dear husband and father? I'm no political man. I simply want what's mine by rights.'

'You shall have it. All of it. You know I've won the canteen concession at Lyness?'

'I don't want to go there again.'

'Why not? It would be a way of showing the ones who sacked you that there are others who appreciate your value.'

Bostock thought of that. It pleased him.

'You'll be governor of the place. There's good bed and board goes with it.'

'With best wages?'

'Yes.'

'There's something else.'

'Yes.'

'I want the right to come into your house and sit to dinner.'

'That's a matter for my wife to decide.'

'You're the husband and master,' Bostock nearly shouted. 'You'll speak to her. You'll tell her I'm to have the child call me Grandpa and she's to call me Father. I will have some respect.'

Suddenly there were tears threatening to spill from the man's ravaged eyes.

Will reached out a hand to calm him. Unbelievably, Bostock began to slobber and cry. Will suddenly understood the man's pain of wanting a measure of respectability and kind affection. They were brothers in that regard.

'All right, man. All right. I'll speak with her.'

Bostock drew himself up. The fear was gone, the plea for respect, the threatening tears. Instead, there was arrogance and cunning.

'See that you do, Hartz.'

He walked away, scraping his shoes along the shingle. Will watched him go. He was amazed at the man's ability to change his strategies so swiftly. Surrender and attack, weakness and vainglory, supplication and threat. It was a marvel.

Bostock had left him with another thought. There was no safety for him as long as Bostock lived to blackmail him. He would have to 'retire' him. He pushed the thought away.

'Good night, Ian,' he called softly as though to give the man at least that much for his pride.

CHAPTER 23

In March, 1939, Germany occupied Czechoslovakia, and that small brave nation ceased to exist. France and Britain did nothing to honor their pledges at Munich to protect Czech integrity. They were, neither of them, prepared for war. The people prayed for peace and fled to caves of rationalization. Hitler prepared his grand design for the invasion of Poland.

Winter battled with spring during the month of April. Halfway through the thirty-one days of May winter capitulated. Bitter cold days and nights had not fled altogether but there were sunny days of such brilliance that they seemed to exist in a case of crystal. It was Will's favorite time of year. He took his son, safe in a life jacket fashioned of two resealed empty ten-pound jam cans, for long sailing trips. He allowed John to hold the tiller and was pleased at the uncommon strength the boy possessed for a child not yet five. He would place his own large hand so that it covered his son's. They laughed into each other's faces.

The Dowdys retired and gave up the flat abovestairs. The rotms were quickly let to new employees of the Admiralty office in Kirkwall. Will spent a full day, every day, in the Fox and Grapes. Julie gave over the day care of Little John to a newly established dame school in the town and served the growing custom of the tavern alongside her husband. Will was glad of her help, her company and her affection. He admitted to himself that the presence of a good island woman, wife to the proprietor, did something to deflect comment upon his accent and foreign birth which might have otherwise come from patrons newly arrived.

There were hundreds of men and women flooding into the area. New reinforcements came to the base at Lyness and bright-eyed girls to the Admiralty office. They spoke in every nuance of the English tongue, the soft trill of the Highlands, the clipped singsong of the Cockney, the hard nasality of Liverpool and Birmingham, the extraordinary musicality of the Welsh. Will's own accent was lost and softened in the babel.

Gun crews dressed in service khaki, heavy-booted and rough-handed, arrived to serve the eight antiaircraft batteries that had, at last, been emplaced to protect against attack from the air. It was generally accepted that air strike would be the logical weapon employed against the great staging base at Scapa Flow.

Sections of the British fleet were arrived at, or steaming toward, the Orkneys. Destroyers, lighters, tankers, cruisers, frigates and battleships were gathering. In event of war they would be dispatched where they would most effectively counter the first smashing blows that were sure to come.

The great battleship *Royal Oak* arrived in the Flow to join the elements of the fleet already at anchor.

The crews were given shore leave in staggered watches, and all of them found their way to the Fox and Grapes sooner or later. There wasn't much time or occasion for Will to know them really well.

There were those who engaged him in conversation comparing the conditions of this coming war to the one that was so soon past. Others wanted to speak of or locate a woman for the night. A few, the younger sailors, boylike, saw in him an old and gentle confidant of their homesickness and loneliness.

A friendly publican was as much a mark of Britain as Mum setting the kettle on the hob for tea or the cries of gulls by the sea and ravens on the shore.

Will's heart went out to them and the trials they must face. They were fresh, ruddy-faced youngsters who spoke softly to him of homely things. They were not at all like the leather-faced sailormen Will knew who'd braved Atlantic gales and would see war as a mere extension of ever-present danger. They were not even like the hardy, salt-cured island youngsters who accepted the sea as home, hearth, mother, God and all and who, with the perversity of youth, were in great part joining up in the Army or RAF for the changed adventure of it.

Will found it impossible to see these boys from farm and village colliery and city streets as his enemy. He thought of their German counterparts, blonder, paler perhaps of complexion, but so much the same. He thought of the tourist lads that had come that time ago when he'd gotten drunk with a few of them. They, and these boys he served now, had their youth written painfully on their faces. They made brave boasts, hoping they would become brave deeds.

As it will happen, out of all the faces seen and scarcely remembered, one or two imprinted themselves on Will's mind and affections.

He noticed the first, an old sailor named McLafferty, as he sat beside his friend Skipper Gatt. He was a bosun's mate on the *Royal Oak* in charge of a company of ship's boys. Their training and welfare were his responsibility, and he fretted about them like any mother over her bairn. Will went to join them, and the sailormen tipped a finger to their brows in way of greeting. McLafferty held up three fingers then, and Will served up three pints.

'Is there something troubling you, Mr. McLafferty?'

'Our friend here has the common problem of parent and child.' Skipper Gatt smiled. 'Worse, he's both father and mother to thirty of them.'

'Do you see they're gone from their homes and mums? They want to prove themselves men,' the bosun fretted. 'They strut about and throw out their chests and challenge each other to fight like young bull seals. It's not good for discipline, but still they have to try their new man's strength.'

'I'm certain the old bull keeps the peace.' Will smiled.

'I do indeed. There's other things. They get it into their heads sometimes.'

'Your good example should take care of that.'

'Well, you see, that's just the problem in the matter. I have a fierce and famous reputation for cursing a man out in half a dozen languages. It served well enough until these babes came into the service.'

Will and Skipper Gatt laughed softly in sympathy, for it was apparent the concern was a real one to McLafferty.

'Then there's the women. That's a worry that keeps me from sleep at night. These infants are made friends of by the old boys who take them off with them on leave and show them low places. They arrange carnal commerce between the lads and women of low repute.'

There was a formality in the way McLafferty phrased himself that was gently comedic. A young sailor, come back from the Mens, was approaching.

'Is it whores you mean, McLafferty?' Skipper Gatt teased.

McLafferty saw the boy. 'Good Lord, watch your tongue, man.' He turned and threw an arm about the boy's shoulders.

'Here, Jimmy, I've ordered you a pint.'

Jimmy smiled and two bright spots of color appeared high up on his pale cheeks. He blushed as easily as a girl. He took a swallow and made a face.

'Could I have a lemon squash, instead?' he asked.

'You're serving on a ship of war, lad. A tot of rum would be better, but the least that will serve a man's thirst is a pint of ale.'

It was clear that McLafferty's greatest problem was in deciding which of the ways of men were properly to be taught his young wards. It was equally clear that young Jimmy had no taste for malt.

'Make it a shandy then?' Jimmy compromised.

'You insist on spoiling good ale with lemon soda? All right then.' He patted the boy in the clumsy, loving way old fighting men approach the young, unblooded, untested ones.

Will felt Julie at his shoulder. She leaned a bit over the counter. Will saw her breasts swell warmly over the top of her blouse and thought of how the tiny girl with birdlike wrists had been sent away by a full-bodied wife.

'Jimmy, luv, when you've had enough of old men's lies and boastings, come you back into the pantry. I've a bit of raisin pie and a warm chocolate for you.'

'Mrs. Hartz, ma'am, are you trying to make this fighting man of mine soft?' McLafferty asked in mock reproof.

'I'm trying to save the poor man's stomach.' Julie laughed. She patted Jimmy's cheek. He blushed and was happy for the woman's touch.

Will went off to fill the rounds. He felt light as a young man himself as he tiptoed along the duckboard, pouring gins and whiskeys, pulling pints. A crowded friendly inn seemed to him the best of all possible places to live.

He paused a moment in some surprise. Old Siever Scarff was tucked up in the corner of the public bar looking like a small white sea urchin, his hair poking out beneath his knit cap in spiky disarray. He grinned toothlessly, much pleased at Will's reaction.

'Come to visit you, I have, Old Will. See there, Abel Ewen's come and brought me along.'

A Kirkwall man clapped the old sea dog on the shoulder.

'Have another, grandee.'

'Make it a rum,' cackled Scarff.

They were both, the old sailor and the townsman, on the way to being drunk.

'You're sure that wouldn't be –'

Old Scarff cut the man off at the root of his tongue.

'It's mother's milk to me. Didn't I serve sailing in Her Majesty's men-o'-war? God bless her soul. Dear Victoria.'

'God save the queen,' shouted the townsman and the assembled company named the royal heads of England from Henry VIII on forward, blessing them all, one and all.

A querulous man, a Mr. Teplow, who was a provisioner of the town, was sitting with a mate from one of the picket ships.

'Does this gathering of ships mean there will be war?'

'Just a precautionary measure, mate. Just a small training cruise as it were.'

'Then do you think the bloody Hun will really start up again?'

'Indeed, if he does, we'll give him hind tit to chew.'

'Old Neville Chamberlain said he came back with "peace in our time," ' someone remarked.

'What does old Churchill say?'

'He's painting pictures. All's right with the Empire.'

'God save the king.'

'God save the Virgin Queen.'

'God save Henry.'

'God save King George.'

'God save England.'

'I don't see you joining us in our toasts to king and country, Mr. Hartz,' Teplow said.

The remark rang loudly in one of those unpredictable silences that sometimes falls upon large companies of talking people. It remained like words written on stone.

'My hands are full with serving people, Mr. Teplow.'

'I wondered, that's all.'

'What did you wonder, Mr. Teplow?' Skipper Gatt asked.

'Well, everyone knows that Will Hartz is a foreigner,' Teplow said bravely, trying to make the best of what he'd got himself into.

'What does that mean, Mr. Teplow?' Abel Ewen asked and his words became thick with extended vowels. It was a sign of his anger.

'Nothing at all, except he's a stranger among us.'

'How long are you to the islands, Mr. Teplow?' old Scarff asked with wavering, honeyed tones.

'I'm here these twelve years,' Teplow blustered.

'A stranger you are. We should have you deported.'

'I'm an Englishman,' Teplow brazened.

'So is my husband, Mr. Teplow,' Julie said.

Will poured a whiskey and placed it on the bar in front of the man.

'That's by way of forgiveness for your rudeness, Mr. Teplow,' Julie said.

'And by way of accepting your apology,' McLafferty added.

Will wanted the awkwardness done with. He wanted the talk and the laughter to begin again. He wanted no apology. But the others would have it.

Teplow dipped his head. 'It was foolishness, Mr. Hartz. I regret it.'

The laughter came, but Will felt, somehow, that there were those who had been set to wondering about him again.

CHAPTER 24

On July 27 Julie, leaving young John in Will's care, journeyed to Stromness.

It was a charitable mission on behalf of her brothers and sisters. During their infancy and early childhood they had played together as all young animals will do. But in the life of the jackal's cub or eagle's fledgling, the moment of leaving comes very early on. After a passage of time, when remet, they approach each other with the same wariness they afford to strangers. Man is not so well gifted with short memories. Recognition of face and form, a remembered voice recalls old blood and associations, imposes fresh duty on long-dead responsibilities.

The brood spawned by Ian Bostock had lost the tender ties of brother and sisterhood very early on, almost as quickly as the jackal and the eagle. But enough was left that Julie felt a need to see her own in this time of trial.

She found the broken-spined croft empty of any but the life of the usual vermin that had infested her home since as long as her memory served. She began to make a half-frenzied attempt to push the filth away from bed and kitchen, but it was a vain task and one in which she could place none of her heart.

Her brother, next eldest to herself, arrived at the cottage sometime near the fall of dusk. He was a big quiet man of twenty-two, who bore a strange soft look about the eyes and mouth. Some of his father's brute coarseness of feature already marked his young face and frame, but the eyes and mouth gave the lie to the brutality there.

'Come, Paulie, where are the others?' she asked softly as he startled at the sight of her.

'Richard's gone from the islands these two years.'

Julie dipped her head in the shame of not knowing.

'Ruth?'

'Gone. Taken a lesson from you.'

'Don't hurt me so, Paulie.'

She looked at him and saw his face innocent of any cruelty. He smiled softly.

'No meaning to hurt you, Julie. I always thought you did the proper thing no matter what might have come of it.'

'The youngest?'

'I took the smallest by the hand. I found a place for them, for Morgan and Elizabeth. For Rebecca too.'

'Are they well?'

He brushed his hand along his chest in regretful apology.

'They're children of charity in the people's houses. They're treated kindly, I'm sure.'

'I am sorry.'

He reached out a great, gentle hand.

'Don't misread my meaning. We've been managing in one way or another for a long time. The old man's been no use these years. It was easier, if anything, when he went his way.'

'You did it all, with no help from me.'

He smiled and shrugged his heavy shoulders in a revealing sign of his patience.

'I've been no good sister to you.'

'Hush. You've a husband and a child of your own. Cares enough. I've taken care with no great hardship to me. I'd have them all together still but I've enlisted in His Majesty's forces and I'll soon be off to Aberdeen for training.'

'What of Robert and James?'

'Still with me, but Robert's soon to go into the army as well.'

'Both of you gone to the army?'

'We thought we might try the feel of things away from the sea.'

'I don't mean that. I mean to say that Robert's only a baby.'

'Ah, no. He's sixteen and a big lump for his age at that.'

Julie began to sob for all the lost things. Her brother took her into his arms. She had come to do what she could, offer what help and comfort she was able to give, and here she was, instead, being comforted by the little brother who had become a man.

Bostock appeared in Kirkwall. He entered the Fox and Grapes and took a place at the bar. He ordered a double tot of whiskey. Will served him and didn't ask for payment. Bostock asked for a word in private.

Will asked Skipper Gatt to tend the bar while he went to the cellar to tap a new keg. Bostock followed him down the flight of wooden steps.

The cellar seemed fresh and cool away from the heaviness

of the smoky air above. There was a loamy smell to the place and something of the odor of rotting salt fish which was not at all unpleasant. Will sat down on a cask of wine and waited for Bostock to speak.

'Have you told Julie I'd be coming to dinner?'

Will avoided a direct answer, for he hadn't approached the subject with his wife. 'Julie's at Stromness seeing to her brothers and sisters.'

Bostock read censure in the mention of his abandoned children. He hurried on to the primary purpose of his visit.

'I've heard something you'll want to know.'

'Have you?'

'The submarine nets at Hoy and Switha sounds are to be taken up.'

'They were only just this past month put down.'

Will felt a quickening within him. Perhaps he was a hound fashioned for the hunt after all.

'Makeshifts,' Bostock said with a superior air. 'Just a great show until the job could be done properly.'

'How do you know?'

Bostock placed a finger alongside his nose and winked an eye. He suggested that he was a clever fellow. Will knew he'd got the information because he was a dog in a corner that went unnoticed.

'When will the nets be taken up?'

'Then it's information worth something to you?'

Will considered the offer. Bostock suspected enough to jeopardize him as it was. Would a full admission of his true purpose and identity prove to be a fatal lack of caution? Although his own friends and acquaintances would give small notice to anything Bostock might say against him, there was always the danger that the drunkard's words might reach the wrong ears and an investigation might be launched. But Will knew he had little choice if he wanted the information Bostock had.

'Yes,' he said at last.

'I expect to be paid. Paid damn well.'

'I know that you do. I'll see that you are.'

'Where will you get the money? From your German bosses?'

'Yes.'

Bostock crowed like a rooster. 'I knew it. I knew it. Didn't I know it?'

'You're a clever man. When will the nets be taken up?'

'I want a hundred pounds in money. I want you to call me Ian. I want you to make me your manager in the Fox and Grapes. I want you to treat me with respect. I want John to call me Grandpa. I want Julie to serve me at her table and call me Pa the way she did when she was a child.'

He wanted, wanted, wanted. He sang the whole sad, sorry litany of wanting pride restored.

'The date?'

'In six weeks' time. No more.'

'I will have to have the dates more exact than that.'

'I'll see you get them. Now what about me?'

Will reached into his back pocket and removed his worn purse. He extracted twenty pounds, nearly all that was there, and handed them to Bostock.

'The balance when you bring me the rest of what I need.'

Bostock took the money eagerly in his maimed hand. He tucked the banknotes into his pocket, from which they would quickly flee in a half week's drunkenness.

'And the other things?'

'I can't make you the manager of the Fox and Grapes right away, Ian. You can understand that.'

'Yes, yes. And in Lyness I'm in a better place to listen. It can wait.'

'I will treat you with respect as long as you treat me with equal respect.'

'Fair enough.'

Will felt sick with the petty bargaining.

'I cannot order Julie's love for you or demand that she call you Pa but I'll have you at our table as I've promised before.'

Bostock nodded in reluctant agreement.

'And how can I control the words of a child?'

Bostock waved that much away. It seemed almost an embarrassment to him to have demanded such a small thing.

Will stood up, prepared to leave the cellar. 'Remember that you work for me.'

'I'm not likely to forget it.'

'If you do I may have to remind you.'

After Julie's return she seemed troubled but she took care not to burden Will with her regrets. She lavished young John with a mother's love, often to his annoyance. She babied Will shamelessly, and he was pleased by it, for he sensed her need.

There was so much love remaining that she cast about for persons upon which to discharge her affections. She brought Jimmy into the circle of those who enjoyed the gifts of her generous caring. She made a son of him or, more correctly, a dear brother. McLafferty, because of his companionship to the boy and because he seemed to have the same need to keep Jimmy safe, was included as well. They were her special sailors of all the legions of them that passed through Kirkwall.

They were invited as members of the family, as was Skipper Gatt, to John's birthday party when he became five. They sat together with Will. Julie smiled at them often. Will could see she saw a husband in himself, a grandfather for John in Skipper Gatt, a favorite uncle in McLafferty and a brother to her son in Jimmy.

When Jimmy bent close to share some secret with John, his fair hair was nearly a shade with the boy's. They indeed looked like brothers.

When Jimmy went off to supervise the games of the children, the men talked of war.

Skipper Gatt wove a cat's cradle with a length of string. His hands were uncomfortable and unhappy unless at some task.

'War will come. It's in the German nature to make a plan and to execute it no matter what stands in the way.'

'The Nazis must see we'll fight and France as well,' McLafferty said.

'No matter. Once started, they don't know how to stop. There's a stubbornness in them. A blind spot. They're like lemmings running into the sea. Into certain death. They'll run the way their prows are pointed, no matter how strong the running of the storm.'

The men nodded, and Will nodded with them. Suddenly he saw himself from outside his skin. He saw an anxious, solid tradesman, homeowner, father and husband agreeing that the enemy was impossibly foolish and impossible to deal with. He was that enemy.

He excused himself and went off to capture his son where the children played at tag. He carried him to the party table. Julie brought out the cake and the refreshments. She called the children and other guests. Will toasted his son's fifth year.

In the evening he held the child, pleasantly weary with the festive excitements, in his lap. They murmured between themselves about the day and the gifts. Will coaxed the boy to reveal the favorite among his new toys. It became a teasing game. Will tickled young John with a blunt finger. John laughed, and Julie came in to urge him on to bed. John stilled his laughter to steal a few more moments. He asked a question he thought interesting to divert his mother from thoughts of bedtime.

'What is a Nazi bastard?'

'That's no word for you to speak,' Julie scolded.

'Which word?'

Julie laughed. 'Well, both are curses after all.'

'Why do you ask, John?' Will felt a slender sickness in his throat.

'At the play school, there's some who say that's what you are.'

Will wondered how he could make a simple answer to his son's simple and direct question.

'I want to tell you –' he began slowly, but Julie cut in gently.

'It's time for your pillow,' she said lifting John from his father's lap. 'Say good-night to your da and kiss him well.'

When she had the boy to bed, Julie returned and sat on the stool at Will's feet.

'So, old husband, were you about to give the boy a solemn lecture on the nature of vicious gossip?'

'I . . . wanted to make him understand –' he began.

'Who can understand black hearts?'

She placed her head upon his knee. Will touched her hair.

'Husband?'

He increased the pressure of his hand bidding her to go on.

'There's trouble in my heart.'

'I know. I've been waiting.'

'I want to go to Stromness again to say good-bye to Paulie and Robert.'

'Soon?'

'Yes, they'll be away soon.'

'What else?'

'I want to gather up the brothers and sisters and bring them here.'

'I can think of no better thing to do.'

Julie took the hand that stroked her and turned its palm to her lips. Will heard her murmur something into it with the kisses. Something about how good he was. He felt the pain of it.

CHAPTER 25

Both bars of the Fox and Grapes were filled nearly to overflowing. It was Friday, September 1. Julie was gone to Stromness to gather up the children. Germany had attacked Poland.

Will felt mightily alone despite the gathered crowd.

The place was suspended in a cube of smoke, the smell of bitters and the chatter of many voices. The radio played musical selections. From time to time the BBC announcer broke in to report on the progress of the ultimatum sent to Germany by France and the United Kingdom. Will remained open till well past midnight, but still nothing had been decided between the nations. As he bid the last sailor good-night, Bostock appeared out of the darkness. He was well on his way to being drunk. He was at that place where a drunk stands most firmly upon his dignity.

'I've come to have dinner at your table, Will.'

'It's well past dinnertime.'

'Even so.'

'Julie's not to home.'

'Never is when I come to call, is she?'

'She's off gathering up your children, her brothers and sisters.'

'As well she should. She should have a little love and care for her own. You're rich enough to give them what to eat and a place to sleep.'

'Come inside.'

'I want to go to your home.'

'Come inside while I get John from his bed.'

'You've got the boy sleeping in a tavern? That's not a very good atmosphere for a small boy, is it?'

'Come in, damn you, and stop playing the fool.'

Will gathered up his son without awakening him. He wondered what he could do with Bostock.

'Why have you come?'

'The new submarine nets have arrived. They'll be taking up the old ones soon.'

'When?'

'We'll discuss it over a meal.'

There was nothing for it but to take the man along home with him.

Once there, Will put young John down in his bed right off. The child still slept. He gave Bostock a chair by the fire and set out a table of cold meats, cheeses and bread. He placed a bottle of wine beside the dishes. There was a jug of island whiskey warming on the hearth. As he went about the homely and hospitable tasks, he became suddenly aware of a prophetic excitement growing within him.

They ate – Bostock with relish, Will without savor in the food. Bostock emptied his glass of the water Will had poured him. He reached for the wine bottle. Will removed it from his grasp.

'Here what's this?' Bostock complained.

'You're not to drink anymore.'

'The hell you say.'

'We may soon be at war. We must keep clear heads.'

'My head's bloody well clear.'

'Not for the business we're about.'

'Business? What bloody business?'

'Espionage. We're spies, you and I.'

'I'm no fucking spy.'

Will leaned forward and poured himself a glass of wine.

'You're something that people regard as far worse. You are a traitor.'

'I'm not,' Bostock nearly screamed. He stood up in a sudden violence of self-awareness and repeated his innocence for the sound of it in his own ears. The chair tipped and fell.

'Pick up your chair,' Will suggested softly. 'Sit down.'

When it was done, he went on.

'You've delivered information into my hands. You've known for a longer time than I've admitted that I am an agent of a foreign power.'

'All I wanted was a place for myself,' Bostock moaned in self-pity.

'I've given you that. That and payment.'

'I wouldn't take any more.'

Will shrugged and spread his hands in a gesture of acceptance.

'I won't take any more of your filthy money,' Bostock said again.

'You have taken it and spent it.'

'I'll give it back.'

Will smiled and felt a vagrant sorrow for the man who was being cruelly shown his own true face.

'None of that matters. You've done a job of work against the interests of your country.'

'I'd do nothing to hurt my own people,' Bostock protested. 'I'll go to the Admiralty and tell them what I've done. I'll tell them what I know about you.'

Will grinned. It was a reaction to a warning that grew within him. He knew it appeared to be a grimace of threat to Bostock.

'What do you know?'

Bostock folded over his hands a bit and directed his words to them.

'I saw the radio.'

'I will have it hidden the moment you leave to inform upon me.'

Bostock brought his head up sharply and stared at Will with sullen bewilderment.

'Give me a drink.'

The excitement which had been growing within Will seemed to come together in a tiny crystal of expectation. He recognized it as the beginning of a deadly resolve.

He wiped his mouth with his napkin. 'No! I want you sober.' He placed the whiskey jug and the remains of the bottle of wine in a cabinet. He locked it with an air of finality.

'We're in this business together now, and I intend to get good value for money out of you.'

A shard of light gleamed in Bostock's eye, caused by a quick motion of his head that marked the coming of a thought. He shot a swift glance at Will to see if he had been witness to it.

From the corners of his eyes Will could see the process as Bostock sorted out his subterfuge and strategy. It seemed clear that he would pretend to fall in with Will and then inform on him from a position of safety. Foxlike, he would concoct a tale for the authorities that would make of him a minor hero who had seen villainy in Will when everyone else had been hoodwinked.

'You can see that you have no weapon to use against me,' Will said.

Bostock nodded with a show of resignation. 'There's not much choice left to me, is there?'

Will became hearty. 'Come along. I'll show you my

darkroom. You've only just seen it through a peephole in the windowpane.'

He made the mild joke to put Bostock off his guard. As they walked to the cellar door, his legs seemed to be made of columns of fragile coral full of channels that drained his strength away. On the cellar steps he wondered for a moment if Bostock could truly accept the easier and safer course. Could he continue to work for Will to his own profit? If he could, there might be hope.

But the crystal of Will's resolve had become a matrix, a structure. It had become very nearly an irrevocable decision. It grew out of the inescapable fact that, no matter what decision Bostock made under pressure, he would present an ever-growing threat and problem. As a co-conspirator his demands would inevitably increase. As a drunkard there would be the co stant fear that he would make the fatal revelation through accident or design. The resolve challenged the slender hope and killed it.

Will unlocked the door to the darkroom. He bade Bostock enter and seat himself upon the high stool.

He forced the solution to his problem to remain just beyond the reach of his conscious will. But the resolve already knew what it would do.

Bostock gazed with bright-eyed pretense around the small cluttered room.

'So these are the play toys you fool away your time with?'

'No, these are the means by which I secure my privacy and explain a locked room.'

Bostock grinned and winked.

'It might be a good idea if you pretended an interest in my hobby,' Will continued. 'It would provide a reason to give to Julie when I tell her I intend to have you as a frequent visitor here.'

Bostock laughed out loud. 'She'd never believe I'd want to fool about with such things.'

'We'll simply tell her it is so. There's not much difficulty to it. These trays are for the various chemicals.'

As Will watched Bostock nod his head, the certain knowledge that he must act to neutralize the man came to his conscious awareness in lines of simple black and white. He felt the pulse at his throat begin.

'Developing solution. Fixing solution. Alcohol to chill the emulsion when making gum-bichromate prints.'

Bostock's eyes fixed themselves on the bottle of alcohol that Will pointed out.

A rage of excitement gripped Will in his chest and throat.

'Did you hear something?'

'What?' Bostock said as a man speaks when disturbed from sleep.

'I thought I heard young John cry out. Excuse me. I'll just run up and see.'

He left Bostock alone in the darkroom. He went upstairs in the quiet house. He looked in upon his son. The child was sleeping peacefully as he knew he would be. He'd heard no outcry. He returned to the stairs and, suddenly weary, sat down.

He faced the simple fact. At the moment of Bostock's threat of exposure, perhaps even at the moment when he entered the tavern from out of the night, but certainly at the moment when his pulse told him of his intent, he had resolved to take Bostock's life. Still, he'd hesitated to act face to face. He was leaving it to fate.

If Bostock resisted the desire for a drink, if he'd indeed brought the spine of the idea that he would be a man bent on important actions, he might resist the beckoning bottle of alcohol. If he had any knowledge of the danger implied in drinking a fluid that was used solely for the purpose of its chemical reaction, he would be saved. At least for this night.

He heard, or thought he heard, a muffled crash from the cellar. He went unhurriedly downstairs. He paused in the doorway.

Bostock hadn't been able to resist the bottle for more than a minute. Had he intended to replace what he drank with water? It was a foolish, vagrant thought.

Bostock stared up at Will as he writhed on the floor with eyes so dilated as to appear totally black. His flesh had assumed a bluish tinge. The first violent irregular seizures had flung his body about the confined space, and the floor was littered with broken glass. Those first convulsions had spent themselves. He was gasping slowly for breath, and he was held by paralysis in a grotesque running posture.

The cyanide of potassium, a chemical known to be frequently used in photography, a chemical that had been laced in the alcohol, was working as swiftly as Will had read it would on the warning label.

Bostock's body was suddenly torn by a new series of

spasms. Will closed the door. He had no wish to be witness to the moment of death.

Will was waiting on the quay the following midmorning when Julie arrived back in Kirkwall with her gathered family aboard Abel Ewen's fishing craft. Even before she set foot upon the pier, long before she could really discern the subtle expressions on his face, she was aware of tragedy. It was in the manner in which Will held himself, tight and contained, as though protecting himself against repeated blows. Her first thought was of her son.

As she walked to Will, her face grown pale, he intuited her natural concern and moved quickly to assure her that young John was well and even now playing with his toys in the backyard of the Fox and Grapes under the careful eye of young Jimmy.

'What then, husband?' Julie asked.

'Your father is dead.'

The color flooded back into Julie's cheeks. She felt momentarily giddy from the relief that nothing was wrong with John. Or perhaps, in that single instant, she felt regret for the passing of someone who was, after all, of her blood. If it were so, the twinge passed quickly and so lightly as to have the substance of memory before it was truly fact.

'Accident or drink?'

'Both. He's not been happy in Lyness.'

'He'd be happy nowhere,' Julie interjected.

'He complained again that we were not treating him as we should.'

'He was treated far better by you than I would have treated him if I'd had the say of it.'

'I asked him to come home with me for a late supper and a chat since you weren't at home. I thought I could reason with him. He became quite jolly. We had a cold supper, and he had nothing to drink. I could see he wanted to prove to me that he intended to change his ways, to make himself welcome.'

'Bless the sinner,' Julie murmured, more through rote than belief.

'I even had a glass of wine with the meal and he refused. I had a whiskey after and he refused again. It was hard for him, but I believe he meant to abstain. We went into the cellar and I showed him the darkroom. He seemed mildly interested in it all. We talked about cameras and photography in general. Yes, he seemed interested.'

'Anything to make himself pleasant to you because he wanted something of you.'

'Perhaps. I thought I heard John cry out in his sleep, and I went upstairs to see to the boy. I wasn't gone more than five minutes. When I returned, he was lying on the floor in pain. I could see after the first shock and confusion what had occurred. I'd pointed out the various chemicals that were used in making prints. One of the bottles contained alcohol. Apparently he felt it safe to take a drink of it without my knowing.'

Will felt a sadness in him as though this story of an alcoholic who had struggled a scant hour or two against the need for drink and couldn't resist any longer were true.

'Refusing the wine and the whiskey must have been a greater struggle than I knew. He couldn't resist any longer.'

'So drink did kill him.'

'There was a chemical in the alcohol used to fix images on the paper. The poison killed him.'

Julie was silent for a long moment, regarding Will with eyes that only now grew misted with threatening tears. Tears for Will, not for the dead father. She reached to kiss him on the cheek.

Will shivered in self-revulsion.

Julie placed her hand on his cheek. 'Have you caught a chill?' Her concern for him shriveled his soul. 'You've had a bad time of it,' she went on softly. 'And here I've come with new troubles for you.'

'Take the children home.'

He returned to the tavern. It was, if anything, more clotted with people seeking comfort in human contact than on the day before. Will felt heavy with the death of Bostock. He retreated to his small office for fear his face was written over with his guilt. He stayed there through Saturday most of the time, alone with the memory of the dying Bostock. The police had taken the body from Will's home that very morning. Still, he remained very near to Will. He dozed and was awakened by the face of Bostock with its stained and twisted mouth. It screamed in Goldman's voice, and the eyes that accused him were those of Jakob-Salomon.

On toward evening the police constable came to inform Will that a coroner's inquest would be assembled on Monday next.

He assured Will that the verdict would surely be death by misadventure.

Will sent a message to Julie that because of the Polish crisis, he intended to keep the tavern open as long as it was useful as a meeting place.

The hours passed, drinking slowed. Some of the service personnel returned to duty. Many stayed on. They drank sparingly, chatted hoarsely or slept on their arms.

At eleven ten on Sunday morning, from 10 Downing Street in London, Prime Minister Neville Chamberlain made an announcement to the world:

'I am speaking to you from the Cabinet Room from 10 Downing Street. This morning the British ambassador in Berlin handed the German Government the final note stating unless we heard from them by eleven o'clock that they were prepared to withdraw their troops from Poland, a state of war would exist between us. I have to tell you now that no such understanding has been received, and consequently this country is at war with Germany.

'You can imagine what a bitter blow it is to me that all my long struggle to win peace has failed. Up to the very last it should have been quite possible to arrange a peaceful settlement between Germany and Poland –'

The address was repeated many times during that Sunday. Will sat in the office space of the tavern. Through the glass he could see the civilians and military that had gathered to listen to the address and the news attendant to it over and over again. He could read the fear, the terrible relief now that the sword had at last fallen, the arrogance of youth and certainty of British resolve. He saw old Scarff getting steadily drunker as he told his stories of Britain's past glories and victories for a tot. In Skipper Gatt, who employed a knife quietly on a bit of scrimshaw, he saw the patient acceptance of one more storm to be ridden and weathered. He saw John Kendrick in the man's eyes and in the set of his shoulders.

Will charged to his feet as though impelled by the need of action, the need to outrun time. He rushed to the door to let more of the sounds of men come to him. He was lost in a flood race as fierce as that which guarded Holm Sound. He must have intercourse with other men or drown. Chamberlain was again in the midst of his declaration of war.

'When I have finished speaking, several detailed announcements will be made on behalf of the government giving you plans under which it will be possible to carry on the work of the nation in these days of stress which may be ahead, but these plans need your help. You may be taking part in one of the fighting services or one of the other branches.

'It is of vital importance that you carry on with your jobs. May God bless you all and may He defend the right, for it is the evil things we shall be fighting against – brute force, broken promises, bad faith. But I am certain that right shall prevail.'

The assembly in the Fox and Grapes stood as one person and began to sing the national anthem. It had been happening through the day each time the address was repeated or some communiqué was marked by the playing of 'God Save the King.' They seemed unaware that they might have sung it a half dozen times before. Each time it stirred the air with patriotic fervor. Will found himself singing with the others.

He felt a chill rise along his spine that he recognized as one of pride in this community of men and women. It was followed by a shudder of self-revulsion. He felt himself somehow obscene. A parasite thrilling at the grand emotions of the host it was sworn to destroy.

Will moved through the days, his senses blazingly aware of every least thing, his emotions charged to that point where the sight of a shaft of light haloing his child's head would bring unbidden tears to his eyes.

At night his body seemed to have acquired that vision over its entirety that they say some of the blind possess in their hands and faces. The length of Julie was more than warmth and pressure. In the dark hour before false dawn, lying with her alone in his wakefulness, her body was light and shadow, rosy hues and blue-saffron shadows.

There was a night revival of his appetite for her, and she, with unasked questions behind her eyes but sensing a deep hunger in him, responded with an even greater sense of discovery between them than that which had existed in the weeks following her seduction of him.

His tongue became acute to the taste of salt in the air.

The very breath he took in was formed and shaped; a palpable thing.

His mind wouldn't give him rest. Neither would it come to final grips with the vast indecision that gripped his soul.

CHAPTER 26

When Sean Selene came to the pub on the evening of Tuesday, October 3, Will had played a strange and beneficial trick upon his mind. He had so completely divorced himself from the conundrum that faced him that he was genuinely surprised when Selene drew him off alone and murmured to him in conspiratorial tones.

'I have a bit of information that can do for the British if the Germans are quick enough. Orders came into the Admiralty to bring up the submarine nets.'

'You shouldn't be so free with such talk,' Will cautioned, and Selene smiled a crooked smile.

'Now there's good droll, dry bit of German humor.'

Will answered the smile, feeling disconnected from himself.

'How long will the sounds be unprotected?'

'At least three days. Maybe more. Now if the Germans have the stomach for it, they can get a U-boat in there and kill like a fox in a chicken run.'

When Selene had gone, Will thought with bitterness that he might have, after all, continued his denials of espionage to Bostock. He might have found some way, other than murder, to defuse the threat the man presented, but he had foolishly revealed himself and dealt with Bostock. He'd allowed himself to dance to the tune that the drunkard played. They had indeed danced together and there was little to choose between them. They had both given up pride, character and conviction. In that moment Will, stooping to the level of the sot, had no other recourse but to murder him. He'd comforted himself with the knowledge that he had extracted valuable information from the conspiracy of cooperation. But he had as yet done nothing with this information. And here was the same intelligence come again. Having received it from Selene, he could no longer allow himself to delay his commitment. He must act.

Schedule C, that transmission rota under which Will was presently operating, accorded him the full attention of the German listening post each Friday between the hour of midnight and one o'clock. In the event of urgent intelligence he was to discard 'C' and broadcast the first five minutes of each hour until his control acknowledged the message. All communication was to be broken off at that moment. It was expected that such regular and frequent transmission would vastly increase the chances of British monitoring stations pinning down the radio location. It was to be considered of no use from that instant and was to be destroyed.

Much of the British war fleet lay at anchorage in the Flow. The ships were kept under steam at all times, in constant readiness for departure at a moment's notice. There had been much coming and going; ships ordered elsewhere and other ships come to the gathering place.

A U-boat creeping through one of the unprotected passages, unseen, could wreak havoc among the vessels which were, after so many years of neglect and months of hopeful shortsightedness, less protected than trapped by the rocky arms of the Flow.

Will sent no messages.

On Saturday Will played with John and managed to stay very close to Julie during the whole day until at last, with housewifely irritation touched with humorous affection, she told him to take himself and his noisy offspring elsewhere to roughhouse at their games. They found young Jimmy sitting by the sea, and they spent an hour collecting winkles from the tide pools.

On Sunday Will went along to church with Julie. She'd taken to going some time past for the good instruction of little John. They were accompanied by the new additions to his family. McLafferty had, after protest, come along with Jimmy. They occupied a full pew in the small church. Will felt himself the patriarch of a clan.

When the minister prayed for the safekeeping of Britain, their islands, the men who fought and would fight on land and in the air, when he called down a special blessing on the men who sailed in the ships at sea, Will cried 'Amen' as fervently as any of the assemblage. He touched the hand of the young sailor Jimmy, who sat at his right shoulder, and prayed the boy would be kept safe.

There were rumors in the Fox and Grapes that next night that U-boats had been sighted in the North Sea. Most were comforted by someone's remark that the fishermen had probably sighted a pod of whales.

Monday was traditionally, as in most public places, a quiet evening at the Fox and Grapes. The locals, despite the drama and the need for mutual bolstering of spirits created by the war, tended to see Monday as a stolid day of the week. A day that must be spent setting the tone of the days to follow until the weekend, even if the fine plans and great dreams fell apart come Tuesday morning.

In the five weeks since the outbreak of war the brave talk and resurrected slogans against the Hun had worn out their flavor. There was instead the certain knowledge that the conflict was to be a long and arduous one and that they were stationed for the present at the lonely tip of the world.

A girl dressed in the uniform of the Women's Army Auxiliary rose from a table near the fire. She was small and very trim-looking. Not pretty, but with the fresh-lipped charm of a Devon girl.

'My turn for a round, is it?'

Jimmy stood up, his young face flushed with the pleasure of being among his elders, among fighting men and women.

'I should get them.'

'Now sit you down,' the Devon girl said. 'In this madhouse of a station we're all military personnel under the king's orders. Are you sure, Jimmy, you won't have a whiskey?'

The boy ducked his head and turned a shade or two brighter.

'I don't really fancy the taste of it.'

McLafferty grinned broadly and put a rough hand on the boy's sleeve.

'Come off it, girl. The lad's only fifteen.'

Mary Ann smiled and gave her order to Will, who stood watching them with a terrible affection shining from his eyes. To the object of his regard he no doubt looked as though he were sleepily staring off into space.

Iris, a slender girl from the streets of London, born within hearing of the Bow bells, added her opinion.

'If Jimmy's old enough to serve aboard the *Royal Oak*, he's old enough to have at least a glass of bitters.'

'He's not that long from his mother's tit that he can stomach ought but milk,' McLafferty replied, and squeezed the boy's arm to let him know there was nothing but fondness for him in the banter.

'Leave off that talk,' Iris giggled in reproach. 'You'll be corrupting the boy.'

She leaned across the table and kissed young Jimmy on the corner of his mouth.

'Never you mind that dirty old Scots devil hiding behind an Irish name.'

'Here now, who's to be corrupting who? Kissing him that way very nearly on the mouth.'

Iris winked.

'Next time I'll adjust my sights, Jimmy dear.'

'Oh, you are a dirty old woman.' McLafferty laughed. and the girl gone to war, twenty-three years old, laughed as well.

Up at the bar, standing there with one foot apiece propped up on the shining brass rail, members of crews from other vessels chatted. Two men from the *Oak* were with them.

Merton Jekyl had seen much of the world and little of the oceans, for he'd labored as stoker in the bellies of a hundred ships. He shrugged when a man called Barclay opined that the men of the *Oak* would be staying at Scapa Flow yet awhile.

'The devil you say,' wondered Jekyl.

'Then off to the Mediterranean,' informed a Liverpudlian called Say When for reasons he himself had all but forgotten.

'I was told they were off to join the picket craft out in the North Sea,' offered a man from Birmingham. 'I'd like to know the reason for all this shuffling about.'

'Use your nob, man. Mother England was caught with her knickers down. She moves the fleet about to keep from being raped.'

'No safe harbor for the armada anywhere.'

'We're in safe harbor here in the Flow,' Say When boasted.

Jekyl snorted derisively. Say When bristled.

'See here, she couldn't be breached in the last war.'

'Twenty years and a world's age ago. Look at it now. Blockships rusted and falling apart, string and paper sub nets put down and already to be taken up for repairs, eight bloody pop guns to protect the flock. The *Oak* herself is anchored off in the far northeast corner of the Flow because she trusts her own guns to protect her more than those eight at Lyness.'

Say When swirled his head around in an exaggerated gesture.

'Here now, watch your talk.'

'Yes, I can see we're in the middle of a covey of spies.'

Will shook his head and smiled and walked up the bar a pace to join with Skipper Gatt where the fisherman sat in his favorite corner.

'Scapa Flow in danger? The whole world is in danger of being found out for the fool it is,' Will said.

Skipper Gatt glanced at the Navy men.

'Those men should know better than to go on about such things in a public place. Still, is there any place we can't stick a finger and find dry rot? Scapa Flow needs repair, it's true. The fleet is scattered and spread far too thin.'

'Part of the foolishness. All of it. War. Damn foolishness.'

'Not much old gulls like us can do for it, Willum, one way or the other.'

Will shivered.

'Lord, the nights grow cold.'

It was colder still at two o'clock Tuesday morning. Cold as death in a land where summer was often a brief few days, spring no more than a promise, autumn heavy with winter's weight and winter itself a tomb.

There had been no sleep for Will. He'd spent the hours impaled upon a sharp knife between the past and the present. He searched through all the philosophies that he could remember in hopes of finding some clue that should recommend a following action. But he found in the end that philosophers, in most part, were better able to order the cosmos than decide between the left and the right hand.

In this fashion at the hour of four when false dawn brightened, then died in the sky that met the sea, Will sent the message, the urgent intelligence that Scapa Flow was open to attack. He did it with a mind focused at a neutral place within himself so that it was an automatic response to a remembered order, a culminating act in a pattern of habit, like rinsing the glass after brushing one's teeth.

He went to his bed then gathered his wife to him as she moved to his familiar warmth in her sleep. He lay there, reading the pattern of his life across the shadowed ceiling until the days of his life reached the present and beyond. But beyond was the window growing gray and empty.

He slipped away to transmit again at five.

Again at six.

Each time he returned to the bed. Each time Julie sought shelter against him. When next he attempted to slip stealthily from beneath the covers, Julie's eyes opened and regarded him with the childlike solemnity she always awakened with upon her face.

She smiled to let him know what she was about to say was said with tender, teasing affection.

'Old husband, you've been no good pillow for your wife this night.'

He patted her awkwardly on her shoulder as though embarrassed at a display of love he couldn't contain and murmured something without consequence.

He took up his robe and slipped his feet into his slippers.

'I'll put the teapot on the hob. Will you watch it? There's a picture I did during the night drying in the cellar.'

Julie clicked her tongue and shook her head in fond remonstrance of a child too eager to play with toys to be about the serious pursuits of men and she was happy for it.

Will sent the message at seven. He repeated it for the full five minutes.

When he was done, he sat staring at the key feeling an overwhelming weariness in him.

The reply, the one signal the wireless had ever received, startled him.

'Message acknowledged,' he read.

He'd lighted the fuse. Whether or not action would be taken to attempt an attack upon Scapa Flow was of no further concern to him.

His duty was done.

He had committed himself to complicity in anything that was to come by an act of obedience and loyalty which was also an act of treason and treachery. He had removed himself from the right to feel human concern, from the right to ask human understanding.

In the end of it there was only one thing he had done really well. He had sat and waited to fulfill his duty and obey his orders with less reason than a dog has waiting for a promised meal.

He had sat and waited. Now it was only necessary for him to sit and wait a little while longer.

On the morning of the thirteenth Will discovered that the major units of the Home Fleet had left Scapa Flow under cover of dark.

Where the *Royal Oak* lay anchored in the northeast corner, she had only the old battle cruiser *Repulse* and the seaplane carrier *Pegasus* for company. One other, the *Daisy II*, lay ready to service the *Royal Oak* while she was in harbor.

In the early hours before noon the island mail packet was sighted and shortly after tied up at the pier. Will took the excuse to leave the house, which somehow oppressed him that day. He walked the two miles to Kirkwall.

He went to the post office to secure any mail that might have come for him. Wiley, that small, ugly, twisted man, put his claw on Will's arm as he stepped out into the sunshine. Will felt a painful start of revulsion.

Wiley handed him an envelope covered with special service stamps and endorsements. Will began to open it.

'Never mind that. It's just the excuse for my seeking you out. What happened to your goddamn wireless?'

'I destroyed it.'

'Damn fool, you almost cut your lifeline.'

'What are you talking about? It was part of my standing orders to destroy the radio immediately after I found it necessary to broadcast on the emergency schedule. I did so.'

'All right then. Just another jolly fuckup. I had to weave some fancy tales, I'll tell you, to get the captain to arrive here some three days before time. I never asked for any damn thing in all these years of any captain that ever sailed that bloody packet boat. Asking favors draws attention to yourself.'

It seemed inconsequential, yet Will was compelled to ask Wiley what tale he had spun.

'I made it out that a woman who gave me room in her bed was leaving the islands to do war work in Liverpool,' Wiley answered, and the man's mouth twisted with bitter pain. 'Do you see, the captain thought he was doing a poor damned ugly creature like me a great favor. A last fuck with the only woman anywhere about who'd be mad enough to do the dirty with me.'

He spat, clearing his mouth of the words.

'Enough of that. There's plans to attack the Flow.'

He looked off to the anchorage.

'Not much reason for it with nothing anchored here to speak of. But I suppose it would mean something to show the bloody British that Scapa Flow ain't the impregnable fortress they think she is. No matter. If they pull it off, you're to take a small boat. There'll be confusion and hell aplenty all around. You're to make your way to Swona.'

'It's no small row from here through Hoxa Sound to that island.'

'That's your worry, not mine. It's your ass you'll be rowing to save. If the submarine makes it back out to the open sea, they'll figure her fled and gone. But she'll lie doggo off the southern point of South Ronaldsay for a day and a night. The next morning following, before first light, she'll poke her tower above the sea. You're to row out to her. They'll take you aboard and back to Germany so you can receive your plum cake for the good job you've done.'

'Can such a ragged venture hope for success?'

'Who the hell knows or much cares, for that matter? We're expendable, old cock. They want you back to make a show of their cleverness and their victory. Besides, the English counterintelligence will be taking a close look around here. Your ass is up for grabs.'

Will released the flap of the letter and looked at the blank page, and somehow it seemed a message of great import to him.

'Well, then, Mr. Hartz, I've said it all.'

He turned away.

'Mr. Wiley.'

Wiley looked over his shoulder. He gave every appearance of being an inquisitive crab.

'There is something I want to ask you.'

'Go on then,' Wiley urged when Will hesitated.

'A long time ago a horse was seized with a fit at the quay in Stromness.'

'I'm not likely to forget.'

'It killed itself.'

'And you damned near killed me.'

'You laughed, Mr. Wiley. I wonder if you would tell me why you laughed.'

Wiley stared at Will as though Will himself had just gone mad like the island pony and was about to beat his head against the stones.

'Crazy foreigner,' he muttered and scuttled away.

Will walked home.

During the hour that Julie went to the school to fetch young John, he packed a small gladstone bag with an extra suit and a change of linen. He included an enlargement he'd made of a portrait of his wife and child that had particularly pleased him at the time of his taking it. He packed those fictional papers that proved his heritage as a Swiss. He took the bag into the yard and concealed it in the small tool shed at the back of the garden.

Will went to sit in his rocking chair. He didn't answer when Julie came home with their son and called to see if he were home. She assumed he'd gone to the pub and went about the household tasks and prepared the evening meal. When by chance she went into their bedroom, she found him in the gloaming, staring out the window toward the sea.

He seemed so solitary she didn't speak but was impelled to place a loving hand upon his head.

'I've done it,' he said.

'Done what?'

Will shook himself, looked up at her and smiled.

'I must have been dreaming.'

'A good dream, Willum?'

'Yes. A long, good dream.'

CHAPTER 27

There was no peace for Will in the familiar bed. His inability to capture sleep transmitted itself to Julie, and she woke to inquire after his well-being.

'I feel well enough. What time is it?'

She glanced at the clock on the side table. Without his glasses the face of it was unreadable to her husband.

'On to three o'clock.'

'Perhaps if I got up and took a walk in the air.'

'It's winter cold out.'

He was already out of the bed.

'I'll bundle up warm.'

He dressed himself, Julie watching him, her eyes growing heavy at last. He helped her settle in the warm bed and kissed her mouth. She was asleep in a moment, his tension flowing out of her at his leaving.

Wrapped in his sailorman's greatcoat and wearing a knitted cap, Will rode the two miles to the Scapa pier on his bicycle. He stood in the deep well of blackness staring out across the Flow to the place where the *Royal Oak* was at rest.

She was blacked out under wartime conditions, as were the town and the hills all around. Try as he would to pierce the dark, he could not be certain if the *Oak* really lay anchored out there. But he saw the bulk of her in his mind, if not in his eye. He saw her decks and the silent seamen stationed about her on the dog watch. He fancied he could see the glow of the cook's stove and the smoking lamp swinging gently overhead, a sailor warming his hands around a great white mug of coffee. He heard the gentle and not so gentle sounds of men and boys sleeping, the sudden outcry of dreams. He saw the face of McLafferty and next to it Jimmy's shy face with the spots of color high up on his round cheeks. He felt the intimate warmth of the sleeping quarters and the breaths and the pulsing blood of men about to engage in the madness of war.

He shivered within the coat, within his skin. He was not certain of the purpose of the vigil he kept. He realized, suddenly, that it was a desperate prayer that when the dawn rose, the great shape of the battleship would still be picketed there. He would, he knew, be drawn to keep this same vigil every predawn until the danger was past, the *Oak* sailed away or the attack launched.

Perhaps Will, of all the people of the islands, the garrison at Lyness, the night plane watchers, the civil wardens, the police, the sleepless mothers with ailing children, the men of the *Oak* herself, was the only one whose senses were so alerted as to know the exact moment when the first torpedo struck.

At 4:02 on the morning of Saturday, October 14, the *Royal Oak* was struck forward by a torpedo launched by the submarine U-47 commanded by a fresh-faced, handsome tourist boy now grown to manhood and in command of the underseas killer. His name was Günter Prien.

A strange waiting silence followed the first dull explosion. Then a shuddering roar shook the old warship.

In the documents of war great disasters tend to numb the senses. They become statistics. The roll call of the dead becomes a litany of names and numbers. Only the individual identity of the singular dead is magnified upon the gray lists, comes forward to engage the heart and become an object of deep sorrow.

The men thrown to the decks from their hammocks, out of their deepest early-morning sleep, would remember, only if they survived and after a long time, how they felt in that disordered moment. Only then would they recall the shudder that fled along the bones of the battleship into their own, the sharp spray of water knifing across hatchways from burst pipes, the pretty veil of rainbow mist beyond which they heard a man screaming. They would recall, for a longer time still in their nightmares, the friend pierced through and bloodied. They would feel upon their faces the terrible heat and in their legs the chill of the northern sea. Those who died, in the moment of their death, were part of the great death struggle of the ship herself and screamed their last breath with her voice.

Will ran down to the slip where he kept his small sailing craft moored. He untied the painter of the dinghy from its stern.

He stepped aboard the rowboat and pushed off into the Flow.

At 4:14, twelve minutes after most of the ship's complement had awakened from dream to nightmare, the second torpedo struck. A great column of water vomited up from the sea, nearly as high as the spotting top.

There were men who died in their sleep, torn apart and never knowing their ship was under attack.

McLafferty struggled to gather up the boys in his charge. He slapped, then soothed a boy who screamed in his terrible awakening, perhaps believing the reality to be a child's night horror come true. He noted, even as he labored to achieve order out of chaos, the splendid white-faced courage of most of them, moving to help their fellows. He saw Jimmy, the shy, nearly girlish youth become a man before his eyes, as he lifted an unconscious shipmate, his weight and more, upon his shoulder. Jimmy came to stand before him silently awaiting orders. In that brief and brilliant moment, McLafferty for the first time in a wandering, roving seaman's life regretted the wife and son that never were. Blood trickled from a cut above the boy's eye. McLafferty moved his hand to brush it away. He turned and led his charges, stumblingly, toward the ladder and the deck above.

Aboard the *Daisy II*, Skipper Gatt was startled awake. He made the deck and conferred briefly with the marine who was the officer of the watch. They agreed that one of *Royal Oak*'s fifteen-inch guns had somehow been fired.

As they watched, the third explosion wracked the battleship. Skipper Gatt put his vessel under way. Great gluts of flame rose from the *Royal Oak* amidships just forward of the mainmast. Fifty men and more died that moment in her belly. A pall of smoke rose above them darker than the sky.

Half a dozen of his boys were on the ladder when McLafferty felt the third shattering explosion. He tried to free the last of them from the tumbling bodies that fell. Flames rushed down the well. He was driven back by a giant's fist, and when he was recovered, his boys were charred and dead. The compartment was burdened with great heat. It threatened to cook them all before bursting out the seams of the ship. Clutching at Jimmy's sleeve, he dragged the boy and the unconscious sailor he carried toward the starboard passageway. They moved through a heavy pall of burning cinders and bits of cloth that, aflame, glistened in the gloom like fireflies.

Will rowed toward the stricken vessel like an automaton. He reached out the oars, dipped and pulled against the sea encarmined with flames. He turned to see the *Daisy II* reach the *Royal Oak*, and he was nearly beside her a moment later. As he glanced a second time, the *Oak* fell off fifteen degrees.

Men were leaving her, leaping into the killing sea. In waters of 48 degrees Fahrenheit, they would become benumbed, cast into shock and finally would die in a matter of minutes.

McLafferty and Jimmy, still bearing the body of his friend, struggled through the passageway and climbed a ladder hot with the radiation of the fires below. The icy air caught at their lungs, and the glory of it set them to choking. Jimmy knelt on the deck. He felt the weight of the sailor removed from his back. McLafferty laid the young boy out upon the deck. Jimmy looked into his face. Only then did he know his shipmate was dead. McLafferty grabbed his hand and drew him to his feet. The deck canted. The ship's broken body screamed. Jimmy went sliding away. McLafferty grabbed a trailing rope and shouted out to the boy.

Will tried to maneuver his cockleshell in the tragic sea. From the shore men and boats were beating their way toward the rescue. He heard as clearly as a voice at his shoulder the name 'Jimmy' shouted above the confusion of fearful and dying men. He cast desperately about for sight of the pale-skinned, shyly loving boy. He must save him even if he were able to save no one else.

The *Royal Oak* had given a great lurch to starboard. Men of the Devon moors, the alleys of Liverpool, the hills and the long farms of Wiltshire, the shadows of London Bridge and the collieries of Welsh villages with outrageously melodic names slid along her decks and left their blood upon them.

The dead sailor boy slid past Jimmy, where he clung to a bollard, and fell into the sea. McLafferty reached Jimmy. The ship was going under, and he knew it. He led the boy to the ship's rail. There were small craft below. Pray that they would be picked up. There was nothing left for them but to leave the *Royal Oak* and commit their bodies to the sea. They went into the water together, holding hands in a fiction of innocent lovers.

Flames illuminated the waters of the Flow. Capriciously, a quarter of the port side of the ship suddenly blazed with lights. Antiaircraft beacons came on, thrusting their fingers into the sea as though belatedly seeking the enemy that had not arrived from above but below. In the blaze of a light that spotted and followed them two men swam in a ragged line toward Will's boat. He shouted encouragement and pulled hard to shorten the distance between them. He put the oars aside and knelt in the stern, reaching his hand out to a man whose face was a mask of oil. The man grinned at him in wild happiness. Will saw it to be McLafferty and the man he kept afloat must be young Jimmy. McLafferty thrashed painfully and awkwardly as the probe of light fled away. Will's eyes tried to adjust to the greater dark that fell. He cast wildly about, trying to judge the drift and tide's direction in those few seconds. He found McLafferty, who held Jimmy before him. Will reached out and grasped the sleeve of Jimmy's shirt. McLafferty smiled. The blackened skin of his face seemed to shatter with crimson fissures. He fell back and slipped into his grave.

A surge of tide dragged at Jimmy's body. Will felt his shoulder cringe at the pain. He shifted his stance and reached down with both hands. Jimmy's eyes opened. He lifted his arms. Will was reminded, wrenchingly, of the gesture of the infant John reaching up from his crib for Will's strength and comfort. He grasped the boy's arm above the wrist. The arm from elbow to hand peeled back, the skin eroded from flesh and bone by flame. Will's eyes were fixed, filled with inexpressible pity at the arm, welling red with blood from beneath the black oil. Jimmy went under, his mouth wide as though inviting a swifter death.

Will screamed a bitter, blasphemous protest. He went into the water and dived beneath it, searching for the boy already a corpse and lost to him.

The cold gripped at him, shriveling his heart and sending lancets of pain through his groin. He searched, and soon he felt his warm life leeching away into the sea around him. He ceased the search and his struggles. He floated peacefully. He would soon be dead.

The cries and pleas of desperate men aroused him from the beginnings of a warm sleep. He forced his body back to urgent life. He cast about for sight of his boat. The movement of contradicting eddies had left his craft only a few feet from his questing arm. He had been condemned to live.

He was crying and didn't know it. He wept all through the night. The tears were as cold as the sea spray.

He labored. As a fisherman takes up the harvest, Will took up the harvest of broken men. He gathered them into his fragile craft. He saved some and told others they must wait as he rowed for the shore. Upon his return they were gone. Saved? He would never know. He shouted in a voice of terrible rage. He bade men cling to the gunwales of the rowboat. They slowed his already-slow progress. Some were soon taken by the stricture of death and lay back to die quietly in the sea's frigid embrace.

The *Royal Oak* was sinking fast. The antiaircraft lights went out, their generators overcome by the water. A great flower of fire and sound took her amidships and blew a gaping darkness in her that was swiftly flooded with the black of the sea. Men around her were sucked into the vortex and died with her.

Slowly she fled from sight below the surface, carrying with her eight hundred men. She vomited up her oily blood.

Will served the needs of his fellow men and the truest promptings of his soul that terrible morning. Toward the end of it he was overcome with a weariness so great that he tumbled to the bottom of the boat in the act of dragging a man aboard. He recovered himself and clutched at the man. The sailor fell away from him, rolling on his back, neck taut and mouth agape, in that final posture that had grown so familiar to Will. Will watched helplessly as the turbulence carried the man away. He entered the sea again, swam to the sailor and ptured him. He all but shouted into the sailor's eyes that he was saved, saved. The man stared back with a lifeless stare that held a terrible accusation.

'Oh, the humanity! The humanity!' Will heard a voice cry. He came to realize the cry was his own.

Will found himself adrift well beyond the glare of the burning *Royal Oak*. He was in a wilderness of darkness. He began to row without any idea of his purpose or direction. After a long while he became aware that the cries of stricken men and searching rescuers, though still in his ears, had taken on the echoing lost quality of distance. He gazed up at the sky. It was washed by dawning day. The pole star still shone dimly and marked his place. He made a dead reckoning and pulled for the passage through Hoxa Sound. The flood, moving out of the Flow, helped speed him along. He set the oars aside and beat himself with his arms to restore his warmth. He sighted the small bulk of Swona Island.

CHAPTER 28

A bone-chilling wind drove in with unremitting force on the unprotected rocks of Will's last waiting place. Each wave that broke against the rocks of tiny Swona was shorn of a cap of foam which, wind whipped, scudded into shore to collect in gray-white billows. The spindrift piled up in milky masses that seemed solid to the eye.

Will sat wedged in a cleft of rock a short distance up a cliffside. He huddled there like some ancient eremite self exiled from the company of man.

Indeed he felt like such an exile. Without excellence at any particular thing, without ambition and drive, he had been no more concerned about or in control of his future than a bit of that stained foam. He'd blown like a leaf through the youth that was past. He'd become a spy by default as it were. He had been so passionless as to forsake home and loved ones and had conveniently replaced them with a fiction called duty and love of country.

He had passively accepted a role that had been thrust on him without the demonstration of any will of his own. He'd lived a fantasy, never truly believing that he would ever be called upon to act in behalf of a Germany that had become stranger to him, against a nation that had become his home and his life. Yet in service to an improbable future circumstance he'd suffered a love to be deferred past bearing and finally destroyed.

With it all, he'd found a measure of happiness. He'd been the steward of a small warm inn that had grown into three separate, bustling establishments that drew a thousand friends to his hearth.

He'd gathered prosperity, respect, dignity and vast measures of human regard.

He'd befriended a waif, bedded a whore and found a wife who brought him tenderness and comfort and gave him a son.

He'd spent twenty years in the fashioning of a real life, and then, in what seemed the mere passage of days, he had attended the kidnapping of one man, murdered another and been the instrument of a crime of mass murder so horrible that the shame of it heated him while the terror of it chilled his blood.

Time had played him false. Jakob-Salomon seemed but a moment away in his agony from the person of Ian Bostock, and he but a tick from the agonies of the many faces in the sea.

Now it was the morning of a last day. He waited for the submarine that would take him away from his home and return him to a place where he would be a stranger.

Perhaps the U-boat would never make the rendezvous. There was no urgent reason that would prompt the commander of the war vessel to risk it and his crew for a single man. Will didn't care if the rescue ever took place. He would sit on his lonely rock until privation and cold killed him. They would find him there, and everyone would puzzle about the man who had kept a solitary and mysterious vigil.

The waters some two hundred yards offshore broke into turbulence and foam. A monolithic shape appeared like a plinth from some long-submerged structure of an ancient city. A figure appeared and raised an arm.

Will roused himself and launched his small boat from the cleft of rock where he'd beached her. He rowed out to the undersea craft and moments later was taken aboard.

The sailor who escorted him was silent and carried with him the smell of fear. The man wanted to be well away from the battleground.

Below, in the ship's bowels, he was scarcely noticed as commands were issued for the craft to seek the safety of the depths. Only when this was accomplished did the captain turn to Will.

There was a shock of recognition, but Will couldn't say where or under what circumstances he'd met this man. Somehow the recall was accompanied by the feeling of a happy time, of holiday and of sun. The captain was handsome in the way of the ideal Nordic prototype. He failed to extend his hand in greeting, though he bowed slightly from the waist.

'Welcome. This is a ship of war without facilities for civilian personnel. I ask you to accommodate yourself to the needs of the ship. Quarters will be provided. I suggest you replace your clothes at once. There was considerable danger in this mission. Unnecessary danger in this aspect of it. We wouldn't want you to take ill and die.'

'It would be an inconvenience,' Will said, and allowed a sharp edge of satire to shine in his voice.

The captain suddenly smiled and extended his hand as though official concerns and warnings done with, he could remember the courtesies.

'Welcome once again, Mr. Hartz. Perhaps you remember me?'

Will narrowed his eyes. 'I felt a start of recall just a moment ago.'

'We shared a bottle together. It was many summers ago, and I was just a boy.'

'Yes, yes,' Will remembered. 'You were a student on a touring vessel.'

'My name is Günter Prien, Mr. Hartz.'

'My name is Wilhelm Oerter, Captain.'

They made directly for Germany.

Wilhelm Oerter was going home?

All the cold, dreary day the men and women of the towns ringing Scapa Flow searched for the dead. They took them up from the sea and gathered them in Lyness and in Kirkwall. They laid them out on plain planks in the schoolhouse and along the quays. They were there in long rows. Some were dressed and some were only in singlets. Some were naked. They were all covered with rough blankets. Their faces were covered only to be shown when identification was attempted. They were named and tagged and sorted out.

Later the women washed them and made them clean of blood and oil. Julie worked with the other women. There was a keening in the air like the mourning of seabirds. She asked after her husband, Will Hartz.

Everyone, or nearly everyone knew him. No one had seen him since the hours before when he'd rescued, some said, two dozen men or more.

After a time Skipper Gatt found her. He was red-eyed with fatigue and thick in his speech.

'Mrs. Hartz.'

Why, she wondered, did their old friend address her in that formal way? Then she knew that it was the formality that accompanied the announcement of death.

A while later she began to hear stories from men who came to console her. They told her of her husband's wonderful courage that terrible night. One man believed he'd seen Will sucked down into the grave of the ship when he'd dived into the frigid water in a vain attempt to save a young sailor's life. But the man couldn't be sure.

Julie questioned everyone, trying to pinpoint the moment of his passing as though only that could affirm the reality. She traced his passage from one heroic act to another. The record was confused, and the moment couldn't be fixed with certainty. Will Hartz was gone. Young Jimmy was gone. McLafferty was gone. More than eight hundred men were dead and gone.

Most bodies were returned for burial near their homes. Some, the homeless and unidentifiable, were buried en masse in the rocky slopes of the island. Many were given burials in the waters of the harbor, so they might join their ship in its final resting place.

A service was read, and a stone placed above an empty place in the cemetery. Hundreds of people came to honor the memory of Will Hartz.

Molly came from Stromness. She stood beside Julie and held her hand. They cried together over the uncommon goodness of the common man they'd known. Molly stroked young John's head. She murmured his name and treasured the sound of it.

Will's son cried for the sadness of the grown-ups. Julie gathered them all, her brothers and sisters, Skipper Gatt, Molly, Wee Jock and his wife, the Dowdys, Mr. Cockburn and all, all those who'd loved her Will. They returned to the house and sat the wake.

Young John went alone, unseen, to the lunette of beach. He fashioned a small cross of driftwood and planted it in the cold October sands.

A week later Will's rowboat was found drifting, driven by the tides, near the tiny island of Swona in the Pentland Firth.

The ocean washed the little cross away.

CHAPTER 29

Wilhelm Oerter was met at Bremerhaven by one Joachim Werner, a minor factotum of the German secret service, who took him in hand as though he were a visiting dignitary of some minor and obscure alien culture that must be treated with carefully measured respect until his status was reaffirmed by the actions of those superior to Werner. With his stiff-winged collar, after the fashion of men in the foreign service, he was the archetypical German civil servant with a spine that had a built-in calibrator that seemed to know instinctively just how far to bend the back on a scale broken into fine shades of respect.

They journeyed to Berlin in a private compartment of a luxury train. On the way Werner gave Wilhelm a nonstop lecture on the glories of the Third Reich, the stunning victories of its military forces and the sainthood of its leader, Adolf Hitler. The man's conversation was sprinkled with slogans. It was obvious that he would have preferred company other than Wilhelm, who sat next to the window and tried to believe he was a hero returned but couldn't capture the sense of it.

In Berlin he was afforded certain goods and services which were checked off a list by the meticulous Joachim.

Registration first at the Leiderhof, an exquisite and discreet residence hotel overlooking the river. A suite of two rooms and a bath, beautifully furnished and appointed, had been arranged for him. Joachim Werner had somehow sent notice ahead of the time of their arrival and a bottle of Riesling was chilling in nearly unmelted ice in a silver bucket on the sideboard. A bowl of fruit and a tray of cheeses flanked it on either side.

Werner pulled the starched collar away from his prominent Adam's apple. It was a queer gesture. It was as though he were suddenly overcome by the need for air and was prepared to throttle himself in order to obtain it.

'So? Everything is to your pleasure?'

'It seems very nice. Is this where I am to reside?'

'That is not my department. The rooms have been engaged for an indefinite period. I should guess that they will be made available to you until you are assigned a position and given the opportunity to make arrangements of your own.'

Wilhelm nodded and went to a large overstuffed chair near one of the tall windows. He sat down gingerly as a man unused to such luxury might do. He lay his head upon the chair back and closed his eyes. Was there a sound to be heard, a texture to be felt, a smell whose aroma would call up a sense of homecoming?

Werner's guttural voice shocked his nerve ends. He had discovered on the submarine and since that only with an effort of translation was he able to follow his native speech. He had used his language so little these past years and the hinges of fluency were rusty. He looked at Werner inquiringly, begging for the statement to be repeated.

'If you would like to bathe and shave, the necessary equipment is in the lavatory. Two suits, one evening wear, six shirts, two pairs of shoes and a pair of boots, underlinen and so forth and so forth are in the armoire in the bedroom.'

'Suits? Boots?'

'I believe they will fit. I'm sure they will fit.'

'Yes, I'm sure of that. You're most efficient.' Werner grimaced. It was meant to be a smile but apparently had become aborted someplace between the thought and the lips. Clearly he didn't know how to handle the mild compliment since he was still most uncertain about Wilhelm's precise status. He hid in further details.

'After six this evening you will please to keep yourself available.'

'Yes?'

'It's my understanding you are to be afforded a great honor.'

'An honor?' Wilhelm shook his head. He was responding like a parrot. It was a habit that came upon him in times of weariness.

'Perhaps I have already revealed too much.'

'It's not my birthday, Herr Werner,' Wilhelm smiled. 'Nor do I like surprise parties.'

'There is to be a reception for the heroes of the great victory at Scapa Flow. Commander Prien has already made his report, I've been told. We've proved the British fleet is not so invulnerable behind her defenses at Scapa Flow. One German U-boat destroyed that myth.'

'It did?'

The automatic echoing response was not fatigue but wonder.

'It is, I'm told, a thrilling account of great courage. The British allow that the *Royal Oak* was sunk, but we know that the battleship was only one of many ships, cruisers, destroyers and auxiliary craft, that were torpedoed and sunk. We know the extent of the victory. But of course you know better than any. You were there.'

'Yes, I was there, and I know.'

The reception was held two nights later in the grand ballroom of the opera house.

Werner negotiated a fine, delicate line from the moment he met Wilhelm at his hotel.

He walked around Wilhelm, pursing his lips and clutching at his throat like a mother sending her son off to his first day at dancing class. Apparently Wilhelm had cleaned his fingernails and washed behind his ears, for Werner, though not overwhelmed by the figure Wilhelm cut in the evening dress, was nevertheless grudgingly satisfied with his charge's appearance.

With it all he managed to play the role of the manservant proudly preparing his master for a reception at court.

On the way to the opera house he kept up a constant chatter of trivia, naming the luminaries to be present and assessing the altitude of the affair by the status of those who were to be there. Wilhelm scarcely listened. After all, the names meant little or nothing to him except as references in newspapers he'd read at home, he thought.

At home. Did they know back there what he had done? The terrible deception he had perpetrated? Did Julie find the bed cold and empty in the early hours of the night? Did little John ask where his father, his loving father, had gone?

'There is every hope that Goebbels himself will be there. If so, tonight's occasion will be a glittering one. In some circles to have the Minister of Propaganda attend the party is considered even more socially notable than if the Führer himself attended.'

'I find that incredible.'

'Please understand,' Werner amended hastily, 'it is not to say Goebbels' presence adds greater importance to the affair. Just that the Führer is well known for his love of society – he is a friendly, open man – but Goebbels is known to be a private person.'

Wilhelm was about to speak but thought better of the desire to tell this posturing fool that Goebbels' attendance or lack of it was of absolutely no concern to him. He felt no part of this playacting. He was simply and patiently following orders.

The official host seemed to be Admiral Walter Wilhelm Canaris. He was not in uniform but was dressed instead in a plain business suit with a light chalk stripe running through it. He acted as though he had stopped in for a glass of champagne on a break between business matters.

But if he was unresplendent in mufti, there were enough uniforms, sashes and medals about to create a blaze in the eye. Canaris came forward and all but ignored the nervous introductions offered by Werner.

He shook Wilhelm's hand warmly and looked deep into his eyes.

'You had a long, long wait.'

Wilhelm nodded.

Before anything more passed between them, there was a flurry at the doorway. Canaris made a sound that was very like an expression of impatience and left Wilhelm.

But he was not left alone. Werner was there, and in a moment three couples, as though under instruction, came to introduce themselves and welcome him back to Germany. The women were very beautiful and wore evening dresses such as Wilhelm had never seen before. There was much naked flesh: shoulders and arms, long necks and white breasts. He would have been embarrassed for Julie to see her dressed so, he thought.

He maneuvered his way in small steps so that, looking beyond the polite eyes and politely commenting mouths of these people, he could see the newcomer. It was Günter Prien. He was dressed in the black dress uniform of the Navy, trim and severe. He looked very tall and very blonde, but there was a sardonic smile that seemed uncomfortable on his fine mouth, as though he were fighting an illness.

He was surrounded by older officers. Ladies were gathering to him. He was the very symbol of Nordic youth. A demigod.

Looking at him, Wilhelm remembered the boy who had come on holiday to the Orkneys. The boy whose manner had given Wilhelm hope that war would never engage his country again. He remembered how they had drank schnapps together.

At that moment, Prien seemed to hear his thoughts and

glanced his way. His eyes touched Wilhelm's and he smiled brightly, comrade to comrade, friend to friend.

Wilhelm felt lost in the glittering assemblage. He applied himself to the lavish buffet that occupied the four white-clothed tables that were placed to one side of the room, although he really had no appetite.

Practically no one knew who he was or why he was there. They treated him with a kind of oblique deference as though unwilling to place him anywhere on their scale of importance for fear his humble appearance was a mask for a man of great but secret eminence.

After an hour Wilhelm desperately desired the opportunity to go back to his rooms. He felt suspended in an alien place and hoped to arrange his thoughts and the pattern of his new life in solitude.

There was a sudden stir. The bright people moved about and rearranged themselves. Wilhelm was reminded of a school of silver herrings disturbed by the arrival of a predator fish. The guests lined themselves up along the back and the side of the room opposite the food-laden tables. There seemed to be a remarkable tendency for uniforms to join with uniforms of the same service, for beribboned evening dress to consort with one another and for those who appeared to be minors in the drama to herd together.

There was a cattlelike quality about it all. A feeling of animals lining up for inspection by a feared but adored executioner. He saw Werner casting about. When his guide and watchdog spotted Wilhelm among the canapes and herrings in tomato sauce, he charged toward him, intent on putting his clutching hands upon his charge.

There was a stillness that settled over the room like the compression of air before an explosion. The room was a held breath.

Werner stopped in mid-stride and turned. Wilhelm turned his eyes to the broad entry doors.

A fat man in a white uniform came through with every appearance of a ship of state. He moved with surprising lightness of step. He seemed to float rather than stride. Over the resplendency of the bemedaled uniform rode a face in full moon, all smiles and pleasant glow. More sinister figures in black made a phalanx behind him. It parted, and a small man in a drab uniform paced in.

He wore a hat whose shining leather peak very nearly

obscured his eyes. There was a smudge of mustache beneath a witchlike nose. The figure smiled. It was the smile of a marionette much in keeping with the jerking strides of the booted legs. Hitler removed his hat and smoothed his hair to his head. Göring moved to his side like a benevolent whale.

The room released its breath, wanting to shout, to scream, to adore.

Wilhelm found himself before the Führer. Canaris was swiftly outlining the exploits of one Wilhelm Oerter, the amazing spy who had patiently waited for the single moment and then struck a stunning blow for the Fatherland. Much of the swift German was lost to Wilhelm. He became aware of Commander Prien standing at his shoulder. He wanted to look at the face of the man, the only man in the whole company he might call an acquaintance, but he intuited that such a break in his attention upon the form of Adolf Hitler would be a breach of etiquette so severe as to be unthinkable.

He noted that Hitler's smile was pasted on and that the eyes were tired. He nodded his head several times, affably at first but with growing impatience. Canaris turned to a uniformed aide. A flat velvet box was transferred into his hands. He opened the blue plush covers. Two medals were revealed. Simple crosses of iron suspended from ribbons of silk.

Hitler took them up and pinned one upon the breast of Prien's tunic. He shook the officer's hand and said something.

Wilhelm felt greatly excited.

He received his own medal from the savior of Germany. He felt a pride, not his own, well up in him. He recognized the pride as that of his father. This, then, was the high point of Wilhelm Oerter's life?

The attention given him increased the moment Hitler turned on his heel and strode out, followed by his entourage. Everyone knew who he was finally. He was a hero. He was a man who had been decorated personally by Hitler. He was a celebrity.

Wilhelm sought the privacy of the balcony that overlooked the opera house gardens. He stood near the balustrade, looking out to the velvet dark of the linden trees. Where the lights of the ballroom touched the ground, it was rusty with fallen autumn leaves. He heard a step behind him.

He turned to face Günter Prien.

The naval officer addressed him in German.

Wilhelm knew the man's remarks to be in the way of congratulations and replied haltingly in kind.

Prien smiled. 'You have difficulty understanding German?' he asked in English.

'You must understand it has been twenty years since I've spoken, as a matter of daily habit, in my native tongue. It is easy to forget. And, too, there is this excitement. It makes it difficult.'

'I will speak in English. I was congratulating you on the honor paid to you.'

'And I congratulate you.'

Wilhelm was shaken by a sudden tremor of the arms and shoulders.

'It is not too cold for you?' Prien asked solicitously.

'The wind blows much colder than this at home. I mean to say....'

Prien interrupted him. 'I understand. Home is a matter of habit. A phrase. A thought. I think of the sea as home.'

He leaned against the marble balustrade.

'You've read the reports of our amazing accomplishment?'

Wilhelm shook his head and wondered at the note of sarcasm that touched Prien's words.

'I've had no opportunity.'

'It bears little resemblance to the facts. According to the official document, the harbor was well lit and alive with British destroyers.'

Wilhelm shook his head and shrugged, wondering if a comment was called for.

Prien laughed.

'In this way our accomplishment is maximized to the world. But do you know, it has somehow been made smaller for me.'

Wilhelm glanced at the man sharply. The voice was that of the boy from that summer's holiday long ago. The voice of a young man who had dreamed of honor and service and a shining glory.

'They are, I understand, preparing a book concerning the exploits of that hero of the Reich, one Günter Prien, who single-handedly took on and defeated the British Fleet at Scapa Flow,' Prien continued.

He waved his hand vaguely and grew silent.

Then he looked at Wilhelm for a long, probing moment.

'Mr. Oerter, will you miss it very much? The Orkneys?'

'I am a stranger here.'

Prien nodded.

'I'm beginning to feel the chill,' Wilhelm murmured. 'I would like to go back to my room if it's permissible?'

'Don't ask permission. Tell them you are heavy with honors and wearied by a surfeit of heroism.' Prien laughed.

He touched Wilhelm's jacket as though adjusting a scarf about the neck of an older man.

'I shall be returning to duty before very long, but until then and whenever I'm in Berlin, I would like to call on you and ask after your welfare.'

'That is very kind of you.'

'We are neither of us heavy with friends. But I believe we are both heavy with loneliness.'

He turned away and left Wilhelm to find his own way back into the reception.

At the end of two weeks the wonder of Scapa Flow was permanently amberized and set aside in official statements that proved the British fleet far from invulnerable. Wilhelm Oerter's part in it was never made public after all. He was politely informed that the suite of rooms in the hotel had been engaged temporarily. He was expected to find suitable accommodations for himself, by himself. Werner gave him no help, but a secretary from the Office of Naval Intelligence came unannounced and offered to help him in the city that was strange to him.

Her name was Ilsa Schaff. She was a woman in her middle forties. She was large-breasted and solidly built. She was a friend of Günter Prien, and it was he who had suggested she might help the unknown hero of Scapa Flow find a place to sleep. She was efficient in the task and procured a small apartment for Wilhelm. It was furnished and had a bed. She offered to join him in it. Wilhelm courteously refused, and he never saw her again. He was certain she was not too upset by the refusal. She would have enjoyed the celebrity of having slept with a genuine, iron-medaled hero, but it would not have been, after all, an act performed with a public hero and would have been, therefore, less desirable.

He bought a rocking chair and waited for a summons from the Office of German Intelligence concerning his future employment.

He rocked back and forth until it became the thrust of John Kendrick's fishing craft against the sea. Sometimes it became the gentle lifting of his own cockleshell. He could feel his son's small hand beneath his own on the tiller.

In the day he stared out the window until the street below dissolved away and he could see the cliffs of the Orkneys and relish the distant spot of white that marked Molly's cottage.

He often thought he saw Julie walking down the market street.

In the night he saw the quiet reaches of Scapa Flow.

There was madness in the fantasies he fashioned. He knew it and welcomed such gentle madness.

At last he was called to present himself for assignment. He was given employment in a department that translated and evaluated material taken from the English press.

He went to the office at eight o'clock and remained until six o'clock in the evening. His desk was exactly the same as forty-nine others in the room. He wanted it no other way. He embraced anonymity.

He was shortly summed up by his fellow workers as a man made arrogant and proud by some mysterious association with active intelligence operations in the field. They disliked and feared him to some degree. His stolid manner and refusal to gossip marked him as a possible informer. A spy who spied upon spies.

Wilhelm didn't care for the friendships denied him. He went home each evening and drew his rocking chair close to the stove that gave heat to the bed-sitting-room. It was his nation. His piece of England in an alien land.

CHAPTER 30

The German papers were filled with the latest swift, blazing invasion of the invincible German armies. On April 9, 1940, they had occupied Copenhagen.

Because of the plan of Winston Churchill, 'the century's greatest warmonger' and the First Lord of the Admiralty, to police Norwegian and Danish waters against the wills of the two countries, Hitler had resolved to take over the protection of Danish and Norwegian neutrality and guard the countries during the war. Germany had been forced into the act of prevention so that Britain might not be allowed to expand the war.

Another item in the same day's paper commanded even more of Wilhelm's attention. It concerned the German report of an attack on several heavy units of the British fleet at Scapa Flow.

At the translation office he read in the London *Times* that no hits had been made on any heavy elements of the British armada. It did say that a civilian had been buried under debris by a high-explosive bomb but had sustained no injury beyond shock.

The article brought sudden living fear piling in upon Wilhelm. How little, he realized, could the articles printed by either side be believed. The statement that one man was trapped but rescued, small sections of heather set afire without further injury, one farmhouse scorched and nothing more brought visions of a Kirkwall laid waste. He saw his own home bombed to rubble. He saw Julie dead or dying among the wreckage. He saw his son flung and shattered by the giant hand of explosives. Had the people of the Orkneys evacuated the children, at least, to safer places in the heart of Britain?

He was sick with fear and worry. He had no means to discharge them and no one to express them to.

He went to a rathskeller two blocks from his flat and sought the company of men. That first night he entered into no conversations.

He drank heavily, which was not his usual custom. The alcohol left him comparatively unchanged. It brought no forgetfulness or comfort to him. Instead, the vivid pictures of Julie lying twisted, one hand flung toward the protection of young John, already shattered and dead, began to merge with the recall of the upflung arm and his touch upon it. The arm that had risen from the sea to implore and accuse him. The arm that had been stripped of its living envelope as he'd touched it.

He felt madness coming upon him and began to curse the liquor that had vivified his nightmare visions instead of wrapping them in the opacity of forgetfulness. He struggled home to his lonely bed, feeling as though he were trodding through icy water filled with dead men's fingers clutching at him.

The triumphant celebration of German victory went on. A drum roll of the dead. A parade of nations fallen.

The Netherlands, Luxembourg, Belgium – all were invaded on May 10. They were occupied in order to protect their neutrality from the British lion, the German press said.

Britain occupied Iceland to forestall a German invasion of the strategically valuable former Danish dominion.

Broken bodies of women and children lying in deceptively peaceful landscapes dotted by windmills, barges sunk leaving a floating debris of human parts, toy soldiers winnowed by a scythe of steel – all came to join the sailors of the *Royal Oak* in Wilhelm's sleeping and waking dreams.

He went to the same rathskeller every morning and remained there late, drinking steadily, hunting an anodyne.

He entered, at last, into the conversations of other men. The atmosphere of common fellowship and ease, so like that which he'd enjoyed in his own pubs, lured him with the false face of normality. It often seemed strange to him to be on the wrong side of the bar counter. He often had the nearly overpowering desire to step behind it and play at proprietor. There was companionship and a man, Karl Hauser, he considered a friend.

'Do you know,' Wilhelm said, 'it is almost amusing how the great nations go about protecting the small ones? They take over, invade, occupy. Always for the protection of the weak. Great nations are endowed, it seems, with a certain built-in nobility.'

'How exactly do you mean that, Wilhelm?' Hauser asked.

'Do you see that Germany "protected" the neutrality of the

Danes and the Norwegians? She is now protecting the Lowlands. Meanwhile, Britain protects Iceland and seeds the waters of Norway with mines.'

'Wilhelm, it would be better if you didn't speak this way in front of people.'

Wilhelm looked at his friend with some surprise at the sharp tone of his voice. Hauser went on. 'In some quarters such remarks would be considered more than indiscreet; they would be considered treasonable.'

'Certainly the irony of the situation is obvious.'

'What is obvious is often treasonable. An expression of the truth is often disloyal. Upon this and other paradoxes, nations survive. To know the truth and act counter to it is often the greatest of patriotic gestures; to ask for an explanation of contradictions often the direst treason.'

Wilhelm celebrated his fifty-sixth birthday in tears. He decided to return to his boyhood home in Garmisch on a visit of hope and nostalgia.

Since his return to Germany he had avoided asking himself if his mother or perhaps the servant girl Katy was still alive. The certainty that his father was long dead had never left him. He had sorrowed in his heart that there were things between them left unsaid that would never be done with. Now he had a sudden longing to see old streets and familiar faces.

He took the train into Bavaria. He saw few familiar faces. A whole world had died and a new one been born and raised since last he'd walked the streets. His old house was there, nearly unchanged. He rang the bell and waited a long time before a suspicious eye finally appeared at the door.

'Pardon me. I'm trying to locate a family by the name of Oerter.'

'Not here.'

'It would be some years ago.'

'How many?'

Wilhelm shrugged. 'Twenty years. Perhaps as long as that. Probably not so long.'

'What was the name?'

'Oerter.'

'There was an Oerter lived here. The husband died ten years ago.'

'And the wife?'

The door opened further to reveal a crabbed chin and an ancient nose.

'What business is it of yours?'

'None, none. I would simply like to find the Oerters.'

'I own the house.'

'Is it much changed?'

Suspicion dripped from her eyes with a watery rheum.

'It was left me when the wife died.'

Wilhelm backed off a step, nearly stumbling over the boot scraper that had come partially loose from the concrete step.

'Katy?'

'My name is Katerina Myers.'

The door opened wider still. The old woman clawed at a shawl, food-stained and worn. She wore a pair of men's shoes too small for her splayed feet. They were cut at the sides to relieve the bunions and other growths that deformed her toes.

Wilhelm reached out a hand and supported himself on the doorjamb. She retreated as though she believed he was going to strike her.

Her voice sounded far away to his ears.

There was a terrible shift of time. Was this the Katy, the servant woman who had been so sturdy, who always smelled of spices and flour?

'It is me, Katy. It is me, Willy.'

He watched her face collapse into the most terrible wreckage of conflicting emotions. Disbelief, joy, regret, fear – all passed about the raddled features. She threw the door open and allowed the shawl to slip to the floor. She held out her arms, and he went to her.

They stood in that fashion for a long, long time until the pain was gone somewhat. She began to fuss at herself, knowing that the immaculate Katy of this man's boyhood had allowed herself to become a sloven. She drew him into the house. It smelled sour with the sweet overlay of a sickroom.

They sat in the kitchen, and she forced some small foods and a cup of tea upon him. The rest of the house, except for her old bedroom, was left unoccupied and unused.

She related the details of his father's death at great length for the comfortable sound of it to her own dying ears. She detailed the illness and passing of his mother. The deaths were as commonplace as the lives and deaths of most people. She told him that they had been informed by the authorities that their son had been killed in the last attack launched by the German Army in the last desperate days of the Great War.

How efficient were the authorities, thought Wilhelm. They'd remembered to declare him dead for his cover's sake.

She asked that he stay the night. She wanted to prepare his old room for him, but he begged urgent business back in Berlin.

When he left, she touched his sleeve to stay him for a moment.

'Why did you never write and let your mother know you were alive, Willy?'

'It wasn't possible.'

She nodded as though that were some explanation of the general madness of living.

'Your mother never believed you were dead. Even at the last she said that you were never dead.'

It seemed a fact of great wonder and significance to the old servant woman. Wilhelm understood it to be the expression of love that every mother held concerning a child dead, lost or stolen.

Wilhelm returned to the city of Berlin. A city holding a great, boastful cry of vengeance achieved in its lungs and belly, for it was June 5, and France had been attacked.

There was in the eyes of even his mildest acquaintances, the passersby on the street, a blood madness that frightened Wilhelm.

The cry burst forth on June 14. Paris had been declared an open city for the protection and preservation of its beauty, and German soldiers were marching through the Arc de Triomphe.

Germany was plunged into the wildest of celebrations. Wilhelm spoke softly to his friend Karl and drank to excess. The exuberance of the city was too much for him. He went to his rooms and for a while remained there in the evenings.

The French signed a truce in a railroad car in the forest of Compiègne at 6:50 P.M. German time, on June 22, 1940, and Hitler executed an amusing dance step.

Britain was alone. Wilhelm felt a strange pride as he read the British papers and the statements of Britain's leaders. They were so full of patient resolve, courage, discipline and the absence of despair.

CHAPTER 31

It was August, and the stories in the British press gave a sober view of the Battle of Britain.

They made little attempt to minimize the rigors to which the British people were being submitted or the effectiveness of the German air raids.

The Berlin papers were equally full of the conflict. They were triumphant and predicted an early collapse of the island kingdom that foolishly refused to see that its destiny was linked with that of Greater Germany. The stubborn British were forcing their cousins to annihilate them.

It colored every conversation in the rathskeller. Wilhelm sometimes found his heart touched with rage when someone mouthed a particularly offensive insult against the British.

He very quickly had his fill of the society of friends and acquaintances who projected estimates of the time and the manner of Britain's final capitulation. Even Karl Hauser, with his quiet ways, was no good companion to Wilhelm, and he shortly excused himself and made to leave. Karl begged him to stay a moment longer.

'Please, not yet, Wilhelm. My sister has come to Berlin. She's to meet me here.'

'I didn't know you had a sister.'

'That's true. We've never spoken of our families. She's lived in Dusseldorf with an aging aunt these past six years or more. The old aunt died this past week, and Gisella has come to stay with me.'

Wilhelm made a small mew of sympathy over the death of Hauser's relative. Karl waved a hand.

'Thank you, but she was very old and, I think, tired of life. I saw very little of her. In fact, I felt that Gisella was wasting herself caring for the old lady, but my sister was afraid to have her put in a home for the aged.'

Wilhelm made no comment, but his manner suggested he was curious about the reasons behind the sister's reluctance to give up her burden and afford the ancient a more efficient routine of care.

'The aunt was senile and childish. She had no control over

her body functions. Indeed, I don't believe she even recognized anyone these past three years or so. Gisella had heard tales that old relatives put into state institutions were soon dead.'

Wilhelm continued his silence. The implication was clear, ut he was reluctant to make any comment.

Karl stood up.

'My sister is a fussy but loving person. She was easily frightened by fairy tales when she was a child.'

He took a few steps, and Wilhelm turned and stood in the same motion. It gave him a sudden stricture along his ribs. From a position, awkward and crablike, one hand to the small of his back, he saw Gisella Hauser for the first time.

He experienced, as he had before upon rare occasions, an overwhelming sense of *déjà vu*. She was tall for a woman, taller than her brother. She was, Wilhelm reckoned, in her middle forties but scarcely looked more than thirty-five. She wore her hair in great coils of hair that was the color of dark wet wheat. He knew what it would look like loosened and hanging down her strong back. Her breasts were high and thrusting, and he was sure they were not the product of a garment maker's art.

When Karl introduced them, she reached a hand out to the one he was using to support the pain of his back and grasped that wrist instead of offering her right hand to be shaken.

'Please be seated. I'm afraid you turned too fast.'

'I was clumsy.'

'It happens.' She smiled lightly and sat down at the table.

Wilhelm relaxed into the chair with a sigh of relief and caught her eyes upon him. She laughed lightly as though they were old, old friends or even bed partners sharing a secret joke that only people of long experience with one another might share.

She was, Wilhelm considered, not a beautiful or comely woman. She was what one might call a 'handsome' woman. Her eyes were notable. They were large and luminous and straightforward in their regard of him. He remembered thinking such thoughts before.

He remembered Molly.

Gisella refused beer or schnapps but allowed that she would take a glass of hock.

The room suddenly grew warm and cozy in her presence. Wilhelm listened to the brother and sister making plans.

Gisella was, for the moment, staying at a small hotel. Karl had been, till this moment, sharing rooms with two other bachelors. He was obviously careless about his surroundings. ow they planned to acquire a small flat, and she would make a home for them.

Wilhelm remarked that an apartment might be found in his own building. Gisella turned her smile on him once more.

'That would be nice. We would be neighbors, Willy.'

The small word of affection.

The small claim announced?

Wilhelm sat in his chair in his room and lowered the paper that told of the German invasion of Yugoslavia and Greece. It meant surprisingly little to him.

He stared out through the window. It was little more than an arm's length away. Beyond the pane he could see the faint gray of gathering dawn, and he imagined the sea not far beyond the scattered rooftops and chimney pots within his vision. The North Sea crashing at the shores of the Orkneys. Driven from his bed by nightmare, he returned to it and Gisella lying there.

He felt the long, soft length of her lying next to him. The touch of her was a blessing. He turned his head from the view through the window and his back on that past and those women, Molly, Julie, that intruded on the space that contained himself and Gisella. She lay deeply sleeping in the way of a healthy animal, her mouth slightly opened and the tip of a pink tongue gleaming.

He had been amazed at the thrusting potency of his body that night before. It was the first night they had come together in this way after many, many nights of coffee and quiet talk at the kitchen table in the Hausers' small apartment but two floors below.

He wondered at it again as he felt an erection that any lusting eighteen-year-old would be proud of. The urgency of his desire communicated itself to Gisella, even in her sleep. She opened her eyes, fully awake and unstartled, to see him watching her. Her hand enclosed that youthful part of him. She rolled over onto her back and drew him on top of her.

'Willy, fuck me good morning,' she said in the smallest of voices.

CHAPTER 32

The work in the office of translations was far from demanding. It offered absolutely no challenge and was, therefore, eminently suited to Wilhem's temper.

He found in the pages of the British press and periodicals the same self-serving, public-duping distortion of the news that appeared for the very same reasons in the German press. He, of course, only assumed the distortions since there was no way he could know what really was happening.

This whole business of truth, or the interpretation of truth, as a means of public control, solace, enthusiasm, loyalty, sacrifice and entertainment only served to reconfirm the sense within himself that all men, and perhaps himself most of all, were actors in a play without a playwright. The circumstances exploded upon them, they were acted on for reasons of survival, and later those actions were carefully explained and analyzed to prove one's own cleverness and the enemy's stupidity.

On rare occasions he would note some obscure fact in the welter of information and link it to another item equally obscure that together added up to a significant bit of knowledge useful to the game plan. He was once commended upon his acuteness. The commendation took the form of an official letter printed on fine vellum paper and emblazoned with the German eagle in bas-relief. He had been the envy of his fellow translators.

It was that night he offered his medal, awarded by the Führer himself, to a merchant in such trinkets. With the proceeds he bought a copper machine that, after much fuss and fury, delivered a scant two cups of very thick, but very good coffee. It was a samovar but wasn't called a samovar, for Germany had gone to war with the Soviet Union.

After dinner in the Hauser apartment with coffee served from the machine, Karl invited Wilhelm to join him at the rathskeller. It came as no surprise when Wilhelm demurred. In the past weeks when he had been a frequent guest to dinner, only once had he gone along with Karl to share a glass of beer.

This evening there had been a tension between Gisella and Wilhelm. Karl presumed things had not gone well in bed the night before. Did his friend seem a trifle drawn? He had the feeling that his dear sister had an insatiable maw between her legs. He shook his head in pity. A man of Wilhelm's age should have long since afforded his penis a proper place in the scheme of his life. It was, Karl thought, best used as a discharge valve for a bladder overloaded with beer. It was less complicated and far less demanding.

When he was gone, Gisella went to the sink behind the curtain at one corner of the living room and washed the dishes. It was done with dispatch in the manner in which she accomplished all household tasks. She came back drying her hands on her apron.

'Shall we go to your rooms, Willy?'

He hesitated. She roused desire in him easily, but there was a frantic quality to it as though they were making up for lost time, lost orgasms. In the maturity of their time they went at the business of sex like those newly arrived to the passionate landscape, and it left its own bad taste of urgency when it was done.

In the long days of his marriage there had been none of that sense of time challenged and fought. The sexual life he enjoyed with Julie had been paced to a kind of special time that encapsulated them both. There had been long seasons of near abstinence that carried no feeling of loss, full seasons of slow and explorative sex that seemed to ripen and burst like a peach on a summer tree and violent appetites that flared like rockets filled with breath-catching excitement followed by utter exhaustion, cool and refreshing. But it was all part of a single piece of cloth, a tapestry of days shot through with a thousand different colors given to the nights.

With Gisella it had taken on, once the novelty of such abundant carnality after a long abstinence had waned, the aspect of a sport or a contest, an almost military accomplishment.

He shook his head. She sat on the footstool at his feet and fixed him with her large, luminous eyes.

'Willy, there is a flat that will be to let in a building on the Parkstrasse. It's a nice building closer to your work. It has a large salon and two bedrooms. There is a proper kitchen. A good friend of mine is giving it up, and in this crowded city we might not have a chance for such a place for a long while.'

He scarcely heard her, though he nodded. He felt that this was the prelude to the main theme that she'd been composing as she hummed at her chores.

'With two wages, yours and Karl's, we could easily afford it.'

'Two bedrooms?' Wilhelm was struck by the thought that whenever he was in doubt, or whenever he could see no way to stave off the words that would demand a decision or statement of him, he would dumbly repeat some phrase plucked from his confrere's speech.

'One for Karl and the other for us.' There was a crisp overtone to her voice like the sound her white teeth made when she bit into a raw turnip. She liked raw turnips, and it was another thing Wilhelm found difficult to understand.

'Ah.'

'I'm saying, Wilhelm, that it is perhaps time for us to be married. There are advantages.'

'I can see that there would be.'

A great silence lay between them, not so long as deep.

'You're a fearful man,' she condemned, though her voice was soft.

'I have no courage,' he agreed. He'd amended the word, for a lack of courage seemed, somehow, a more courageous admission than to agree that one was fearful. A sound escaped him that sounded uncomfortably like a giggle.

'I've noticed that about you, Willy. You let life happen to you.'

His head raised sharply, and he looked at her as though she had uttered an expression of great wisdom.

'So do we all. Don't we?'

'Perhaps there are things we can't control, but there are many things we can judge and act upon. We have enjoyment in bed?'

In the moment it seemed startlingly true, and he felt a surge of desire.

'Much enjoyment.'

'And the other things, the cleanliness, the cooking, the talk is all good?'

'I think so.'

'Then we should be married. We are, neither of us, getting any younger.'

Wilhelm wished desperately that she hadn't added the last phrase. He was acutely aware of the years passing, and it made more acute the certain knowledge that those years would not be half so burdensome if they were to be spent with his wife and son. As the boy grew, it would be as though the years that were draining from his cup of life, and those that fled from Julie's cup as well, were filling the body and bones of the life they'd made. Where would Gisella and he place the years? Into what receptacle?

'Do you think,' he asked, 'the owner of this other apartment building would allow us to have a dog?'

They were married in the office of the city clerk two weeks later.

CHAPTER 33

A half year of his new married life had left Wilhelm with the uncomfortable feeling that his inability to decide on a course of action had led him into commitment prematurely and the comfortable feeling that matters had turned out, for him, very well indeed.

His brother-in-law seemed less pleased by the new arrangement. Gisella extended her pride in her husband's appearance and well-being to her brother as well, and it didn't suit Karl at all. In spite of the fact that he had the convenience of a neatly brushed suit and polished shoes with no effort to himself, he regretted the loss of his carefree bachelor ways. At last he informed his sister and Wilhelm that he prized his solitude far too much to allow him to continue in the arrangement.

Gisella offered a dozen arguments against his departure. He undoubtedly ate better, slept cleaner, presented a finer appearance altogether. He grinned and agreed that all this was true enough, but it should be apparent if he wanted such riches he would have married long ago. Gisella then spoke more sharply of economy, responsibility to Wilhelm and herself and his sworn duty to the oral contract that had made the acquisition of the new apartment possible.

Karl studied his sister blandly as though she were some strange creature that had invaded the placid pond of his life. He allowed the practical justice of her arguments and packed his few belongings. With a cheerful air he left the admittedly bright and spacious apartment for the cramped, shared quarters of an old crony.

Later, in the rathskeller, he pretended great surprise when Wilhelm joined him.

'Has she let you out then?'

'I don't understand.'

'Marriage seems to be the catalyst in a strange alchemy that affects women. They are overcome by a certain madness to dust, to clean, to polish not only tables and shelves but any male that comes in range. With tender and loving tyranny they present men with clean shirts, warm meals and all manner of rules and regulations.

'I remember my little sister' – his mouth quirked at this description of a woman larger than he – 'as being an exceptionally pliable little girl. By a certain meekness of manner she secured dictatorship over my father's heart. When she took on the care of my ancient aunt, she was a willing and untiring servant. She displayed extraordinary patience with the old lady. Upon reflection I wonder if it was all an act. I wonder, too, if the old woman pretended a failure of her senses just to soothe the tiger that pretended to be a kitten.'

'I wonder' – Wilhelm laughed – 'if you are not just too old a dog to be housebroken.'

Karl leaned back with a stein of beer in one hand and his smelly pipe in the other. He eyed the smoking bowl with ludicrous intent. He puffed on it furiously, sending up clouds of smoke, and challenged Wilhelm with a twinkling smile.

'Yes, yes, I know. Gisella prefers pipes to be smoked outside the house. She says the smell clings to the curtains.'

Karl nodded sharply, his argument proved. 'Yes, these quiet, willing ones present a picture of great docility until that moment comes when they have a home of their own in their control.'

Wilhelm was about to say, but did not say, that such things as the restriction against smoking was a pleasing one to him. It afforded him a simple ready excuse to leave the starched bright rooms and seek the silence of the stars.

Karl put down the glass and pipe and clapped his beefy hands together. He peered into his palms one after the other.

'Is that a fly?' he asked with heavy humor. 'No, it is a husband,' he answered himself.

They laughed over the humorous burlesque. Suddenly Wilhelm realized that there was a deeper well of disquiet within him. Why else did he often use his pipe or any other excuse to escape the apartment? Karl might well believe it was because of the sexual demands Gisella had so obviously made upon him during their courtship in addition to the restrictions of her house. In truth, the very nearly desperate bedroom activity that had preceded their marriage had fallen off considerably. Often, before those far fewer occasions when they enjoyed each other in married fashion, he would become aware of her silent regard. She would have about her that quiet sense of preparation one has when about to enter a battle or stand to trial.

Was it because she found intercourse with his aging body

distasteful to her? Honestly, no. Once engaged in the act, she responded so fully it sometimes frightened him.

Was it because some deep-set morality or childhood training made such abandon unbecoming for a middle-aged matron? If it was a question of morality, certainly the sex before the wedding would have been even more sinful and improper.

Was it fear of pregnancy? They'd never given any care or conversation to birth control. Wilhelm assumed she'd reached her menopause.

Whatever the root cause and true nature of the slight alienation between them, in the moment he clearly saw that it was at the very center of his disaffection.

He must think about it and decide what to do about the matter.

There was no small dog in the apartment. Three days after his conversation with brother-in-law Karl, Wilhelm decided he would make a small assertion of his own will. He did not intend to appear henpecked in Karl's eyes.

'I've not forgotten that the landlord allows us to have a pet. I've been thinking about the sort of dog we should get.'

'Dogs are dirty things. They leave their hair about the furniture.'

'I think perhaps an imperial French poodle. They are beautiful and not often seen.'

'Dogs are smelly.'

'We'll go to the market tomorrow.'

'I won't have a dog in the house.'

'I will go to the market tomorrow on my lunch hour and buy such an animal.'

Their eyes touched and locked. Gisella dropped the point of her sword first.

'If you will have a dog, wouldn't it be better to have a shepherd? It is at least a dog of this country.'

Wilhelm conceded the point. He was unwilling to press total surrender on her.

He acquired an undersized shepherd with intelligent eyes that was already a year old and housebroken. He'd wanted a male, but at Gisella's prompting, the dog was a female. Gisella felt they were gentler and more tractable. The dog was spayed at once. Gisella didn't feel it necessary for the bitch to fulfill the female destiny and bear pups.

The bitch was named Blondie at Gisella's request because that was the name the Führer had given his dog.

In private Wilhelm called the dog Boola, which meant nothing. The name with no meaning suited Wilhelm's general mood when he sought escape walking the streets with the dog on leash. He'd not yet broached the subject of their sexual life to his wife.

After victory piled upon victory and even with the entry of the United States of America into the war, the triumphant feeling run rampant throughout Germany went on unabated. Until, after four nights of bombing by the RAF, eight thousand dead and more than thirty thousand made homeless, the Fatherland came to the shocking realization that it, too, could be wounded and would bleed.

As the first refugees from the massive attack on the port of Rostock began to filter into Berlin, Gisella went at once to the office of the Refugee Relief League and offered the room that had lain empty since Karl's day of departure. Wilhelm had turned it into yet another refuge against the subtly reproachful attitude of his wife. He'd placed a writing desk, his rocking chair and Boola's basket there.

The offer of succor for some poor people deprived of their homes and possessions did not seem entirely an act of kindness on Gisella's part. Wilhelm felt, with some small sense of shame and disloyalty, that the offer had been made to prevent the authorities from otherwise commandeering the space without payment.

He realized that what seemed to him devious talents might more properly be considered superior organizational skills, yet he could not shake off the feeling that there was little spontaneous charity in her acts. She returned that night not only with a short list of unfortunates that were in need of shelter but with paid employment in the welfare organization.

Wilhelm could imagine her with her vast bosom and compassionate, overflowing eyes, intricately woven with that air of crisp efficiency she carried with her like a shield, volunteering her services, mentioning the long years of faithful care of an aging relative and dropping the hint that it was painfully difficult to provide a hero of the Third Reich, Iron Cross, Second Rank, with a suitable home after the years of rigorous service he'd suffered for the Fatherland.

Her salary was small to begin with, and she made it her own entirely.

In her new position she was able to escape any official inspection of their premises; her description of their quarters was taken at face value. The first beneficiary of her charity was a young couple who were childless. The wife was not very clever. She was, in fact, somewhat dim-witted, but she was quick to learn the housekeeping techniques that Gisella employed.

The husband was not much brighter. He was thirty-five and robust. Some disability, vague but documented, had so far kept him from service in the armed forces. He found employment easily enough or, rather, Gisella found it for him. From his paycheck she extracted payment for their food and lodging.

Two weeks after their arrival in the apartment Wilhelm had occasion to come home at midafternoon. The wife, Lenni, was not at home, apparently off on some errand or other.

Boola had been locked in their 'guests'' room. The husband, Hugo, was in Wilhelm's own bedroom. Indeed, in his own bed.

Wilhelm quietly shut the door. He could not be certain whether or not Gisella had spied him over the young man's shoulder. He chose to believe, for his pride's sake, that she was too lost to passion to have seen him.

CHAPTER 34

If the reports of the British offensive in the Egyptian desert in October, 1942, were shrouded in secrecy as they were written in the British press, the very existence of such a major defeat suffered by the elite Afrika Corps and Germany's hero-as-minor-god Rommel was all but ignored in the official German communiqués. But somehow the long shadow of disaster had fled darkly across the burning sands, crossed oceans and probed with a terrible finger at the vitals of the German people.

It was the talk of the gathering places, and Wilhelm indiscreetly mentioned to Karl that his translation of the London *Times* had sounded a triumphant note unusual to date in British reports of the war.

Early in the following week Wilhelm was called into the office of the chief of the division for which he worked. Dr. Prinz had been a professor of languages at Leyden University before the war, and his pale-blue eyes always seemed filled with the longing for the cloistered halls of academia. He was a skillful man at his job, a fair administrator, but he gave no enthusiasm to his responsibilities. He simply managed them with a minimum of fuss and a maximum of goodwill among his employees.

He rose to his feet as though startled when Wilhelm knocked on the half glass of his office door and beckoned him in with a gesture that was broader and more effusive than any he had ever used before.

The man sitting in the wooden chair at the side of the desk didn't rise to the introduction. He neither smiled nor offered his hand to be shaken. He sat low on his spine, nearly sprawling, with an insouciance that bordered on the insulting. There was that in the man's manner and a certain slovenliness in his appearance that reminded Wilhelm unpleasantly of the silent assassin Harold.

Professor Prinz offered Wilhelm a seat. There was fear and concern in his manner. Wilhelm was certain the silent figure was Gestapo.

'Last week you were assigned to the translation of the London *Times*?'

Wilhelm nodded. The question was largely official, for the doctor was well aware that Wilhelm was most usually at the translation of items from that newspaper, the Manchester *Guardian*, and an occasional popular magazine.

'You noted the front-page article concerning the supposed British breakthrough in the Western Desert at El Alamein?'

'I did.'

'You translated it for official attention?'

'A great deal, but not all of it.'

'You felt it of no particular significance?'

Prinz was carefully leading him, and Wilhelm was ready to follow the moment he saw the way.

'Significant only as an expression of the propaganda techniques the English employ upon their citizens.'

'Explain!' The word coming from the slouching figure shocked Wilhelm as Harold's final resort to speech had dismayed him those years ago.

He, therefore, looked dumb.

'You believed the lies were of no special importance then?' Prinz asked, leading Wilhelm to a safe path.

'I translated a reasonable portion according to standard procedure. I deemed it certain that the authorities were aware of the lies. The piece was red-lined in the event that the entire text was asked for in translation. No such request was made.'

'Naturally our superiors are aware of the deviousness of English methods,' Prinz agreed. 'You spoke of this during the course of the day?'

'No.'

The Gestapo agent removed a small notebook from his pocket and flipped over a few soiled pages.

Wilhelm felt a start of fear. Was he to be officially accused and faced with some obscure treason? He frowned, giving his face the appearance of thought. Prinz leaned forward, trying to will him to remember and to tell the truth since it was, apparently, already known.

Wilhelm felt drops of sweat form on the backs of his knees. It was an acute and amazing sensation.

He began to speak but stammered and held his words for a long moment. When they came, they seemed steady enough to his own ears, and Prinz smiled encouragingly.

'I did perhaps mention it in passing to my brother-in-law.'

'Where?'

Wilhelm felt his head jerk around to face the man. He was reacting shamefully, he thought, to the single words as though they were the crack of a punishing whip.

'At the rathskeller near my home.'

'Who else was present?'

'No one. Only my brother-in-law.'

The Gestapo man looked hard at Wilhelm, then at Dr. Prinz. He seemed to have exhausted his need for speech. Dr. Prinz took up the interrogation.

'Did you suggest when you, indiscreetly perhaps, mentioned the English newspaper article, that they were telling the truth and that the alleged victory was indeed genuine?'

'No.'

'But you had reason to comment upon the article. I mean to say that the English were filling their people with lies?'

'That seemed obvious.'

The Gestapo agent closed his book with an air of completion. He stood up and nodded to Prinz but made no further recognition of the presence of Wilhelm.

When he'd left, Prinz visibly shrank into his chair.

'You were most indiscreet, most foolish.'

'It was a passing remark, no more.'

Prinz shook his head, and his desire to be out of even such unimportant corridors of intrigue was most obvious.

'You are employed in a sensitive capacity by a branch of German Intelligence. Nothing, not even a sign over the water cooler, is to be mentioned outside this office.'

'The speculation that this English offensive is of vital concern to the German people and the outcome of the war is common talk wherever one goes.'

'It is a matter of obedience to orders. I'm afraid I've been asked to sever your relationship with this operation.'

'But why?'

'They told me that you were married to an Englishwoman and have an English son.'

'I was instructed to maintain British citizenship and to become, as nearly as possible, a member of the community in which I found myself.'

'Please don't confuse the issue or me with the application of logic.' Prinz smiled at his small professional joke. 'It seems they suspect you may possibly have succumbed to a certain sympathy to the English cause because of the wife and child and those long years in England.'

'I was ordered to play the role,' Wilhelm nearly shouted in frustration.

Prinz was silent. He turned his gaze to the window. Perhaps he saw ivied walls and long rows of books in burgundy leather bindings. The blue eyes grew soft, nearly weeping.

'You are a good man, I think. An honest and honorable man, if such a thing is possible of someone who lived such a deception. Were you always comfortable in the part?'

Wilhelm was about to answer, to react to the expression of empathy and understanding. He stopped the words in his throat. Could this gentle old man be leading him into a trap? Was he being tricked into condemning himself as disloyal, at the least unreliable?

'I obeyed my orders.'

Prinz nodded, indicating an understanding that existed on more than one level. He was embarrassed somehow and became brisk.

'There's very little I can do. I've been asked to relieve you of your duties.'

'What am I to do?'

'I have no way of knowing.'

He lowered his head to his desk and began to read a report lying before him. Wilhelm accepted the action as dismissal. He rose and left. He stopped at his desk. There was only a pipe and a bit of tobacco in the bottom of a two-ounce can. When he'd placed those in his pocket, he'd taken away every trace of his connection with the office.

CHAPTER 35

They sat, the five of them, in his living room.

He glanced at Gisella and thought of her as a full-bodied, lecherous, domineering, flour-handed, spice-smelling matron, wife and, somehow, incestuous mother.

Hugo was the thirty-five-year-old 'son' and lover. He sat hunched over the beer glass clutched in his hands as though trying, by the awkwardness of his physical attitude, to convey the impression that he was listening with heart and reckoning mind to the radio voice as Hitler addressed the German people.

Lenni, the pale, ghostly inhabitant of Hugo's nighttime bed, inactive and suppliant, gazed with eternally questioning eyes at the dog, Boola, who returned her stare as equal to equal.

Karl belched hugely and hid his smile behind his hand as his sister looked at him with bland disapproval. Her annoyance seemed not so much because of his rudeness, for she was used to the boorish habits of her brother, but at the implied insult to the Führer as he spoke from Munich.

Gisella had revealed herself as a most political person in recent weeks. There was the implication that her husband and her brother would best serve Germany with a gun in their hands despite their age.

And there was himself, Wilhelm Oerter, the father of the house. No, the grandfather of the house. Past jealousy, past sex, past passion and loyalty. Past usefulness.

Wilhelm's mind drifted to the girl he'd seen in the park that very day. Since his dismissal from his post he went there each morning about eleven o'clock. In this manner he avoided the sighs and contemptuous glances of his wife and absented himself in the event Hugo returned at the meal hour ready for something other than a cold table.

The girl had been twenty or so, small-boned and fragile. She walked with a lifting step like the stride of a water bird and her head thrust forward slightly as though daring the wind. As she'd passed Wilhelm seated on the slat bench beneath a linden tree, a gust caught at the edge of her skirt and lifted it above her stocking tops. She'd caught at it, hiding the sudden flash of white flesh, and smiled the briefest of understanding smiles into Wilhelm's eyes. Her teeth were like tiny seed pearls, small and even.

Wilhelm had felt the color rise to his face. It was not a displeasing embarrassment. He was aware that young girls often flaunted themselves a bit at old men. It afforded a sense of daring to them without the cost of real danger. It was a gentle cruel game they played. It satisfied as well a subtle need for assurance. To stir the nature of a young man was no great task, and there might be consequences. To rouse some old one past the sharp appetites of the flesh was, in its fashion, a finer victory.

Wilhelm felt a warm flush suffuse his face, and he plucked at the wattles of his neck. Tomorrow, he decided, he would be certain to be on the same bench at the same time. Perhaps the girl would stride by again. Perhaps the wind would blow, and he would be better prepared for it.

Gisella looked at the doltish Hugo and decided she would make arrangements very soon for the couple to secure lodgings of their own. His employment, received from her hands, gave him the funds and the privilege to secure quarters elsewhere.

She tore her thoughts away and concentrated them on the words of Hitler with a sense of shame at the moment's inattention.

Wilhelm saw her glance and read her thought. He smiled to himself until he caught Karl's glance on him, and then they smiled together.

Neither man heard much of the long, long harangue. They nodded from time to time, smiled and scratched themselves until it was done.

Hitler shrieked from the speaker, weaving his sorcerer's spell.

'They shall find out over there that the spirit of German inventors has not been resting and they shall get an answer which will numb their senses.'

It was a moment before the assemblage at Munich realized that the Führer's speech was done. Then they exploded. The riotous cheering faded as the transmission dimmed. The five people looked at one another like sleepers awakening from private dreams.

Karl rose and excused himself and was gone from the room

before anyone else spoke or moved. Surprising himself, Wilhelm chased after Karl with scarcely a good-bye.

The two men threw their legs out as they walked to loosen the cramps gathered there from the enforced inactivity.

'What did you think of our leader's speech, Wilhelm?'

'I have no opinions. I have no feelings except those any loyal German would feel.'

Karl glanced sharply at Wilhelm from the corner of his eye.

'I thought it idiotic. An apology for failure before the final evidence of failure.'

'That's dangerous talk, Karl.'

'Dangerous to speak my mind to my friend and brother-in-law?'

'I have similar attitudes. Apparently they placed me in a position of some jeopardy. Because of it, I've lost employment and who knows what will follow?'

Karl pulled himself up and grasped Wilhelm's arm with the strength of anger.

'What are you trying to say?'

'I made some small comparison between the reasons for German invasion of nations and British "protection" of nations. You warned me not to speak of such matters.'

'In the rathskeller. In public,' Karl protested.

'I mentioned the British offensive at El Alamein.'

'Everyone was talking about it.'

A shock of revelation passed across Karl's face.

'You think that I reported you?'

Wilhelm returned his fierce stare with one of accusing calm.

'If not you?'

'I told no one. No one.'

They began to walk again. They drew closer together.

'You were overheard,' Karl mused. 'Perhaps.'

'That is most certainly it.'

'But you know that others were offering speculations about the British attack.'

'No one who has a post in a sensitive government office.'

'Sensitive?' Wilhelm snuffled vehemently. 'The information disseminated by the Allies is known to the German public in a matter of hours.'

Karl nodded wisely and then began to laugh.

'It's all so foolish. Can they overhear all conversation? Can they watch every soldier and worker? They can try, but the derisive laughter and defeatist talk goes on. So they watch as many as they can. Not so high up as to be privy to real secrets. Someone far below who works in what appears to be a secret organization.'

He sobered suddenly, and his eyes grew wide for a moment.

'You must be very careful of what you say from now on. To anyone. To me. To Gisella.'

'I will be. For my own sake and for the sake of the friend who unloaded an unwanted sister upon me.'

'You must forgive me that.'

'No matter. She's an excellent cook.'

'You must believe me, it wasn't because I believed she'd be difficult for a man to live with.'

'A husband but not a brother?'

'I swear.'

'I forgive you. I'll see that you are not made guilty by the association with me.' Karl's laughter caught in his throat. Fear touched his eyes.

'Would they accuse me because of that?'

Wilhelm didn't answer but nodded comically instead.

The two aging men laughed again. It was the laughter of madness in an incomprehensible world.

On January 30, 1943, at the precise moment that Reich Marshal Hermann Goring was to begin a broadcast in Berlin celebrating the tenth anniversary of Hitler's regime, the RAF launched the first daylight attacks against the German capital.

The friends privately laughed hugely over the Nazi humiliation.

CHAPTER 36

Wilhelm went to the park. He sat and waited for the girl to pass by, for the wind to lift the edge of her skirt above her thighs. Though he waited many hours, she never passed again.

On the following Monday he took the public transport to the factory to which he'd been assigned. He wasn't certain how he was to dress, so he wore a suit and tie. He was given a broom to sweep up the shavings of bright metal spun from the lathes. Some of the workers laughed at the sight of a man in a business suit sweeping the floor, and Wilhelm didn't mind.

In Stalingrad one hundred thousand German soldiers were killed, more than forty-six thousand captured. The commander of the crushed German Sixth Army, Field Marshal General Friedrich von Paulus, and sixteen of his generals were taken prisoner as well.

It was no longer possible to keep any part of the desperate state of the war from the people. In Berlin and across the breadth of the nation the evidence was all around them.

A new timbre drowned out the beat of the drum of German victories. The Allies landed in Italy. Marshall Badoglio formally agreed to an unconditional surrender.

On September 9 the American Fifth Army landed at Salerno.

On January 22 the Allies landed at Anzio and Nettuno.

In Germany itself death and destruction was the daily bread.

Hugo's disability no longer kept him exempt from military service. He was called up and went off to war. Gisella kissed him on the cheek as a woman might do a nephew. Lenni left to live in a dormitory for soldiers' wives.

Other roomers came to share the apartment with them. Sometimes they were couples, sometimes two or three men together sharing the living space. Never were they women alone. Gisella apparently saw to that. Wilhelm made it a point never to come home outside the normal schedule.

After a time it was announced that the allocation of living accommodations was to be taken out of the hands of the relief organizations and placed under the command of the Office of the Plenipotentiary for Total War Effort. Gisella could no longer pick and choose her houseguests. Wilhelm was surprised to notice that the new arrangement seemed to make no difference to her.

The Oerters were allowed the smallest of the rooms in the apartment in which to live and sleep and eat. They shared the toilet with twelve others. Wilhelm noted other subtle changes in Gisella. He realized with a small twinge of curiosity that she had ceased her activities with other men. She gave no notice beyond a neutral shielding smile to any of the men that occasionally passed in the halls. She gave her interest entirely to housewifely duties, prepared extraordinary meals on the hot plate and kept the small room as bright as a great palace. She developed a certain affection for the dog. She called her Boola in imitation of Wilhelm's affectionate way. The animal transferred the weight of her love from the master to the mistress. Gisella sat for long periods of time humming to herself. She took to looking at Wilhelm with what might be called gently adoring and affectionately amused glances.

One evening they sat comfortably in the small space which somehow gave a greater impression of being a home than any he had experienced since the house in Kirkwall.

'Do you feel you've made a bad bargain, Willy?'

The question roused him from a reverie, and Wilhelm scratched his head like an old dog stalling for time.

'Have I cheated you?' she continued.

'You followed your nature.'

'No, Willy!'

There was anger, pain and indignation in her voice.

'To sleep with many men is not my nature.'

Wilhelm pushed his glasses up on the bridge of his nose and threw his head back so that he could observe her clearly in the optical center of the lenses.

'Did my eyes deceive me when I opened the door to my bedroom by chance and saw you in the arms of that –'

The name could not be recalled. His sternness dissolved in some confusion. He felt embarrassed at not being able to remember the name of the man who had first cuckolded him.

'Hugo,' Gisella said for him.

'Yes, Hugo.'

'I was told he was sent to the Russian front and killed the second day there.'

'I'm truly sorry to hear that.'

'He was run over by a German truck by accident.'

'Hugo was not very bright,' Wilhelm said.

He was about to go back to his reverie. He lifted his paper to hide behind it.

'I wanted a child. All my life I wanted a child,' Gisella said. 'Nothing served to fill that desire.'

Wilhelm lowered the newspaper.

'Why didn't you marry when you were young?'

Gisella shrugged but didn't explain. A thousand reasons perhaps, but that had nothing to do with the truth of her feelings or the facts of what she had done.

'Did you hope to perform a miracle with so many younger men?' Wilhelm asked softly. 'I can understand that. Yes, I can understand that.'

'No miracle, Willy. I'm young enough. I still have a woman's monthly flow.'

Wilhelm found himself nodding as though he were a gynecologist giving attention to the symptoms of a patient. He even pursed his lips while he wondered at a relationship that had managed to avoid such intimate knowledge.

'It would have been better if you'd told me you wanted a child.'

'Could you have done anything about it? We had sex night after night, time after time.'

So it wasn't enjoyment alone but practicality that had prompted her unusual demands, Wilhelm thought.

'I've no way to explain it. After all, I have a child.'

She stared at him as though he had confessed some unbelievably obscene sin.

'You have a child of your own?' she asked in a voice heavy with disbelief.

'If you saw him you'd have no doubts. I was married to an Orkney woman. Yes, I'm a father,' he said with pride.

'I am going to have a child as well,' Gisella said.

A sea of silence occupied the space between them. They both seemed afraid to tread upon its still surface.

'How old are you, Gisella? I never thought to ask.'

'Forty-one.'

'We must find the best obstetrician. It is sometimes difficult for a woman of your age to have a first child so late in life.'

'But not too uncommon?'

'So I understand.'

He leaned forward a bit, and the old rocking chair creaked.
'Do you know the name of the father?'
'No. And I'm happy for that.'
Wilhelm smiled. 'Then I am the father.'
'Yes, Willy. Will I make you a cup of hot chocolate?'

CHAPTER 37

Upon the occasion of the startling revelation that he was to become a father again, Wilhelm buried the true knowledge that the child could not be his own and lived in pleasurable anticipation.

A week later, still smiling foolishly over his secret delight, he was met by Günter Prien. Wilhelm had left his machine at the noon meal rest and gone to his solitary place on the edge of a loading dock where a stubbled field offered the illusion of free space, to eat the sandwich prepared for him by his wife.

He looked up at the sound of approaching footsteps and was mildly surprised to see the slender figure of Commander Prien, dressed in a dark great coat, approaching him. Since that night when he had received the Iron Cross, he had never en the sailor, though he'd sometimes read of his exploits in the popular press. He'd never really expected the man to fulfil the intentions he'd uttered on that terrace so long ago.

Wilhelm stumbled to his feet and extended a hand stained with his labors. He felt himself old before this man who seemed to have grown younger. Close to, as Prien gripped his hand with every evidence of being greatly pleased at seeing him again, he noted that age had indeed touched the schoolboy he remembered from a summer's day. The eyes were etched all around with the rings of years like the core of a felled tree.

'So, old friend,' Prien said, 'you thought I'd forgotten the pact I made with you.'

'No, no. I didn't expect you'd be able to fulfil the promise. I was grateful enough for the kind thought at the time.'

'Yes, I've been much at sea. Sit down, sit down.'

He himself sat on the edge of the dock and dangled his half-booted feet over the edge.

Wilhelm sat and began to offer half the sandwich to Prien and then laughed apologetically.

Prien patted Wilhelm's knee.

'I've always kept track of you, though, meaning a hundred times to look you up. But one thing and another.'

He gestured vaguely, suggesting that Wilhelm, himself a man of affairs, understood the pressures of time and duty.

'I went to your office. They said you'd left but wouldn't tell me anything further.'

'I was discharged.'

'Yes?'

'They seemed to feel that my marriage to an English girl, my son, my years in the Orkneys, might have left me with some sympathy for the English cause. Apparently there was reason to feel that I would disseminate the news which I translated from the English press. News unfavorable to the war effort.'

'News which thousands of Germans were receiving on their radios against the express orders of the government.'

Wilhelm looked at Prien and caught him staring intently at him a moment before the commander dropped his eyes.

'Did you feel the dismissal unjust?' Prien asked.

Wilhelm shrugged his shoulders. Prien looked at him again in a challenging manner.

'You have no opinion?'

'It's of small concern.'

'No feelings about it?'

Wilhelm realized Prien was asking for a statement that would create a bond of trust between them.

'I felt it was remarkably foolish.'

Prien laughed shortly like the barking of a dog.

'They do much that is damned foolish. They throw armies to their deaths when all hope of victory is lost. They send exhausted men and ill-equipped ships out into the sea in some mad attempt to extract a last ounce of blood from an enemy heavy with the blood of success. They harass small men for imagined disloyalties while Germany howls in pain. Hitler is quite mad, you know?'

Wilhelm made no response.

'I have placed my safety in your hands, you know?' Prien said after a long while.

'Who would believe anything I had to say?'

'Hitler is prepared to believe much that would seem unbelievable to any sane man. He's seeking scapegoats for his failure. He looks for new traitors to excuse this war as he used old traitors to create reasons for it. He fears the career military. Most of all, he fears the Navy. They're the most conservative in matters of tradition and his hand has never been as manipulative among us as it has been elsewhere.'

'Why do you tell me this?'

'I've come to offer you a position of trust.'

'A position that carries with it certain services against the government?'

'Against Hitler, if at all.'

'How can you trust a man you can so casually approach upon a matter that might very well be treasonable?'

'We consider you intelligent.'

Wilhelm made a small deprecating sound in his throat. Prien went on quickly.

'We know you to be patient and loyal to your principals.'

'I've always condemned myself for not having any. I have a history of vacillation and lack of determination to prove it.'

'You think very little of yourself,' Prien remarked with a certain sadness in his voice. 'I meant by principals, those who were in authority.'

'I give a good day's work to the shop foreman, and I obey my wife's edict that there be no pipe smoking in the house,' Wilhelm said with wry humor. He went on in a more serious vein.

'If I am such a faithful servant, then I must continue to serve the German war effort in any position in which I've been placed.'

'The greatest loyalty of all is to the Fatherland itself. Do you agree?'

'Yes.'

'That is the final authority for which I work and which I ask you to serve.'

'I am not a decisive man. I've experienced the inexpressible frustration and weariness of fighting with the conscience and the logical mind. I have no talent for polemics.'

Prien stood up briskly.

'I trust you will keep this conversation confidential?'

Wilhelm nodded, and Prien turned to walk away.

Wilhelm raised his voice, half hoping it would still go unheard. 'What is it you wish me to do?'

On February 1, 1944, Wilhelm took up his new duties in a small office in the building that housed the Abwehr, the Wehrmacht's Intelligence arm.

He was interviewed briefly by Admiral Canaris, who recalled immediately and in detail the circumstances of their first meeting.

Wilhelm was told of his duties. They were childishly simple. He was, in effect, a glorified mail boy. He was the spout of the funnel through which would pass papers, reports and documents scheduled for dissemination to the proper eyes. There was little that was sensitive in the material. He had only to stamp the papers with the proper official seal and with the proper routing schedule.

He thanked Canaris for the post and was told that when Canaris had heard that a hero of the Reich had been so shabbily treated, he'd made it his business to see that such unusual service was properly rewarded. Canaris gave the impression that, godlike, he was aware of the plight of the least fallen sparrow.

Nothing was said of the real duties he would be expected to perform. He had the feeling that he was once more in a web whose intricacies he could not possibly understand. That he had been placed on a spoke of that web and would be maneuvered, from time to time, closer to the vital hub.

He had been chosen because he was insignificant and nonthreatening to anyone. He could be easily overlooked. If not, he could be easily dispensed with.

On February 18 the Abwehr was dissolved, and Canaris made the chief of the Office for Commercial and Economic Warfare. It was a powerless post. Somehow, in the shakeup and dissolution of staff that followed, Wilhelm Oerter remained at his desk.

The Allied Expeditionary Forces launched the great invasion through France. The first communiqué from Eisenhower's Supreme Headquarters came into Wilhelm's hands. The last line of it brought a bitter smile to his lips. All leaders had the glowing phrases with which to lead little men to acts of destruction.

'To members of resistance movements, whether led by national or outside leaders, I say: "Follow the instructions you have received." '

Wilhelm waited to be told what was to be expected of him.

CHAPTER 38

Gisella, heavy with the child they had easily come to call 'their child,' often looked at her husband with her disconcertingly liquid eyes.

Wilhelm knew that she was perplexed but pleased at the new position that had been given him. From time to time she'd even made veiled remarks suggesting that his apparently innocuous employment as a translator upon his triumphal return to Germany had been a cover for far more important activities more deeply concerned with the heart of espionage or counterespionage. She'd apparently come to believe that his dismissal and disgrace, the suspicions against his loyalty, slender and unfounded, were part of the same intricate and devious structure that allowed him the freedom to go forward with his work. The fact that he had been so soon reinstated in a position of trust confirmed her in the belief that her husband was engaged in affairs of great moment.

Wilhelm did nothing to dissuade her from the view. He even played the game a bit and enforced his image by quickly avoiding references to clandestine operations and murmuring such inconsequentialities as 'One should know only what one needs to know.'

Another aspect of her new regard for him was her obvious contentment with her pregnant condition. She, long before he himself, had come to speak of the happy event as a product of their love discovered and come to them comparatively late in life. He was happy for the fiction and contemplated the arrival of a child with quiet joy.

Her attitude in bed had briefly flared into the same urgency she had displayed early on, but that had burned itself out, and at a moment when she perhaps felt that she had made recompense for her sins of adultery and denial of him, a new sexual easiness grew between them. They truly enjoyed each other in a quiet way in which frequency or lack of it was no part of the consummation.

One other thing seemed covertly indicated in her frequent examination of Wilhelm. She had, he was certain, developed intense curiosity about his child in the Orkneys, the wife that bore it and the aspect of his life there in general. She never asked, for she apparently presumed it came under the same prohibitions that guarded the lives of all men employed in secret affairs.

Wilhelm was glad of that as well. He had no desire to speak of Julie to this wife. No wish to conjecture on how the new child soon to be born should compare with John. He wanted to keep the parts of his life carefully separate. He felt it would be a dishonor to Julie to anatomize their relationship with this woman who was a stranger to her. He tried not to allow even the thoughts of his Orkney family to intrude upon the greater part of his present life with Gisella. To think of them too much would be a dishonor to her.

His domestic life was a muted backdrop for a more immediate concern. He couldn't understand why he had been overlooked in the general reconstruction of the Abwehr. He assumed it was because his introduction to the service so shortly before Canaris' discharge and the destruction of the Intelligence arm had gone unnoticed. He wondered fearfully if the Gestapo continued to watch him because of his minor indiscretion that had caused his separation from the office of the translators. Were they indeed watching, perhaps assuming that he had been placed in his present capacity by a far-seeing Canaris, who wanted any small bit of access to restricted documents he might afford himself? Were they waiting for him to be called on by his new masters in order to destroy them? What did these new masters want of him? He felt hollow and useless, like a puppet dangling from its strings waiting to be manipulated. It was a feeling he had lived with for many years, and it was surpassingly unpleasant and terrifying to be so disposed once again.

He felt that within the German government there were forces at work against each other that would soon explode into hate, madness and mutual destruction. If the leviathans of power came to grips, he was afraid that he would be crushed beneath them.

Meanwhile, he stamped the documents that flowed across his desk.

Even before mention of the new secret weapon, the pilotless bombs, reached the press, he knew of them.

The first robot attack on England was given as proof in the German press that Hitler's promises of visiting the apocalypse on the enemy were coming true. Those more intelligent, analytic or simply informed saw it as the thrashings of a creature mad with the pain of its own death agonies.

Wilhelm was visited shortly after the introduction of the destructive but strategically doubtful robot bombs by his friend Commander Günter Prien.

Prien invited Wilhelm for a stroll in the public gardens that were some blocks from Oerter's office.

The gardens were not places for the quiet contemplation of nature's beauty. They were trenched and sandbagged scars no longer green, haunted by bomb-shattered trees and the decapitated granite busts of old war heroes. They were used by the people more extensively perhaps than when they had been arboreal havens. The parks afforded a measure of privacy, and that was a commodity beyond price in Berlin.

They strolled along. Wilhelm was pleased that Prien matched his own younger, long-legged stride to his own.

'You look tired, my friend,' Wilhelm offered.

'Yes, tired. Weary of lost war.'

'It's a certainty?'

'The only thing in question at this time is the extent to which the professionals can prevent Hitler from bringing about the total destruction of Germany and cruel reprisals to pay back the vicious cruelties he's employed in the conduct of this war.'

'What can you possibly do?'

'We can remove him from Olympus.'

'Depose Hitler?'

'Destroy Hitler.'

The expression of the intent shook Wilhelm so badly that he faltered in his step, and Günter reached to take his elbow and led him to a stone bench. Wilhelm took several deep breaths and clenched his hands to keep them from trembling so.

'You expected a call to be made upon your services, didn't you?' Prien asked gently.

Wilhelm looked at the younger man with stricken eyes.

'I lived twenty years waiting to be called upon. Twenty years, and in all that time I never knew when the call would come or what would be asked of me finally. They asked me, at last, to send nearly a thousand sailormen and boys, much like you, to their deaths. Not in honorable combat.'

'According to the accords of war,' Prien said defensively.

'Not as you. Not as you. You entered into perilous battle as you were trained to do, required to do. I sent a simple signal through the air with no great danger to myself. How could there have been danger for me? I was well liked, unsuspected, even loved. I was a traitor.'

'You were a patriot.'

'I was a traitor to my own heart.'

He wrapped his suit coat about his body in sudden chill and agitation despite the warmth of the night.

'I never once asked myself what exactly it was I was being asked to do. Not to defend my Fatherland or even to carry the battle to the enemy. I was asked to lurk in their midst and to come to love them. And then with their arms still warm about me and a child's kiss still wet on my cheek, I was asked to kill the love that was there and flee the one place on all the earth that had become my home. I was such an ignorant and unquestioning fool that I didn't even know it was my home until it was gone from me.

'Now you tell me I'm to be asked, once again, mindlessly and without knowledge of the consequence, to lend my incredible talent for mediocrity and anonymity to a venture whose value I have no way of judging.'

'Its purpose is the very same purpose that led you to sit those years out in Scapa Flow. Germany! Your homeland.'

Wilhelm waved his hand in small circles and smiled and put a mocking lilt into his words.

'Oh, yes, the Fatherland. The English fight for Mother England, and the French for La Belle France, and we fight for the Fatherland. This is not my Germany. This Hitler's cesspool of fear is not my country. I am not home here.'

'Then all the more reason for you to lend your help to this enterprise.'

'Don't misunderstand me. I have a home. It is a small apartment. There is a rocking chair in the one room of it and a box filled with such oddments as a butterfly captured by a child, a bit of shell taken from a stormy beach. It's a box of memories. The means to tell me that I once lived a life of twenty years' duration. And in that house is another woman who is about to have another child. My child.'

Wilhelm raised a hand for fear Prien in some manner knew of the conception of the unborn infant and would tell that he knew the truth of it.

'I'm a bit old for becoming a father again, and yet it seems fair enough that I should have this, even at this time of life. To have a wife, older and fuller than the one I knew. To have a son, perhaps, that I can pretend is that other son, separate but the same. It's a warm house, and there's love in it. You're welcome, my friend, to join us at our meal and in the quiet conversation of the evening.'

'You refuse then?'

'I refuse. Quietly but with all the strength that I possess, I refuse. I expect your purpose is worthy. I know the death of this monster can bring nothing but good. And I know that innocent men will die because of it.'

Prien peered at him in the gathering dusk.

'No,' Wilhelm said, 'I'm not afraid for myself. It's just that I'm not innocent. Not any longer. But I will not be a small piece in a large game, moved from square to square as though I were filled with sawdust. I won't be used for high and mighty intrigues anymore.'

Prien stood up.

'You'll have to report this to your superior?'

Prien nodded.

Wilhelm smiled cheerfully.

'There will be reprisals against me then if you're successful in your enterprise. I will be visited, no doubt, by persons who, having stilled the terror of Hitler, will create new terrors for the good of Germany and the purging of its soul.'

Prien looked thoughtful, and Wilhelm reached up to touch the sleeve of his uniform.

'Don't put yourself in jeopardy trying to find ways to excuse my disaffection with your leader's cause.'

Prien walked away.

'Don't concern yourself, old friend,' Wilhelm murmured when the figure was past hearing. 'I will survive. You see, I am a patient man and easily overlooked.'

CHAPTER 39

On July 20, 1944, the conspiracy against the life of Hitler and the subsequent take-over of the government of which Wilhelm had been asked to be a part were executed and failed. Hitler had suffered a narrow escape, but he went on the air before 1 a.m. to address the German people:

'My German comrades!

'If I speak to you today, it is first in order that you should hear my voice and should know that I am unhurt and well, and secondly, that you should know of a crime unparalleled in German history.

'A very small clique of ambitious, irresponsible and, at the same time, senseless and stupid officers had concocted a plot to eliminate me and with me, the staff of the High Command of the Wehrmacht.

'The bomb placed by Colonel Count Stauffenberg exploded two meters to the right of me. It seriously wounded a number of my true and loyal collaborators, one of whom has died. I myself am entirely unhurt, aside from some very minor scratches, bruises and burns. I regard this as a confirmation of the task imposed upon me by Providence. . . .

'The circle of these usurpers is very small and has nothing in common with the spirit of the German Wehrmacht and, above all, none with the German people. It is a gang of criminal elements which will be destroyed without mercy.

'I therefore give orders now that no military authority . . . is to obey orders from this crew of usurpers. I also order that it is everyone's duty to arrest, or, if they resist, to shoot on sight, anyone issuing or handling such orders. . . .

'This time we shall settle accounts with them in the manner to which the National Socialists are accustomed.'

A wave of terror swept across the entire spectrum of officers in all services. Men of great rank, Rommel among them, were allowed to take their own lives by poison or gun. Others were gunned down where they stood without the formality of arrest or trial. Still others were placed on public display, tried in viciously partisan courts and hung like cattle, suspended by their necks, wrapped round with piano wire, from butchers' hooks.

In the following weeks Wilhelm was able to piece together a mental list of the suffering caused by the abortive assassination attempt. There had been well over seven thousand arrests. Nearly five thousand were purportedly on a death list. He knew for a fact that generals, officers, pastors, professors and professionals, men of wisdom and strength, had been taken to their deaths. In all the names, that of Commander Günter Prien did not appear, but it was reported sometime later that the hero had gone down with his U-boat in an engagement in the Atlantic.

Admiral Canaris was ordered tried by a summary SS court, but somehow the trial was delayed, and it was said he had been taken to the concentration camp at Flossenburg.

Whatever punishment the enigmatic man may have had planned for Wilhelm Oerter for his refusal to join in the conspiracy was no longer a threat. But there was still great danger in the fact that Wilhelm had been given his present position in communications through the offices of the admiral. Small men, innocent men, had been gathered up in the general dragnet of conspirators. Any least doubtful association could be a death warrant.

Strangely, Wilhelm felt no great fear nor even exceptional concern. He was far more interested in the swelling belly of his wife.

He did wonder what part Canaris and Prien had expected him to play. He pieced together some factors about the nature of the plan. Some time before the actual murder attempt, General Olbricht was to order the Berlin garrison to march against strategic points of command within the city and environs. Wilhelm could assume that those orders were to have been issued from his office under the authority of the stamp his insignificant hand wielded. It seemed amusing to him that such extraordinary powers had somehow, through oversight or other caprice, been vested in someone who was nothing more than a lowly mailman.

He thought of a dozen other ways in which they might have used him. It was all conjecture. All valueless. Even if he'd agreed to be part of the conspiracy, he could have done nothing toward its success. Its failure came from sources far above him. It was done. He had only to sit and wait patiently and with good humor for whatever his fate had left for him.

There was fear and relief and patience left in him. Above all, there was a strange antic emotional reaction to it all. Though he was happy to have escaped, so far, the hangman's noose, and though he had been proud of his refusal to join the conspiracy, now that the assassination attempt had failed, he was beset by a feeling of guilt. In some subtle fashion he felt he should have agreed to participate, agonized over the failure and suffered the consequences with the others. It was a feeling that was hard for Wilhelm to shake off. It clung to him through the days of August and the day of the liberation of Paris.

It lingered until September 4. That night the district in which the Oerters lived was struck by British bombers in a nighttime raid. As the citizens flowed out of the building at the warning sirens to make their way to shelter, Wilhelm, slowly and with great care, helped his pregnant wife down the staircase and along the passage to the streets. A bomb fell nearby at 2:37 a.m. No one was killed or seriously injured, but Gisella was thrown violently to the ground.

Shortly after she was wracked by birth pains and taken to the hospital.

She was delivered of a premature baby girl two hours later.

The baby was placed in an incubator.

Gisella Oerter did not survive the rigors of the traumatic birth.

Wilhelm went to the hospital and viewed the child in its tomb of glass and prayed for its survival. On the fourth day he received orders to report within one week for induction into the armed forces of Germany.

Germany was dying. Joseph Goebbels, Reich Plenipotentiary for Total War, was conscripting schoolchildren. Red Cross workers and men between the ages of fifty and sixty. There were rumors that Hitler intended to mount a great counterattack against the invaders.

The child was alive the day before he was to leave and take up arms. It would be placed in a government nursery. There was no christening, but in his heart he named her Molly.

In the course of his last day at work a sheaf of documents demanding the official stamp reached his desk. He read a copy with little attention at the start. Then he read more closely. It read in part:

'Further hostilities in this conflict will only bring total destruction to Germany, her people and the future of the Fatherland.

'Soon an armistice will be forced upon the nation.

'You are ordered to go underground. You are to make your whereabouts and occupation known to your control and to your control only.

'You are ordered to await further orders.

'The defeat of Germany was brought about by the infamous conspiracy of traitors within.

'This is not a total defeat. It is but one rung on the ladder of eventual victory.'

Wilhelm began to laugh. The corners of his mouth pulled back until his lips ached. He made a game of stamping the papers in a marching rhythm. He laughed and the water ran from his eyes.

'The Reich will endure.'

'The Reich will rise again.'

On Tuesday, December 19, 1944, Private Wilhelm Oerter was killed in action against the enemy in the last great German offensive of the war in an area eight miles southwest of Malmédy.